STACY M. JONES

Sparrow Down

I0693858

First published by Stacy M. Jones 2025

Copyright © 2025 by Stacy M. Jones

All rights reserved. No part of this publication may be reproduced, stored or transmitted in any form or by any means, electronic, mechanical, photocopying, recording, scanning, or otherwise without written permission from the publisher. It is illegal to copy this book, post it to a website, or distribute it by any other means without permission.

This novel is entirely a work of fiction. The names, characters and incidents portrayed in it are the work of the author's imagination. Any resemblance to actual persons, living or dead, events or localities is entirely coincidental.

Stacy M. Jones asserts the moral right to be identified as the author of this work.

Stacy M. Jones has no responsibility for the persistence or accuracy of URLs for external or third-party Internet Websites referred to in this publication and does not guarantee that any content on such Websites is, or will remain, accurate or appropriate.

Designations used by companies to distinguish their products are often claimed as trademarks. All brand names and product names used in this book and on its cover are trade names, service marks, trademarks and registered trademarks of their respective owners. The publishers and the book are not associated with any product or vendor mentioned in this book. None of the companies referenced within the book have endorsed the book.

First edition

ISBN: 979-8-218-67325-3

This book was professionally typeset on Reedsy.
Find out more at reedsy.com

For Liam

Acknowledgments

Thanks to 17 Studio Book Design for bringing my stories to life with incredible covers. Thank you to Dj Hendrickson for your insightful editing and Liza Wood for proofreading and revisions. I am so grateful to these incredible women who ensure my work is professional and interesting to the reader.

Thanks also to my advanced reader team who had first eyes on the finished product. I'm grateful for their feedback and interest in this new series. We are coming to know Fitz and Charlie together.

Special thank you to all my D.C. friends - who cannot be named individually, but you ensure accuracy and took my late night calls with my million questions about all things politics. Any mistakes are my own. I took some liberties for the sake of the story.

CHAPTER 1

As far as Connor Fitzgerald knew when he woke that morning, it was going to be an average Tuesday. He had gotten up with his alarm at five and trained in his home gym for about an hour – heavy weights – before driving over to his favorite trail in Rock Creek Park for a three-mile run.

After he showered, he opted not to shave, ate a protein-packed breakfast, and headed out to work. Lately, he'd been feeling his forty-nine years. Knowing he was on the doorstep of fifty made him start prioritizing his health in a way he hadn't since he was in the police academy.

On his drive to his former rowhouse in Georgetown, he had stopped for coffee for himself and his partner, Charlotte "Charlie" Doyle. She wanted a toasted marshmallow mocha something or other that he had to read from her text to order. For a former CIA operative, she had an elaborate coffee order. Fitz couldn't complain though because she was the best partner he'd ever had and he'd had more than a few when he was working for the D.C. Metro Police Department. He had worked his way up to being one of the best homicide detectives in the district.

Life as he knew it came crashing down when Fitz caught a serial killer who had created chaos for the D.C. metro area. He'd been trotted out to the media as a show pony then told he'd gotten too big for his breeches and sacked. The brass didn't know what to do with him and it's not like Fitz didn't stick out enough already. He was tall, broad, and by all accounts movie star good-looking. All Fitz wanted to do was get back to investigating. Instead, they sidelined him and the parting of ways between him and his job was more than mutual.

That left Fitz without work. As fate would have it shortly after he met John Huntly, the greatest opposition researcher in all of the United States. Huntly was old, ready to retire, and had no kids to leave the business to. The plan was for Fitz to pay Huntly monthly for the business and cover his retirement. A couple of months into the deal, Huntly dropped dead and the business was Fitz's. He got rid of Huntly's physical office and moved the business into his Georgetown rowhouse, which at the time had been falling apart.

The work suited him. Fitz still whet his investigative whistle while doing what he considered a public service. He figured if politicians were supposed to be representing the people, the people had a right to know exactly who they were electing.

Secrets were a playground for blackmail and influence.

It's why the FBI background check was so important before people got security clearances. It was important to know how easily someone with America's secrets could be bought and sold. Fitz didn't realize just how much people were hiding until he started doing the work. A little while into the business Charlie came along looking for work. He had more than enough to share and sensed that she needed something. It took him some time to get the truth of her background from her. She'd been a CIA agent at the height of the War on Terror and she'd seen enough to last her a lifetime.

Charlie was happy to come into a nice office, research clients in ways that weren't going to get her tortured or killed, and call it a day in enough time to take her dog for a walk and make some dinner.

Life had turned out pretty good for both of them. They were a few months apart in age – both on the downslope to fifty, neither had children, and Fitz had been married and divorced. If Charlie was single or dating, he wouldn't know. She was tightlipped about some things. His love life wasn't much to write home about.

Fitz pushed thoughts of his pathetic dating record aside as he pulled into the narrow driveway around the back of the rowhouse. He maneuvered into the back of the house, balancing the coffees in the flimsy cardboard tray with one hand while unlocking the door with the other.

"Charlie, coffee's here!" he yelled as he tossed his keys on the counter in the small recently remodeled kitchen. Even with the conversion to an office, he had left most of the home intact. The living room on the first floor made a nice waiting area and the dining room made a decent conference and workspace if they needed to spread out. Their offices took over the second-floor bedrooms. Fitz had kept the primary suite on the third floor the same in case either of them needed to crash there for the night. His house in Chevy Chase had been a new addition to his life. The suburbs were suiting him well for now.

"Charlie!" he called again as he made his way to the bottom of the stairs, shouting her name one more time for good measure.

A moment later she made an appearance at the top of the stairs and Fitz stepped back. "What did you do to your hair?" When he saw her the evening before, she had shoulder-length auburn hair and now it was up to her chin in a chic bob. It was significantly bolder in color.

Charlie wrinkled up her nose. "It's called Cherry Pop," she said, running her fingers through her shorter locks. "The woman who did my hair convinced me that I should let the red come out more. Is it terrible?"

Fitz shook his head. "Not at all. It looks terrific." He eyed her cautiously. "You know you're not going to blend in as you so famously like to do. This is a stand-out. You're a stunner."

She shoved him as she reached the landing. "I'm an old lady. No one is paying attention to me. I could show up with purple spikes and nobody would care. Where's my coffee?"

Fitz playfully nudged her as they made their way to the kitchen. "If you're an old lady than I'm an old man and I'm not ready for that. What's on the docket for today?" Before Charlie had a chance to answer, the front door shot open, stopping them both cold in the hallway.

A young man with blond wavy hair stood there, catching his breath. "Senator Austin Ford sent me," he managed to get out between gulps. "President Monroe has been shot."

The words didn't register in Fitz's brain fast enough.

Charlie rushed to the door. "What do you mean shot?" She grabbed the young man by the shoulder and ushered him inside, closing and locking the door behind him. She marched him to the conference room, flipped on the light, and sat him in a chair.

"Catch your breath," she commanded him.

The man's eyes were wide as he steadied his breathing. He told them his name was Casey, a staffer for Senator Ford. "He said to find you both. He said you'd know what it's about."

Fitz and Charlie shared a knowing look.

The Warren Circle.

Right after they had exposed the corruption of a Supreme Court pick, Senator Ford had shown up at the office to make them an offer. Join the Warren Circle – a secret ring that worked in the shadows keeping everything in the government even keeled. That's at least how it had been explained to them. It was started by Dr. Joseph Warren during the Revolutionary War. Sometimes the circle acted as a spy ring, other times it worked to ensure democracy remained.

They were the checks and balances for the checks and balances.

Senator Ford's request had been two months ago. When they

decided to join, they were supposed to have called a number Ford had provided and tell whoever answered that Dr. Warren sent them. They hadn't called. They had rolled into the Christmas holiday and then started in January with more work than they had anticipated.

A new president, Abigail Monroe, had been inaugurated three weeks prior. Monroe was a direct descendent of James Monroe, the country's fifth president. She had been a lawyer before her meteoric rise in the Senate. She served two terms and gained a reputation as an intelligent, thoughtful but outspoken member. She didn't always vote along party lines and was known to reach across the aisle to get things done.

She won her primary for president by a landslide and the general election easily.

Monroe didn't suffer fools easily and she didn't seem to care if she was liked or not. She didn't run the D.C. political circuit looking for favors or friends. Monroe was one of the few who if she promised something, she did her best to get it done.

But now, she'd been shot.

Fitz rested his hands on the table so he was more at eye level with Casey. "Is she dead?"

"I don't know," Casey said, his voice cracking. "Senator Ford got the call and sent me over here. I don't know anything more than that. It must be on the news by now."

Charlie pressed him. "You don't know what happened?"

Casey took deep breaths until they became even. "I don't know anything. All I know is I was sitting in the office going through yesterday's mail when Senator Ford erupted from his private office and shouted for me to find you. He said I had to get here as soon as possible." Casey reached into his pocket and pulled out a folded-over orange Post-It note. He handed it to Charlie. "He said to give you this address."

Fitz got up from the table and headed into the living room, grabbed the remote control, and turned on the television. The screen jumped to life with breaking news flashing across the bottom of the screen. The reporter's wide eyes and strained composure immediately told a viewer that something was wrong.

The reporter noted, "President Abigail Monroe was shot at five-thirty this morning on her run along the National Mall. She was shot at the Lincoln Memorial. We know she was rushed to George Washington University Hospital and is currently in surgery. We have sparse details at this time about the incident, President Monroe's condition, or the shooter. The White House is not releasing any information. While these reports are confirmed, there is still more to know. We assume more information will come."

The reporter turned to pundits to speculate about what happened and that's when Fitz turned the television off. He wanted facts, just facts – not speculation, not chatter from talking heads.

"What did you find out?" Charlie asked appearing in the doorway to the living room.

"She was shot this morning at the Lincoln Memorial. I heard she jogs along the Mall." Fitz gave her the same information the reporter gave him. "The Secret Service probably hated that she jogged. It's the same path Bill Clinton took and they were angry then. It's unsecured and they aren't able to fully do their jobs."

Charlie agreed with that. "Doesn't the White House have an outdoor track on the grounds? If my memory is correct, George W. used that track."

"Yeah," Fitz said absently, wondering why on Earth anyone would allow the president to run an unsecured route like that. Abigail Monroe was an avid runner. Everyone knew that. She had been on the track and field team in high school and at Yale. She ran while she was in the Senate and during her campaign.

Fitz pointed to the Post-It. "What's the address?"

Charlie carried over the slip of paper and handed it to Fitz to let him read it himself.

511 10th Street NW, Washington, D.C.

Fitz didn't need a map. He knew the address. Most people who knew history or resided in the D.C. area did – Ford's Theater. He was being called to meet where Lincoln had been shot.

"We're doing this?" Charlie asked, her tone implying that she was doing it with or without him.

"We're doing this," he echoed back.

They sent Casey on his way, armed themselves, and set out on foot toward the nearest Metro stop. There'd never be parking near the theater at this time of day.

CHAPTER 2

"The house or the theater?" Charlie asked as they stood outside looking from one building across the street to the other.

Fitz assumed it was the theater. That was the address he'd been given. The building looked dark and unwelcoming, but that might have been the point. He tried the middle of the five doors under the white archways. The door glided open in his hand. As he stepped into the empty front hall, Fitz wondered if he should call Senator Ford to let him know he'd arrived.

"Senator Ford. Ford's Theater?" Charlie asked.

"I don't know," Fitz said as he turned left in the narrow hallway. They didn't get far when an older man approached from a doorway.

"The theater is closed today for visitors," the man said with a question on his face.

Fitz fumbled for something to say until landing on what Senator Ford had told him early on. "Dr. Warren sent us."

The man offered a gentle nod. "Follow me. Next time don't use the front entrance. I'll show you later where you can enter."

Fitz and Charlie followed him silently, allowing themselves to be led into the main part of the theater. They walked down an aisle of rows of red seats toward the main stage. Fitz glanced up to his left at the box where Lincoln had been shot. The American flag was draped on both sides of the box and across the front. In the middle was a photo of George Washington.

Fitz returned his focus to the white-haired, short man with a rounded middle who guided them up to the stage then to the left in the back. The man stopped short of going behind the stage with them.

He pointed. "Go to the red door. You'll find a narrow passage of stairs, follow that down, take another left then a quick right to the black door. Rap on that five times and repeat what you said to me."

"You're not coming?" Charlie asked.

"No. I'm a guardian like my father and his father before him." He turned toward the open doorway without explaining more. When they hesitated, he rushed them. "Please, go on. When you're done, meet me back here."

Fitz and Charlie entered the space following the directions the man gave. Once they were at the black door, they could hear the murmur of voices behind it. "Are you ready? There's no turning back?" Fitz asked her, suddenly unsure of himself and what would be asked of him.

Charlie looked up at him. "I know you're not used to this cloak-and-dagger kind of thing. A homicide detective isn't cut out for living in the shadows. This is what I was made for, Fitz. I promise you'll be fine. We can always refuse to do something illegal."

Fitz was glad he had Charlie there to steady him. His heart raced as he reached out and knocked exactly five times and spoke aloud the greeting. A moment later, the door creaked open and Senator Ford stood on the other side.

"Glad you're here. Both of you," he said as he ushered them into the small space. There were round tables with chairs scattered across the black cement floor. Photos of various presidents in gold frames hung on the wall. Fitz counted ten other men in the room. Charlie was the only woman.

Ford stepped beside him. "This isn't how I wanted to make your introductions. I had hoped you would have called me weeks ago and we could have eased you in. Given the circumstances, we need you here now. Trial by fire it is."

Ford made quick introductions around the room. Fitz caught every other name. He was sure he'd only remember a handful of them. A couple he'd had as clients. The FBI director, Marcus Kane, was the most known to Fitz. He noted that Charlie nodded to the man by the name of James Blackwell. Ford didn't specify what agency he was from. If he was familiar with Charlie, Fitz assumed the CIA or maybe even the NSA – some intelligence agency for sure. It seemed everyone in the room knew Fitz and Charlie even if they didn't know them as well.

When introductions were done, Charlie asked, "Is this everyone?"

"No," Senator Ford said. "There are fifteen of us at any one time in this circle. No more. We had two vacancies and I suggested you both."

"We don't normally allow anyone to join who is outside of the government," one of the men in the back said. "Ford convinced us that we should expand."

"I saw an opportunity and I took it." Ford's tone indicated that Fitz's and Charlie's memberships had been a hotly debated topic.

Fitz didn't have time for all of this. If they were there for the reason he assumed, he wanted to get down to business. "How is President Monroe? I saw some brief information on the news."

Senator Ford folded his arms across his chest. "Surgery. She was shot once in the chest, nicking her lung, and once in the abdomen. The gut shot missed vital organs by some miracle. She's expected to survive if she survives the surgery. She lost a considerable amount of blood but the Secret Service sprang to action quickly."

"The shooter?" Charlie asked.

"Dead," Marcus Kane said, standing. "The Secret Service killed him almost immediately after the shooting. He was spotted and neutralized."

An attempted homicide was in Fitz's wheelhouse. "What do we know about him?"

Marcus zeroed in on Fitz. "The reason I said yes to your membership is because of your work as a D.C. Metro homicide detective. I think you got railroaded by the brass. You should be out on those streets still."

Fitz extended a hand to the man. "I appreciate that. Hopefully, I can use those skills here in this situation. Won't the FBI and Secret Service be officially investigating this?"

"Killer is dead," Marcus said definitively. "The FBI will investigate to make sure he was acting alone and there's no one else to bring to justice. You'd think it would be a priority but it won't be."

"You're the FBI director. Isn't it your job to make it a priority?" Fitz asked the question, but he already knew the answer. The killer was dead – justice was done. Unless there was another obvious suspect, it would be seen as a waste of taxpayers' money.

Marcus shrugged off the question. "You and I both know that this will hit the media for maybe a month, but the wheels of justice turn much more slowly. I've already put my best agents on this. If there is something there and time permits, they will find it. I'll probably have to pull them off the investigation before too long if nothing comes to light."

"Secret Service?"

Marcus nodded. "Secret Service will do an internal investigation. All the agents who were involved are on leave. They will also explore any recent threats against her, of which there are many."

"Many?" Fitz asked, not thinking of any that had been publicized. "I thought she was popular."

"Monroe is still a woman holding the highest level of power and leadership in this country and there are many who don't like the idea of a woman running the country." Marcus gave Senator Ford a knowing look. "There were some in Congress who didn't want her to win either. None of them would come out and say that outside of a few fringe members. She was well-liked and most knew that their constituents on both sides of the aisle liked her too. There were threats against her."

Charlie tsked. "Insecure men are always threatened by powerful, successful women. I'm honestly surprised she made it as far as she did."

The edge in Charlie's tone caught Fitz off guard. She'd rarely spoken about her time in the CIA, not that she could disclose much because of security clearances. There was something in what she said that indicated to Fitz she might have had a rough go of it. He had never considered what it might have been like for a young woman in the CIA back when Charlie had first joined. He cocked an eyebrow in a question.

Charlie shook her head, brushing him off. "Threats coming from the usual suspects?"

"We are getting ahead of ourselves here," Senator Ford said, slowing them down.

Fitz didn't mean to step on any toes. "Charlie and I don't know how this works. What's the purpose of the Warren Circle in this situation? Can we help?"

Heads nodded and a murmur of yeses volleyed around the room.

"Explain to us how this works then. We have to be read in fully to be able to help." Fitz looked over at Charlie who was agreeing. "I can speak for both of us when I say that we need to understand your purpose and what you do here to understand our role. Neither of us likes sitting around wasting time. If there's something that needs to be done, we want to do it. What exactly has the Warren Circle done throughout history?" When no one spoke up, Fitz pushed harder. "Look, we can go. Read us in or we can walk out of here and pretend this whole thing doesn't exist."

"Time is of the essence," someone shouted from the back.

Senator Ford held his hand up to stop him. "Fitz is right. They need to understand before we ask anything of them. And this situation…" He took a deep breath and let it out in a sigh. Ford gestured for Charlie and Fitz to sit down at one of the tables. He remained standing with Marcus Kane.

Ford gestured out toward the tables. "The people you see in this room are here because their forefathers throughout history have been coming together to support the fragile concept of democracy since the founding of the country. This is a birthright for all of them. As I said at the start, we've never had outsiders in the Warren Circle before. Each one of the men has ancestors who came together to start the Warren Circle back during the Revolutionary War. It was used as a spy network to help the Patriots. Military strategy, too. Whatever George Washington needed. Later, it was used to help democracy hold."

"You keep saying that," Charlie interrupted. "What does that mean?"

It was the man Charlie seemed to know, James Blackwell, who responded. "It means we keep things running on track even if the person in the White House either doesn't care or doesn't know how. The president can bring a lot of unqualified people into their cabinet who can make radical decisions against the best interest of the people and frankly the government. Charlie, you know this firsthand. It's hard to take the intelligence we know and make it actionable. There's a lot you saw and did in the field for the good of the country that never made it back to an official desk."

Charlie agreed. "Can we assume the work you've done here has remained out of the press for the most part?"

"Nearly all of it," Blackwell confirmed. "We have averted wars, stopped assassinations, prevented governments including our own from being overthrown. We have investigated and found the truth to things when others couldn't."

Fitz was interested. "Like what?"

"In time," Ford said, redirecting them. "As I said, the men in the Warren Circle have ancestors going back to the beginning. It was the members' job to recruit someone from their family to take over their role when they retired. Unfortunately, families got smaller over the years, people less inclined to go into government work or others simply not qualified. It's a bit of a miracle we have lasted as long as we have. The last two members to leave didn't have replacements. I thought it was time we brought in some new blood." He looked over at Charlie. "And a woman's perspective."

Although Charlie appreciated that, she squinted her eyes in the way she did when she was concerned. "Neither Fitz nor I have any children to pass this down to when we retire."

"That's fine," Ford assured. "We will work as a group to recruit. No matter what happens, the Warren Circle must continue. There is far too much at stake for it to stop. That's why the group hesitantly agreed to go outside the original member families."

Ford went on to describe a few times the Warren Circle was pivotal, particularly around the Civil War and working behind the scenes with allies and even the enemy during the world wars.

Fitz listened until Ford was done. Then he stated what he had at the start. "Tell us how we can help you now."

Marcus cleared his throat. "There are many questions about the killer still left to be answered. He was part of a religious cult. There could be other threats from them or inside the government."

"How do you know that?" Fitz asked, looking for the evidence.

"We don't know for sure," Marcus admitted. "That's where the two of you come in. We need you to find the truth."

"We need someone from the outside. If there are internal threats, it will raise too much suspicion if we are asking questions," Ford said with an expression that told Fitz there had been more than one reason they had been asked to join. "Are you up for it?"

"I'm in," Charlie said not seeming to feel the restriction Fitz felt in his chest.

"I'm in too," Fitz said after a beat, hoping he wasn't going to regret it.

CHAPTER 3

itz and Charlie sat alone at one of the tables in the basement of Ford's Theater. They had learned that the theater had been the meeting place for the Warren Circle since shortly after the Lincoln assassination. The members had gathered at the scene of the crime to discuss the best course of action. A few didn't believe that John Wilkes Booth had acted alone and were sure it was part of a broader Confederate conspiracy. Bringing those other people to justice had been their goal.

Fitz's mind was still swirling with questions. "Did it sound to you like the members had assassinated people? Like they brought their own justice to certain situations."

"That's exactly what it sounded like to me." Charlie clasped her hands on the table. "This could get messy, Fitz. You and I have different standards for justice. It's why the FBI and CIA don't always play well together. The CIA gets their hands dirty in ways the FBI could never."

Fitz knew some of the history of the agency. The coups they had staged in countries around the globe and the operations that toppled regimes. They even ousted foreign leaders who didn't align with the needs of the United States. Kermit Roosevelt, the grandson of President Theodore Roosevelt, had been an intelligence officer with the Office of Strategic Services, the precursor to the CIA, during and following World War II. He'd been directly involved in the 1953 coup in Iran. The United States and Britain toppled the democratically elected government of Iran run by Mohammad Mossadegh. Kermit was a key figure.

It didn't take long for Fitz to consider the implications of joining the Warren Circle. "I'm not killing people. I'm not an assassin, a gun for hire, Charlie. Not unless my life or the life of someone I care about is directly threatened. Then I'll go after the person with a ferocity you probably don't realize is in me. I can't be involved in toppling governments. I spent my whole career on one side of the law. I can't make that radical of a shift."

Charlie had witnessed him do some crazy things before but nothing that ever crossed the line. On the other hand, she had done a whole host of things she never talked about with him. He watched her expression for any sign that she might echo what he said.

Finally, Charlie shrugged. "I don't think they will have you kill anyone, Fitz. Not anyone good, anyway."

"See that's what I'm talking about," Fitz said, the worry line creasing across his forehead. "Killing people and toppling governments is your thing." He threw it out there to see if she'd bite. When she didn't look away nor confirm, he laughed. "I'm not going to get anything out of you."

"The Russians tried. I have the scars to prove it. They failed and you will too." She laid her hand on the file Marcus had given them before he left. Senator Ford told them they could have the room for as long as they wanted but not to take the file with them. Ford said to give it back to the man who had let them in.

When Fitz asked about the man's role in all of this, Ford said that the Smith family had long been guardians for the Warren Circle. They found them places to meet, made sure their time together remained private, helped with coordination, and used a courier for messages back and forth when needed. They tried their best now to have no electronic communication. It was part of the reason they had remained a secret – they did things the way they had been done during the Revolutionary War. It made it harder now but kept the protection they needed.

The Smiths were not official members but a resource.

The Warren Circle wouldn't have survived without them.

Fitz pulled the single manilla file folder to him and flipped it open. Marcus told them all the information about the killer was in the file. Fitz lowered his head to read. He skimmed over it all once then read aloud to Charlie. "Zachary Steele is a thirty-year-old Army veteran. He was dishonorably discharged from the Army two years ago. He had a few deployments to Afghanistan. He suffered from some post-traumatic stress disorder. His military record indicates that he refused treatment but the outbursts and violence continued. That contributed to his release from the military."

"What was the final straw?" Charlie asked. "Dealing with PTSD is run of the mill these days. There had to be more than that."

Fitz turned to the military record and skimmed the page. He winced. "Steele attacked two men in his unit. Fellow soldiers turned him in. There was a military hearing and he was dishonorably discharged. I'm sure there was more in between the incident and his dismissal but it's not in the file."

"There is probably a lot more."

Fitz focused on the report. "He was originally from Kentucky but found his way to Virginia. He had trouble finding work after he left the Army and fell in with a group known as Last Covenant, a radical religious cult. There he found camaraderie for his racist and misogynist views."

Charlie shifted in the chair. "That's usually how it works. People like Steele are easily radicalized under those circumstances." She paused for a moment as if waiting for Fitz to go on. He could see she had more on her mind and encouraged her to continue. "Racist and misogynistic views are broad. There are so many hate groups out there with so many differing agendas. What exactly does that mean for Steele? What's Last Covenant all about?"

Fitz glanced down at the file and gestured with his hand as he spoke. "You know the usual stuff – white power, against race mixing, Holocaust denial, anti-immigrant. It looks like he hated everyone who wasn't white, straight, and his brand of dystopian Christian. He fell into the more extreme misogyny right down to wanting to strip women of the right to vote. They should be back in the kitchen and having babies. Forced marriage, forced sex, and forced birth if they didn't want to comply. Last Covenant was a mix of a militia group, a hate group, and a doomsday cult. They believed that the world was coming to an end soon if their radicalized ways of life didn't become law."

"They lobby?" Charlie asked.

"I don't know but they certainly protested at several places even going as far as to harass female professors and college students on campuses they deemed as havens for Satan. This is like the Westboro Baptist Church on steroids. More extreme than even the KKK."

"I can see why he wouldn't like a woman president." Charlie's breath caught in her throat.

Fitz closed the file. "Are you okay? You've had a look on your face that I can't explain since we got to this meeting."

"I'm fine." Charlie shook off whatever she was feeling. It was clear she didn't want to take the deep dive Fitz had been hoping for. She wore her emotions close to the vest and didn't allow herself to wallow long in her feelings. As a result, Fitz rarely knew what she was thinking and feeling. It annoyed him because he wanted to know and more importantly he wanted to help.

"I know you're not fine," Fitz said to her scowl. "I also know not to push it."

Charlie did what she did best and reframed the conversation. "I think the question Marcus was asking of us is if Steele acted alone or had an accomplice. Maybe some grander plan inside Last Covenant cult."

"Possibly," Fitz said slowly, not sure that's what Marcus meant at all. "He certainly was already radicalized to the cause and had the military connection. He would have been easy to track down. I'm sure the FBI has this group on a watchlist of some kind. I believe Marcus and Senator Ford were suggesting someone used him to do their dirty work."

"I'm sure he was highly motivated to sacrifice himself for the cause. If it's someone in government, they are going to be protected. There won't be an easy-to-find paper trail."

Fitz agreed. "The FBI investigation will look at the surface and make sure no one from Last Covenant was also involved. If there's a government connection, it's going to be buried deeper than the FBI agents will find. It would probably take Marcus suggesting looking for a government connection for the agents to explore that. I assume that's what Marcus was trying to avoid. Why do you think that is?"

Charlie sat for a moment to consider. "Because someone in the Department of Justice is going to be looking over his shoulder. Congressional committees are going to be looking for answers. If there's someone on the inside, any investigation will alert them immediately. They will cover their tracks."

Fitz agreed with that. "Whoever did this is going to see the FBI coming and take the appropriate steps to either get the investigation shut down or hide whatever evidence there is. They aren't going to see the Warren Circle coming because they don't know it exists. I think the goal is to pacify them with the FBI investigation while we dig around behind the scenes."

Charlie asked, "Won't that ultimately make the FBI look bad if we uncover a plot they missed?"

That brought Fitz right back to his initial concern. "That's why I asked about their end game. Say we investigate and find that there is a broader conspiracy. What then?"

"I'm sure Marcus will find a way to utilize the FBI to bring it to light."

"Or take out the threat themselves," Fitz said, expressing his earlier concern.

Charlie shook her head. "Don't assume that. The Warren Circle has been doing this work for more than two centuries. They don't seem like an assassin group. I assume if they find something, they handle it in the most appropriate way possible. We just have to trust them on that."

"Is trust that easy for you?" When Charlie didn't answer, he shoved the file aside and leaned his arms on the table. "I know you can't tell me about your time in the CIA. I'm lucky you even finally told me the truth that you were in the CIA. I used to have more trust when I was a detective. I've lost a lot of trust in the government since I started this work. I've seen their secrets and what they hide. I've seen the way they cover for each other and tell one story behind closed doors and another to the public. I can't just trust a secret cabal that's been working behind the scenes for centuries. Men are fallible, Charlie. Speaking of that, you were the only woman in this room."

"We didn't meet all of them," she said, but even she didn't sound convinced. "Government is the oldest boys club in the world. It's changing slowly. *The arc of the moral universe is long, but it bends toward justice.* I've lived by that quote."

"Martin Luther King, Jr.?"

Charlie nodded. "The only person I fully trust is myself. I've extended that to a few of my colleagues in the CIA and you. Others either gain my trust or not. I make decisions accordingly after that." Charlie smiled across the table at him. "I've never seen you so hesitant before. What's going on?"

Fitz couldn't articulate it. The only thing it came down to was his reticence to join things. "I don't want to say I'm a loner, but I'm not much of a joiner. The Warren Circle feels like a lifelong commitment to something I'm not sure I can trust. Now, at one of the most pivotal times in American history, they are handing us a task. It feels as much a test as anything else."

"It might be a test," Charlie concluded. "Whether it is or not, don't you want to know who tried to kill the president? That's what it comes down to, Fitz. That's all they are asking of us right now. Find out who shot the president and why. It doesn't have to be bigger than that."

Fitz knew Charlie was right. He was making more of it than it needed to be. He pulled the file close to him and flipped it open, reading a few more details about Steele. He'd have to commit it all to memory. Marcus was clear that they weren't allowed to take the file or photograph anything from it. He studied it for as long as he could keep focus.

Before closing the file, he fixated on the one single photo of the man – five-foot-ten, sandy brown hair cut close but not a military haircut, a crooked nose probably from being broken a few times, and deep-set blue eyes. The crows' feet around his eyes and deep lines across his forehead made him look older than his years.

When he was done, he spun the file around for Charlie to read through everything again and commit it to memory. Fitz knew once she read something, she wouldn't forget.

Much too soon, the door to the room opened with a groan. The man Ford told him to call Smitty hitched his chin toward them. "Ready?"

"Yes," Fitz responded without a trace of sincerity in his voice. He felt like he just signed his life away.

CHAPTER 4

itz still had a business to run and it required his full attention. After Smitty took them through the secret alley doorway that from the outside looked like it was part of the brick wall, they went back to the office. Charlie retreated to her office while Fitz went to his. Each of them focused on work that had the most pressing deadlines. They worked right through lunch and well into the afternoon.

Fitz was so focused on the task at hand that he didn't hear Charlie call his name. It took her stepping into his office and walking right up to his desk before he finally raised his head from his laptop. "Done?" he asked her.

"Nearly. I went downstairs to make coffee and saw on the news that the president was out of surgery and was in the intensive care unit. She is expected to live. Whether she makes a full recovery is still to be determined. The recovery will take considerable time. All the powers of the presidency have been transferred to Vice President Henry Coldwell for the time being. The pundits are already speculating about what will happen long term."

Along with a dislike for most politicians, Fitz felt the same about the mainstream media. Where were the Walter Cronkites and Edward R. Murrows of his generation? It was all a bunch of talking heads and an effort to sort fact from fiction. It's why he rarely watched the news.

Fitz asked, "Did they say anything about the shooter?" While Ford had a file on Zachary Steele, he'd yet to hear the man's name mentioned on the news.

Charlie moved files from the chair in the corner of the room to the floor and pulled it up to his desk. "They finally released his name about a half-hour ago. No details other than his age and that he was originally from Kentucky but living in Virginia. They are keeping the information locked down for right now. I'm surprised there weren't any leaks to the press before this afternoon."

Fitz was surprised too. There were always leaks, most of them intentional. "Did they give any specifics about how the shooting happened?"

"A Secret Service spokesperson said the shooter was lying in wait at the Lincoln Memorial. The Secret Service didn't say why she was on the monument, only that they were near the statue of Lincoln and Steele was off to the other side. Honestly, the biggest question I have is how the Secret Service agents didn't see him on the approach. He had to have been visible."

Fitz tried to imagine the scene that unfolded that morning. He was having a hard time envisioning the Lincoln Memorial and where the shooter might have been that he wouldn't have been immediately seen. "Monroe ran early enough in the morning that there shouldn't have been too many people out there. I don't know how they missed him." There was a look on Charlie's face that hinted at what she was thinking. "Let me guess, you think at least one of the Secret Service agents knew the shooter was there and let it happen."

"Maybe more than one if Marcus and Senator Ford are right that this was an inside job. Even if someone paid the shooter, he still had to pull it off. It might not be hard to find out Monroe still ran in the mornings, but I assume the Secret Service at a minimum made her vary the route."

Fitz was already making a mental list of the people they'd need to interview. The challenge was they had no authority to interview them. He had been thinking about that for the better part of the day in between working on other assignments. The *why* they were involved kept creeping back to the forefront.

"What do we tell people about why we are investigating this? We are going to need some access. At least the other members of the Warren Circle have the inside track. We are just two civilians butting into something where we have no jurisdiction. Secret Service agents aren't going to talk to us."

Charlie didn't look convinced. "They might. We don't have powers to arrest. If they want to get the information out, clear a guilty conscience, or be a whistle-blower, they might be looking for allies." She considered their options for a moment. "We can always say that we have an official investigation but can't disclose the client. We've had to do that before. The guise of official capacity has never stopped either of us."

That was true enough. Fitz couldn't shake the overwhelming feeling. The last time he felt like this was when he started work on the D.C. serial killer case that ultimately upended his life and got him fired. Maybe that's what it was – some weird feelings from the past creeping into this case.

Charlie was staring at him waiting for a response that he didn't have. He asked her a question instead. "Did you start to look into his military background? Did they mention that on the news?"

Charlie confirmed she had started digging. "The news didn't mention anything other than Steele had been in the Army and deployed to Afghanistan several times. He wasn't a sniper or in special operations. He had ten years in and had achieved the rank of master sergeant in the infantry when the Army dishonorably discharged him. My guess is he went right in after high school and worked his way up.

He was probably going to try to get his twenty years in but that didn't work out for him."

Fitz knew Charlie had ways to get information most, including him, would never be able to access. "Did you get any specifics about what happened there?"

"Not yet," Charlie said, "but I have the names of two of the men who went above his head."

Fitz resisted the urge to ask her how she had obtained that information. "Are they still in?"

"Both of them left the Army shortly after. Manuel Garcia is local. He works for an insurance company. He was the first person to speak up then others followed. I don't have much on him other than where he works and his current address. He doesn't live far from here. Just outside the beltway in Manassas. Probably about an hour's drive from here."

"That's enough to start." Fitz checked his watch. It was nearing three-thirty. If they left now, they'd beat some of the rush-hour traffic on the way out of D.C. at least. "We can probably get there in time for him coming home from work."

"Assuming he works a regular schedule. Given I don't have a phone number, I think we should take a shot at it."

Fitz was eager to get started. Once he got his teeth into the case, he might shake the feeling he'd been having. They gathered up their things to leave. Fitz uncharacteristically double-checked the lock on the door before leaving.

Charlie eyed him. "Paranoid?"

As Fitz got into the SUV and buckled his seatbelt, he admitted, "That might be what's going on. I've never known anything about secret societies that didn't turn out bad. It's like a cult in a way."

"That doesn't sound like what the Warren Circle is all about." She turned in the seat to look at him. "I'm not going to let you get caught up in a cult."

Fitz laughed, shaking his head. "I'm not worried about it being a cult. I was thinking about movies where there are secret societies and once you get in, it's impossible to get out. At least we didn't have to go through some weird initiation."

"Black robes and a candle service? Maybe a blood oath and chanting in a circle in someone's basement?"

Fitz laughed at what she said while not admitting that had been exactly what he thought an initiation into the Warren Circle would have been like. He had expected more formality to it than a meeting in the Ford's Theater basement. It was all rather unceremonious. He was only a little bit glad about that.

Nearly an hour later, they pulled up to a two-story house with white siding and light blue shutters. The door was the same color blue. An older model SUV was parked in the driveway. There were a handful of Legos scattered on the front porch. Fitz didn't see anyone behind the large front window.

They planned to catch the man coming home. They decided to wait until five-thirty and if he still wasn't home to try the door. The last thing they wanted to do was get his wife who'd probably alert him. They didn't know if Manuel would avoid them if given the chance.

At five-twenty, their patience paid off. A man with dark hair driving a Ford pick-up truck passed them on the street, pulling into the driveway behind the SUV. The man parked, cut the engine, and opened the driver's side door.

Fitz was out of his SUV and he and Charlie made their way across the street. "Manuel Garcia?" he asked as he approached the man.

The man pulled a workbag from the truck and turned to the sound of his name. "Can I help you?" he asked, no trace of concern in his tone.

Fitz introduced himself and Charlie as they approached. "I'm a former D.C. homicide detective and run an opposition research firm. I wanted to ask you a couple of questions about the shooting of President Monroe."

"You're here to ask me about Zachary Steele," Manuel said as he closed the truck door, heading down the walkway to the front door of his home. He turned back around to them. "You with the FBI?"

"Not the FBI," Charlie said, not explaining further. "We just have a few questions."

Manuel hesitated for only a second. "We can talk in the living room. I'll have my wife take the kids upstairs." He pushed open the door, called out for his wife, informing her they had guests, then ascended the stairs.

Fitz and Charlie stood awkwardly in the small foyer that had a simple wooden table next to the door with a half-dead plant and a silver wire bin with mail. A moment later Manuel charged back down the stairs having changed his work shirt to a gray tee-shirt.

"Sorry, I should have told you to go sit down. Also call me Manny, no one but my mother calls me Manuel." He led them into a living room, moving children's toys out of the path. "I have two kids under six. It can get messy in here sometimes," he said as a way of explanation. When they were seated, Charlie and Fitz on a small loveseat across from the couch, he raised his eyebrows. "I saw the news so I heard that Zach shot the president. It doesn't surprise me, honestly."

"Why is that?" Fitz asked, still not believing this man would invite them into his home to have this conversation when he could have easily said no.

Manny stared off across the room. "I'm not a rat. I didn't want to turn him in to the Army. I certainly didn't want to destroy the man's career. He was escalating though. Each mission we went on, he was escalating the violence with civilians and the rest of us. I wasn't going to stand around and wait for him to kill someone. It was hard enough over there knowing who was friendly or not. Zach's actions were making it harder for us. We needed people to trust us and terrorizing them wasn't the way to do that."

Fitz could see the man still had some conflicting emotions about having to go over Zach's head in the military. "You did the right thing," he assured Manny. "We need more people like you stepping forward for what's right. Neither of us have any judgment about what you did."

Charlie agreed with that. "Did you have any contact with Zach after the Army?"

"Surprisingly, I did." Manny raked a hand through his hair then clasped his hands in his lap. "He called me a few months ago. He said he got sober and wanted to make amends."

Fitz hadn't seen substance abuse in the file. "Zach was a drinker?"

"Drugs too. Pills. Cocaine. Anything he could find. I don't know how he ever passed a drug test but there are ways." Manny paused for a moment as if he were going to say something else. He seemed to think better of it. He only added, "I was glad he got sober."

Beyond the pause, there was something in his tone that made Fitz take notice. "That's not all you want to say. Be candid with us. Did you not believe he got sober?"

"I believe he did," Manny clarified. "I just don't believe that he did it for the right reasons. He told me about this group he joined. I didn't think being there with those people was going to make his life better. By the end of the conversation, I felt more like he was threatening me than apologizing."

"How so?" Charlie asked.

Manny's features tightened. "He made a few racist comments about me going back to my home country. That it might be better for me. If I didn't, there were people who would make me. He followed that up with some comments about my wife and how she shouldn't be working. He told me I needed to get a better handle on my marriage. That since she had my name, she was my property now and it was up to me to handle my home."

Fitz started to say something, but Manny held up a hand to stop him.

"I was born here in Virginia. My parents were born here in Virginia. There's no country for me to go back to. I'm as American as he was." Manny took a breath, his anger apparent on his face. "My wife can do whatever she wants to do. She loves working as a nurse. Neither she nor my children are property. The guy is messed up." Manny paused and corrected himself. "Was messed up. He's dead, right?"

Fitz confirmed. "You said he was with a group. Do you know anything about that?"

"I didn't at the time. I looked it up after and was shocked by what I read. Maybe it was that group that pushed him over the edge, but Zach had been making threats before them."

"Threats?" Fitz asked.

Manny sighed and nodded. "Zach had threatened to kill female military officers as well as senators before this. The Army knew all of it. It was in the report I filed. Did you see that?"

"No," Charlie and Fitz said at the same time.

Manny shook his head. "Then let me tell you the rest of it."

CHAPTER 5

"It doesn't sound like Zachary Steele needed too much to radicalize him," Charlie said as Fitz drove in bumper-to-bumper traffic on the way back to D.C. "Sounds to me like he was primed and ready. I wouldn't be surprised if he sought out Last Covenant because it fit what he already believed rather than him being some lost soul after the military."

The story Manny told them was of a man who had entered the military already radicalized with racist, misogynistic, and homophobic beliefs. During his tenure with the Army, two female soldiers had reported him for sexual harassment. The result was that the female soldiers were removed and his commanding officers made it a point not to allow women in his unit. It never solved the problem. It gave Steele exactly what he wanted. As time went on, his views grew darker and more violent.

Fitz was so lost in thought that he didn't hear Charlie. "Huh?" he said, turning to look at her. "Sorry, I was thinking about something."

"I was wondering if maybe we are looking for something that isn't there," Charlie said again. "If Steele was this radicalized, it sounds like he could have easily been a lone wolf shooter."

"All we can do is see where the evidence leads us."

"Do you want to speak to anyone else who served with him to make sure Manny was telling the truth?"

Fitz changed lanes to pass a slow car as he contemplated it. "There was the information in his military file that Ford showed us. Manny told a broader picture of what was happening. Do you think we are good?"

Charlie thought they were. "There is enough in the file that backs up what Manny said."

Fitz's shoulder's tightened and he moved his head from side to side to loosen his neck. "Let's skip the rest of the military stuff for now. I think we know enough to get a clear picture of who this guy is. We need to know his last twenty-four to forty-eight hours."

"Where are we starting with that?"

Fitz knew exactly where they needed to start, not that access was going to be so easily granted. "Let's head to the Lincoln Memorial. I want to get a sense of exactly what Steele saw this morning."

"They aren't going to let us through."

"Maybe." Fitz was hoping that the FBI and the Secret Service had finished with the scene and the people left to guard it were some of his old colleagues with D.C. Metro. At the very least, they'd get as close as they could. Fitz drove them the rest of the way moving with the flow of traffic and changing lanes when a car went too slow and started to annoy him.

By the time they made it back to D.C., a drizzle fell against the windshield enough that Fitz had to turn on the wipers. Rush hour had ended and darkness had fallen over the district. Fitz liked this time of the evening. The office buildings were empty and the only people on the street were those who lived in the neighborhood or who were scurrying off to one of the restaurants. It was quiet on the streets, the roads were clearer, and he could breathe.

The only traffic they encountered was a few blocks from the Lincoln Memorial. He had anticipated that people would be out trying to see the area where the president had been shot. He was grateful for the weather because he assumed most people would be heading for shelter. The rain was expected to get heavier later into the evening.

"I'm just going to park here," Fitz said as he pulled over to the curb. It was two-hour parking during the day but that ended at five. He also didn't have to pay for parking at that time of the evening. He pulled his phone out and sent a quick text. He could feel Charlie's eyes on him. "I'm trying to get us access."

"Good luck with that," she said as she slid out of the passenger seat and closed the door behind her.

Fitz had been hoping he'd get a text back from his old partner by the time they made it to the barrier. Nothing came in though. While it was D.C. Metro standing guard, Fitz didn't know the three young officers.

They pushed through a few people heading for the far right side of the memorial steps. It was on the right side behind one of the pillars that Marcus said Steele had positioned himself. Fitz and Charlie were able to get right up to the barrier as the sea of people started to retreat as the rain grew heavier.

"This doesn't make any sense, Fitz," Charlie said after only a few seconds of standing there. He was thinking the same thing. "If she was on a run, why was she up there on the memorial? There is also nowhere for Steele to have hid."

Everything Charlie said was true. Fitz stood there staring at the monument, calculating angles and looking in every direction trying to make sense of it. He couldn't.

Fitz left Charlie standing there as he made his way over to one of the uniformed officers standing guard at the barrier. The rain pelted the young man's uniform and hat, leaving drips from the brim down the front of his face.

"Officer," Fitz said to get the young man's attention. He hadn't known the young cop when he was a detective. Still, he introduced himself as a former homicide detective. "I realize you probably don't have a lot of details and this isn't information you could share anyway but this crime scene doesn't make any sense. Do you know where President Monroe was standing when she got shot? I was told near the statue of Lincoln. But if that's true, and she and her Secret Service were up there on the memorial, there'd be nowhere for Steele to hide."

The young cop shifted his attention to Fitz. A light smile graced his lips. "I know who you are, Mr. Fitzgerald. Everyone does." He leaned into Fitz. "At first I was told she was shot on the stairs on her jog up. Then we were told she was standing near Lincoln. Neither story made sense to me either."

"Why was she off her running path?"

"Above my pay grade, Mr. Fitzgerald. They just told me to stand here and guard the area. As you can see, there are a lot of people who came to the spot to see. Not much to see though. The crime scene team was here early this morning and gone." He hitched his chin toward the stragglers still there. "I never understood people who want to come see tragedy."

"People want to be a part of history," Fitz said absently. "Did you see the crime scene techs out here or only hear about it?"

The young cop cocked his head to the side. "What do you mean?"

"Well, did you see them out here working, or were you just told they were out here?"

"Told. What does it matter? I'm never out at a scene when the techs are doing their thing. It wasn't D.C. Metro techs either it was the FBI. They are the ones in charge of the investigation. We are just here protecting the area."

Fitz knew he wasn't going to get anything else from this young man. He thanked him for standing out in the rain and following orders. He made his way back to Charlie. "Something is off. If she was out for a run, why go up on the memorial? If they are going up, why didn't the

Secret Service search it first? There is nowhere up there to hide."

"I've been standing here thinking the same thing."

"I don't think it happened here," Fitz finally said after reflecting on it. What he couldn't articulate was why he felt that way. He had no evidence of that. Everything *felt* off. Fitz had learned a long time ago not to dismiss that kind of feeling when it rose in his gut. He had solved more than a handful of cases by trusting it.

Charlie turned her head to look up at him. "I've been running every scenario in my head. If stopping here was random, the shooter would have no way of knowing. If she was called to meet someone here, wouldn't the Secret Service sweep the area before her arrival? They would have sent an advanced team or at least an agent or two."

Charlie was asking all the right questions. They weren't going to answer anything standing here in the rain. He nudged her shoulder. "Let's go back to the office and start writing down all these questions. We can watch the news to see what they are saying. Maybe there are more details now than earlier reports."

They made it back to the office forty minutes later, after picking up some dinner on their way. Fitz's stomach needed to be satisfied if he was going to give any of this his full attention.

They were mid-way through dinner with the news turned up loudly in the background when a knock on the front door had them both crane their necks in that direction. Even when they did have clients in the office, it was scheduled and during the day. No one should have been knocking on their door this late at night.

Charlie started to stand, but Fitz gestured for her to sit. "Let me go." She wasn't going to let Fitz go alone, even to answer the door. She followed him down the short hallway. Fitz glanced over his shoulder, chuckling at her overprotective stance.

He glanced out the top of the window more confused than worried. He unlocked the door and pulled it open. "Burrows, what are you doing here in the rain this time of night?"

Charlie gasped behind him. Fitz heard her footfalls as she hightailed it back to the conference room. FBI Agent Josh Burrows had met Fitz on a previous case. His relationship with Charlie pre-dated that. Fitz was still waiting for her to tell him about it. Burrows had been the one to tell Fitz that Charlie had broken his heart. It was a vulnerable admission from a tough law enforcement officer who had proven valuable the last time Fitz got too mixed up in government corruption.

"Are you going to let me in or leave me standing out in the rain?"

"Of course," Fitz said, backing up to allow him to enter. He closed and locked the door behind him. Without being asked, Burrows made his way toward the conference room. Fitz had no choice but to trail after him.

"Charlie," Burrows said, his tone curt but the smile on his face told Fitz he was glad just to gaze upon her face.

As usual, Charlie remained unaffected. She barely glanced up at him as she dug back into her food. She offered him a nod, not even an offer to sit.

"What's brought you out here tonight?" Fitz asked, pointing to one of the chairs. "I'd offer you some food but there's not much left."

Burrows glanced down at Charlie, regret etched on his face. "Not a social call, unfortunately." He sat in the chair next to Charlie, across from Fitz. "I'm sure you've heard the president was shot."

Fitz nodded. "We have." There was a lingering question he didn't articulate.

"I can trust you, right? We have a certain rapport?"

"I didn't think that was a question at this point."

"I always like to know where I stand, Fitz." He cast a glance over at Charlie. "When a man knows where he stands, he knows who he can trust."

It was a dig at her for ending the relationship without giving him much of a reason. Fitz understood he was still hurt, but he wasn't going to let Burrows come in here and jab at her. Not that Charlie needed his protection. She could snap Burrows in two if she chose. Still, what kind of man would he be?

Fitz said, "If you can't trust us, you know where the door is."

Burrows shrugged off Fitz's tone. He shifted his eyes toward the ceiling. "Are we alone?"

"No one's here," Charlie assured him. She had stopped eating and while she wasn't making eye contact with him, her body had shifted slightly toward him.

That was enough for Burrows to continue. He leaned into the table. "President Monroe isn't my case. There are other FBI agents assigned to it. I'm here because I need your help." He paused as if he wasn't sure he could say the words aloud.

Fitz had a sense of what was coming. Yet he was still taken aback by it.

"I don't believe the official story," Burrows admitted. "I don't think there's any way that it could have happened like they are saying. That means we aren't even twenty-four hours into it and there's already a cover-up."

"We agree," Charlie said, more readily than Fitz would have.

He wondered if they were the only three people in D.C. who knew this.

They were being tasked with the *who done it,* not the how, but it seemed figuring out the how might just lead them to the who.

Burrows seemed pleased they were on the same page. "I assumed you would feel that way too. That's why I'm here. I want to run a parallel investigation and want your help."

CHAPTER 6

Neither Charlie nor Fitz flinched at the admission by the seasoned FBI agent, who was setting a path to go rogue. Fitz didn't want to show his hand too soon.

Charlie wasn't going to either. "Shouldn't you be bringing those concerns to your boss instead of us?"

Burrow gave an emphatic no. "If there is a cover-up this soon, it means those in the know are hiding something big. If it's that big, who knows how far this goes up the chain of command. I don't trust anyone right now other than the two of you."

Neither of them said a word.

Burrows laid out what he had uncovered. "I'm sure it's occurred to you both that you each have a specific set of skills that when combined cover law enforcement, international intelligence, and an understanding of the geopolitical landscape that most in Washington don't have."

Fitz eyed him. "We're aware of that."

"I've been out of the game for a long time, Josh," Charlie said, using the man's first name causing both of them to zero in on her. Burrows's expression softened and Fitz held back a smile. It was like a crack in a wall had opened up and a little glimmer of light shone through.

"Do you still have your security clearances?"

"No. I'm out, Josh. Completely out, which is exactly what I want."

She asked the question that was on the tip of Fitz's tongue. "Why do you believe there's already been a cover-up? The news is admitting the White House has been slow to release details."

"I think it's because they have been slow to release details and can't even answer the most basic questions, like why was President Monroe at the Lincoln Memorial at that time of morning? There was no way she was shot running past."

Fitz stopped him. "The D.C. Metro cop I spoke to said Monroe was near the statue of Lincoln when she was shot, not running past. That's at least more plausible."

Burrows digested that new information. "If that was the case, then Secret Service agents would have checked that area ahead of time." He paused for a moment. "There's no blood."

"What do you mean?" Charlie asked.

Burrows wasn't going to slide past that. "I was out to the scene earlier before most of the rain started, soon after the crime scene techs were there and there was no blood anywhere. Not on the sidewalk or the stairs or even up on the landing, except where the shooter was killed. The crime scene techs thought it odd and inquired. They were told that when Monroe was shot she collapsed onto Secret Service agents who got her out of there. Any blood was absorbed by their clothing, which conveniently wasn't available. That's unlikely."

Charlie jerked her body forward. "What do you mean wasn't available? Anything in that crime scene including what those agents were wearing, especially if they got blood on them, should be a part of the record."

Burrows agreed with her. "If the Secret Service has them, they are refusing to turn the clothes over."

"How did she get to the hospital?" Fitz asked, assuming that an ambulance had been called. He hadn't given it too much thought until that moment.

"Secret Service vehicle, which they claimed was out there with them while she was jogging. I'm sure it was close by as that's protocol. It was also confirmed that she arrived at the hospital by Secret Service. One nurse said that the agents who carried her in did have blood on them. One agent said he didn't have any details about the shooting and the other was quiet. The hospital staff said it was an odd scene. There were also no witnesses. The FBI hasn't been able to find one witness to this shooting."

Fitz shifted in his seat, the unlikeliness of that made his heart race. "Not one? I know the streets of D.C. aren't busy that early in the morning but not one witness? There was not one person in the area who heard the shots echo?"

"Not one."

"Then she wasn't shot there," Charlie said definitively, saying aloud what they were all thinking.

Fitz wasn't ready to jump to that conclusion so quickly. "I don't think it's that simple. She was shot someplace. That's not contested. Why hide it?"

"Distraction," Burrows said. "Cover-up."

"But why?" That still didn't make any sense to Fitz unless the answer was so bad that it could…he wasn't even sure. His mind couldn't fathom a reason to conceal where the president had been shot. Neither had an answer for why, so he asked, "Are there any witnesses who saw her jogging this morning and might be able to corroborate at least the path she took?"

"I don't know," Burrows admitted. "As I said, this isn't my case. I know the lead agent, Isabelle Conklin. She's good and thorough, but she's territorial. She's not going to share much with me. The information I got was from the crime scene techs."

He focused his attention across the table directly at Fitz. "There's not been one witness who has come forward on the news either. I know reporters have been begging for witnesses and no one has come forward. A reporter from CNN went down to the Lincoln Memorial and asked people in the crowd what they knew. There was not one person who'd been a witness to it."

Charlie countered, "Couldn't the FBI and Secret Service have asked the witnesses not to give any interviews? This is a sensitive matter. Maybe we are expecting far too much too soon."

"No," Burrows said with a shake of his head. "If the shooter was still alive or if they didn't stop him and he's out there in the wind, maybe they ask to hold back certain evidence from the news. They aren't going to be able to stop people from speaking out. It's not information that people are going to keep quiet. You saw them out there today at the monument."

They talked about the lack of evidence and the sheer amount of conflicting evidence for a few more minutes. Fitz couldn't sit there speculating anymore. He needed to bottom-line it. "I think we can all agree this shooting didn't go the way the media or the officials involved are portraying it went. What do we do about it?"

"I want to look into it and I want you to help me," Burrows said without any hesitation in his voice. "I don't think the FBI is going to figure out what's going on. The shooter, or the person they believe is the shooter, is dead. The case is a wrap as far as the FBI is concerned. They will do some cursory digging, making sure no one else is involved, dig up some background that shows why the shooter is the guy and that's it. It will become a footnote in history."

It was basically what Marcus had told them that morning.

"Do we know for sure Zachary Steele is the shooter?" Fitz asked.

"I'm not convinced," Burrows responded evenly. "I saw his body at the morgue. He was killed with a shot to the chest and one to the head. Either shot would have killed him. The medical examiner believes the shot to the chest was first. Here's the thing though." He paused, possibly for dramatic effect. "The medical examiner told me confidentially that the shots were fired at close range. That directly disputes the story given by the Secret Service."

Burrows had laid a lot of groundwork for only a few hours.

Fitz asked, "How are you getting so much information if you're not officially involved in this case?"

"People trust me, Fitz. I've been working here in Washington D.C. for a long time. The medical examiner, Dr. Ingrid Barnes, found some inconsistencies in what the Secret Service agents were telling her about the shooting of Steele. She tried to tell Agent Conklin and she said she felt brushed off. She's going to write it in her official report but wanted to run it by me to hear what I thought."

Fitz raised his eyes to Charlie. "Access is helpful." The information Burrows was bringing them now might have taken them days and even weeks to uncover if they uncovered it at all.

"It is helpful," Charlie echoed, turning to look at Burrows more directly than she had since he arrived. "How do you think we can help you?"

"This is too big for one person and I'm already at the max with my caseload. I'm afraid this is going to be swept under the rug. If Steele didn't shoot the president, then President Monroe's life is still in danger. If the Secret Service is lying about what happened, I want to know why."

"Was the intention to kill her?" Charlie asked. She saw the look of confusion on Fitz's face. "If this was someone inside the Secret Service, they have access to her. She'd trust them the most. They could have easily killed her. If it's someone close to her, the same logic applies. Was the shooting meant to kill her or just incapacitate her for a while?"

Burrows and Fitz shared a look. It was clear neither of them had considered that. "Does anyone know what her relationship is like with her husband?" Burrows asked.

Fitz was ready to dismiss that outright. He forced himself to sit with the idea that the First Gentleman, Richard Avery, might not be the kind, loving, supportive husband he appeared on television. Monroe was well into her political career by the time they met and she did not take her husband's last name, something reporters asked them about all the time, and a decision he had championed. He saw no reason for his wife to take his name. The media propped him up to be the perfect modern man.

There were a lot of firsts happening in the White House. Fitz recalled the images of Richard Avery on the campaign trail. Happy. Engaged. He had been a United States Attorney like his wife. He had kept his job during her rise even during the time she was in the Senate.

Once Monroe had secured the presidential nomination, Richard quit his job to take an active role in running her campaign. There were rumors of tension among the team once he got involved. That's all they were though, rumors. But Richard's demeanor had even changed in the footage Fitz saw of them on the campaign trail and during television interviews. The man had gone from happy-go-lucky to downright aloof, even seeming sullen at times. Fitz had chalked it up to the tiresome grind of campaigning. Now, he wondered if it was more.

He had to admit that Richard could be a possible suspect. "We can't rule him out," Fitz said finally. "What motive would he have? Would a man wait until his marriage was on the biggest public stage in the world and then try to take out his wife?"

"Leading cause of death for pregnant women is homicide, Fitz. Never underestimate what a man will do when he wants out of his marriage and can't leave," Charlie said with no emotion in her voice. She seemed resigned that it was inevitable that Richard would *and should* be a suspect.

Burrows seemed on the fence. "If it was Richard, wouldn't he have chosen a less public method of killing her? At least one that doesn't have this many holes in the story."

Fitz considered that. "I don't think we can say either way right now. Then there's Zachary Steele who pulled the trigger. He must fit in somewhere."

"Allegedly," Burrows and Charlie said at the same time. He shifted his eyes to her, a slow smile spreading across his face.

"He's dead. Shot by the Secret Service," Fitz argued, not sure what they were suggesting.

"That doesn't mean anything, Fitz," Charlie explained, her voice too calm for his liking.

Fitz sat back, folding his thick arms across his chest. "What are you suggesting? That this whole thing is some kind of operation – some curated crime scene for the public?"

"That's exactly what we are suggesting." Burrows looked to Charlie to back him up. All she did was offer a stiff nod. He turned his attention back to Fitz. "I think we need to start at the beginning and understand all the people who could want Monroe dead and who might have the best access."

Fitz couldn't recall one case in his career where they were starting at such a deficit.

"Are you willing to help me?" Burrows asked, looking between them.

Fitz couldn't tell him they were already investigating. Senator Ford said the Warren Circle had to remain a secret – he never told them they couldn't seek outside help. "I'm in if Charlie's in."

With all eyes on her, Charlie kept her features neutral giving nothing away. "If the three of us can't solve it, then I don't think anyone can." She turned her body fully in the chair to look at Burrows. "I'd be happy to help you," she offered, extending her hand, which was about as much affection as Fitz had ever seen from her.

Burrows took it gently as if he couldn't believe it was happening. "Let's get down to work."

CHAPTER 7

After tossing and turning all night, not able to think of anything other than the attempted murder of the president, Fitz got out of bed, put on running clothes, and left for his favorite running trail. Instead of driving to the park, he started his run at the end of his driveway. His feet pounded damp pavement through the city streets to the entrance of Rock Creek Park then picked up the pace once on the trail.

Fitz always ran to clear his head. It was a trick he found a few years after he became a detective. He'd been bogged down by a murder case, in which they hadn't had much evidence and no suspects. He went for a run to burn off some pent-up energy when he couldn't stop thinking about the case.

Fitz forced himself to think of nothing other than putting one foot in front of the other and how the air filled and depressed his lungs. He ran until his calves cramped and his lungs burned.

It was exactly what he needed this morning.

Fitz pushed himself as hard as his body would allow, his breath coming in ragged gasps, his feet pounding the dirt trail as the first light of dawn kissed the horizon. The cool air clung to him, a welcome contrast to the sweat that tickled his brow. The rhythm of his footfalls was his only focus.

A bird screeched overhead and he pushed harder, his legs aching with each stride as the trail twisted deeper into the dense woods. Rock Creek Park was serene this time of the morning, the quiet broken only by his labored breathing and the occasional rustle of the trees. He welcomed the solitude, the calm before the storm of the day that would demand his focus. But as he veered left, steering his body away from the main trail and deeper into the trees, a shiver ran down his spine.

Footsteps. An echo of his own, possibly.

Fitz had heard them moments ago, soft but steady. The subtle crunch of dirt underfoot, the light shuffle. It wasn't an echo. Fitz wasn't alone but that didn't necessarily mean anything. Many people jogged in the park at that hour. Despite all rational thought, something quickened his pulse.

His brain screamed *don't turn around.* The paranoia crept in against all logic. Fitz pushed forward, faster now, each footfall a beat of rising urgency. He ducked beneath low-hanging branches, his breath ragged and thick in his chest. Still, the footsteps remained behind him, unrelenting.

His instincts kicked in – something wasn't right.

With a sharp turn, Fitz veered deeper into the shadows of the woods, his muscles tightening as he reached the more isolated parts of the park. No one came here unless they were looking for something…or someone.

He slowed, his feet barely making a sound. It was only then he turned.

In a flash of movement, he turned his back to the nearest tree, eyes scanning the slivers of light between the trees. He expected to see a man – a shadow in the dim morning light, maybe a jogger who had come too close – but nothing. Silence.

Fitz's breath rasped in his throat, his hand instinctively reaching for the gun holstered at his side. The presence in the woods with him was undeniable. He could feel it – *someone was there.* Fitz tightened his grip on the hilt of his weapon, his mind locked in that state of sharp, focused clarity only a cop would know. The hairs on the back of his neck prickled as he tried to hear anything that would give him a clue as to what was happening.

From behind him – movement. A flash of a dark shape, too fast, too deliberate. Fitz spun with the speed of instinct, his heart slamming into his ribs as he raised his gun.

The figure wasn't a jogger. This was someone stalking him.

The man's eyes focused on Fitz. His breath was heavy as if caught off guard. With a low growl, Fitz rushed the man, slamming his shoulder into him. The man stumbled, but Fitz was on him, grabbing him by the shirt and slamming him into the dirt with a satisfying thud.

The ground was rough beneath him, his breath hot on the man's face, adrenaline surging through him, pumping more fury into his veins than he'd ever felt before.

"Who are you?" Fitz growled, his grip tightening on the man's throat. The stranger's wide eyes flared with panic, but his lips remained sealed. "Tell me who you are!"

The man turned his head, struggling to raise a hand in surrender. "I need to talk to you."

Fitz didn't believe that for a second. Why would he stalk him in the woods if he just wanted to talk? Fitz put a knee to the man's chest, pressing just enough to cause pain. "I'm not letting you up until you tell me who you are and why you are following me."

The man winced at the pressure Fitz caused on his chest. "My name is Wyatt Standfield and I'm with the Secret Service."

Fitz cursed in his face, not believing him for a second. "Don't play me."

"I'm not. I swear. I've been on desk duty for more than a year due to an injury."

Fitz instinctively released his knee from the man's chest, allowing him to struggle to a sitting position. "Show me your badge. Slowly."

"It's in my pocket. You can grab it if you want." Wyatt stared at Fitz's gun still in his right hand. "Can you put that away? There's no need for it. I'm here to talk to you. I just can't be seen talking to you. I figured out here in the woods was best."

Fitz holstered his weapon and patted the man down feeling the outline of a cred pack in his pocket. He released the man from his grip and leaned back on his haunches. "Get your badge yourself."

Wyatt struggled to sit up wincing as he moved. He dug his hand into his pocket and pulled out his Secret Service badge, turning it so Fitz could read it. "I can't be seen speaking to you. I didn't mean to startle you."

"It's barely morning light, thick in the woods. You're lucky I didn't shoot you."

"I admit it's not the best-conceived plan I've ever had." He put his hands behind him and started to push himself up, but Fitz still loomed over him. "You think we can stand and have this conversation? I could barely keep up with you running and you knocked the wind out of me with ease. I'm out of shape."

Fitz knew it had to have taken a lot for him to admit that. He pushed himself up to his full height and extended his hand to Wyatt, who slapped it away. The man still had his pride. "How'd you injure yourself?"

"I hurt my back during a training exercise. I had surgery and have been rehabbing for a year." Wyatt moved his hands behind himself, braced his lower back, and stretched. A wince appeared on his face once again. "I'm still in pretty bad shape."

"I hope that hit didn't knock anything lose." Fitz shrugged off any guilt about potentially hurting the man. He should have known better than sneaking up on him out in the woods. "Who told you I run out here in the morning?" Fitz knew if it was that common knowledge, he'd need to start varying his routine.

Wyatt didn't seem bothered by the question. "Fitz, I don't think there's anyone in D.C. who doesn't know who you are. Everyone in politics has been watching your rise carefully. You are the keeper of a lot of secrets and more feared than you know. I think most are regretting that D.C. Metro homicide ever let you go. You hold a lot more power than you realize. Certainly, more power than John Huntly ever had."

That was news to Fitz but still didn't answer his question. He asked it again and still Wyatt refused to answer. "Why the interest in me? I'm not beholden to anyone or any political party."

"That's exactly why you're feared." Wyatt leveled a look at him. When he realized Fitz wasn't convinced, he went on. "In a place where everyone has a price and most would sell their soul to get or keep power, you're one of the few who can't be bothered with it. You can't be bought off, bribed, or threatened and people know that. Huntly was good but didn't have your moral character."

"What does that mean?"

Wyatt cocked his head to the side and ran a hand down his stubbled chin. "He could on occasion be bought off."

Fitz wasn't sure he believed him. He wanted to know more but held himself back from asking. Huntly was dead. It didn't matter now anyway. That's not why they were standing in the middle of Rock Creek Park. Not in motion now, he could feel the cold creeping into his joints. He'd be stiff soon if he didn't get back to his run.

"Why are you here? You still haven't told me that."

Wyatt grew quiet as his facial features tightened. "I found something and I was told you'd be the guy to bring it to. You're a helper, a fixer of sorts. I figure you'd be the one person in all of D.C. that I could trust."

"Okay," Fitz said slowly, not sure he wanted to hear what the man had to say. He was embroiled in enough of a mess as it stood. When Wyatt hesitated again, Fitz nudged him. "Look, it's cold out here. I have to get back to my run. If you have something to say, I'm going to need you to come out with it or make an appointment to speak to me later."

"We can never speak in public." Wyatt's blue eyes dilated in fear. "We never met, Fitz. You have to promise me that. I could lose my job or worse. I don't know how high this goes. My life could be in danger."

Fitz fought the urge to shake the information out of him. Too calmly, as if he were talking to someone on the brink of a panic attack, Fitz assured him, "We never met. I got it, Wyatt. I still need to know why you're out here. You sought me out so I assume you trust me. Now out with it or I'm going to start running again."

"I found something related to the attempted assassination of President Monroe. It pains me to say this about my own agency, but the Secret Service is lying about what happened."

Fitz's whole body jerked toward him. Wyatt had his attention now. "What did you find?"

Wyatt held his hand up. "I'm going into my back pocket to get my phone. I don't have a weapon."

Fitz had already patted him down. "Get whatever you need."

Wyatt got his phone, scrolled through a few photos, and turned the screen to Fitz, who couldn't quite make out at first what he was seeing. "Yesterday one of the Secret Service agents on the president's detail rushed back to the Murry Lane office after the shooting. He slipped something out of his pocket and put it in his desk then took off out of the office again. I didn't see him after that. He didn't see me in the office. I was in the back. He was looking around as if looking to see who was watching him. He came back for it later and left with it."

Fitz examined the photo closely and had many questions running through his mind. He knew exactly what it looked like, but he couldn't make his mouth say the words.

"Spent bullets," Wyatt said it for him. "Two in a Ziploc bag he put in his desk drawer. Retrieved later."

"Evidence," Fitz said in a whisper. Then caught himself. "That doesn't mean that it's from the president's shooting. How can you be sure?"

"I know the agent and he's assigned to the detail," Wyatt countered, his tone growing frustrated. "When he came into the office, I didn't know about the shooting right then. It was announced soon after he left. That's when I rushed to look to see what he had put there. What else could it be?"

"Why would he hide evidence in the office where anyone could find it?"

"He probably didn't know what else to do with it. The FBI got involved soon after."

Fitz started to ask a question then stopped himself. He was trying to make sense of the kept bullets and couldn't. "You've had a long career in the Secret Service. Based on what you saw and heard, what do you think happened?"

"The official story isn't true," Wyatt said, stating what was now obvious to Fitz. "That Secret Service agent is protecting whoever shot her. There's no other reason to take the bullets. A shooter is dead. There's questions surrounding that too."

"What questions?"

"How it all went down. Everything from A to Z. Rumors are swirling around the office that one of the agents on her detail went rogue."

Fitz's stomach groaned. "Would they do something like that?"

Wyatt could see Fitz wasn't convinced. "Look, you're asking me to guess based on very little evidence. I don't know how exactly it went down. All I know is taking bullets from a crime scene doesn't make any sense."

"Why me?" Fitz was starting to wonder if the guy was a plant from the Warren Circle, maybe a test to see if he'd spill the secret or if maybe Wyatt had found out about it and this was a test.

"The president's detail are some of our most senior agents. If this is a conspiracy to murder the president than who knows how high this goes."

If a Secret Service agent was saying that, then Fitz had to listen. His worry for President Monroe grew. "Who is with her now at the hospital?"

"Another team. Everyone who was on her detail that morning has been suspended," Wyatt assured him. "That's unusual too. Everything about this is unusual."

"Will you share with me the agent's name who had the bullets?"

Wyatt shook his head. "Not now. If you find something, then maybe."

"I have nothing to investigate. You said the bullets are gone. How can I figure anything out?"

"I'm sure you'll figure it out. I was told you're the best," Wyatt said, backing up slowly until he turned around and disappeared into the woods.

Fitz remained there against the tree, the cold settling into his joints. He'd gotten himself into a mess.

CHAPTER 8

"The bullets could have been from anything," Charlie countered. They were sitting at the conference table discussing Fitz's early morning visitor. "I understand the timing is suspicious. We don't know where they came from though."

"You're absolutely right," Fitz said, leaning back in the chair. He had also considered Wyatt was lying about the whole thing and it was nothing more than a test from the Warren Circle. Wyatt seeking him out in the same way that Agent Burrows had was suspicious. Maybe they were watching Fitz and Charlie to see what they'd do. Sending Wyatt in the same way Burrows arrived was too coincidental. Fitz hadn't mentioned that to Charlie. He wanted to see if she thought of it on her own. So far, she was just discussing the merits of the evidence.

Charlie stared at him across the table. "If I'm right, then there's not a lot we can do with it. What did Wyatt expect you to do with the information?"

"Investigate it." Fitz had also run every scenario he could think of in his head on the way back home and in the shower. Not to mention the time he spent driving to work. He hadn't even turned the radio on. He drove in silence thinking about those bullets.

"You're frustrated already," Charlie said noting his tone.

There was no denying it. That was the constant state of emotion since they had agreed to help the Warren Circle. There was something about the way she was looking at him that told Fitz she had more to say. "Talk to Burrows again?"

"Not Burrows. You weren't the only one with an early morning visitor."

Fitz raised his eyebrows. "Someone sought you out with evidence?"

"Not so much evidence but more speculation."

Fitz pointed down toward the table. "They showed up here to talk to you?"

Charlie shook her head. "Never here, Fitz. They dead-dropped a message. I met them early this morning, earlier than your morning visitor sought you out."

Whoever had contacted Charlie had to be within the government and working in one of the security agencies. Otherwise, they wouldn't need to be so covert. "Did they have information for you?"

Charlie gestured with her hand while she spoke. "They had heard rumors and wanted to run a few things by me. See if I had heard anything given what we do and the number of people we come across. This shooting has sparked a lot of internal chatter within government circles."

Fitz assumed big things like this usually did. "What did your contact say?" As much as he wanted to know, he avoided asking about their identity. He knew Charlie wouldn't tell him, but she looked like she was on the verge of telling Fitz something big.

"My contact suggested that there's chatter the shooting took place inside the White House."

"What?" Fitz asked, his tone dismissing it outright. "How is that even possible?"

"That's what I said too." Charlie leaned back in the chair. "One of the Secret Service agents saw a Secret Service SUV pull out of there at a little after three in the morning, tires screeching. He thought he noticed the president slouched over in the back next to one of the other agents. When he asked about it, he was told that he was wrong and that it was just one agent in the back of the SUV. There was no explanation of where they were going and he didn't see the SUV until later in the day. His shift was over at that point, but he'd come back to the White House in search of the SUV. He made up some excuse about why he had returned between shifts. Something about missing house keys."

The speculation around the shooting got weirder by the second. Fitz shook his head as if trying to jar something lose. "They aren't usually at their stations alone. Was there another witness?"

"The other guy had run inside to use the bathroom. There isn't much action at that guard station in the middle of the night. It's not a change of shift and there's hardly any cars coming or going. He just happened to be out there alone at the time."

"How did the information make it to your source?"

Charlie shrugged "I don't know. All I know is it landed with my friend and he passed the information on to me to see what I thought."

When Charlie grew quiet, Fitz gestured for her to continue. "Did your source believe the information?"

"He dismissed it at first. But he thought about it overnight and wanted my take. Why would the Secret Service agent at the gate lie? He doesn't benefit from disclosing the information. I believe at the time he told his supervisor, nearly right after it happened, the president hadn't been *officially* shot yet. He was asking his supervisor more or less to know if there was some kind of threat. He was dismissed outright. Told he didn't see what he saw and that's when he got suspicious."

Fitz sat with the information, trying to process any scenario where a shooting inside the White House would even be possible. He came up blank each time. "How would that even happen? Wouldn't everyone have heard?"

"I would assume so. I don't know how many people other than the Secret Service are in the White House at night."

Fitz kept coming back to the same question. "The president is never alone, Charlie. The Secret Service is always there. They monitor everything and the entire White House is under surveillance inside and out. The perimeter of the White House is watched. There are surveillance cameras everywhere that are being monitored in real-time. There is at least one agent near the president while they are sleeping. Food is prepared under Secret Service watch. They are never alone. How would it happen in the White House and where was the president's husband if it happened in the middle of the night?"

"These are all the same questions I had, Fitz."

He could feel his already intense frustration growing as it tensed his neck and shoulders. "This person that contacted you had to have some credible information or a working theory about what happened. What's the theory?"

Charlie's tone was even and calm. "I was told that the working theory is that a Secret Service agent woke her in the middle of the night and told her there was an emergency she had to address. She was brought out of the Executive Residence probably to the West Wing. There was some confrontation with someone and she was shot in the process. They assume that other Secret Service agents not involved in the plot rushed in and got her out of there to the hospital."

Fitz backed his chair up, scraping the legs on the floor. "That would mean she was in the hospital far earlier than was released. It would also mean that the crime scene is not in front of the Lincoln Memorial but in the White House. It would also mean that someone high up in government is involved because they got access to the White House and the Secret Service agents felt comfortable enough to leave her alone with the person. That's a lot of balls in the air to manage, Charlie, especially if the shooting happened spur of the moment."

Charlie didn't have answers for him. He got up and paced around the room to think. He could feel her penetrating gaze on his back. "Fitz, we took in a lot of information in less than twenty-four hours. No one expects you to solve this overnight. Everything is an unknown right now and that's okay."

Fitz turned to face her. "I don't know how we are supposed to solve anything when all of the president's information is a secret, we can't access the White House, won't be able to speak to witnesses, and have no access to the evidence to even see if it's real or fake. We've been tasked with an impossible mission."

Charlie shrugged far too casually. He knew her back had been up against the wall during her time in the CIA and not much fazed her. "You've had tough cases in your career. Also, we have someone we can interview." Charlie pulled a slip of paper from her pocket and slid it across the table. "My contact gave me the name and address of the Secret Service agent at the gate. He was put on leave for now."

"On leave? For what?"

Charlie smirked up at him. "Now that's the question, isn't it? He reported what he saw immediately to his superior. He was told that's not what he saw. A couple hours later the president was shot. There are far too many holes in the official story. If we can start proving that the story is fake, maybe some truths will start to slip through."

Fitz couldn't disagree with her. "What about Burrows? Do we bring him in on this?" Charlie's eyes darted to the side and he couldn't tell if she was considering it or if she was annoyed the man's name was raised. "Charlie, listen. I know you have a history with him. If this is going to be a problem, tell me. I don't know what we'll do, but I'll figure something out."

"It's not going to be a problem." Charlie got up from the chair, pushed it into the table, and turned to him. "I admit Josh and I have a few personal things to work through. I was wondering if this is why he brought this to us. He's looking for a way to get back in my life."

Fitz had considered that too. He hadn't dared speak it aloud to Charlie for fear that she would have nixed Burrows's involvement at all. "How do you feel about that?"

"I don't know." Charlie glanced down at the table and took a breath so deep it made her chest rise. "Maybe it's not the worst thing. He's a really good guy."

There was a lot Charlie wasn't saying and Fitz didn't want to push her too hard. He settled on keeping it professional. "Then let's bring him in on this."

Fitz had also wondered how Marcus was going to play into this. He was the FBI director, after all. Shouldn't he be giving them access to evidence as they needed? Fitz didn't know. The members of the Warren Circle didn't offer them much direction. It was going to be trial by fire, he assumed. "Let me call Burrows and see if he wants to go with us."

Charlie reached out to stop him. "Let me. I think it's time he and I start repairing what I broke."

Fitz held back the smile but cocked an eyebrow. "Like getting back together?" He knew from Burrows that's exactly what he wanted.

"Settle down," Charlie chided him with a laugh. "Don't get ahead of yourself. I only meant that I should start being nice to him so we can have a smoother professional relationship and I stress professional. The rest..." she trailed off and didn't finish her thought.

Fitz ran back up to his office to grab a few things while Charlie contacted Burrows. When he got back downstairs, she was already waiting in his SUV. As Fitz slid into the driver's seat, Charlie explained Burrows had a meeting on another case, but that he'd be happy to meet after work to discuss. He had found out a few things too.

"I didn't tell him what we found, specifically," Charlie noted. "If anyone intercepts our communication it could be bad for us. I was intentionally vague."

That was good thinking on her part. Not that Fitz doubted Charlie's ability to be covert. She told him the address of Ethan Thompson and they headed north out of D.C. to Silver Spring, Maryland.

Fitz pulled to the curb in the suburban neighborhood. Ethan lived in a small split-level house on a narrow tree-lined street. A black Ford pick-up truck was parked in the driveway.

"Curtains are closed and it doesn't look like anyone is home," Fitz noted as he cut the engine. The house appeared eerily quiet. The home was well-kept and the lawn was cared for by someone meticulous about it. While he was focused on the home and property, Charlie was in the passenger seat looking in front of them and behind.

"I want to make sure we aren't followed," she explained. "My contact said that someone might be watching Ethan. I don't see anyone. It's a quiet neighborhood, not many cars on the street. I feel like if someone were watching him, they'd stick out."

Fitz did the same cursory surveillance of their surroundings, not spotting anything out of the ordinary either. "If someone is watching him, they are better at hiding than most. I think we are in the clear."

Charlie agreed with that. She opened the passenger side and was up to the front door knocking before Fitz hit the sidewalk. He watched as the curtains parted, a man stared out and waved them off. Fitz wasn't going to give up that easily.

"He's in there," he told Charlie when he reached her at the door. He knocked and shouted, "Ethan, we just want to speak to you. We aren't the cops."

"That was loud," Charlie said with a laugh. "I think you just announced yourself to the whole neighborhood."

It had the effect Fitz had hoped. If the man didn't want to speak to them that was one thing. No one wanted two strangers standing on their porch shouting about the police. The door opened enough that the man leaned into the space. "Who are you and what do you want?"

Fitz leaned toward the crack of the door and introduced them both. "We are *very off the record* investigating the presidential shooting. We believe you have some information that might help us."

"How'd you get my name?" he asked suspiciously.

"You're Ethan, right?" Fitz asked, realizing they had been assuming. When the man nodded, Fitz said, "We were told you were one of the agents at the gates and might know a few things. We were also told that the Secret Service was trying to silence you."

"I've been suspended." Ethan opened the door a little more. "Got any identification?"

All Fitz had was a business card. He held it up for Ethan, but when he tried to hand it to him, the man wouldn't take it. "We promise you we aren't here to do you any harm. We just need to know what you know. The Secret Service shouldn't be trying to silence anyone."

Ethan agreed with that. "We can't talk here. There's a park not far away. Make sure you aren't followed and I'll meet you there in an hour." He closed the door before Fitz could ask him the name of the park or an address.

"I know where he means," Charlie said bounding down the porch steps back to the SUV.

At least that made one of them.

CHAPTER 9

After leaving Ethan's house, Fitz drove around for a bit trying to burn off time and make sure no one was following them. Charlie ran into a shop to grab them coffees and returned with the phone in the crook of her neck holding the cups out to him. She couldn't open the passenger side of the truck.

Fitz exited the driver's side and came around to help her. He took both cups from her hands and hitched his chin toward the phone in a question.

"Burrows," she mouthed in return. She focused back on the call as she leaned against the SUV. "It's better you don't show up to the meeting. Ethan will get spooked if we bring an FBI agent with us, even off the record. Plus, it would probably compromise you." She rolled her eyes in Fitz's direction as she continued to listen to Burrows on the other end.

Fitz assumed he was most likely arguing his position about meeting with them. He knew that's what he'd be doing if he was in Burrows's position. Charlie was right that Burrows shouldn't be there. It would compromise him and he was already putting himself in a sticky situation running a counter-investigation to the official FBI one.

Fitz glanced over at the row of parked cars behind him, looking for…well, he wasn't exactly sure. He had a sneaking suspicion that someone from the Warren Circle might be tailing them to assess their progress. The way they had handed them this assignment and backed off wasn't sitting right with him.

Fitz didn't see anyone out of the ordinary – men and women rushing in and out of the coffee shop, probably heading to meetings and grabbing coffee just to get them through. An older lady pushing a stroller with a baby under a thick blanket. She smiled and nodded at Fitz as they passed. He returned the gesture.

As Charlie finished the call, she glanced up at him. "No one tailing us?"

"I don't think so. I've been keeping watch and I assumed I'd have spotted them by now. Did you convince Burrows not to come to the meeting?" Charlie opened the passenger side door as Fitz handed her the coffee cup.

She slid inside. "I didn't give him an option. I didn't tell him where we were meeting." When she noted Fitz's confused expression, she added, "I said we should keep him updated. I didn't say we should give him enough information so he compromised himself. We have far more leeway than he does. He's still on the FBI leash and he's got a year to official retirement. There's no point getting fired now."

Fitz agreed with that. He wasn't sure why Burrows was sticking his neck out anyway. As Fitz put his cup in the holder, he turned to Charlie. "Did you tell him about my morning visitor?"

"I did. He didn't know what to make of it either. The shooting doesn't make any more sense to him than it does to us. I think he was even more adamant that the shooting didn't happen inside the White House than you were." Charlie reached behind her and buckled the belt. "That said, he heard from a source in forensics that the crime scene at the Lincoln Memorial isn't adding up. The FBI is already starting to question the official story – quietly that is."

Fitz recalled what Marcus had told them about the FBI not looking at it too hard. He might have discounted his staff. "Was that an on or off-the-record conversation?"

"Off the record. Burrows said that there is some pressure from above to close it quickly." Charlie gave him a knowing look. "Do you think Marcus wants the official record to state the Secret Service story? Why send us to investigate behind the scenes when the FBI could do that themselves?"

That was one of the questions that had been plaguing Fitz through this whole thing. "Unless Marcus is getting some pressure to close the case."

"I don't know how he'd be getting pressure from anyone when it all just happened."

Fitz knew a lot but he didn't know the inner workings of all the offices. Although the FBI director should be one of the most independent positions in the federal government there is oversight. The position is appointed by the president and confirmed by the Senate. They answer directly to the attorney general. If pressure was coming down, it might be coming from inside the attorney general's office.

As if reading his thoughts, Charlie said, "Congress." She turned her head to look at him. "You mumbled attorney general. I figured you were trying to figure out who could pressure Marcus. It's the attorney general or someone in Congress – directly or through the attorney general."

Fitz hadn't realized he'd spoken aloud. Charlie was right, those were the only options. "Maybe Marcus anticipated it."

Charlie shrugged. "He might also have suspects in mind. Instead of going at the case directly, which might get him nowhere fast, he's taking a back door approach."

"The agents aren't going to like that," Fitz said as he signaled and pulled out into traffic. He listened as Charlie gave him directions to the park. They were about fifteen minutes early, but it would give them time to scope out the location ahead of the meeting.

Fitz's tires crunched over the gravel as he pulled into the park, the midday sun struggling to break through the grey clouds overhead. He pulled next to Ethan's truck as he stared out the windshield. He wasn't surprised Ethan was there early too.

The park felt strangely still, like the air itself was holding its breath. Fitz assumed it would have been lively with joggers and families. It was deserted except for Ethan, leaning against a rusted lamppost near the edge of the tree line. His silhouette was sharp against the dull sky, standing motionless.

Fitz killed the engine, the SUV's idle noise dissipating into the quiet of the park. He opened the door as a lone crow cawed from a nearby oak. He turned back to Charlie. "You said you know this place. Is it always so quiet? It's creepy, like something out of a horror movie." Even though there were jungle gyms and swings off in the distance, he couldn't picture the place full of kids.

"Never been here in the middle of the day," she said dismissively. When Fitz asked her when she had been to the park, she chuckled. "Most of my work goes down in the darkness, Fitz. Both literally and figuratively. Come on. He's waiting and Ethan doesn't strike me as the kind of man who's going to wait for long."

They followed a concrete path until it became a worn dirt path that had been sketched into the grass. Ethan pushed himself upright from the pole as they got closer.

"Thanks for coming alone," he said. "Let's start with how you got my name."

Fitz instinctively turned to look behind him but saw no one. Ethan's tone had a tinge of sarcasm that made Fitz wonder if they had been tailed. There was no one but their two vehicles in the parking lot. He refocused on Ethan. "Charlie got it from a source that we can't disclose. I told you at the house we aren't here for any trouble. We heard that what you saw was dismissed by your supervisor and we think it was important."

Ethan didn't respond to Fitz. Instead, he turned his head a little to the left to look at Charlie. "Who's your source?"

She did not give the name. "We're allies, Ethan. We don't mean you any harm. We believe there's something more than a little odd about the official story of the shooting of President Monroe."

Ethan was no fool. "The official story is barely out. What gives you both the right to investigate this?"

Fitz explained to him his business and how he's connected to the government. "I was also a homicide detective with D.C. Metro for a long time. Let's just say that our connection to this case and what we are doing comes from people who care about the truth."

Ethan absorbed the information without seeming to have any reaction to it. He contemplated for a moment, then said, "I could get fired for talking to you. I was told to forget what I saw and that's what I was inclined to do until you came knocking. I don't want to lose my job."

"Why are you willing to speak to us?" Charlie asked.

"As he said, the truth matters."

"What's your truth, Ethan?" Fitz pressed him.

Ethan's tongue snaked out and licked his lips, the first sign of nervousness creeping in. "I saw a Secret Service SUV race out of the lot at eleven minutes after three in the morning. It was driven by Sebastian Cole, the head of President Monroe's Secret Service detail. The back windows of that SUV are tinted as you are probably well aware. That said, I was close enough that I'm sure I saw another agent in the back holding President Monroe who seemed to be slumped forward in the seat. They raced out of there like something was wrong. I barely even got a chance to get the gate up for them to leave. Sebastian didn't make any eye contact with me and I couldn't make out who the agent was in the back. They took off out of there going significantly over the speed limit. That's why I wondered if there was a threat. If there was we should have been notified. That's not usually how they move the president in those situations."

"How do they move the president then?" Fitz asked.

Ethan shook his head. "I can't share that with you."

"Understood." Fitz hadn't thought he would. "Given the tint of the windows, how can you be sure it was President Monroe in the back and not someone else?"

"The long hair for one. It was half pulled up in a ponytail but looked messy as if she'd been asleep and dragged from her bed."

"Was she awake? Eyes open?"

"I don't know. Her head was down." Ethan lowered his head until his chin was basically resting on his chest and angled it away from Fitz, showing how the president had been. When he righted himself, he said, "It was like that. There isn't another woman in the White House that would be escorted out of there like that."

"What about another Secret Service agent?" Charlie asked. "Could someone have been injured and brought out like that?"

"It wouldn't have been a secret. They could have called an ambulance and told us at the gate."

Fitz had one question that seemed most pressing. "Could you tell if President Monroe was injured?"

"That didn't occur to me at the time," Ethan said with regret. "My first thought was a security concern. That's what prompted me to call inside to my supervisor. I wanted to know if something was happening. If we were under attack or there was some known threat. As I said, that's not normally how the president would have been secured if there was. But at that hour and the way they tore out of there, it was anyone's guess. I immediately called and asked. I was told something surprising." He paused and his eyes darted back and forth from Fitz to Charlie.

They remained silent waiting for him to go on. The tension rose among the three of them. Fitz knew whatever he was about to say was critical to the story and he seemed to be having trouble saying the words.

Finally, Ethan's shoulders dropped. "I was told that Sebastian Cole was inside the White House and that another agent had left in the SUV. I was not told who it was or why they left."

Charlie's head turned sharply to lock eyes with Fitz. "A denial of what you saw?"

"An outright denial," Ethan confirmed. "Not a flimsy excuse about what might be going on or even a lie about what they were doing – an outright denial of what I saw. I was told that there was no way I saw Sebastian Cole because my supervisor was looking at him in the office as we were on the phone and that President Monroe was safely in her bed."

Ethan chuckled lightly, a contrast to the man's rigid body language and serious expression. "The funny part is I never said anything about the president. All I said was I saw a Secret Service SUV driven by Sebastian Cole tear out of the residence. I didn't even get a chance to mention seeing the president when my supervisor cut in and told me that I couldn't have seen Cole because he wasn't on shift that night. A direct contrast from being told Cole was in the White House seconds earlier."

"Why bring up the president if she was asleep in her bed," Charlie said what they were all thinking.

"Exactly. My supervisor made two critical mistakes." Ethan took a breath. "I've been on the nightshift for a long time. I wasn't a newbie who wasn't used to the hours and sleep deprived, seeing things that weren't there. I know what I saw and who I saw. But for some reason, the Secret Service wants to deny my reality. Why? Then she was shot at the Lincoln Memorial two hours later. Nothing adds up."

"Were you there when President Monroe would have left in the morning to go jogging?"

"Yes." Ethan frowned. "But she didn't leave the White House that morning for a run."

"There are other ways she could have left though," Fitz argued.

"Yeah," Ethan said with a nod. "Except every morning they went jogging, they left out of my front gate. President Monroe would have the window down enough to give me a nod or say good morning. They'd drive her to the path she took. This happened roughly three to four times a week. You're telling me all of a sudden this morning they changed how they leave the White House. Why?"

Fitz didn't have an answer for that. "Is there anyone else in the White House who was there that you trust?"

"Reggie Malloy. He's been the White House executive chef for two decades, through several administrations. We became friendly awhile back. When my shift ended, I saw him briefly. We locked eyes and I'll tell you there was fear in that man's face. He didn't tell me what he saw but he saw something inside the White House that shook the man to his core. If you know Chef Reggie, you know that nothing scares that man." Ethan looked around Fitz and then back at them. "I have to go. I don't know anything more, but if you're really after the truth, then I hope you find it because that shooting did not go down the way they are saying."

"What do you think happened?" Fitz asked, wanting more time with him.

"I don't know. If I were a betting man, President Monroe was already shot when she left the White House. Whatever went down, went down inside. I'd stake everything I have on that."

"Wouldn't you have heard the shot?" Fitz asked.

"Everything is so soundproof in there. I might not have, but I've been wondering if Reggie did. I haven't reached out to him because I don't want to compromise him. If I've been suspended, who knows what they are doing to him? I've said enough."

CHAPTER 10

Fitz reached out his hand to stop him. He came a few inches shy of actually touching him. "You can't drop a bomb like that and run. Tell us why you think this shooting happened in the White House and how that would even be possible."

"I've spent enough time with you already."

It wasn't Fitz who moved to stand in Ethan's path but Charlie. "I can't tell you what I did for work. All I'll say is I gave my blood and sweat on the most dangerous and secret missions. I've sacrificed relationships, a stable homelife, and my body for the United States. I swore an oath to the Constitution to protect. Just because I left my job doesn't mean I can deny that oath now. I know you took a similar oath. It's time we did what is right even if it's not easy."

Ethan's eyes darted away from her. "I have no proof of anything. Inconsistencies. That place is like clockwork. There are systems, protocols, and procedures in place. The whole place had an unusual feel that night. I don't know if I could put it into words if I tried."

"Try," Charlie commanded him, her tone firm. She wasn't going to let him off the hook that easily. She could be tougher than Fitz most times.

Ethan toed the ground with his sneakers. He gnawed at his upper lip before turning his head to lock his gaze on her. "My supervisor was changed that night. Now I know you'll say maybe my regular supervisor was on vacation or was sick. I know the rotation. I called him and he'd gotten word from above that he had to use his time off. That was the only explanation, so he's in the Bahamas this week."

It was interesting to Fitz but it didn't mean a whole lot. He didn't know the inner workings of the Secret Service. Not a lot of people did. "Maybe he had time to burn that he'd lose otherwise."

Ethan shook his head. "I was told Barry, my normal supervisor, was out sick. That he had the flu. Barry told me he was on vacation. Why lie? The guy in charge was David Sparks. He's the one who told Barry he had to take a vacation. Originally, he was supposed to take it in March. Then the day before Sparks told him he was on leave from that afternoon forward for a week. Sparks was there that night instead of him."

Charlie asked, "Were some of the president's normal detail around?"

"I know Sebastian Cole was there that night no matter what anyone tells me. He shouldn't have been. He had worked all day. I don't know what brought him back but something did. He was there as were two others. I didn't go fully into the command center to see who was there. I never do. There would have been no reason to. I just noted the oddities and kept it moving. At that time, it didn't mean much to me and was above my pay grade. It was just after I saw Sebastian drive out of there with the president and I was told I didn't see that so I started to question everything, especially after hearing President Monroe had been shot."

"When was that?" Fitz had to keep a working timeline – the one that was the official story and what he was coming to learn was reality. "You said you saw her leave eleven minutes after three. You also said you didn't see her leave for her morning jog. What time did you hear she had been shot?"

"That's the thing, you'd think there would be mass panic when the news came in, right? We should have been notified of a higher threat alert. That never happened. We didn't get official word outside. My partner got a text from another agent asking him what he thought. We had no idea. The official word came in around six, from their account more than an hour after the shooting happened. We should have been notified immediately. Nothing about any of this adds up. No protocol or procedure was followed. It was either a massive failure of the Secret Service or an inside job followed by a massive cover-up. I believe the latter."

He still wasn't getting to Fitz's initial question. "How was it done then? How could the president have been shot inside the White House?"

Ethan didn't have a good answer for that. "I assumed you'd have to look to the unknown people. Why were they there and what was their role? The president's husband was rushed out of there to the hospital right after we were notified, so I assume he had no idea what was going on. I don't think she was shot in the Executive Residence. They might have called her down for a meeting and shot her. Maybe Cole got a conscience and took her to the hospital."

"The timing doesn't match up," Charlie stated the obvious. "From when she was raced out of the White House to the time she ended up in the hospital. It's hours later. Surely, she would have died if she'd been shot inside the White House."

Ethan suggested something else. "The hospital lied." When he noted the disbelief on Fitz's face, he shrugged it off. "Listen, I understand you were a detective. The White House is not law and order. If the Secret Service wants you to do something, you do it and don't ask questions."

Fitz couldn't believe what he was hearing. He could feel his heart start to race. Before he could ask the question, Charlie confirmed that Ethan was right. "I don't see how we are going to be able to figure anything out when we are up against the Secret Service who can get people to lie and change the official story."

"That's just the way it goes," Ethan said with a hint of sarcasm. "This is the United States government you're dealing with here."

Fitz waved him off. He was nearly to the point of disgust where he didn't want to hear anymore. "You said Reggie was there at the end of your shift and seemed to be a bit freaked out. Do you know what time he came in?"

"He worked overnight. He was there when I got there at midnight. I think he was working on some new recipes. A few big dinners are coming up. President Monroe was hosting some foreign leaders and Reggie was planning the menu. He frequently works overnight to try things out like that. The kitchen is quiet then and he can focus."

Fitz asked for a way to reach Reggie as well as some of the others involved. "What's your take on Sebastian Cole?"

Ethan looked right at Fitz and didn't waver. "Up until this happened, I would have told you he was the best we have. He's been a Secret Service agent for more than twenty years and he's dedicated and committed. He served on President Monroe's detail back when she was primarying. He quickly won her trust and support. She asked specifically that he remain the head of her team after she won. I'm having a hard time believing that he's involved somehow. Yet, I know he was in the White House, not on his regular shift, and he brought her to the hospital."

Fitz would have to take the time to dig into the man's background. "Is it possible that he was in the White House for some other reason that night?"

Ethan nodded. "Anything is possible. However it went down, I don't think the dead guy was the shooter."

Fitz was hearing what he was saying, but it still didn't mean much. He didn't know if when President Monroe was being escorted out of the White House she had been shot at that point or not. He was trying to make sense of the nonsensical and it was giving him a headache.

Charlie wasn't deterred. "What about the president's husband? You suggested that you were sure he didn't know what happened. Could there have been domestic violence? Maybe it escalated and Richard Avery shot her."

Ethan countered as he considered. "There's never been any suspected domestic violence that I've heard. Except..." He trailed off not finishing his thought.

"What is it?" Fitz asked, sensing the man was remembering something.

"It might be nothing," Ethan admitted. "When President Monroe first moved into the White House, the couple had a screaming fight in the Executive Residence. The Secret Service was there, but they raged on at each other. It was so bad that some of the staff became concerned. I'm only aware of that one incident though and not sure that's indicative of bigger problems in the marriage."

Fitz had a delicate question and was not sure that Ethan would even know the answer. "What about infidelity? Was either of them known to stray in the marriage?"

"If they did, I wouldn't know that. Their Secret Service detail would know if affairs went on during the campaign or after."

A familiar crunch of gravel echoed off in the distance. A small four-door blue sedan pulled into the lot. It was parked to the side of their vehicles so Fitz wasn't able to see inside. It was enough to spook Ethan.

"I have to go," he said, staring into the parking lot. "I shouldn't have said so much."

"You did the right thing," Charlie said, trying to appease his guilt of betraying the Secret Service. "When is your suspension over?"

"Next week."

"You're going back to work like nothing has happened?"

"That's the only thing I can do. I have a family to feed. I love my job." Ethan stepped back from them both. "I can't leave the agency now. I only have a few more years until I'm eligible for retirement. Please don't tell anyone we spoke."

"We aren't looking to get you in trouble," Fitz assured him. "Would you be willing to call us if you found out anything further? You're in a great position to be our eyes and ears on the inside."

"No. Absolutely not. I'm going back and keeping my head down and doing my job." Ethan's tone didn't give Fitz any wiggle room. "You're lucky I met you here to talk. I told you what I know, now do something with it. I did my part."

"At least give us the names of the other Secret Service agents there."

"No one is going to speak to you."

"Let us worry about that," Charlie said, assuring him that they wouldn't tell anyone they got the information from him. "When we contact them you can complain we tried to speak to you too but refused."

Ethan refused to give them more information. "Good luck but don't contact me again." With that, he walked past them without looking back.

Fitz and Charlie stood there watching him walk to his truck, unlock it, get in, and drive away a moment later. No one had exited the sedan that had pulled up. Fitz wasn't in any hurry to rush over to his SUV to see who was in the parking lot. Instead, he walked the other way, deeper into the park. He found a bench and sat, folding his arms over his chest.

Charlie took a seat next to him. "Processing?" she asked, staring over at the empty swings. One of them moved slightly in the breeze.

"I'm not sure what to make of that conversation. Did we learn much of anything useful? A lot of it was speculation on his part. We don't even know President Monroe's condition when she left the White

House."

"It sounds like this starts and ends with the Secret Service, Fitz. You have them taking the president out of there two hours before they said they did. So far, we've been able to get information from two Secret Service agents – Wyatt Standfield and Ethan Thompson. Both of them said something was off with their agency. I think we need to speak to Sebastian Cole next. If he's the head of Monroe's detail, he's going to be the one with most of the information."

"The one with the most to lose if he did something wrong," Fitz said, mostly to himself. He wasn't sure they were in a position to go to Cole next. "I want to see if we can gather other information first."

"Senator Ford," Charlie said after a few moments of contemplation. "Surely, he'd be able to access the Secret Service agents working that night."

"Let's start with Ford. Then I want to try my contact at the hospital. She's an emergency room nurse, a trauma nurse to be more specific. I've used her as a source before. I know she still works there. She might be able to find out what time President Monroe was brought in." Fitz glanced over. Charlie was staring at him with a smirk on her face. "What?"

"A source or someone you sleep with occasionally?"

Fitz rubbed at the back of his neck. "Both, I guess."

Charlie shook her head in dismay. "When was the last time you spoke to her?"

"About a year ago. It ended on good terms. She got a boyfriend and stopped coming around." Fitz didn't know if the woman would be willing to speak to him, but he had no other resources at that hospital to get to the truth. He felt like pinning down the time the president came into the hospital might be one step in creating a real timeline of events.

"It's worth a shot," Charlie said as she stood.

They were nearly out of options and had only just started.

CHAPTER 11

Amy Singleton had reluctantly agreed to meet Fitz late in the afternoon for coffee not far from the hospital. He didn't tell her why he wanted to meet, only that he wanted to talk to her. She was hesitant in their text exchange but willing. She reminded him she had a boyfriend and that if his request was anything romantic the meeting was pointless. Fitz assured her that while he enjoyed their time together he was happy she was happy.

Charlie had stared at him while he was texting as he struggled to get the words in the text just right. Then she teased him when Amy said she'd only meet if it wasn't romantic. If Fitz ever got too full of himself, Charlie was right there to bring him back down to Earth.

Fitz had arrived at the coffee shop before Amy and waited for her at a back table. He sipped his latte and raised his hand in a wave when she walked in. He couldn't deny that she still looked good. Her long dark hair was braided at her back and her blue scrubs fit her curves in a particular way that still stirred a feeling of lust. He let his gaze focus back on the cup and he asked her if she wanted anything while she approached the table.

Amy shook her head as she pulled out the chair. "You look good, Fitz. Then again you always did. Looking good was never your problem."

He smiled and bit. "What was my problem?"

"No," Amy said with a shake of her head. She was smiling too. "I'm not going there. We both ended up where we needed to be. I have a great relationship, which is why I nearly said no to your request. I figured you needed something if it wasn't romantic. You're a smart guy and never desperate, so I know you didn't drag me here to try to convince me otherwise."

"You're right about that." Fitz put his coffee cup on the table and leaned forward. He glanced to the side to make sure no one was close enough to listen. He dropped his voice low. "I've been tasked with finding out what *really* happened to President Monroe and I know that you work trauma in the emergency room where she was taken. I also know the hours you used to work and I assume by your scrubs that it's still the same." He watched as Amy pulled back from the table ready to deny him information. He asked her to hear him out.

"I'm not asking you to betray HIPAA," Fitz assured her. "I don't even need her status. What I want to know is simple."

"Nothing is ever simple with your work, Fitz," Amy said with a sigh. She remained quiet for so long that he thought she was going to deny him. Finally, she asked, "What do you want to know?"

"I want to know what time she was brought into the emergency room."

Amy's eyes darted to the side. "I can't see why that's important."

He knew just by her facial expression that something was off. Amy had unintentionally given herself away. Fitz didn't call her out on it, not yet. "It matters because there are some discrepancies in the official story and I'm trying to get to the truth. Knowing what time she arrived at the ER would help me to work through a few theories. That's all I need. The time. The truth."

Amy stared at him across the table.

Fitz knew he was asking a lot of a woman he hadn't seen in more than a year and had probably, without realizing it, disappointed with their romantic situation. He hadn't been the best at committing. Not that he was playing around with multiple women. He just didn't have the heart to get too involved in a relationship since his divorce. Now, calling her a year later and asking something like this of her, might be too much.

Fitz leaned more into the table. "I've spoken to a few Secret Service agents who are questioning what went down. I've also heard from an FBI agent who has said things aren't adding up. I wouldn't be coming to you if I wasn't desperate. I know if I go to the hospital in an official capacity they aren't going to tell me the truth. I won't even get past the front door." Fitz paused and started to go on when she cut him off.

"It was three-twenty-three to be exact," Amy said softly, raising her eyebrows. "As you know, the news is reporting that she was shot just after five. At first, I thought the reporter had bad information. Then I was told by my supervisor that given the investigation they weren't releasing the real details. It hasn't sat right with me, but who am I to question it? What does it matter what time she was brought into the emergency room?"

Fitz wasn't sure if that was a question for him or something she had been pondering. He answered anyway. "It matters when it comes down to who is responsible. Who brought her in?"

"Fitz, you told me one question," Amy countered, looking uncertain. "Don't you want to know who shot the president?"

"The Secret Service got the guy. The shooter is dead."

Fitz shook his head. "A guy was shot at the Lincoln Memorial just after five in the morning, nearly two hours after you're telling me the president was in the ER. If the time is different, the whole narrative of the shooting is out the window. I'm just trying to get to the truth."

Amy sat back and watched Fitz closely from across the table. She let the silence between them sit for longer than comfortable. "She was brought in by two Secret Service agents. Sebastian Cole and Ian

Drake. Cole is the one who called it into the ER and was driving the SUV. We had a team waiting outside when they arrived and she was rushed into surgery. Drake was in the back supporting her as she was slumped over. I don't know how they got her into the SUV like that. I rushed with the stretcher into the surgical suite and wasn't there for the explanation of what happened. I was focused on saving her life."

"Understood." The story matched Ethan's and now he finally had the name of the other agent. He wondered if that was the agent who had hidden bullets in his desk. "Were you involved in the surgery?"

"No. I worked on her initially until we got her into the OR suite and other medical staff took over. I went back to the emergency room, changed my scrubs, cleaned myself up, and went back to work. That's what we do, Fitz, even when it's the President of the United States. Other patients needed care."

"Do you know what happened to the bullets removed from the president?"

"I'd have no idea," Amy explained. "I wasn't in surgery. I can tell you that even in the ER when we have evidence like that it's bagged and handed over to law enforcement. There's a protocol for that."

Fitz wanted to remind her that the hospital also had protocols in place for noting the time someone came into the emergency room and received treatment. There was no point chastising her when she hadn't made the decisions. He considered what questions he could ask given she seemed willing to talk.

"I don't want to test your HIPAA limits," Fitz admitted, "but I'd like to know if you sensed anything wrong when she came into the hospital. I know you said you only worked on her for a few minutes before the surgery. Was there anything that struck you as odd?"

Amy could have refused to answer or she could have told Fitz that was enough. Instead, she sat there and considered the question. "It was a blur of activity. We got the call that the president had been shot and she was being brought in by SUV. Once they arrived, an ER doc assessed her before we even got into the emergency room and rushed her to the operating room that was on standby. Everything on our end went according to protocol. Later, we were told by hospital administrators that we were not allowed to speak to anyone about what we saw or anything about the situation."

"Is that normal given HIPAA? I wouldn't think you'd need the reminder."

Amy offered a dismissive gesture. "We knew there'd be a media circus. That's what hospital administrators do, cover the hospital. None of the staff was going to speak to the media. We'd comply with the investigation. There wasn't a reason to reiterate it to us but no, it's not uncommon with a high-profile case like this."

Fitz took a sip of his coffee. "Why are you willing to speak to me then? You could have walked out by now."

Amy didn't even need to think about the answer. "What you said about finding the truth. If there is a cover-up and it starts with the time she was brought into the hospital, then I don't want to be one of those women being interviewed twenty years from now and having to answer why I didn't tell the truth. As I said, when I saw it on the news, I assumed the news got it wrong. Then the hospital administrator told us we weren't releasing the real details. It didn't make sense. Not that any of us were coming out to say anything different. We know better than that. Until this conversation, I was prepared to stay quiet about it in the interest of national security, which is I guess what the Secret Service told the hospital. What's really going on?"

"I don't know much more than you," Fitz admitted. "I can't say what the reason is for the lies about the timing. The FBI investigative team is already suspicious that the supposed scene of the shooting isn't adding up. We have other Secret Service agents who have seen and heard things that don't make sense. None of it adds up to the official timeline."

"That's why I'm sharing this with you. I'll tell you that the paperwork I submitted had the right time. I'll have to check my online records to see if it's been changed. If they are actively manipulating medical records and not just manipulating the media that's a whole other ballgame."

"Please do that," Fitz encouraged her but followed it with a warning. "If it is changed, I suggest keeping quiet about it. I'm not sure who we can trust right now. I have no idea how far this might go." Fitz had another question but it would probably violate HIPAA. Amy had been so kind speaking to him he didn't want to press his luck.

"You have something else on your mind. We might not have spent that much time together, but I can read your face well. You don't exactly have a poker face."

Fitz laughed, releasing the tension that he hadn't realized he was holding in his shoulders. "I know you probably can't answer this. I'm going to ask it anyway. When the president came in, did she have injuries other than the gunshots?"

"Like what?"

"Bruising new or old. I don't know how much of her body you saw. I was curious about any domestic violence."

Amy winced. "Are you serious? You think her husband did that to her?"

Fitz held up his hand to stop her. "I don't know who did this to her. I have to explore everything. This is probably the most difficult case I've ever been involved with and I have no leads."

Amy shook her head. "I didn't see any bruising, not that I was intensely looking for it. We were trying to stop the bleeding. I can't imagine that the couple I saw on television…" Amy didn't finish her thought. Fitz assumed it was because she knew that it didn't matter how a couple presented, what went on behind closed doors could be something else entirely.

Fitz knew that sometimes domestic violence was only known when it was too late. "I can't prove anything. Not yet anyway. I know I don't need to tell you that it wouldn't be wise to say we spoke."

"I'm not telling a soul. I'm simply meeting with a friend at a coffee shop." Amy looked toward the door then back at him. "Can I ask a question?"

"Ask away. If I can answer it, I will."

"Why are you involved in this? You have a nice business that has nothing to do with this kind of investigation. Someone must have roped you back in. I know you wouldn't go back to D.C. Metro, so who was it?"

Fitz nearly sighed with relief that it hadn't been about their relationship. "That's the one thing I can't tell you. All I'll say is that this isn't an official investigation and some powers that be have asked me to look into it. It's a hard thing to turn down."

"I understand that. I'd just hate to see something happen to you. If the Secret Service, or whoever is involved with this, is covering it up, it must be pretty bad."

Fitz had been thinking that too. The deeper he got involved, the more he worried for himself and Charlie. "Have you heard how she's doing?"

Amy shook her head. "She's still in intensive care surrounded by a team of Secret Service agents. They have the whole unit locked down. I'm not sure she's going to make it."

Fitz cocked his head to the side not sure he had heard correctly. "Is that official?"

"About as official as you're going to get. I've spoken to the emergency room doctor who treated her. We were both surprised she made it through surgery. It was a shot to her chest and a gut shot. I'm not even sure how she survived it and made it to the hospital. She's a fighter but she lost so much blood. Even if she survives, it's going to be a very long recovery." The sadness in her voice was apparent. Amy lowered her gaze to the table. "I can't believe this happened."

Fitz promised her he'd do everything he could to find the truth. "If you hear of anything else, will you call me?"

"I will," Amy said as she stood from the table. Before she left, she gave him a meaningful look. "Please be careful. Even if things didn't work out between us, I do like you. I wouldn't want to see anything bad happen to you."

The regret of losing her crept into his belly. He had let a good one go and he knew it. Fitz wished her well. "Tell that boyfriend of yours he was smarter than me."

Amy laughed. "He knows."

Fitz knew it too.

CHAPTER 12

L ate that evening, Fitz, Charlie, and Burrows sat around the conference room discussing everything that had been uncovered that day. They were eating Chinese food from a shop around the corner from the office. Burrows had called them at the end of his shift and offered to pick up dinner. He wanted to know the progress that had been made.

Fitz was surprised that he hadn't heard from Marcus or Senator Ford all day. If there was someone from the Warren Circle they were supposed to report to regularly, they hadn't been told. He assumed someone would be checking on them. Fitz also had questions as to what other members of the Warren Circle were doing or if this had been fully handed off to him and Charlie.

He could not disclose any of that to Burrows. It was a lie that was going to have to remain between them – for now anyway.

"I'm surprised you were able to confirm the time President Monroe was brought into the hospital," Burrows said between bites of sesame chicken. "I wasn't even able to confirm that. The FBI is still being given the time of five-twenty-five. It's in the official paperwork. Are you sure your source is correct?"

Fitz had no doubt Amy had told him the truth. He was surprised however that the hospital was lying to the FBI. "She was the trauma nurse present when Monroe was brought into the hospital. She had no reason to lie to me. I'm surprised the hospital is lying to the FBI and even more surprised that the time has been forged in the official paperwork."

"The time is backed up by Ethan's statement," Charlie added, getting them a step ahead. She asked Burrows if he wanted them to start there.

"Start wherever you want. I know very little at this point. All I know from the FBI team is that it's the weirdest investigation they have ever encountered and they are being pressed to close it given the death of the shooter. No one to arrest and prosecute."

It's exactly what Marcus had told them would happen. Fitz asked, "Do you have any sense where the pressure is coming from to close it so quickly? This is the attempted assassination of the President of the United States. You'd think the powers that be would want a thorough investigation."

"Unless the powers that be know that something is hinky about the whole thing," Burrows said with a shrug. "We should be throwing every resource we have at it, which is why I'm working with the two of you."

"Does Marcus Kane know you're investigating this off hours?" Charlie asked, making Fitz's eyes go wide. He had no idea she was going to address the elephant in the room head-on like that.

Burrows didn't even flinch. "He doesn't need to know."

There was tension in his tone that Fitz didn't understand. "Do you *not* like the director of the FBI?"

Burrows rested his fork down on top of his napkin. "I don't know the man well. He's been director for all but three years of my FBI career. He's good and solid. The agents like him. I've never had a problem with him. He normally backs us up and he doesn't bow to outside pressure. He makes sure the agency isn't politicized. There's just something…"

"Secretive?" Charlie asked, filling in the blanks.

Burrows's head rose and he looked across the table at her. "Yeah, secretive. I can't put my finger on it. It's like there's something he's hiding. None of the other agents I've spoken to have noticed. There's just something I can't quite put my finger on about him."

Charlie smiled at him with her full face. Fitz had never quite seen her as animated. "Kind of like when you didn't know I was working with the CIA?"

Burrows chuckled. "Exactly like that. I don't think Marcus Kane is secretly working for the CIA or is a spy. There's just something he's not telling the rest of us."

"Let him have his secret. It will come out when it's supposed to come out or it won't. The main thing is you trust him, right?"

"Absolutely."

Fitz watched the volley of conversation between the two of them. He knew exactly what Charlie was doing even if Burrows hadn't quite picked up on it. She was assessing Marcus's trustworthiness while also normalizing the man keeping his secrets. She was reinforcing Burrows's trust in the man while testing it at the same time.

With that settled, Fitz asked his question again. "The pressure to close. Is it coming from Marcus?"

Burrows nodded. "I assume from outside the agency. Marcus would normally have us dig in until we uncovered every rock. He seems almost afraid of what they are going to find." He sat back and folded his hands on the table. "That doesn't make a lot of sense, I know. I've never seen Marcus Kane afraid of anything. That's the feeling I get about it from the things he's telling the agents directly involved."

"You have a source?"

"I told you I know the agent leading the case – Isabelle Conklin. She's good, maybe too good for this case."

Fitz was more focused on what the FBI was or wasn't finding. He wanted to start there. "Let's start with what the FBI knows. Then we can contrast that with our witness statement rather than going the other way."

Burrows agreed with that. He shoveled a few more bites of dinner in his mouth then pushed the nearly empty plate forward. "The official Secret Service statements match with each other. Monroe had three with her on the jog. According to the statements, including the First Gentleman, Monroe woke around four-thirty, put on her running clothes, and left with her team."

"Did you find out where exactly she runs?" Charlie asked.

"That was hard to get, but given she's not going to be running for a long time, the Secret Service offered it up. Either they drive her to a dirt trail along the Potomac or they leave from the 15th Street side and run off the White House grounds heading toward Constitution Avenue toward the Washington Monument. She takes a path directly up and around the monument on National Mall grounds and heads along the path on the north side of the Mall. She runs past the Reflecting Pool toward the Lincoln Memorial. For some reason on that morning, she chose to go up the steps at the Lincoln Memorial and to the statue of Lincoln. The Secret Service tried to get her to move along. Before they could, she was shot."

Fitz held his hand up to stop him. "What is the rest of her route?"

Burrows explained that after passing the Lincoln Memorial she'd run down the other side of the National Mall to the Smithsonian National Air and Space Museum back up toward Constitution Avenue to the National Gallery of Art before heading back to the White House. "It's a path they ran fairly frequently. The Secret Service would vary the days she was allowed to run it, only three days a week. They'd also vary the route direction. She wouldn't be allowed to run it in the same order every time she went out there. The Secret Service only had so much control. I think the reason she was even allowed was because of the early morning hour. That, of course, in hindsight was a poor decision."

Fitz considered what Burrows was saying. With the varying days and changing routes, unless someone was sitting out there determined to shoot the president, it probably wasn't going to be a one-and-done situation. They could have been watching long enough to uncover a pattern to the Secret Service variation but Fitz knew it wasn't a one-day event.

"If this remains the official story, there are still problems with it," Fitz noted. "There had to be planning on the part of the shooter or they had insider information."

Charlie asked, "Did they say why she liked to run the National Mall?"

Burrows explained. "Monroe started running that route when she was in Congress. She felt safer running the National Mall than she did in the woods and she enjoyed starting her morning among the monuments as a physical reminder of the weight of her work. As I'm sure you can imagine, it's been a nightmare for the Secret Service in trying to keep her secure." Burrows reached for his plastic cup and took a long sip of soda. "The problem is, although the statements of all the Secret Service agents match, the physical evidence doesn't bear out. Now you're telling me even the timing of her arriving at the hospital doesn't match."

"We'll get to that," Fitz said, still pushing him. "Tell us more about what the FBI found."

"The scene at the Lincoln Memorial doesn't make sense. There wasn't any blood found where Monroe would have been shot. A Secret Service agent claims that most of her blood was absorbed by his clothing. There was blood over to the side where Steele was shot. But as I said, he would have been shot at a distance not close range like the medical examiner saw. He was dressed all in black and armed."

It was the first time something occurred to Fitz. He didn't want to get them off track but it was important. "What were the president and Secret Service wearing when she was brought into the emergency room?"

Burrows opened his mouth to speak but shook his head instead. "I don't know. I didn't see that information in the report. Tell me what you think you know."

"I don't know anything about the clothing," Fitz admitted. "If she was out running, they'd all be dressed in running clothes. If she wasn't, they wouldn't be. If the scene was staged, how are they going to account for that? That's a pretty glaring investigative gap."

Charlie scribbled the question down on a notepad in front of her. "Didn't the FBI get her clothes as evidence?"

Burrows looked at them wide-eyed. "It didn't even occur to me to ask. I was more focused on the location of the crime scene. I know we don't have the Secret Service clothing. They also initially refused at first to be interviewed. They refused to speak at the hospital and were only interviewed much later in the day after President Monroe was out of surgery and had been stabilized. They were wearing suits when they were interviewed. I know that much. What happened to the clothes they were wearing at the scene – I couldn't tell you. I'll inquire about it tomorrow."

"You said things aren't matching up," Fitz reminded him. "Did they recover the bullets from Monroe's body?"

Burrows released a frustrated sigh. "It's a 7.62×25mm Tokarev cartridge widely used in former Soviet states and China, among other countries. It's still used in Russia today. Not normal ammunition for a former Army soldier."

"You think Russians did this?" Charlie asked with a hitch in her tone.

Burrows shook his head. "There's been no speculation of that with the FBI. The ammunition is odd but Steele had no ties to Russia."

Fitz thought back to the agent he met in Rock Creek Park. He told Burrows about his interaction with the man and the ammunition in the drawer.

Burrows interrupted. "Why you? Why not the FBI?"

Fitz couldn't answer that. He suspected that it was the Warren Circle's doing. "He tracked me down based on my previous reputation with D.C. Metro and the work I do now. I can't explain his actions. I've not been able to corroborate what he told me. He saw a Secret Service agent come into the office and put spent bullets in his desk then leave later with them. The agent I spoke to wouldn't give me any more details than that. He showed me a photo though, of inside the man's desk and the bullets."

"What kind of ammo?"

"One of the bullets looked like a 9mm and the other I didn't recognize. It would be the ammunition you mentioned."

"You have no idea what they were from or why he was putting them in his desk?" Burrows asked with a trace of skepticism in his tone.

"No," Fitz said, understanding why Burrows felt the way he did. Fitz felt the same way. "I'm not saying the story is credible. I'm telling you the information that was brought to me. I've not been able to verify any of it. Did you see any medical reports?"

"I didn't see any report," Burrows clarified.

"Who were the three Secret Service agents interviewed?" Charlie asked.

"Sebastian Cole, the head of the team. Ian Drake and Graham Westbrook, both men were on her team since before the inauguration. All three are senior members of the Secret Service. All decorated and trustworthy."

Fitz thought back to the interview with Ethan and what Amy had told him. Two of them had been in the SUV taking her to the hospital. One of the men was missing. He repeated the last line to himself a few more times. It meant that it could have been Westbrook who was hiding the bullets.

Fitz suggested, "I think we have to set aside the bullets for now until we can sort out a few more things. The information given to Charlie proved much more fruitful."

Burrows looked at Charlie. "Someone came to you, too?"

She nodded. "A former co-worker."

"A spy?" Burrows asked with an edge to his tone. He knew Charlie wasn't going to answer that. "What did he say?"

"He gave us the name of a witness I mentioned to you earlier." Charlie paused and zeroed in on him.

"You didn't say the information came from a spy."

Charlie didn't take the bait. "Do you want to know what the witness said or not? I promised you we'd tell you."

"Then tell me."

In a rush of breath, she said, "Nothing about his story supports President Monroe leaving the White House for a jog. All of it supports her being shot at the White House."

CHAPTER 13

All of the air was sucked out of the room.

The weight of what Charlie said hung over them. Even though Fitz knew the information, hearing Charlie say the words aloud, the implication of their meaning settled over him for the first time.

Someone inside the White House shot the President of the United States.

That left very few suspects.

Burrows took a moment to absorb it and immediately started denying the possibility. "There is no way the shooting took place at the White House. It's not possible. There are too many people around. This Secret Service agent must be wrong. He must be lying to you." His denials went on and on. Finally, Burrows settled in. "He said he only saw two people leave in the SUV with President Monroe?"

Fitz wasn't sure why that was what was top of mind. "He did. Why does it matter?"

Burrows gathered himself. "There was a statement from an ER nurse who initially said there were *two* Secret Service agents with President Monroe. The agent wrote that down in the statement. She was the only one who had said two. He called her back to see if she had misspoken because the doctor reported three agents. The nurse wouldn't change her statement. She said she was sure there were only two agents. The one driving and the one in the back with President Monroe. She helped move the president out of the SUV herself. She knew how many agents were present in that SUV."

"That matches Ethan's statement," Charlie said evenly. "Was there any explanation from the Secret Service?"

"It didn't seem important at the time. My friend only followed up because he noticed the discrepancies. He assumed in the flurry of activity she didn't see the other agent. Of all the inconsistencies that one seemed like it didn't matter. She could have missed seeing the other agent easily in all that chaos. It's just..." Burrows didn't finish this thought.

"It's just now that a witness has come forward, she might be right and the doctor is lying? But why?"

"There were three agents supposedly with her on the jog that took her to the hospital. That's the official report," Burrows explained. "Not two. One is missing. Can you tell me the name of the nurse you spoke to?"

Fitz promised Amy he wouldn't disclose her name. "Do you remember the name of the nurse who said there were two agents?"

"Amy something or other. I'd have to look at the witness statement again."

Fitz didn't confirm it was the same person but the forced look he gave Burrows conveyed the message. "I believe the medical staff at the hospital lied to the FBI because they were asked to by the Secret Service as a matter of national security. I'll get to what my nurse friend said in a moment. I want to stress that Ethan has been with the Secret Service for a long time. His normal supervisor wasn't there that night. He knows what he saw and yet he's being told he must be mistaken. There is surveillance video all over the inside and outside of the White House. Surely, the FBI must have it."

Burrows shook his head. "The FBI isn't pulling surveillance footage at the White House when the shooting officially took place at the Lincoln Memorial."

Fitz cursed loudly. "We need the surveillance video. It's the only thing that will definitively confirm what Ethan saw that night. He had no reason to lie or make this up."

"Do you think they are going to keep that, Fitz?" Charlie asked. "If they are trying to hide something, they aren't going to hand it over. It's probably been destroyed already."

Fitz agreed with that. "Then that's an answer. It means they are hiding something." He turned to look at Burrows. "Do you think you can convince them to ask for it?" Fitz considered for a moment how Marcus might feel about Fitz asking an FBI agent to get information when he could probably call the director himself. If Marcus and Senator Ford wanted Fitz to do the job, they were going to have to give him leeway to do it his way. He felt a surge of confidence growing in him that he hadn't felt since he got the message from Ford at the start of this.

Burrows wasn't sure the FBI would make the request. "All I can do is ask. They aren't going to see any reason to do it though."

"Make them." While he was at it, Fitz had more tasks for the FBI. "We also want to know why there was a different supervisor there that night. There was also the White House chef there working on some dishes for upcoming events. He said that was normal but he's another person we can interview. Does the FBI have a list of everyone present in the White House that night into the morning hours?"

"No," Burrows said, growing frustrated. "They aren't focused on the White House at all. You really believe the shooting took place *inside* the White House?"

"I can't say for certain it happened in the White House, but evidence is pointing in that direction." Burrows started to argue again but Fitz finally went into details about his interview with Amy without mentioning her name. "Look, I've known this nurse for a long time. She's highly skilled at her job and isn't someone who lies or would make up a story to impress me. She was hesitant to speak to me but her conscience got the better of her. She laid out some pretty damning evidence."

Fitz let his words hang in the air before dropping the bombshell. "She can confirm that *two* Secret Service arrived in the SUV with Monroe at three-twenty-three in the morning. It was not after five as in the official report. It was after three, a full two hours before they said she was shot. So you have Ethan seeing the SUV rush out of the White House lot with two agents and Monroe and you have a trauma nurse at the ER confirming that the SUV arrived there with two agents and Monroe shortly after that. These are two people with no reason to lie, Burrows. No reason."

"Fitz," Burrows said his name in a rush of frustrated breath. "That would mean Secret Service agents are lying to the FBI. Other hospital staff are lying to the FBI. The First Gentleman of the United States is lying to the FBI."

"What do you mean?" Charlie asked, interrupting him.

Burrows had been holding back. "I read the statement Richard Avery gave to the FBI. He said his wife woke up at her normal time, kissed him on the cheek goodbye, and she left in her running clothes. That was the last time he saw her. He was just getting up when a Secret Service agent rushed to tell him that she'd been shot. He went directly to the hospital. The statement was brief because the man had been asleep for most of it. Do you think Richard Avery is going to lie to the FBI?"

Charlie shrugged it off. "He's going to lie if he's the one who shot her."

Burrows cursed so loudly that Fitz wondered if the walls were going to rattle. "How can you say something like that? Richard Avery did not shoot his wife."

Charlie's cheeks burned pink as she raised her voice. "Why would that be so different to the countless homicides of women across the country murdered by their husbands and boyfriends? Do you think a woman's job makes her immune to domestic violence? This kind of violence happens to women all the time, regardless of their status in society. I'd venture a guess that women with more to lose might face bigger obstacles in getting out of that kind of relationship. One of the primary ones is the loss of their reputation."

Burrows stumbled over his words. "Charlie, Abigail Monroe has ultimate protection. Don't you think she would just tell the Secret Service and they'd protect her? Don't you think they'd have seen it? Don't you think she would have found a way to remove him from her life a long time ago?"

Charlie rattled off the bad deeds of past presidents in front of Secret Service protection, making a strong case. "They are made to be invisible. They are secret keepers by their nature. Maybe the abuse didn't start early on in the relationship. Maybe it started late when her fame started to rise and Avery couldn't handle that. That's certainly been a trigger for domestic violence."

Fitz swallowed hard as he watched Charlie go off. He'd never seen her this close to losing her temper before. He knew she was still in control, but the non-emotional logical woman he was used to seeing became unfurled through the conversation.

He raised his hand slightly to signal her. It took a few moments to get her attention. When she saw he had something to say, she pushed her chair back from the table and stood. Burrows was already in the process of apologizing for upsetting her.

"It's a heated discussion because we are all passionate about finding the truth," Fitz told them. Then he directed his words to Burrows. "Charlie's right. We don't know what is going on inside their marriage.

What we do know is that Avery is the one person who has unfettered access to Monroe outside of the Secret Service. For all we know there was an argument in the middle of the night or one of them uncovered infidelity. It could have been an accident for all we know and the cover-up is misdirection. I think the country can better handle an assassin than a fight between the president and her husband that turned deadly."

Burrows conceded the point. "How would we even start to investigate something like that?"

Charlie put her hands on the back of her chair. "Let Fitz and I take care of that. There's no point having the FBI go down that road. What about the suspect? Has the FBI uncovered much about him?"

Burrows offered Charlie a puppy-dog look. "Are we okay?"

"We're fine. Just don't be such a—" If Charlie was going to insult him she stopped herself. "Just be open to all the possibilities until we can pin down some real evidence."

Burrows took another sip of his drink. "The FBI knows far more about Zachary Steele and his involvement with Last Covenant than they know about the actual shooting. It turns out we had a guy undercover with Last Covenant for some time last year. They are buying guns and other explosive materials. Your usual cult-like behavior. The end times aren't coming fast enough for them, so they are going to move it along. Some charges are coming for the group. He wasn't there after the election."

"Not anything recent?" Fitz asked, not sure he was surprised. "Not even when she was campaigning?"

"Nothing. At least no planning back then. The FBI believes Steele probably worked alone."

"Based on what? It's not even been forty-eight hours. What was his motivation?" Charlie asked.

"They are still trying to figure that out. He was a rampant misogynist and didn't believe a woman should be president. He was a good marksman in the Army. The FBI can't escape the guy was dead at the scene."

"Dead men don't tell any tales." Fitz folded his arms over his chest. He'd been hoping to hear some evidence that Steele had told someone of his plan ahead of time or that Last Covenant had been involved. "Has the FBI talked to any of his friends or family?"

"Not a lot of either. He was connected to the cult and that's about it. His family lives in Kentucky and hasn't had contact with him since his discharge from the Army. He was the epitome of lone gunman with the emphasis on lone."

"Where was he living?" Charlie asked.

"He had an apartment in the southwest part of the city. A rundown apartment building, mostly transients, people getting out of rehab. The landlord rents to people down on their luck. The FBI swept the whole place and didn't find anything."

"Electronics?"

Burrows nodded. "There was a phone in his pocket and a laptop found in his truck. FBI forensics are going through all of that now. He had two additional guns in his truck as well as a slew of ammunition."

"Any of the Russian ammo?" Fitz asked.

"I don't believe so," Burrows said, confirming once again for Fitz that none of this smelled right. "Even if this did happen at the Lincoln Memorial, he must have had a death wish. There wasn't anywhere for him to have run. He had to know the Secret Service was going to shoot back at him."

Charlie agreed with that. "Either he was trying to get himself killed, he was a complete idiot, or he was the perfect patsy. I was hoping something definitive would have told us he was the guy."

"He was shot by the Secret Service. That seems like a pretty good clue," Burrows argued as he received an alert on his phone. He reached for it in his pocket and read the words, his face betraying him.

"What's wrong?" Charlie asked, leaning forward on the chair.

Burrows raised his eyes from his phone. "They caught a man trying to break into Monroe's ICU room. He posed as a hospital employee down to the scrubs and identification badge. One of the Secret Service agents got suspicious. When he approached the man, he pulled out a knife and tried to stab the agent. The FBI has him in custody. He's refusing to speak. The Secret Service is assuming he was there to kill President Monroe."

Fitz cursed softly as he raked his hand down his stubbled face. "Connected to Steele?"

"They don't know. He doesn't have any identification on him and they don't have his prints in the system. He's an unknown right now."

Fitz had the sudden feeling that whoever it was that was trying to kill the president would keep trying. "They have to move her," he insisted. "They can't keep her in that hospital in that ICU. Too many people know she's there."

"They can't move her, Fitz. She's not stable," Charlie countered.

"They are going to keep trying to kill her before she has the chance to wake up." Fitz's words settled over the room filling the silence with a heaviness. They all knew he was right.

CHAPTER 14

Fitz woke the next morning before daybreak to the sound of a buzzing phone on his nightstand. He went to bed at close to one in the morning and planned to skip his run in return for sleep. That wasn't to be.

He rolled to his side, reached for his phone, and slid the screen to answer. "Amy," he said his voice still groggy. "Are you okay?"

"Not really, Fitz," she said in a hushed tone. "Someone tried to kill President Monroe…again. The place is swarming with Secret Service agents, one of whom cornered me in the emergency room. He tried to convince me that I saw three agents that night and that I needed to change my FBI statement. I know what I saw, Fitz. I also know what time they came in and who said what to whom. I'm calm under pressure. I'm not so sure now I should have lied to the FBI about the time."

"Where are you?" Fitz asked, hearing the real fear in her voice.

"I'm in my car in the hospital garage. I don't know what to do. My shift is over for the day. I'm afraid. Should I call the FBI agent and tell him the truth? Will the Secret Service know?"

"How did you leave it with the Secret Service?"

"I got called away and we didn't finish our conversation. He was still outside of the emergency room waiting for me when my shift ended. I slipped out a back door to avoid him. I'm sure he knows where I live. They are the government, Fitz. They can do anything they want."

"Do you know his name?"

"No, he didn't tell me."

"Come here to my house," Fitz said without thinking about the implications. His offer was met with silence. "I'm suggesting you come to my house in Chevy Chase. I don't live above my office anymore. I bought a house and you'll be safe here until it all blows over. I have a few questions for you anyway."

"I don't know."

"You're scared to go home. Take a few days off work and come here. I'll keep you safe. No one will know you're here. The house is so big you can have a whole floor to yourself."

"My boyfriend," she said. "I don't want to tell him I'm coming to your house. He'll get the wrong idea."

"It's better if you don't tell anyone. Leave your cellphone, too." Now Fitz wasn't sure if he was being paranoid. He sat up in bed, letting the sheets pool at his naked midsection, trying to think of the best thing to say. He settled on the truth as simple as it was. "You have a right to be concerned. The Secret Service should not be lying to the FBI and should not be asking a witness to lie. I'm having a hard time understanding why the hospital would comply with that. There's something strange going on. If they can go after the president, then they can go after you."

Amy sucked in an audible breath. "That's what I've been thinking about since the agent approached me in the ER. He wouldn't tell me his name but kept insisting I had to do the right thing and change my statement to the FBI. I thought about calling the FBI agent, not to change my statement, but to tell him. I didn't and I'm not sure why not."

It was probably safer that she didn't. "What do you want to do?"

Amy grew quiet for a few moments before finally relenting. "I'll come to your house. Do you think it's safe to go to my house first?"

"No. I'll go there with you later. Come here now." Fitz gave her the address and directions from the hospital. "I'll see you soon."

Fitz called Charlie to tell her he'd be late coming into the office and that he'd explain later. She didn't question him because she was buried in research for the clients that had been left pending while they chased down leads on the president. Fitz would have to find a way to better manage what the Warren Circle needed and his commitments.

As he sat at his kitchen table waiting for Amy, his phone rang. Thinking it was Charlie he answered without looking. "Problem with one of the cases?" he asked off-handedly.

"In a matter of speaking," the voice said on the other end of the phone.

Fitz didn't recognize the voice. He pulled the screen back and looked – Marcus Kane. "Director Kane, I apologize. I thought you were Charlie. What can I help you with this morning?" Fitz wasn't surprised the man was calling him. He had expected it would be sooner.

"Why is Agent Joshua Burrows spending so much time at your office?"

That confirmed what Fitz had suspected – they were being watched. "We struck up a friendship. He had a previous relationship with Charlie. Nothing more than that."

"Has he spoken to you about the assassination attempt?"

"He has," Fitz said as if it were no big deal. "It's on the minds of a lot of people. I think he's frustrated like many of us."

"Have you discussed it with him?"

"In general terms, yes, of course. Have we discussed anything else? No. Charlie and I both take vows of confidentiality seriously. Agent Burrows is an asset to the FBI. He's intelligent, thorough, and a good agent."

"I know that."

"Then what's the problem? You can't assume Charlie and I are going to cut off all contact with everyone we have known. Furthermore, to expedite work, we are going to have to rely on sources that we have always used. Those relationships help us gather information and we can do so without disclosing the whole farm."

Fitz was specifically staying away from words to indicate the Warren Circle because he assumed that's what he should do. No direction had been given to them about phone communication with other members.

Not dissuaded by Fitz's words, Marcus asked, "Do you know Burrows is running a side investigation into the shooting? He's not happy with the FBI official investigation."

"I don't think I'd call it a side investigation. He's quite busy with his current caseload. He doesn't believe the FBI is getting accurate information."

"They are working at my direction," Marcus said with his commanding tone.

"Why is that? Why are you rushing the official investigation? I'm having trouble understanding with the wealth of resources and the importance of the investigation, why are you directing agents to rush it along? Why are Charlie and I even needed?"

Marcus remained quiet for a few beats. Fitz could hear him breathing. He skipped right over Fitz's question and came up with one of his own. "What have you found about the shooting so far?"

"That evidence is scarce, but what we have found from witnesses doesn't match the official statements being provided to the FBI. The shooting did not take place while she was jogging. It most certainly didn't take place at the Lincoln Memorial." Fitz did not go as far as to say it took place in the White House. He wasn't sure why he held back the information. He didn't feel right sharing it.

If Fitz expected Marcus to sound shocked, he was disappointed. A little too calmly, Marcus said, "I have my reasons for limiting the FBI investigation. We will be issuing a formal statement soon closing the investigation."

"I assume you know someone tried to finish the job with President Monroe at the hospital last night? I assume the FBI has that person in custody."

"They do and he isn't speaking. We have no prints for him in the system. He had no identification on him. He's a ghost, an unknown."

"Facial recognition?"

"We are working on that. Right now he's in a cell waiting to be processed. I have one of my best interrogators coming in today to try to break him."

Fitz was going to offer but he couldn't see how that would work. "Is President Monroe being moved to a more secure floor or facility? Preferably something unknown to the public?"

"We are in the process of that. As you know her condition is still tenuous. There is a discussion with the doctors about a move and how that would work. Until then, the FBI has added security there with the Secret Service, for obvious reasons."

"Should I trust the Secret Service?"

"No," Marcus said without explanation. "There are very few you can trust, Fitz. I thought we had discussed that."

Fitz had asked the question for one specific reason and it brought them right back to the start of the conversation. "That is partly why when Agent Burrows came to us for dinner the other night talking about the shooting, we allowed it. Encouraged it even. He's able to access information for us. I didn't think that I could run to you with every question and it would be suspicious if we were suddenly snooping around the FBI."

"You've turned one of my agents into an asset then?"

Fitz couldn't tell from the man's tone if that would be a good thing or a bad thing. He took a middle-of-the-road response. "I don't think I'd go that far. We are friends and Burrows came to us with concerns about the shooting. We were already working on it, so we decided to join forces. We didn't see any harm in it."

"Fine, then."

"What does that mean? Are you going to reprimand Burrows for working on this?"

"No," Marcus said. "This may turn out in our favor. It's another way to make the FBI look good when we have to walk back our official investigation. Burrows might even get a promotion out of the deal. Just watch what you say to him. Loyalty in friendships is no reason to break other loyalties."

"Understood," Fitz said and meant it. He had no reason to disclose anything to Burrows. "While we are talking…what should Charlie and I be doing with what we find or if we have questions? Can we contact you?"

"I don't recommend that. If you need something go to Senator Ford unofficially."

"I can do that." Before Fitz could say anything else, the line went dead. "I guess that settles that," he said aloud to himself. He started to send a text to Charlie then thought better of it. He'd tell her in person. Fitz scrolled through social media reading the headlines and the news updates about the assassination attempt, speculation, medical updates on the president, and what factual news he could decipher from some of the reports.

Amy arrived about twenty minutes later. Her face was flushed and her hair tied back in a ponytail with strands around her face that came undone. "I don't think I was followed. I'm not sure how they could have followed me. I did everything you said, kept pulling from one lane to the next, and got off an exit to only get back on it. I stopped at two stores and watched to see if there was anyone around. If they are following me, they are invisible."

Fitz guided her to the kitchen and offered her some coffee. Amy declined but asked if he had some juice or water. He poured her a glass of orange juice and got her cold water from the fridge.

As she sat down at the dining room table, she glanced around the eat-in kitchen. "This is certainly an upgrade from your rowhouse. Business must be doing well."

"It is. I sometimes miss living in Georgetown in the thick of it. But there are benefits out here too."

"Like hiding people who have gotten themselves in trouble with the Secret Service," Amy said wryly. "I don't know what I've gotten myself into. I reported what I saw like I do all the time. My medical records have to reflect the facts. I'm coming to understand the Secret Service doesn't operate in facts. I changed the time when requested but nothing else."

"Were your official records in the hospital system changed?"

"They were." Amy exhaled a breath.

"Did you have any concerns about lying to the FBI? You know that's a crime?"

"I had a lot of concerns and I brought them to Dr. Alex Hayes, who is the ER doctor. He didn't want to lie to the FBI either. Word came down from the hospital administration that we had to do what the Secret Service said. Dr. Jonathan Pierce, who was the surgeon, was also told to do what the Secret Service said. It didn't sit right with me. I guess when I gave the statement, I hadn't been told I had to lie about how many Secret Service agents were there. The FBI came back to me to ask if maybe there were three. I was adamant that there were two."

"What specifically did the Secret Service tell you to say to the FBI?"

Amy cradled the juice glass in her hands. "They were mostly focused on the timing that they arrived and that the president went into surgery. I assume the others got the message that there were three agents there. I didn't hear that and it didn't make any sense why that was something to lie about."

"What details about the shooting did you hear?"

Amy shook her head. "I didn't hear those details. Just that she was shot twice and she was bleeding out. Sebastian Cole, the driver, told us that she had been shot fifteen to thirty minutes before. I remember him specifically saying that when he found her he carried her to the SUV himself to bring her to the hospital. It sounded to me like there might have been some arguments about whether to call an ambulance or not. Agent Cole took charge and decided to bring her in himself. He said it would save time."

When he found her. That meant he hadn't been present for the shooting.

That statement alone was a direction for the investigation.

CHAPTER 15

Fitz knew he needed to get to work. He wasn't going to leave until he extracted everything he could from Amy. "How was President Monroe dressed?"

Amy pulled back surprised by the question. "I'm not sure I remember. We were in a hurry to cut her clothes off."

"Close your eyes. Look at her and tell me what you see." Fitz didn't know if that would work, but he had used the technique with witnesses before.

Amy did as he asked and within seconds she had an answer. She opened her eyes. "It was a soft yellow long-sleeve shirt and blue pants. Not yoga pants but the same kind of material but loose on the legs."

"Something she might have jogged in?"

"Possibly." Amy turned her head to the side taking some time to remember. "She wouldn't have been running though with the sneakers on her feet. They were the slip-on kind. Like the Sketchers I have for grocery shopping or running errands. Not something I'd exercise in."

"Do you remember the color?"

"Blue like the pants. There was blood on the shoes. There was blood everywhere. I remember wondering if the shoes had a design before I realized that it was blood. Her clothes were all blood. The shirt almost didn't look yellow anymore."

"Do you know what happened to them?"

"I don't know." Amy turned back to Fitz. "I was busy cutting her out of them and trying to address the bleeding. Everything else was cast to the side. I assume someone picked them up and bagged them. That's standard protocol."

"What should have happened to them?" Fitz had been on the receiving end of clothing from the emergency room in past homicide cases. He knew they were bagged with the date and the initials of the person who bagged them. While medical care was the priority, he had met wonderful medical staff who understood the importance of evidence collection and worked to help the cops.

"I don't remember who collected them. As I said, it was a whirlwind. They would have been turned over to the FBI."

"Could they have been turned over to the Secret Service?"

Amy started to answer then hesitated. "Given everything that's happened so far that wouldn't surprise me."

"What about what the agents were wearing? Do you remember that?"

"Not suits. I know that much. Agent Cole looked as if he'd been dressed for bed. I think he was even wearing pajama bottoms and a sweatshirt on top. His clothes were covered in blood, more so than anyone else."

Fitz already knew the answer. "Would you say any of them looked like they came from a jog?"

"No," she said with a shake of her head, "no one looked like they were out on a run. Who runs before three in the morning?"

Fitz knew Amy would make a solid witness when the time came for it. "Do you remember seeing the bullet wounds?"

"Yes. I was trying to put pressure to stop the bleeding. Most of us didn't even think she'd make it into surgery before she bled out. There were two wounds." Amy pointed at the top of her right breast then lower closer to her stomach also on her right side. "I didn't see the back of her. If you're going to ask me about exit wounds, I don't know. She was on her back on the stretcher. We were working on her as we were transporting."

Fitz considered what else he needed to know. "Did the Secret Service agents go with you?"

"They remained outside the surgery room door. The surgeon wouldn't let them in."

"Did you have any conversation with them or overhear any conversation?"

"No. I didn't speak to either of them. There was an odd tension between them though. I thought it at the time and chalked it up to the fact the president got shot on their watch. Who wouldn't be tense under those conditions?"

"What was the tension?"

She refocused on him. "Cole was calling the shots. He was the one giving information to the doctor and then the surgeon. He was stressed when the doctor asked him questions about what happened and he couldn't answer. He said he got there after the fact. He didn't think there was time for an ambulance, so he scooped her up and brought her to the hospital himself."

"It doesn't sound like he was there for the shooting."

Amy agreed with that. "Once Monroe was in surgery, Cole was focused on the other agent, Ian Drake. Cole said something strange in the hallway. He got right up in Ian's face, pointing his finger, and asked how he could let this happen. Then he asked if he was involved. I understood the first part. That makes sense. If Agent Cole wasn't the one protecting the president at the time it could have been Ian. The shooting happened on his watch. I didn't know what he meant by *involved*. It was an odd exchange looking back at it now."

That was interesting. It also meant that Graham Westbrook was probably the agent who went back to the office with the bullets.

Sebastian Cole wasn't present for the shooting. "What about the president's husband, Richard Avery? Was he at the hospital?"

"No. The only two people there with her were the two Secret Service agents."

"Who was the one that asked you to lie? When did that happen?"

"That came later in the day. I was told to stick around after my shift ended to speak to the FBI. The directive came down from the hospital administration before I met with them. I didn't feel comfortable, but I went along with it because I felt like I had to. No one told me that I needed to say there were three agents there. I never saw three agents."

"The Secret Service agent that came to you at the hospital today. Have you ever seen him before?"

Amy shook her head. "Never. I have no idea who he is. He flashed a badge but didn't tell me his name. I didn't see his name on the badge long enough to register it. I didn't see him speaking to anyone else at the hospital either."

Fitz knew they were working to make sure their cover-up stuck. If they were willing to shoot the president, then anyone who crossed them could be in danger.

As if reading the worry on his face, Amy asked, "Who do you think could have done this?"

Fitz didn't see any reason to lie to her. "We believe the shooting might have taken place inside the White House rather than the street. If that's the case, then we are dealing with very few suspects and there'd have to be coordination with someone within the Secret Service for them to access the president."

"Who has access to her at that time of night?"

"A handful of well-vetted White House staff. If it was one of them, the Secret Service would not protect them. This had to be someone high up. There must be some kind of conspiracy. The Secret Service. The First Gentleman, Richard Avery. No one else is there that time of night unless there was an unofficial meeting."

Amy took that in and asked an insightful question. "Who would the president get out of bed to meet with at that time of night?"

That list could be much longer, especially if a well-placed ruse was utilized. "Any of her cabinet members. Someone high up in Congress – like one of the heads of her committees. The vice president, of course."

"You're never going to be able to access who was in the White House that night."

"We have to do something." Fitz knew the real evidence was slowly showing itself. "Will you be fine here while I go into the office? Later, we can get your things."

"I called my boyfriend before I left to tell him I had to go out of town for a few days and I might not be reachable. I left my phone in my locker at the hospital. Do you think they bugged it or something?"

Fitz wasn't sure. "Did you get off easily?"

"I never take time. It's been accruing and accruing. I think the hospital was happy I was finally using some of it." Amy looked down at her scrubs. "I could use a shower and a change of clothes. I worked all night and could use some sleep too."

Fitz reassured her that he had everything she needed. "Let's get you settled and I'll head to work."

He arrived at the office in time to meet Charlie in the hallway headed toward the kitchen. "I need coffee," she said while holding three thick file folders.

"What are those?" he asked as he leaned against the counter.

"I ran some background on all three Secret Service agents. I wanted to know everything I could about Graham Westbrook, Ian Drake, and Sebastian Cole."

Fitz was impressed at not just the speed but her commitment to the task. "Did you find anything interesting?"

Charlie didn't respond. She slapped the folders into his middle and focused on her coffee. "Can I get you a cup?"

Fitz smiled down at her. She rarely offered anything that could be considered domestic. "Yes, please." He reached around her and grabbed one of the chocolate chip muffins from the plastic container. "Can I have one of these too?"

"Your fingers are all over it, so you better eat it," she said in a teasing tone.

Once they were in the conference room seated at the table with Fitz's muffin half gone, Charlie finally started going over what she had found.

"Ian Drake is in his late thirties. He played college football for Alabama. He was in the military for a short time before joining the Secret Service. As you would expect there is nothing in his criminal background check. All the agents have security clearances, so the background check is rigorous and includes a polygraph and drug testing. He's been with the agency for more than a decade working his way up to this detail. He first was assigned when President Monroe was on the campaign trail for the presidency."

"Graham Westbrook?" Fitz wanted to save Sebastian Cole for last. He had a lot to say about the man.

"He went from high school into the infantry in the Army. Spent a few years there. Had one tour in Iraq then joined the Secret Service when he got out. He's thirty-three. The youngest member of the team and the newest. While his background is clean enough to have passed the background check, he did get in trouble in high school. Some public intoxication and a few minor public fighting incidents that were wiped from his record officially."

Fitz knew Charlie had used some back channels to dig into their background. He didn't like doing that with regular clients because it wasn't what anyone else could access. This time though, he appreciated she went the extra mile. "I think we've narrowed down that Westbrook is the one who hid the bullets while the two others took Monroe to the hospital. We have to consider him part of the conspiracy for now."

"What about Sebastian Cole?" Charlie asked.

Fitz filled her in on what Amy said about Cole at the hospital. "He admitted he wasn't there during the shooting. He attacked Ian in the hallway and asked if he was a part of it. Cole rushed Monroe to the hospital. I don't think he worried that getting an ambulance there would take too much time. I think he didn't know what happened and was protecting her. The word came down from the hospital administration that they were to lie about the timing. What they forgot to tell Amy was that she was supposed to say there were three Secret Service agents there. They are covering for Westbrook." He looked down at the file. "What's all this say about Agent Cole?"

"Your summation of his actions is a summation of the man's career. He's the oldest on the team at forty-five and the most senior and has been with President Monroe since her time in Congress when she first decided to run. He's been leading the team from the start of the primaries all the way through. She demanded to have him in the White House with her. She trusts him completely."

Charlie reached for the file and flipped it open. She didn't read but told Fitz from memory. "He went to West Point, did a stint in the Marines, and then came to the Secret Service. He's a highly decorated agent. Stellar background check. He's unmarried and has no children. All three of them are unmarried with no children. I don't see anything in their backgrounds that would appear on the surface to cause alarm. There couldn't be or they wouldn't keep their security clearances."

Fitz remained quiet as he considered what she said. His thoughts swirled with the senior positions these agents held and the power within their jobs.

"I didn't expect to find anything in the background checks that would indicate a smoking gun. It's not like we were going to dig into them to find one of them had been radicalized. If one of them was convinced to allow the shooting of the president or they did it themselves, then something along their trajectory went very wrong."

"Money issues?"

Charlie shook her head. "These weren't men who were radicalized by money. Power, maybe. Depending on what was promised. I'd say if one or two of them were involved it was ideology and that's something they would have remained very quiet about."

The implication of what she was saying was clear – it was time for them to hit the streets and start talking to people in the lives of these agents.

"Let's start with Sebastian Cole first. I want to see what he knows and what he's willing to tell us."

"He hasn't even given a full statement to the FBI," Charlie said, causing him to sit back in surprise. "He gave them a brief statement that he wasn't there and wasn't sure what happened. He said he had to get back to the White House and so far hasn't shown up to provide a formal statement."

"Is that from Burrows?"

"I spoke to him this morning." Charlie didn't meet his eyes when she said that.

He wanted to ask her exactly how early in the morning she had spoken to him. Like did she roll over and have the chat? Fitz held back the question and the smile he felt forming on his lips. "Let's find him."

CHAPTER 16

They arrived at the only address Charlie had for Sebastian Cole. It was a small ranch house on a quiet suburban street at the end of a cul-de-sac in Tacoma Park, Maryland. It was on the Red Line on the Washington Metro and a little more than six miles outside of Washington D.C. The drive took them about a half hour from Georgetown with traffic.

The house was well-kept but nondescript. The blue siding was in good condition and the paint on the shutters appeared fresh. The lawn was mowed and free of leaves. The walkway even looked like it had been recently swept. There was no car present, although there was a windowless garage at the end of the driveway. Even if nothing more came of this than checking out where he lived, Fitz thought it worth the trip.

The suburban neighborhood was eerily quiet, the kind of place where nothing ever seemed out of place. Fitz and Charlie stood on the curb outside the modest house, the air around them still. The sounds of traffic buzzing not far in the distance.

"Something's off," Charlie muttered, her sharp eyes scanning the house. The front door was ajar as if the owner had forgotten to close it – or as if they'd fled in a hurry.

Fitz hadn't seen it at first. The door was blocked by one of the porch pillars. He leaned in closer to Charlie to see from her vantage point.

His expression remained a mask of quiet calculation.

Charlie knew what he was thinking. "Sebastian Cole isn't the kind of guy who runs from his responsibilities unless something is seriously wrong."

Fitz nodded then set out to the front door. Charlie followed, her movements deliberate, alert. They reached their destination and Fitz knocked lightly, pushing it open. No response.

"Sebastian Cole?" he called, his voice low but firm. No answer. The only sound was the faint rustle of papers inside.

They stepped into a hallway lined with dark wood paneling, the smell of sweat hanging in the air. The silence felt too thick. Fitz's heart beat a steady thump in his ears.

Charlie was the first to notice the papers scattered across the floor, a laptop open on the counter, its screen flashing warnings about unauthorized access. With a glance to her left, she spotted a half-packed duffel bag on the sofa, clothes and gear spilling out.

Fitz took a step deeper into the house. "Cole?" he called again, louder this time. Still nothing. He knew they weren't alone, but they had no choice but to keep moving forward.

A door slammed in the back of the house, followed by the sound of something heavy hitting the floor.

"Get down!" Charlie hissed, grabbing Fitz by the arm and pulling him toward the nearest cover. But it was too late. Cole appeared at the doorway, his face wild, eyes darting from one to the other as if trying to place them, to decide whether they were a threat.

Fitz muttered a curse under his breath. He saw the gun Sebastian was holding – a sleek, black handgun, fingers tight around the grip as if he was ready to use it.

Sebastian's eyes flicked nervously toward the window, then back to them. "Who are you and why are you trespassing?"

Charlie held up her hands in a show of peace. "We're not here to hurt you. We need to talk to you." She paused then added what she probably didn't need to. "About President Monroe."

Sebastian's face twitched, and for a moment, his guard dropped. "I don't have time for this. I don't have time for reporters." His voice broke, and for the briefest moment, he seemed human.

Neither one of them dared move with the gun still trained on them. Fitz held his hands up like Charlie's. "We aren't reporters. I'm Connor Fitzgerald, I run the opposition firm in Georgetown. I used to be a homicide detective for D.C. Metro."

Sebastian blinked in recognition. "I thought you looked familiar." He jutted his chin toward Charlie, expressing a question without words.

"I work with Fitz. I used to work for the government too. State Department." She had told the lie for so long that it sounded like the truth even to Fitz.

Sebastian didn't buy it. "I know what the State Department means for women who look like you."

"Women who look like me?" Charlie asked, no trace of the sarcasm Fitz would have assumed.

Sebastian rolled his eyes. "Hot without trying to be. Good muscle tone like you lift a few times a week. Eyes like you're scanning for trouble. CIA?"

Charlie conceded. "Retired. I still care what happens inside the government. It's why we are here. There's an FBI agent who doesn't believe the official story. We don't believe the official story. We want the truth."

"The truth?" he asked in a forced laugh. "You think you're entitled to the truth? Lady, I can't even get the truth and I was there." He turned his back on them heading back down the hall from where he had come. He shouted from the back of the home. "They're coming for me. I can't stay here. Someone shot up my house last night. I'm locked out of my email and my work website. I got a notice that my security clearances are suspended."

"Shot at you?" Fitz asked too quietly for Sebastian to hear while looking down at Charlie. She seemed as surprised as he. Fitz couldn't stand in the living room and wait this out. He took off through the living room in the same direction as Sebastian.

Fitz found him in the room at the end of the hall. Sebastian was bent over his bed throwing clothes from a nearby closet into a suitcase. Fitz took a slow step forward, keeping his hands visible. "Who shot at you?" He scanned the room for visible signs of bullets realizing then that both windows didn't just have drapes half covering them. They had been boarded.

Sebastian gestured toward the window on the far wall on the left side of his bed. "Around two in the morning, the first shot came through that window over there. Then the window above my head. I raced out when the shots stopped but didn't get there in time. I saw the black van screeching down the road. I'm a liability to them now."

"You brought Monroe to the hospital – alive. How can you be the liability? The FBI investigation is pointing the finger at Zachary Steele at the Lincoln Memorial. No one thinks this is your fault."

Sebastian's jaw tightened. "You don't understand. This goes deeper than you know. No one is blaming me but they want me to keep my mouth shut and they know I won't."

Fitz felt Charlie at his side. He turned his head as her eyes flicked toward Fitz. She'd been in situations like this before – people on the run, people with secrets they couldn't keep. It was always a balance of tension, of getting them to trust you just enough to let something slip. He'd let her take this one.

"We're on the same side here," Charlie said, her voice calm but urgent. "Help us and we can help you."

There was recognition in Sebastian's eyes. "You don't believe it was

Zachary Steele?"

Fitz wanted to shorthand this for him. "We don't believe the shooting even took place at the Lincoln Memorial." He paused and clarified. "Let me be clearer. We know the shooting didn't take place at the Lincoln Memorial. We suspect that it might have taken place inside the White House, not that we have solid evidence of that. My understanding is it was you who got her to the hospital. But we know that occurred roughly two hours before the official statement says you went to the hospital. We know that you were there with Ian Drake and that Graham Westbrook was back in his office hiding bullets in his desk. What we don't know is why all of this happened, who really shot the president and who is behind it all."

Sebastian's eyes flickered to the door, then back to them. He exhaled sharply, running a hand through his hair as if trying to clear the fog. "How can I trust you?" he muttered. "How do I know this isn't a test? You come here sent by them to see what I know then you report back or worse try to kill me."

"If we wanted you to be dead, I'd have killed you already," Charlie said eerily calm. "I wouldn't have done something so messy as shoot up your home in the middle of the night. I'm sure that triggered the cops coming out and your neighbors."

"It was a nightmare. I never went back to sleep. I'm a bit surprised it hasn't made the news. I told the detective I didn't want a spectacle and my neighbors know what I do. They are respectful."

"So," Charlie started again, "as I was saying, if this were me and I wanted to know what you know, I'd employ techniques I used at the agency then I'd dispose of you."

Fitz coughed back the emotion rising in him. Fear, maybe. He'd never heard Charlie speak like that. It was as if she was a different person right before his eyes. This was the most Charlie had ever hinted about that facet of her former work. Fitz tried to forget everything other than she had government resources he didn't have that helped their business. He hadn't ever wanted to know the nitty-gritty of her former life.

Sebastian didn't seem at all concerned about what Charlie was capable of doing to him. He glanced over at her with a steady smile hinting at the corners of his lips. "Then I should be grateful the CIA isn't involved. We can cross that agency off the list."

Charlie disagreed. "I wouldn't cross anyone off the list until we know more. Why have you stuck around so long if someone tried to kill you?"

"I had a meeting this morning at the White House. I told my boss about the shooting at my house. I thought he'd want to know. Discuss it." Sebastian stood to his full height, turning to them with his hands on his hip. A blue shirt still gripped in his hand. "Do you know what he said? He told me that I just need to keep my head low and stick to the party line and it will all blow over. The attempted assassination of the President of the United States. I was directed to lie about what happened. I was shot at and then told it would all blow over soon." Sebastian shook his head. "I'm not that stupid."

"You did lie though?" Fitz pressed.

"I did what I thought I had to do before I thought better of it. I wasn't in the room when the shooting happened. I wasn't there to protect her. My one job and I failed." Sebastian raised his head to the ceiling. "I was suspended and rightly so. It's what I deserve allowing an assassination attempt to happen."

Before Fitz could respond, Charlie said, "Two assassination attempts. You know that, right? At the hospital, someone tried to access the president again. They had a knife. The FBI has them in custody, but he's not talking."

Sebastian lowered his head and cursed loudly, a string of frustration escaping his lips. "No. I didn't know that because the only information

I've been able to get since the incident has been on the news. My agency has shut down all communication. They won't even let me near her. They have another team protecting her."

"I assume they are going to move her or add more protection," Charlie confirmed.

Sebastian licked his lips and his eyes watered.

Fitz was picking up something from the man he couldn't quite put his finger on. There was something emotional about Sebastian's response. Overly emotional for a Secret Service agent. His eyes connected with Sebastian's. "Did you have a personal relationship?" Fitz faltered to speak the rest of it. He was suggesting that the President of the United States was having a personal, intimate relationship with the head of her Secret Service detail. Nothing like that had ever happened to his knowledge. Then again the former presidents were all men.

While he was having an internal struggle with the idea, Sebastian and Charlie stared at him. It was almost like Fitz was having an internal struggle and no one was coming to his rescue.

Charlie had no problem saying it. She wrinkled her nose at Fitz and then turned to Sebastian. "What Fitz is poorly trying to ask you is if you were screwing the president?"

Sebastian winced his eyes shut, pinching the bridge of his nose. When he opened his eyes again, he looked at Charlie, not Fitz. "I wouldn't put it like that. But yes, we were having a relationship. No one knew and it went back years. Her marriage has been over for a long time."

Fitz found his voice. "Did Richard Avery know that?"

"That the marriage was over? Yes. That we were having a relationship? No. No one knew that." He watched the two of them carefully and while Charlie did a good job of keeping her expression neutral, Fitz knew his face gave him away.

"I don't care about your judgment. I love her. I loved Abigail Monroe long before I was on her protection details and long before she even thought about running for president."

"Good," Fitz said, recovering. "Then you're going to be motivated to help us take down whoever shot her."

Sebastian cast a glance at his suitcase. He reached for a pad of paper and a pen on his nightstand. He scribbled down something and handed it to Charlie.

Fitz leaned over her shoulder and read.

There was an address in Northern Virginia and a meeting time for later that night.

Sebastian met Fitz's eyes. "I'll do whatever I can to figure out who shot her, even if it means sacrificing my own career."

Fitz and Charlie retreated from the house without saying another word.

CHAPTER 17

The drive took longer than expected. Fitz kept his eyes on the road, the headlights illuminating the curve of Route 211 as they wound deeper into the foothills of the Blue Ridge Mountains heading toward Shenandoah National Park.

Charlie sat beside him, her gaze flickering between the darkened trees and the rearview mirror. The air outside had grown colder, the scent of damp earth and pine thickening with every mile. They hadn't spoken much since leaving Fitz's house after a long day of waiting. There hadn't been many leads to run down or at least none they wanted to do before talking to Sebastian.

In the early evening, Fitz had taken Amy to her house so she could get a few things. After he told her about the shooting at Sebastian's, Amy had grown more afraid for her safety. That night while he was gone, Fitz asked a security guy he knew to stay with her at his house. With her secured, he could focus on other things.

Charlie was the lookout on the drive. It had been tense and they hadn't spoken much about what Sebastian had told them. Fitz was still working to put his judgment aside and Charlie just didn't have much to say. He glanced over at her, his jaw tight, as if he was waiting for her to speak first.

"You think we're being followed?" she asked, her voice just above a whisper.

"I don't know. Could be or just paranoia." Fitz adjusted his grip on the steering wheel. "If Sebastian is right about someone coming after him, they're not going to find him here."

"None of this feels right," she said, still staring out the window. "Sebastian was too close to Monroe. He just happened to be there the night she was shot, even though he wasn't working. This could be a set-up. We don't know that he didn't shoot her. A lover's quarrel gone wrong."

"I don't think so." Fitz couldn't see the seasoned agent going that rogue. Affairs happened. Murder was something else. "I don't condone the affair. You could see on Sebastian's face that he was afraid. He wasn't lying either. He didn't know about the second assassination attempt." Fitz's voice was quieter now, thoughtful. "He's running. That counts for something."

Charlie didn't answer. Her eyes stayed fixed on the road behind them, scanning the headlights of every passing car. They were alone in the woods now – no sign of traffic, only the occasional flicker of their headlights against the tree trunks that lined the narrow road. The cabin Sebastian had summoned them to was in the middle of nowhere, tucked away on a small property just shy of the Shenandoah National Park.

They finally made the turn onto a gravel road, the tires kicking up stones as the cabin loomed ahead, barely visible through the thick trees. It was more rustic than Fitz had expected, the kind of place that looked like it belonged to a hunter or someone who didn't want to be found. A low, wooden structure with dark beams and a slanted roof. A fire crackled from the house, sending wisps of smoke curling into the night.

Fitz slowed the car, his foot hovering above the brake as he took in the scene. It was just a house in the woods. Sebastian's truck was parked next to it.

Charlie rested her hand on the door handle. "It's too quiet."

Fitz wondered who else might be out there. He wasn't worried he was walking into a trap set by Sebastian but whoever was after the man. He had no way of knowing if they had already gotten to him, meaning Charlie and Fitz were next.

They parked the car at the foot of the driveway and got out. The crunch of gravel underfoot was the only sound in the stillness. The cabin windows reflected the pale light of the half-moon. The air had a strange chill.

Charlie led the way, her boots muffled by the thick carpet of needles beneath them. Fitz followed close behind, his hand resting near his sidearm, eyes scanning the woods. They reached the door, and Fitz knocked once, the sound echoing in the night.

A moment passed and the door creaked open. Sebastian stood in the doorway, his face drawn and tense, but without the frantic edge he'd shown earlier. He stepped aside, wordlessly inviting them in.

Inside, the cabin was modest but well-kept. A fire burned low in the stone fireplace, the glow casting shadows on the walls. The atmosphere was calm, serene almost.

Sebastian closed the door behind them and moved into the small living room area. He didn't meet their eyes as he moved toward a small table in the corner, pulling out a chair for each of them.

"You're alone, right?" Fitz asked, watching Sebastian carefully.

Sebastian nodded, his jaw set. "No one knows about this place. My name isn't listed on the deed. I never told anyone I came up here. No one should know about this place except the pair of you. I'm going to assume given your training you weren't tailed."

"We weren't tailed," Fitz assured him. "Who does the cabin belong to?"

"An uncle that died years ago. He left it under the name of a corporation for the family to use. I'm the only family left other than two cousins out in California I never see. There's hardly a way to connect this back to me."

"Okay, you got us here," Fitz said as he sat. The silence that followed was thick with tension. "Start talking."

Sebastian's eyes shifted toward the fire, and for a moment, it seemed like he was somewhere far away. Then, slowly, he exhaled, the weight of his decision hanging in the air. "All right," he said, his voice barely a whisper. "I'll tell you everything."

They waited for several beats for him to start but he stared at them.

He licked his lips and parted them. "You're not recording, are you?"

"No," Fitz said. "We have no reason to record this. But we don't have all night."

Sebastian sat back with his hands folded in his lap. He didn't meet the gaze of either Fitz or Charlie. "Abigail and I met when she was first in the Senate. We'd see each other in passing and we were cordial. She got lost once and I gave her directions. After that, we would smile and say hello. It started simple enough. Nothing unprofessional."

"When did it change?" Charlie prodded.

"About six months after that first meeting. We were both in the Senate building late. I was waiting for the person I was protecting. I needed to walk him to his car but he was in meetings and had dismissed me for a while. I wandered through the halls and came upon Abigail's office. She was crying."

Sebastian stared back over at the fire taking a break or recalling the memory of it, Fitz wasn't sure. He turned his head and locked his gaze on Fitz. "I knocked on the door and asked if she was okay. Abigail was startled. I don't think she realized anyone but building security was still there. And they were in the front of the building, not near the offices. She tried to pull herself together and assure me she was fine. It was obvious that she wasn't. I admit I forced myself into the situation. I could have respected her privacy and left. I didn't.

I remained and wouldn't leave until I was sure she was okay."

"Did you ever find out what was wrong?" Fitz asked.

"Marital issues. She had caught her husband cheating. They were struggling with her new role in the Senate. They had talked about divorce, but it wouldn't have looked good for either of them. She said they were trying to decide what to do. They wanted to be logical and rational about it. There was already talk about Abigail's rise in politics. She said she knew if she were going to get divorced the time had already passed. She was too public now. Richard Avery didn't want the divorce. He also said he didn't want to give up his mistress. He was looking for a way to have both."

Charlie cursed a little under her breath.

Sebastian looked at her. "I had the same feeling. I'm not too proud to admit that I encouraged her to get a divorce. A lot of people in politics are divorced. Better that than carrying the potential for scandal down the road." Sebastian continued with his tale of how that night they formed a bond. Friends at first but over time they each found themselves seeking out the other.

Sebastian gave them a faint smile. "We were drawn to each other. I didn't want to get involved with a married woman. A couple of months in, Abigail said she had agreed on an arrangement with her husband. That was the deal they had worked out. If they were going to stay married, then the marriage was open. They both had to make sure not to cause the other scandal and things had to remain as private as possible. Neither wanted to know what the other was doing. It wasn't hard because they both worked so much."

Fitz shook his head, not understanding. "Wouldn't this kind of arrangement be ripe with the potential for scandal?"

Sebastian agreed with that. "I spoke to Abigail about that a lot. I was worried for her. She said they were both good at keeping secrets. We'd meet in her Senate office after hours. If we went anywhere together it was far into Virginia. People knew who she was and no one knew who I was. She told people I was her Secret Service protection and that was easy enough to pass off to people who didn't know better. That wouldn't work in D.C. where people knew she didn't have protection. Everywhere else, no one even questioned it if they recognized her at all."

Charlie told him she could see how that would be possible. "As her fame grew though, people knew her. She was all over the news and social media. Abigail Monroe is a woman who is vocal about the causes she supports and the opposition. For an onlooker, it was like she joined the Senate and within a year she was the star, the one to watch."

Sebastian nodded. "Her rise was fast. Too fast almost for most of us to keep up. It was hard on her too, but she is incredibly intelligent."

"What was the course of the relationship once she was being touted as the next president?"

"It got even stronger. Abigail needed people around her she could trust. Richard wasn't doing that for her. He was working and had women on the side. At that point, they lived in the same house but barely spoke. I kept pushing her to divorce before it was too late. Not because I wanted her to do it for me but because it was a toxic relationship for everyone involved. Their secret never got out." He looked at them with surprise on his face.

Fitz had the same emotion. No one had ever heard even a blip that there was trouble behind closed doors. "What I hear you telling me is that President Monroe did what she had to do to succeed."

"Don't most politicians?" Sebastian asked with his head cocked to the side.

Charlie agreed with him. "I don't fully understand why she made the choices she did, but I can respect she did what she thought was right. You were on her Secret Service detail at some point during the end of her Senate run?"

"When the former Speaker of the House retired, I was without a placement. There had been threats against Abigail early on, so she was given a small protection detail and she requested me. I remained on that team for the rest of her Senate career, her primary for the nomination then her presidential campaign. She kept me on after she was elected."

"I suppose it made the relationship easier to pull off," Fitz said without meaning quite the edge in the tone that was there. He was still trying to drop the judgment of the whole situation. Fitz knew he was coming up short.

Sebastian raised his eyes to him. "It did. Richie, as Abigail called him, might have looked good when out on that campaign trail. He might have looked to the American public like he was a supporting, loving husband who had given up his job to support his wife. He begrudgingly gave up his job and he hated Abigail at that point. He regretted not allowing the divorce to happen back when she was in the Senate. He told her that often. Given I was the head of her detail, I had a front-row seat to the fights."

"Did he know you were sleeping with her?" Fitz asked.

"No," Sebastian said definitively. "No one knew. There isn't anyone who knows except the two of you and I'm not even sure how you figured that out."

Fitz wasn't sure how he had come to it either. "Call it a gut instinct. Was there any physical abuse between them?"

"Nothing physical that I saw or she told me. I believe she would have told me."

Charlie asked, "Is there anything else about your relationship with her we need to know before we go on?"

Sebastian considered the question. "It was as close to a loving normal relationship as one could get in the situation. We spent considerable time together given my position. We were able to be alone together and I was someone she trusted completely. One of the few." Sebastian pinched the bridge of his nose. "Maybe the only one she trusted. Abigail learned quickly once she got into the White House that everyone was after something. Even her allies were only there to use her. The men around her thought she could be lied to and manipulated without consequence."

"Who were those people?" Fitz asked.

"The ones closest to her. Her cabinet, Congress, and her vice president. They were also some of the people there that night she was shot."

If Sebastian had leaned across the table and punched Fitz in the face, he might have been less stunned by the admission.

CHAPTER 18

"What did you say?" Charlie asked while Fitz was still reeling. "Did you say there were representatives and the vice president at the White House the night President Monroe was shot?"

Sebastian took a long breath through his nose and out again. "I did. Let me explain."

"Take your time," Fitz encouraged him. While Charlie was sitting on the edge of her seat to get to the meat of the story, he wanted the lead-up. When he was investigating homicides, it was often that information that revealed more about the killer than the murder itself.

Sebastian slowed his breathing as his chest rose and fell. "Since she took the presidency, Abigail has been dealing with threats against her. Some people simply do not want a woman for president. She has good policies and good relationships with both sides of the aisle. The hate was honestly surprising."

"To men," Charlie said, interrupting. When he raised an eyebrow, she said, "It was surprising to men. Women deal with this kind of hate all the time. It doesn't matter how qualified or how hard she's worked to achieve the position, there is still hate from some factions for what she has accomplished. Women should be pregnant, rearing children, and in the kitchen taking care of their husbands. Anything else is…not acceptable."

Sebastian thanked her for the clarification without wading into it. "There were threats from all sides. Too much to keep up with. We never made it public. She didn't want anyone to know it was getting to her. We gave her the name Sparrow. The Secret Service has a name for everyone. She had a little figurine of a sparrow. She said it meant joy, resilience, and hope. That's what Abigail was hoping to bring with her presidency. She liked the resilience part. I'd call her Sparrow from time to time to remind her of her strength. It wasn't easy for her in the White House, especially with the men who were supposed to be on her side."

Fitz and Charlie remained quiet while he spoke. It was like a long draw for information, but Fitz knew he'd get there.

Sebastian explained, "The threats were why we wanted her to run. The days leading up to the shooting were stressful. She had meetings with several people in her cabinet. There were members of the House of Representatives and the Senate asking for her time on many issues. She had foreign leaders jockeying for her time too. There were many, many late nights. I don't think she was sleeping well."

Fitz asked, "Doesn't it come along with the job?"

"Not like this," Sebastian said with a shake of his head.

"Was there any specific credible threat?" Fitz knew there was a difference between the generic threats most presidents received and the ones with credible intelligence where the threat was specific and actionable.

"Zachary Steele made direct threats to kill her. He was number one on our watch list. Secret Service and the FBI both visited him in the weeks before the shooting." Sebastian grew quiet for a moment, looking down at the table. "He was the perfect patsy."

Fitz lurched forward. "You're confirming that then? Steele was killed to make it look like he shot her?"

Sebastian shook his head. "He wasn't in that room when Abigail was shot. I can only assume someone brought him to the Lincoln Memorial and shot him. They staged the crime scene for the FBI."

Charlie grunted. "Why?"

"The country can't handle the truth. We had to give them something palatable."

"Were agents involved in the shooting?" her voice rose an octave as she asked.

"I honestly don't know. We have a traitor among us."

Fitz held his hand up to stop him. "Take me back to the night of the shooting."

"I had worked during the day. I left around seven that night. She was still in the Oval when I left. I asked if she wanted someone to bring her dinner. She agreed when I reminded her she needed to eat. There were deep circles under her eyes. As I was leaving Richard showed up. I came through the door and heard him arguing with her. I figured it was nothing new and headed out. Things felt off though."

Fitz knew he had been working on instinct then. "What do you mean?"

Sebastian admitted, "Something about the vibe of the White House seemed off. I can't explain it better than that. I was having a hard time leaving the White House. I forced myself though."

Charlie caught Fitz's eyes. The tension in the room rose. She said, "We heard there were some staffing changes that night. Is that true?"

"It is but I didn't know it at the time," Sebastian responded. "After I left Abigail in the Oval Office I went home. I wasn't there more than an hour when I came back to the White House. I decided to just spend the night and start my shift first thing in the morning. I couldn't shake my feeling. It was years of training and risk assessment bubbling up in me. Yet, I didn't have any tangible threat. I don't know if either of you can relate to that."

Charlie's expression didn't change but she told him she understood.

"I had to rely on that kind of gut feeling throughout all of my career. I couldn't always see or hear the threat. I just *knew* it was there. It's in the subtle shift in tension in the room or a person's micro-expressions. Most people can't read those, but we're trained for that."

"Where was Abigail when you came back?"

"She was upstairs in the living quarters. I didn't tell her I was back." Sebastian closed his eyes again as if remembering. "No one was happy I had come back."

"What do you mean?" Fitz asked.

Sebastian opened his eyes and tapped his finger on the table as he spoke. "David Sparks was there instead of our regular supervisor Barry. Sparks is several ranks ahead and I haven't known him to take a supervisory shift like that in years. He was the most senior Secret Service agent in the White House that night. He asked why I was back. I just said I had an early morning and wanted to stay. He didn't say anything, but I could tell he wasn't happy."

"What about the others on her detail?"

"Ian Drake didn't seem to care one way or the other. Graham Westbrook, however, seemed downright angry. He questioned me as if he had a right to. I was his superior on the team. I called the shots. We got into it a little bit in the office. He was angry I was there. He said I didn't trust him. It was an odd thing to say now looking back."

Charlie asked, "What did you do next?"

"I went to bed."

"What woke you?"

His eyes flicked over to her. "The gunshots." Sebastian explained he heard one pop of a gun followed by several more shots. Then frantic voices. "I was out of bed fast and racing toward the sounds. The voices were coming from the Oval Office. I got there and couldn't believe the scene."

Fitz leaned forward. "Who was there?"

"Ian and Graham, who I expected to see. Richard Avery, Representative Adrian Mercer, Speaker of the House Victor Graves. Someone was leaving from the other door through the president's private quarters off the Oval. I only caught a glimpse of them. I'm honestly not sure if it was one or two people."

They were in territory now where Fitz excelled. "Did you have an instinct about who it could have been at the time?" When Sebastian stared at him uncertainly, he explained, "You caught a glimpse of them. You're trained to see and recognize the smallest of threats. You know that our brains can piece together some pattern recognition. For example, I'd probably only need to see Charlie's hand to know it was her or the back of her head. My brain would know even if I wasn't registering it consciously. When you saw the person did anyone spring to mind?"

"I'm hesitant to say," Sebastian admitted.

Charlie pushed the issue. "If you think you know who it was, even speculating, it's vital. They were at the very least a witness."

"You don't understand. If it's either of the men I think it might have been, it means that this conspiracy, and that's what I think we are looking at, goes all the way to the top."

The words caught in Fitz's throat. "Are you suggesting it was Vice President Henry Coldwell?"

Sebastian tipped his head back and looked at the ceiling. When he lowered his head again, he didn't say the word. He just nodded.

"The other person you thought it might have been?" Charlie asked. She too seemed to have trouble believing the Coldwell was in the room when the president was shot.

Sebastian had less trouble naming the other potential. "Marcus Kane, the FBI director. You know he and Coldwell have the same height and build."

If Marcus Kane was in that room, it was plausible that was why he was shutting down the FBI investigation. He wasn't getting pressure from above, he was protecting himself. He had to have known that Fitz and Charlie would uncover it at some point.

Charlie was staring at him, probably wondering if he was going to say what he was thinking. Fitz couldn't explain himself. He shifted the focus back to Sebastian. "When did you see the president?"

"Not at first. They were standing in a huddle almost, shouting at one another. I can tell you this, no one was attending to her." Sebastian winced his eyes shut as he remembered the horrific moment of seeing Abigail, the President of the United States to almost everyone else.

His eyes flew open. "I rushed past them to her. She was on the floor on top of the presidential seal. The blood was everywhere. I checked for a pulse and to see if she was still breathing. When I realized she was still alive, I just scooped her up and ran out of there with her. I didn't know who had done this and I wasn't sticking around to ask any questions. I don't even remember getting from the Oval out to the parking lot. I realized once I was out there that Ian had followed me, helping me get her into the back of the SUV. I tore out of there, nearly took down the gate as I left."

It matched the story that Ethan at the guard station had told them. Given that situation, Fitz might have done the same thing. "Is that the reason you didn't call for an ambulance?"

"Honestly, I didn't know who was the threat. I didn't know if there was someone in that room or if the person had escaped. I wasn't taking any chances with anyone. I also thought I might be faster than an ambulance."

Charlie's voice had grown softer. "Did you see the gun or anyone with a gun besides the Secret Service agents?"

"I wasn't even looking," Sebastian said, the weight of the moment on his face. "My only focus was on Abigail. When we were in the SUV, I was shouting at Ian to tell me what happened, but he said he hadn't been in the room. He had been outside the door when the shots rang out. I don't know if I believe him because he was in the huddle with the rest, shouting."

"Are there always late-night meetings like that?" Fitz asked, considering who was in the room. "Those are some heavy hitters with a representative."

"Not just any representative," Charlie corrected him. "Adrian Mercer is former CIA and head of the foreign affairs committee."

"Do you know him?" Sebastian asked.

"I know him," was all Charlie said. Her tense jaw indicated to Fitz what she knew about the man wasn't anything she liked. "Please don't think I'm outing a fellow spy. He wrote a book on the subject and outed himself years ago."

Fitz pressed Sebastian. "You don't know why they were meeting?"

"I didn't even know the meeting was taking place," Sebastian said as he stared past Fitz. "There were tensions in her party over what to do with looming threats. They had met before at odd hours. It often turned to yelling."

Charlie leaned on the table. "What were the arguments about?"

"There were the typical threats from Iran and Russia she was dealing with. I know Abigail wasn't a hardline war hawk like Coldwell, Graves, and Mercer. They wanted war with Iran. They have been itching for it for a while. Abigail was against it."

"War over what?" Fitz asked, not sure if he had missed something big in the news.

Charlie turned her head to look at him. "It could be anything, Fitz. Iran's backing of Hamas. Their nuclear program. They pose certain risks and there have always been members of this government itching to go to war. The money. The military-industrial complex is called that for a reason. It makes people hundreds of millions, billions." She turned to Sebastian. "I don't think the motive matters right now as much as what occurred and by whom."

"I agree with that. I don't know any more than what I'm telling you."

Fitz wasn't satisfied with it, but it would have to stand for now. "What about the cover-up?"

Sebastian threw his hands in the air. "After leaving the hospital, I was informed by David Sparks that I was to go along with what he wanted me to say or lose my job. If I spoke out, no one would believe me as everyone would back the party line. I'd be going up against everyone. I was vague and brief with the FBI. I tried going over Sparks's head. But no one returned my call."

This time it was Charlie who wasn't satisfied with the answer. "You have no idea what happened with Zachary Steele?"

"You got another two hours?" he asked dryly. "I don't know for sure but I can speculate."

"We have all the time you need," Fitz responded, getting comfortable. He wanted the whole story – even if it was conjecture.

CHAPTER 19

The next day dragged on. Fitz had gotten to the office around eight and was immediately pulled in several different directions for current clients. He spent the day in a flurry of research, phone calls, answering emails, and making sure his business stayed afloat. After the conversation the night before with Sebastian and the long talk with Charlie on the way back, trying to process everything they had learned, Fitz had fallen into a restless sleep. He and Charlie had a meeting with Burrows later that night. They had decided that they didn't want to meet in the office since they were being watched.

The only person who interrupted his thoughts throughout the day was Amy. She was safe and secure at his house. She had plans to take some much-needed rest while avoiding the outside world until this all blew over. She told Fitz she had more than enough saved on streaming channels to keep her occupied for a year. There was food in the kitchen and a television bigger than her own. She assured him she was fine and would call him if there was any issue at all. Fitz was glad he could leave and not have to worry. Still, he didn't go the full day without checking on her. She called him a mother hen and teased that he needed to stop interrupting her movies.

Fitz didn't want to admit it, but he liked having her there. Amy had a light breezy air about her that made being in her presence easy. He wasn't sure if it was a romantic feeling or not. He'd set that aside too because there was no time to focus on anything other than the task at hand.

At six that evening, long after the sky had turned dark and the rain had started back up again, Charlie appeared in his doorway. "We made some real progress today. I cleared all the files you had given me. How about you?"

Fitz held a finger up to stop her. He finished typing the last few sentences of the report he'd been working on for the last hour. Then he hit save one more time and closed the file. Fitz raised his head with a satisfied smile on his face. "Done and done."

Charlie retreated back to her office, yelling to him that she'd be right back. She returned with a file folder like the one they had for their client. "I got done about an hour ago. I spent some time reviewing the backgrounds of Adrian Mercer, Victor Graves, and Henry Coldwell. As you might have expected, I couldn't pull a whole lot on Mercer. His background is buried under layers and layers, much like my own, given the CIA background."

"What did he do for the agency?" Fitz asked. He half expected Charlie to tell him to read Mercer's book. Instead, she sat down.

"I can't get into the work we did. We were both stationed in Middle East posts. As you know, I started right after 9/11 and that was where most of the CIA budget was being spent and the highest priority at the time. That's not to say the CIA didn't have other focuses but that was mine. Mercer was a cocky young guy who thought he knew everything. We were supposed to be quietly building assets on the ground, blending in as best we could. Mercer was splashy. I thought for sure he was going to be compromised. It worked for him though and he did develop some good assets. When he started to have a lot more money than the rest of us, the questions started. He told us he invested well. It was so much at one point the station chief pulled him aside."

"Family money?" Fitz asked, already not liking the sound of the guy.

"Not from what he said. I still don't have a real answer as to what was going on. I was head down and focused on what I needed to be doing. My only concern about Mercer was him compromising the rest of us. I read his book and about ninety percent isn't true. He took credit for everyone else's work. There was something in there that didn't jump out to me until I started digging into the pasts of the others."

Fitz folded his hands across his middle as he listened.

"Henry Coldwell and Victor Graves both have stakes in Al-Faris Holdings. On the surface, it's a real estate company. It's not though. It's a dummy corporation that funnels money directly to Titan Tactical, which is a Saudi-based military contractor similar to the ones we have here. Mercenaries really with a few hefty military contracts. Titan has been fighting a proxy conflict with Iran for a long time. Mercer mentioned Titan in his book and the relationships he was able to form with them to get things done on the ground. The Saudis denied that part of his book when it first came out."

"Plausible deniability. That doesn't surprise me."

"Right. The real question we need to be asking ourselves is why two men who hold the second and third highest offices in the land are investing in a Saudi real estate corporation that acts as basically a money laundering operation to fund Saudi mercenaries." Charlie was waiting for Fitz to catch up to her but he was having trouble making the leaps she wanted.

Charlie waved him along with her hand. "If Coldwell and Graves are investing in this group and there is a real war with Iran, the shareholder profits of this group are going to skyrocket. The three of them will make millions, hundreds of millions. Saudi and Iran have been squabbling back and forth forever. There is a fine line of tension that runs between them. Fighting over control of Muslim countries and who is the bigger dog in the Middle East. Both countries have provided degrees of support to opposing sides in nearby conflicts. Like the civil wars in Syria and Yemen and disputes in Lebanon, Qatar, and Iraq."

Fitz still didn't understand. "Why do they need us then if they are already at each other's throats?"

"I'm getting to that," she assured him. Charlie's face lit up when she was talking about a topic she knew well. If she hadn't gone into the CIA, Fitz wouldn't have been surprised if she'd been a teacher. "In early 2023, March if I remember correctly, Iran and Saudi Arabia agreed to restore diplomatic relations. It was fragile without a real framework but regional powers were hopeful. It's proven effective and durable. Even with the Gaza war, the two have been working as a channel for deconfliction. It's tenuous but it's held. As a result of decreasing tensions, stock in military contractors has fallen. Saudi Arabia, in particular, has been working to make sure that a rogue mercenary isn't going to set a match."

"Is that where the United States comes in?"

"Particularly with their support of Israel. Hamas is backed by Iran."

Fitz stared off past Charlie letting all the information sink in. He was still having trouble processing it. He had all the pieces and it all lined up logically. It wasn't the information he was having trouble digesting it was the mere diabolical nature of it that wasn't sitting with him. He turned back to her. "Are you suggesting that these three could have shot the president to replace her with Coldwell in the hopes of going to war with Iran to make money?"

"We'd rely on Saudi military contractors. You'd be shocked at how much money from the United States is mixed up in Saudi business and vice versa."

"Set aside the money aspect of it. Why would the United States want discord between the two? Who helped broker the deal between them?"

"China," Charlie said as if it were the smoking gun.

Fitz cursed softly, not just at the nature of the deal but the international goings-on that he was oblivious to. He watched the news and tried to keep up. He had to admit though, he faltered on international relations. "So if the peace accord between them was broken, it would be a loss for China too?"

"It wouldn't look good. I'm sure there is money wrapped up in there somewhere. It's a tinder box over there. It's not going to take much for the conflicts in Gaza, Lebanon, and Yemen to ignite a broader conflict, drawing in international actors."

"The United States is actively trying to broker peace between Israel and Hamas," Fitz countered.

"Exactly. President Monroe's agenda," she said, stating the obvious. What wasn't so clear to Fitz was what she said next. "We could assume that it wasn't the agenda of others in the party. Even in the same party there are competing interests."

Fitz wanted to brush it all off as complete bunk. The lines were drawn too firmly in the sand for that. "What about Richard Avery? Do you think he's conspiring with them? Sebastian said he was there that night."

Charlie sat back and folded her arms looking over at Fitz with a look of sympathy. "You don't have to divorce a dead wife. You can pretend to mourn with the country and then move on with your life. He can walk out of that White House with the sympathy of a nation. No nasty divorce, no scandal."

Fitz itched at the back of his neck. "I don't know, Charlie. Do you really think…" He couldn't even finish his thought. "All over money?"

"Iraq War," Charlie said evenly.

"I know but…"

"Nearly every war there was a financial gain for someone. As noble as World War II was it helped pull us out of a depression. It takes supplies and arms to go to war. It takes training and people power. That's money, Fitz." Charlie wasn't chastising him. She smiled at him. "You would have made a terrible CIA agent. You are too old to be this astounded by how the world works."

Fitz shook his head, shaking off the feeling. "I get the worst of humanity on a local criminal level. This is all above my pay grade. Where'd you get the information?"

"I can't tell you that. Let's just say I talked to some assets I still have in my back pocket and then I recalled Mercer mentioning Titan in his book. He had connections with them too."

"Do you think it was all of them? Even Richard Avery?"

Charlie looked at him, raising her shoulders slightly in a shrug. "I honestly don't know. We don't even know for sure this is the motive. At least we have the working knowledge of who was there that night."

"Well, not really. We are speculating that it was Coldwell. For all we know it was Marcus Kane who shot her," Fitz countered, still trying to figure out if that's what he thought.

"I don't think it was Kane. There is almost no connection, no throughline between him and the others. Coldwell makes far more sense. It also makes sense why he'd flee."

Fitz laughed. "Coldwell fits your narrative. That's why it makes more sense." He raised an eyebrow, teasing her. "You would have made a terrible detective."

"Touché," Charlie said with a laugh. "If what I found isn't the motive, then there's another one compelling enough that it got Monroe shot by those closest to her. We need to figure out why they were there. That might help us figure out the motive and who pulled the trigger."

Fitz already knew that was the direction to go. The information from Sebastian had been invaluable but it would only get them so far.

"Was there any connection between them and Graham Westbrook? If there's someone in on this conspiracy it would be him. Like Sebastian, I'm on the fence about Ian."

Charlie agreed with that. "We should interview him with the information we have. Pin him down about his statement. Burrows said he was able to get some copies of the official FBI statements for us. We know Ian outright lied to the FBI. If he's not directly involved in the shooting, he's involved with the cover-up."

Fitz was still stuck on that information. They had talked about it on the ride home and came to the same conclusion. For a single Secret Service agent to betray their oath was one thing. For the entire department at the White House that night to conceal the truth was something else entirely.

They weren't just dealing with covering up who shot President Monroe. Someone dragged Zachery Steele from his home and murdered him. Fitz couldn't help but wonder if there was a hidden message of some sort from where they had left his body.

Lincoln had been a divisive man of his time. President Monroe in simply being who she was – a woman in power – was divisive to many too. Fitz wondered if the Secret Service was doing more than just protecting a killer. Finding out the truth might bring down the whole government. Neither Fitz nor Charlie could fault the Secret Service for wanting to protect that even if it meant protecting the person.

This was something they had discussed on the car ride back to D.C. the previous night. They were both on the same page – it didn't matter what they found – they didn't care about protecting the government.

The truth had to come out at any cost.

CHAPTER 20

Burrows, Charlie, and Fitz were in a third-floor two-bedroom apartment that the FBI used as an undercover spot in Adam's Morgan. Agents that had gone undercover for one reason or another used the place as home while they were on assignment. The place was owned by a dummy corporation that would never be tied back to the FBI no matter how hard someone looked.

No one else at the FBI was using the place at the time and Burrows had full access. When Fitz explained that Marcus Kane was watching them and they should probably meet someplace other than the office, Burrows said he had the perfect place in mind. Burrows had pressed Fitz about how he knew the director was watching. Fitz wouldn't explain but assured him it was true.

"How do we know this place isn't bugged?" Charlie asked when they arrived.

Burrows had a broad smile across his face. "Swept it myself. Seriously, no one comes here unless they are on assignment. I'm the only one with the key. The other agents have to go through me to get access. I've used this place on more than a few occasions."

Charlie wrinkled up her nose at that. "Your own little pied-à-terre."

Burrows laughed. "Are you jealous?"

"No," she said with a shake of her head then looked away from him.

Burrows let her stew for a moment before laughter consumed him.

"I've never brought a woman here if that's what you're insinuating. I've used it when I didn't want to drive back home to Virginia if I have a late case or something."

Charlie waved him off, not responding to him. "Let's get down to work," she said, taking a seat at the small four-person dining table.

Fitz asked, "Do you have anything to update us on before we tell you what we found?"

Burrows put his hands on the table, lacing his fingers together. "Agent Conklin is running down leads for the ammunition used in the shooting. She isn't getting far though. She's also been quietly looking at some international threats."

"It's not an international threat," Charlie assured him without explaining more.

Fitz ignored the confused look on Burrows's face. "Anything else?"

"Not yet. Marcus Kane is pressuring the team to wrap up the investigation. The shooter is dead. President Monroe has been moved to an undisclosed area of the hospital. She's being well guarded. The guy they got still isn't speaking. No one wants a long, drawn-out investigation into something that looks cut and dry. You've heard the media pundits. The longer the investigation goes on, the more questions they are asking."

"As they should," Charlie argued back. "The President of the United States was shot. There should be questions and an investigation that takes however long it takes."

"The conspiracies get spinning, Charlie. The FBI doesn't want that."

Charlie dug in. "Is it the FBI who doesn't want that or is it Marcus Kane? You can't convince me that FBI agents who swore an oath to the Constitution want to rush the investigation into the attempted assassination of a president."

Burrows held his hands up in surrender. "I'm not calling the shots here. I'm just telling you what I know. It's the reason I came to the two of you."

"Do you trust Marcus Kane?" Fitz asked.

"I don't know him well. He's been a good boss." Burrows's eyes fixed on Fitz. "Do I have a reason not to trust him? Is there a reason why he'd want this investigation wrapped up so quickly?"

Fitz leaned back in the chair, kicking his long legs out in front of him. He tapped his finger on the table, pausing only for a moment to decide how much he wanted to say.

Burrows looked between them. "I thought we trusted each other. Clearly, you've found out something. Tell me."

Charlie had been the one earlier who argued that it might compromise Burrows to know too much. He'd have an obligation to run to the FBI team and the whole thing could get blown up before any real investigation was done. Fitz reminded her they had to trust him.

In the end, they told him everything including that Sebastian Cole had been having an affair with Monroe. With each new bit of information, Burrows's body twisted in surprise, probably more shock. His mouth fell open then snapped shut. His eyes darted between Fitz and Charlie.

When they were done, Burrows closed his eyes and shook his head as if he couldn't believe any of it. They let him process it without saying another word. Fitz and Charlie had a long drive the evening before and all day to settle into the reality.

This was brand new for Burrows. It would shake anyone to their core.

He got up from the table and went to the sink. He stood there for a few seconds then pulled a glass from the cabinet and turned on the faucet. He filled the glass and drank it all in one gulp.

Burrows turned back to them. "You're telling me Sebastian Cole, the head of President Monroe's Secret Service detail, admitted to you that the shooting took place in the White House and that Marcus

Kane might have been present. Is that what you're telling me?"

"Or Henry Coldwell," Charlie corrected him. "We don't know which man it was, but he was in a hurry to get out of there. That's why Sebastian didn't get a good look at him. You know how much the two men look alike."

"The implications of this…" his voice trailed off. None of them wanted to think about the implications of the act alone and then the cover-up that followed. Burrows took a breath. "Does that mean then Zachary Steele was murdered in cold blood as part of some cover-up?"

"That's what we believe," Charlie said, sitting on the edge of her chair.

Burrows put his hand to his heart, pulling at the fabric of his shirt.

"Are you okay?" she asked, getting up from the chair. She stood there for only a few seconds before rushing to him, taking him by the arm, and bringing him back to the table. She went back to fill the water glass again. Charlie handed him the glass and he took it with a trembling hand. "Are you having a heart attack?"

Burrows shook his head. He could barely get out the word but he squeaked no.

Fitz wasn't sure that his assessment of not having a heart attack was right. All the signs were there. It was that or a panic attack. He didn't want to ask an FBI agent if they were in the throes of a panic attack though. He wanted to give the man a little dignity.

Charlie on the other hand had no problem squatting down until she was right in front of him. "Look at me, Josh. Count to ten slowly while taking some deep breaths." She was good in a stressful situation. It appeared to Fitz she knew exactly what to do.

Charlie caught Fitz's glance. She gave him a look that said this wasn't the first time she had witnessed this happening. She focused back on Burrows and waited for his breathing to become normal again.

Burrows put his hand on her shoulder, thanking her. "I'm fine," he assured her. "I'm fine." It was clear he wasn't fine. His voice shook and the more he repeated the words, the more it was obvious he was trying to convince himself, not them.

Charlie stood from her crouched position. "Do you want to go for a walk and get some fresh air? Maybe we should have prepared you better for what was coming."

"No." Burrows shook it off. "I'm an FBI agent. I shouldn't have to be prepped like a child for terrible news."

Fitz felt for the guy. "It happens, Burrows. It's happened to me before." That was technically a lie, but Fitz knew all too well the rush of heartbeat, the breath that wouldn't even out, and the pain that stabbed in the chest with such force that it felt like his heart was going to explode.

Burrows brushed them both off. His cheeks started to redden. "The implications…"

"Staggering," Fitz filled in what Burrows hadn't said aloud. "We know. Charlie and I talked about it last night. Luckily, other work consumed us today. There's not a lot we are going to be able to do about this. It's not like we can get into the White House and assess the scene. Do you have any ideas? Even if we got in, the Secret Service isn't going to let us anywhere near that Oval Office, which is now occupied by the very man who might have shot her."

Burrows held his hand up to stop him. "That thought right there is what sent me over the edge. We're only going on the word of one Secret Service agent, who wasn't even supposed to be there that night and who was having an affair with the president. This needs corroboration."

"Two," Charlie reminded him. "Ethan Thompson was at the guard station that night. The story that he told us corroborates what Sebastian said."

"There is the nurse at the hospital who confirmed the time they brought President Monroe into the hospital and there's also the agent who came to me to tell me about the bullets," Fitz reminded him. "I believe he saw Graham Westbrook hide bullets in his desk and retrieve them later. We still don't know what those bullets represent. You said the bullets that shot Monroe were accounted for by the surgeon."

"Okay," Burrows said, returning to normal. "We have something to work with. Is there anyone else you can interview?"

Fitz explained who was left. "Reggie Malloy, the White House chef, and Ian Drake, the other Secret Service agent there that night. We haven't been able to figure out if Ian was involved in the shooting and cover-up or if he got there later like Sebastian. You have to remember Sebastian heard a shot and rushed to the Oval. He entered after the shooting had already happened."

"How many shots did he hear?"

Fitz held up one finger. "One shot followed by a volley of shots. He was asleep though when it started."

Burrows couldn't make sense of that. "Isn't he trained for such things?"

Charlie explained that he was trained for it, but he'd been asleep after a long shift. "I don't know the acoustics of the White House either. We have no idea how far away he was sleeping from the Oval. There are a lot of unknown factors still at play."

Burrows wasn't going to let it go. "What about everyone else inside the White House? There had to have been other staff and the other Secret Service agents."

Those were all questions Fitz and Charlie had too.

"Was it planned or did something go wrong in this meeting?" Burrows asked, with an eyebrow arched.

Neither Fitz nor Charlie had given any consideration to whether the shooting had been planned or if someone had acted in a fit of rage.

He admitted that to Burrows. "As we said, we were as surprised as you were to hear this information. We haven't processed it all."

Burrows considered the information and came back with another thought. "There's also the situation room, which is staffed twenty-four-hours, seven days a week with someone on that National Intelligence staff. There's always someone in there monitoring national and world intelligence information. That doesn't even account for all the other Secret Service and police forces guarding that place."

Fitz hadn't considered who might be in the situation room. "As I said, we don't know what we don't know." The more Burrows argued the point, the more Fitz had to concede that Sebastian might have been wrong in what he heard. Fitz imagined that if shots had rung out in the White House for everyone to hear, there'd have to be a lot more people involved in the conspiracy. If there was one thing Fitz knew about governments and secrets – secrets weren't good at being kept. The information would inevitably leak.

Burrows shifted in the chair. "Are you sure you can trust Sebastian Cole?"

Fitz believed they could. "His statement is backed up by other people. He's been put on leave for a month. They are trying to silence him and make sure he remains quiet." In the flurry of other information, he'd forgotten something. "Sebastian also told us that someone shot at him the other night. It's why he ran. He's in hiding, Burrows. He wasn't going to stick around to allow the Secret Service to silence him for good."

Burrows got up from the table and walked to the front window, staring out of it. Fitz watched the man, waiting almost for him to have another panic attack. Charlie quietly told Fitz to give Burrows time. Fitz had no reason to rush the man. He knew what it was like to work a homicide case. Sometimes he just needed to be alone with his thoughts.

Burrows finally turned around. His features were more relaxed, the color was back in his face, and his eyes were brighter than before. There was a determination in his voice. "If there had been a shooting inside the White House, everyone in that place would have known and it would have been immediate chaos. So either Sebastian is lying about the whole thing, which I don't think is what's happening, or there is a broad cover-up. We need to know who was there that night. I'm not going to the FBI with this information. If Marcus Kane is responsible for shooting the president, I don't want him to know we are on to him. Let the official case close. We can take it from here."

"Is there any way into the White House so we can see the scene?" Charlie asked, making Fitz stare at her wide-eyed. "We have to try," she said to him.

Burrows told them he didn't know. "You have to interview the chef. Start there. If he knows something, I don't care what it takes, convince him to tell you. Maybe there's some way he can get you into the White House as a visitor. I don't have clearance to do that. I can't tell anyone at the FBI what I know."

Charlie told him that didn't sound like the worst plan. "We can also see if Ian Drake will speak to us."

"The chef first," Burrows cautioned. "If Ian is in on this, the rest will know and you won't get anywhere near the White House."

"We can do that," Fitz said as he shifted in the chair. "What are you going to do?"

Burrows seemed resolved in his plan. "I have connections and might be able to figure out who was in the situation room that night. I'd like to know what, if anything, they saw and heard. There is no way you're going to get one of them to go along with this kind of conspiracy." He paused for a moment. "What about motive? Do we have any idea why one of them would want to kill President Monroe?"

Fitz started to speak, but Charlie cut him off. "We are still exploring some ideas. I plan to start looking into their backgrounds and see if there's a connection."

Fitz tried to keep his expression straight. Burrows didn't seem to know Charlie was lying or he didn't call her on it. They talked for a few minutes more, planning to meet back at the safe house another night.

With their plans in place, they had work to do.

CHAPTER 21

Before the sun rose the next day, Fitz and Charlie sat in his SUV down the street from Reggie Malloy's rowhouse not far from Fitz's office in Georgetown. While they could have walked to the man's residence neither thought loitering on the street at three in the morning was the best idea. It was better to park and sit in the SUV to watch the house.

The rowhouse sat in the middle of the block. It was painted a barn red with white shutters on the front windows of all three floors. The paint looked fresh and hadn't been worn by years of weather and wear and tear the way some of the rowhouses on the block looked. The porch looked like new concrete had been poured for the steps and the wrought iron railings looked brand new. Pots of fresh flowers for the season took up a row of space on each step. Reggie's was one of the nicest on the block.

Charlie sat on the passenger side of the car, staring at the man's photos. "I can't believe how big he is. Have you ever seen biceps this big?"

Fitz lowered his eyes to the phone once again. Fitz was a big man – over six-foot-four with broad shoulders, thick arms and legs, and a flat stomach. He'd only ever gotten his body weight down enough to see visible abs once. That was once after college while he was in the police academy and it had been a miserable experience. He wanted to be strong and healthy and didn't care much for the aesthetics.

Reggie Malloy, on the other hand, did. There was no denying that he took both his bodybuilding and his nutrition seriously. At six-two, the man's biceps were an impressive twenty-four inches, and he could bench press close to six hundred pounds. At least, that's what the *Men's Health* article said about the famous White House Chef. He had played football for Notre Dame, then went into the Marines where he discovered a love of cooking. Reggie had now worked for four administrations at the White House as a head chef while also championing veteran cases. Fitz wasn't sure where the man found the energy or the time.

"He doesn't look like someone I want to cross," Fitz said absently as he stared off down the dark street, dotted with the glow of lampposts every thirty feet or so. Some of the homes had porch lights on but most were dark. He closed his eyes to take a quick nap knowing Charlie would keep watch.

Nearly thirty minutes later, Fitz woke to Charlie slapping him on the leg. "There he is. He's coming out the front door right now."

Fitz sprung to alertness, focusing his eyes on the rowhouse. Sure enough, the man had his back to them as he locked the front door. He had a chef's jacket slung over a thick arm and a bag in the other hand. He bounded down the front steps toward a Ford truck parked at the curb.

Fitz's feet were on the pavement and he was rushing toward the man, calling out his name on the dark street. "Reggie Malloy," Fitz called again, this time getting the man's attention.

Reggie whipped his head in their direction. "Can I help you?" he asked, his tone cautious yet still commanding.

Charlie came from the other side of the SUV giving him a friendly wave. She shouted out their names before Fitz had the chance. She apologized for ambushing him on the street. "Given your schedule, we figured this was going to be the only time to catch you."

Reggie opened the passenger side of his truck and tossed in the jacket and bag. He closed the door and turned to the two of them. "Why are you looking for me?" He paused and squinted at Fitz. "You look familiar to me."

Fitz got this a lot. He told him he'd been a D.C. Metro homicide detective and reminded him about the infamous case he had handled. "My face was splashed all over the news for a while."

"Yeah, that's right," he said, extending his hand to Fitz. "I wondered what happened to you. I couldn't go a day without seeing your face then you slipped into oblivion. Are you a private investigator now? Is that what you said?"

"Something like that."

"I'm not sure how I can help you."

Fitz didn't want to waste time. "We understand you were in the White House when President Monroe was shot. We are investigating it because word on the street is the FBI isn't going to dig too deep."

Reggie's eyebrows shot up. "You know it happened in the White House? I didn't think anyone was supposed to know that."

Charlie nodded. "We know it happened in the White House. We have been fortunate that some brave people are not willing to go along with the official story. They are off the record with us, just like anything you tell us would be. If it makes you feel better, we have an FBI agent who is working with us who doesn't believe the official story. We aren't just out here going rogue. It's unofficially official if that makes sense. We know you were there that night. You must have seen or heard something."

Reggie sucked in the corner of his cheek and appraised them. "I was there," he said to start. His tone was heavy. "I heard one shot then more. I was in the Marines, I know what an echoing gunshot sounds like. I rushed out of the kitchen and ran right into Secret Service who were scrambling to figure out what was going on. They ordered me back into the kitchen. I did what I was told. You get used to the Secret Service ordering people around. I went back into the kitchen. I realized that the back door to the kitchen, the one that goes into the back parking lot, wasn't locked. It wasn't even closed all the way. I had kept it open to let in a little air. I didn't know where the threat was coming from so I rushed over to secure it. That's when I saw Secret Service Agent Sebastian Cole with President Monroe in his arms. Her body was limp and there was blood dripping to the ground. Ian Drake ran after him and they got into the SUV with Sebastian driving and tore out of there. I don't think any of them saw me. I had an instinct to ask if they needed help, but I didn't. It felt like I was seeing something I shouldn't be seeing. I expected others to rush out after them or the Secret Service to show back up in the kitchen and explain what happened. No one did."

Fitz told him it was probably good he hadn't disclosed what he saw. "What time would you say that happened?"

"The first gunshot was at two-fifty-five. I know that because the first thing I did after hearing it was look at the time. The rest followed right after that. There was a pause in between them, seconds. I figured I'd be questioned and wanted to be precise. I saw Sebastian Cole rush the president out of the White House shortly after three." Reggie stared past Fitz down the street and back at them. "The strange thing is the Secret Service didn't show back up to speak to me until close to six that morning. It was only a few minutes before I heard the radio announcement that the president had been shot."

There was a hitch in his tone that told Fitz that whatever he was about to hear hadn't sat right with Reggie. Fitz encouraged him to speak freely. "What did the Secret Service agent tell you?"

"I was told that an agent accidentally discharged his weapon in the White House in the middle of the night, but that everything was fine. It was shortly after that I heard on the radio that President Monroe had been shot at the Lincoln Memorial. Those two things didn't square with me."

"How did you respond when he came to tell you it had been an accidental discharge?" Charlie asked.

"I didn't," Reggie said his mouth set in a firm line. "I figured it would be better for everyone if I acted like I hadn't seen or heard anything. There's something strange going on in that place. Better that they don't know that I know. The FBI hasn't even come to interview me. You'll have to indulge my curiosity about how you got my name."

Fitz explained, "One of the Secret Service agents who came forward knew that you were in the kitchen that night. They don't know that you know anything, but I just took a shot in the dark. You've stayed quiet, so why tell me now?"

Reggie hitched his jaw toward them. "You're trustworthy. I also figure there's some grave injustice happening right now and someone better be trying to figure out what's happening. I don't know who shot President Monroe though. I wasn't a witness to that. I suspect by the door they were rushing from that it was the Oval or near there. All I know for sure was President Monroe wasn't shot in front of the Lincoln Memorial, which brings up the question of exactly who shot Zachary Steele and why."

"We have the same questions," Charlie echoed.

"I'm glad you're investigating then. I wish I could tell you more. The one thing I will say is that whatever was going on in the White House that night, no one is talking about it. Things are back to normal like nothing ever happened."

Fitz would tuck that information away for later. "What do you think of President Monroe's core team?"

Reggie guffawed. "You want to know my opinion?"

"Of course," Charlie said.

"Graham Westbrook is as shady as they get. I haven't been able to put my finger on what's up with him. He's one of those guys who got too much power early on and it went to his head. I've been in the kitchen at the White House longer than he's been out of diapers. He's too cocky for his own good. Sebastian Cole is as sound an agent as you can find. The only problem is he's in love with Abigail Monroe and I suspect he has been for a long time."

Fitz didn't mean to let his face betray him. When Reggie cocked an eyebrow at him, Fitz admitted, "There's been some talk about their relationship."

"I think that's a stretch. I said Sebastian is in love with Abigail and she like most politicians is in love with herself and power. I don't know if she's in love with him." He held his hands up as if to say he shouldn't be speaking out of turn. "I just think it's highly unlikely Monroe is ever leaving the esteemed Richard Avery for Agent Sebastian Cole, no matter how good the man is at his job. It's a fling that's probably long past its expiration date. He's moon-eyed. Not so much that others would notice but I noticed."

Fitz wasn't surprised by what Reggie said. "What about Ian Drake?"

"He's a tougher read," Reggie admitted. "He strikes me as someone who wants to do the right thing. I worry that he's a little too easily influenced. He might take a bullet for the president, but I don't see him bucking the status quo."

Fitz understood that description perfectly. He'd worked with detectives like that. They were great investigators and did their job well. At the same time, they'd look the other way if another detective did something unethical or illegal. They weren't going to put themselves out on a limb.

Fitz asked, "Did you see anyone else there that night?"

"No," Reggie said with a shake of his head. He glanced down and checked his watch. "I have to get going. There's a lot to be done. Vice

President Coldwell is leaving today for an overseas trip. The White House will be quiet for a few days. Lots to be done before he leaves."

Charlie reached out to stop him. "Can you get us inside the White House?"

Reggie's head snapped up. "What?"

Charlie explained that they needed to get inside the Oval Office to see the crime scene. "I know it's a huge ask. We are grateful you even spoke to us. We need your help." When he hesitated, Charlie pushed harder. "We need to find out who shot the president. They had to move her because someone tried to finish the job while she's in the hospital."

"I heard about that," Reggie said, the shock of the situation registering on his face.

"She's still in danger. We need to see the scene of the crime."

It didn't take Reggie long to relent. "Tonight. I'll give your names to the guards at the gate."

"Ethan knows us. I'm not sure what time he'll be on tonight," Fitz told him. "Do you think he'll allow it?"

"I'll figure it out and make it work. Ethan is a stand-up guy. I haven't spoken to him since the shooting. If he's one of the people who know the truth, he's not going to keep quiet for long. He might be worried about his job right now, but he'll be an ally."

"What about the cameras throughout the whole place?"

Reggie told her not to worry. "I know these guys. Let me handle it for you. If Coldwell was in residence it wouldn't happen. Security will be a little looser with him gone."

With that, Reggie got into the driver's side of the truck and moments later took off down the road, leaving Fitz and Charlie to stand there, adrenaline rushing through them both. They were going to get White House access.

CHAPTER 22

The rest of the day was a blur of starts and stops for Fitz and Charlie. Once back in their office, they went to their separate spaces. Fitz had trouble concentrating for much of the day. Charlie was built for this kind of work – sneaking into the White House. He couldn't even speak the words aloud because the insanity of it couldn't pass his lips.

After lunch, he forced himself to stand from his desk and stretch. His shoulders were sitting close to his ears and the muscles in his back had long since knotted. Every joint seemed to throb. The stress had infiltrated his body and it showed no signs of retreating.

As he was bent over, rounding his back in a stretch, his cellphone buzzed against the desk. Fitz released a deep guttural groan as he righted himself and reached for it. He didn't recognize the number. "Hello," he said, uncertainty in his voice.

Senator Ford barked, "We need to meet as soon as possible."

Fitz's heart slammed inside his chest. *Could he know they uncovered the shooting took place in the White House and they knew who was present? Does he know they suspected Marcus Kane? That they were about to break into the White House?* Every imaginable question ran through Fitz's mind and he was suddenly uncertain if he could trust the Warren Circle. How good could they be if Marcus Kane was present during the shooting?

"Did you hear me, Fitz? I need to see you and Charlie immediately."

"I heard you. Give us ten minutes and we'll meet you there."

The phone line went dead in his ear.

Fitz cursed under his breath. He shoved the phone in his pocket, shouted for Charlie, and the pair of them made their way to Ford's Theater.

Senator Ford was waiting for them when they arrived. He was alone, sitting hunched over paperwork at one of the tables. He raised his head when they entered, pushing his glasses up his nose. "I assumed I would have heard from you before now."

Fitz took a few steps into the room with Charlie at his side. "You didn't exactly give me clear directions on how you wanted us to go about this or who we should be updating. I spoke to Marcus Kane once when he inquired about our relationship with Agent Joshua Burrows."

Senator Ford waved at them. "He told me about that. What do you think about the FBI rushing the investigation?"

Fitz scanned the room looking for…what, he wasn't sure. "Can we speak freely with you? Is there anyone else meeting with us today?" He wanted to ask if he was being recorded but he stopped shy of that.

"It's just us. The rest of them get bogged down in their daily work and don't have time for meetings. I'll tell them what they need to know." He gestured toward the chairs. "Sit. It's just a conversation. Both of you look like you're walking into your execution."

Charlie reached for a chair, pulling it out and sitting down. "We weren't sure why we were being called to meet. What do you know so far about the shooting?"

A smile creased Ford's face. "Are you interrogating me, Charlie? I've been reading up on your file. What I could access anyway, which wasn't much." He looked over at Fitz. "Do you know about any of her fieldwork? The languages she speaks? Her specialty in interrogation?"

He wasn't angry or trying to bait Fitz. His tone implied he was genuinely impressed with Charlie's background.

"I don't talk much about my time with the government," Charlie responded with her back a little straighter. It was clear she wasn't happy he had pulled her personnel file. Fitz wasn't even sure that was legal for Ford to do. "Before we start, we are curious what, if anything, you've been able to find out about the shooting? We know there was a second attempt and Monroe was moved. Would you like me to interrogate the man they arrested at the hospital? There's been no information about it on the news."

"And there won't be. I assume the only reason you know is your FBI contact." There wasn't a question in there. Ford knew that's how they had found out. "President Monroe is secured. The man in custody has not spoken. Will not speak. I don't even know if you'd be able to do much with him. We'd have to go through the agent in charge and she's a tough nut to crack."

Fitz and Charlie remained quiet. They had planned in the short trip over that they wanted to know what Ford knew first before they laid all their cards out on the table. Using silence in an interrogation was the oldest trick in the book.

Ford stared across the table at them. He did what most do and filled the silence. "I don't know much, honestly," Ford admitted. "Marcus Kane is dead set on wrapping up the investigation so it doesn't look suspicious that the FBI is still digging. Zachary Steele is dead and the president is recovering. I know there was the second attempt but no one is even sure it's related to the first or just some opportunist looking to finish the job."

Fitz asked, "What do you think about the FBI wrapping up their investigation?"

"I don't know what to think. The evidence Marcus presented to me isn't compelling. There are a lot of holes in it and I'm not even sure how the public is buying the story. The news has grabbed onto Steele's past and the church he belongs to and is running with it. It fits a certain narrative and people rarely question beyond what's right in front of them."

"Do you believe that Steele is the shooter?" Fitz asked, wanting to get to the point.

Ford gestured toward them. "That's why I called you here. I want to know what you've found. I've not come out with any statement about the shooting and that's unusual for my office. I have reporters calling me day and night. I need to tell them something."

Fitz knew he wasn't going to like what they had to say. "We don't believe Steele was the shooter. We have proof that the shooting didn't happen at the Lincoln Memorial at all."

Ford's forehead creased with deep lines. "Where did it happen?"

"The White House," Charlie and Fitz said at the same time and Ford's eyes grew wide. Before he could argue, Charlie laid out all of the evidence including the witnesses they had, leaving out their names. "We think we might know who was present and why there had to be this elaborate cover-up."

Ford shrank back in the chair as if his body deflated. "Please tell me."

Charlie looked to Fitz to see if he wanted to explain. Fitz encouraged her to go on. She locked her gaze on Ford. "It's our understanding from a witness that Richard Avery, Adrian Mercer, Victor Graves, and one other person were there during the shooting."

Ford's mouth fell open in shock and horror at what he'd been told. "Who was the other person?"

"That's the question we still have," Fitz said calmly. "The witness believes it was either Henry Coldwell or Marcus Kane. He wasn't sure because the person was fleeing the room as they entered and their focus was on President Monroe. We also know Ian Drake and

Graham Westbrook with the Secret Service were present. They were not providing aid to the president but rather huddled up speaking with the men still present. All of them lied in their interviews with the FBI. If Marcus Kane was in that room, then what is he hiding? It might be why he's rushing to close the investigation."

"Oh," Ford said, more of a groan as the two letters escaped his lips. "This is beyond…" He couldn't finish whatever he was going to say. "The witnesses? What is happening with them?"

"They were told to lie by the Secret Service. The cover-up started almost as soon as the shooting happened, probably before they even got President Monroe out of the room." Fitz could see the concern growing on the man's face.

He assured Ford. "We have witnesses we are keeping safe. They are willing to come forward when the time comes if we can ensure their safety. There are still a lot of unknowns. I don't know how you want to address this with Marcus Kane and the rest of the Warren Circle. We don't know if he was there and we can't accuse him of doing anything wrong. We don't even know for sure it was him and not Coldwell."

"Okay," Ford said then said it three more times. "Let's see how this plays out. What are your next steps?"

Charlie and Fitz shared a look. Before the meeting, they had decided the last thing they were going to do was tell him about trespassing at the White House. Fitz decided at that moment that maybe Ford could give them some cover if it all went wrong. He turned back and hesitated for only a moment. "We are going to go into the White House tonight and assess the scene in the Oval Office."

Ford lurched forward as if he were going to throw up. "You can't break into the White House!" he yelled, his voice louder than Fitz had ever heard it.

"We aren't breaking in," Charlie said. "We have a source on the inside who will escort us. We just need to make sure we get in and out of there without the Secret Service inside knowing."

"That's impossible," Ford argued back.

Fitz agreed with him. "Probably impossible. We might very well end up in jail tonight. That's one of the reasons I'm telling you. What kind of cover can you give us?"

"None!" he shouted. "No one knows the Warren Circle exists. When our members are engaged in activities, they are on their own. I thought I made that clear to you. I also thought I made it clear to you that you can't do anything illegal. That should have been common sense enough."

"It's not illegal technically," Fitz countered back, a wave of disappointment that Ford wouldn't be able to offer them any protection. "Do you want to know who shot President Monroe or not? It seems to me like you've got a constitutional crisis on your hands. The second and third in power might have been involved in an assassination attempt. Your Secret Service is lying to the FBI. I think us having an unofficial look inside the Oval Office might be the least of your worries."

Senator Ford, who up until this meeting had been a man of cool, calm resolve, started to melt down in front of them. His face grew red as beads of sweat formed at his hairline. He gnawed at his lower lip leaving it nearly bloodied. "This is…unprecedented. I'm not even sure what to say."

Charlie stopped him there. "If it wasn't for Sebastian Cole, it would have been an assassination. When he entered the room, the rest of them were not even attending to President Monroe. She was lying in a bloody heap on the floor. The poor guy didn't even know if she was alive or dead. Had he not acted so quickly or even been in the White House that night, you'd be looking at an assassination."

Senator Ford held up his hand to stop her. "What do you mean if he hadn't been in the White House? I don't understand what that means."

Charlie's voice was tinged with an emotion Fitz rarely heard. "He couldn't shake the nagging feeling that something was wrong. He came back to sleep in the office. Sebastian wasn't sure what was off. He couldn't put his finger on it. He knew that something was wrong. If he had not been there, President Monroe would be dead. He drove her to the hospital not only because he didn't think there was time to call an ambulance but because he walked into a room with one man fleeing and the rest huddled together not providing aid to the president. He had no idea who shot her. All he cared about was protecting her and the way he could do that best was to get her out of the White House. For his efforts, he was told to lie to the FBI and suspended. Then someone shot up his home."

Senator Ford let out a string of curses. "Is he safe now?"

Fitz explained, "The Secret Service put him on paid leave for the month. He's left D.C. He's essentially in a safe house. I'd suggest not sharing this information broadly. Let them wonder where he went. He's willing to go on record with what actually happened if someone can guarantee his safety."

Senator Ford went back to gnawing on his lip again.

Fitz didn't stop there. "There's another Secret Service agent who saw Sebastian flee in the SUV with the president slumped over in the back with Ian Drake. He noted the time. He was told he didn't see what he saw. He's keeping the status quo to remain safe and keep his job. He's young with a new family. The nurse at the emergency room who doesn't want to play nicely and lie to the FBI is also in hiding." Fitz almost felt bad for the senator. While he and Charlie were investigating this, they had no real power. All of the major decisions were out of his hands. It would be Senator Ford who'd have to engage Congress to act. Not to mention he was in a powerful centuries-old secret order with a potential assassin. Fitz didn't envy the man.

When Senator Ford remained still and silent for far too long, it was Charlie who spoke up. "So you see, going to look at the Oval Office is the least of your worries. We won't get caught. I've breached more dangerous places and extracted myself without being seen. We have to do this though. We need physical evidence to back up the witness statements."

"What if it's gone?" he asked, fear in his voice now.

"The only way we are going to know is if we get in there and see."

Senator Ford rubbed a hand across his forehead. "Call me immediately when you know anything."

Fitz gestured toward the man's phone. "Are we okay to speak freely on your phone?"

Senator Ford hesitated then shook his head. "Code the language so only I understand."

That wasn't the answer Fitz had hoped for – it meant Senator Ford suspected none of them were safe.

CHAPTER 23

The wind whipped leaves across the empty street as Fitz drove the final hundred yards to the White House gate. They were almost to the point of not being able to turn back. The White House loomed ahead, its white columns ghostly in the darkness. Charlie's fingers drummed against her thigh. She might as well have been doing it against the dash. The tapping infiltrated Fitz's brain.

"Stop that," he whispered, though no one could hear them inside the car. "You're making me nervous. You're supposed to be the calm one. You've done this before, remember? You told Senator Ford you've gotten yourself in and out of more dangerous situations."

"I have but this is the White House," Charlie shot back, but her hand stilled. She checked her watch – it was just before ten, right on time for meeting Reggie.

Fitz focused only on the road. He turned into the driveway and eased the car to a stop at the security checkpoint. His heart hammered against his ribs as a figure emerged from the guard station, a tactical flashlight beam sweeping across the windshield. The light lowered, revealing Ethan's face, grim and professional as always. Reggie must have been able to get him on earlier than his midnight shift.

"IDs," he said, giving no indication that he knew them while maintaining the illusion of protocol. Fitz handed over their credentials. Ethan made a show of examining them before handing them back with a curt nod. "You're clear." He finished his sweep of the SUV then went back to the guard station and engaged the gate, which glided open to let them pass.

Fitz guided the car through, following the curved drive toward the service entrance. Charlie's hand found his arm, squeezing once before letting go. "If we get arrested…"

"We are not going to get arrested." Fitz pulled into a spot between two service vans. He didn't like that it was Charlie who was suddenly without her normal steely resolve. He realized then how much he relied on her to be steady and calm even when he was internally panicking. He'd done a lot of things in the name of a case before, but this was something else.

They slipped out of the SUV, their footfalls echoing on the pavement. Fitz was surprised they had even made it this far. The kitchen entrance was lit by a single white bulb, casting deep shadows across the road. As promised, Reggie Malloy stood waiting, his chef's whites stark against the darkness. His face was drawn with tension.

"Quickly," he hissed, ushering them inside. The kitchen was eerily silent, gleaming steel surfaces reflecting the stark white lights. "The Secret Service has already made their nightly sweep down here. We've got maybe an hour before they return. It's less time than you think when in this maze of a place."

"What about the cameras?" Fitz asked. The last thing he wanted was to alert the Secret Service who might shoot them on sight. He also didn't want to get out of there and have footage of their crimes come back to haunt them.

"It's taken care of. Ethan's partner, who is sick of this whole thing too, is manning the cameras. When I give him the signal, he's going to cut them off. He doesn't know how long we have until someone walks into that office and he has to reengage them." Reggie stepped toward them. "I'm going to get you up there but then you're on your own. Do you have an escape plan?"

"We're covered," Fitz said, knowing that wasn't true. "Will you be here in the kitchen for the rest of the night?"

"I'm not going anywhere," Reggie said. "But I'm also not losing my job for this. Worse yet, arrested, tried, and convicted. Do you understand me?"

Charlie assured him that none of this would come back on him. "We just need to see inside the room then we'll be gone like we were never here."

"The *room*," he said stressing the word, "is the seat of power in the United States. Every president since William Howard Taft in 1909 has used the Oval Office. It's more than just a room."

While Charlie was assuring Reggie she understood the weight of what they were going to do, Fitz interrupted. "Really?" he asked. "No presidents before Taft?" He caught them looking at him quizzically as if they needed to explain they weren't there for a history lesson. They were not there for a tour. Reggie shot him a look and Fitz apologized. "I promise. None of this will come back on you."

"Please tell me neither of you were stupid enough to bring a gun in here?"

"Of course not," Fitz assured him. They had decided getting caught without weapons was significantly better than with them. Neither of them would shoot a Secret Service agent. They were better off unarmed.

Charlie checked her watch again, setting the timer. "What if he does his rounds early?"

"He never does." Reggie pointed down the hall. "You're wasting time."

Fitz had studied a map and the structural details of the White House online before they left. He was surprised he had found such plans and had no idea if they were even accurate.

The kitchen was in the northwest corner of the ground floor of the White House. They had to make it clear across the White House to the southeast corner to reach the Oval.

Reggie led them into a narrow hall off the right side of the kitchen. Their footsteps echoed despite their attempts at stealth. They followed through a maze of prep stations and industrial refrigerators toward a service corridor. Reggie held up a hand at the intersection, peering around the corner before motioning them forward.

"Access is through here," he whispered. "Agent Hansen's team always patrols this section. As I said, the hour goes by fast. Don't get lost and get out before you're seen." He retreated toward the kitchen leaving them alone to accomplish their foolish mission.

They continued forward, creeping along the hallways, starting and stopping as they heard echoes of noise around them. When it was clear, they'd move again.

They emerged into a dimly lit hallway lined with historical paintings. The Oval was just around the corner, but the most dangerous part of their mission still lay ahead. They had to cross the main corridor – the one most frequently patrolled.

They sprinted down the hallway, shoes silent on the thick carpet. They entered President Monroe's private secretary's office. Charlie twisted the knob opening it tentatively as if it would sound an alarm. Fitz held his breath until the door was open enough for them to slip through. Once inside, they were at least out of the foot traffic of the Secret Service.

They reached the door to the Oval, but neither of them reached for the knob. The weight of history caught Fitz's breath, and, for Charlie, it was the weight of what they were about to do. She was faster processing the emotion and reached for the knob.

The door to the Oval creaked open. Charlie froze on the threshold, her breath catching in her chest. Fitz, just behind her, hesitated as well, his eyes wide as they took in the room. The grand space, the iconic desk, the thick carpets. None of it seemed real. But there they were standing in the middle of history. For Fitz, the energy of the office felt wrong. The room that had once symbolized power, authority, and the very heart of the nation, now felt cold and hollow.

"How did this happen here?" Charlie whispered, almost to herself.

Fitz didn't answer at first, his gaze flicking over the empty furniture, wondering where the shooting had taken place. This was no ordinary crime scene. This was the seat of power, and someone had shot a president in the very room where history had been made countless times.

He exhaled a slow breath that seemed to drag all the air from his lungs.

Charlie nodded slowly, still standing just inside the door, as if afraid to cross the threshold. The silence was oppressive, a thick blanket over the room. The portraits looked down, their painted eyes frozen in judgment.

"Okay," Fitz said, shaking off the reverence. "We don't have time for this. We need to find evidence." The gravity of the space held them for a moment longer, their feet hesitant as they crossed into the place where history, and violence, had collided.

Moonlight filtered through the tall windows, casting long shadows across the presidential seal woven into the carpet. They split up, Charlie going to the right and Fitz moving forward toward the seal, remembering what Sebastian had told him.

As Fitz stared down at the image he'd seen so many times on television, he struggled to remember what it was supposed to look like because something about this seal was a bit…off. He stared at it for several moments, trying to figure out what looked off to him.

It hit him slowly. The color of the right-hand corner.

It was a subtle difference…but a difference, nonetheless.

Without speaking Fitz gestured toward the right top part of the seal. From the gold tip of the eagle's wing out in a triangle shape through three white stars and the ring of gold and red onto the navy blue carpet, the colors didn't blend perfectly with the rest of the seal. It was clear the section had been hastily replaced, the new carpet subtly different in color. He moved swiftly over it and bent down running his hands over the fibers. The texture was different too.

"Charlie," he called in a hushed but urgent whisper. As she turned to look at him, Fitz was already pulling out his phone to snap a few photos. "Look at this. Do you see it?"

It didn't take Charlie as long to see what he noticed. "It's been replaced." Her gaze fixed on the seal then followed a path across the blue carpet to the side of the Resolute desk. The whole section of blue carpeting had recently been replaced. Her blood must have soaked across.

"I saw something too, Fitz," Charlie breathed, pointing back toward the couch. She brushed past him on her way back over. She bent down to show him. A jagged tear marred the expensive upholstery, poorly concealed by an awkwardly placed throw pillow. It appeared as if a bullet had lodged in the couch. She ran her hand over it, stopping briefly before tugging on the fabric. "If there was a bullet in here it has been removed. This is a bullet hole though. There's no doubt in my mind about it."

Fitz finished taking photos of the carpet and walked over to where Charlie was hunched over the couch. She had tossed the throw pillow and was holding back the fabric so he could take some photos. Unlike the carpet, no one had even tried to repair this. Their only salve was a throw pillow to cover it. Fitz assumed replacing some carpet covered in the president's blood was far more a necessity than fixing a couch they could probably explain away.

They spent the next few minutes scouring the room for other signs of anomalies. President Monroe had been shot twice. Fitz wondered what shot had ended up in the couch. Anything that went through her body would have been fragmented and not left a hole quite so round. He assumed it might have been an errant round or possibly a graze. The shot that ended up in the couch didn't go through her body. If there was one thing he was sure of it was that.

Charlie took one half of the room while he took the other. When he finished he moved toward the Resolute desk, running his hand on top of the fine wood, pushing aside the weight of history at his fingertips.

His eyes scanned the floor, up the long floor-to-ceiling drapes that flanked either side behind the desk. He stopped cold.

"The drapes," he called to Charlie, his voice a little louder this time, marked by confusion as much as in surprise. "There's a hole in the drapes," he noted, moving to examine a ragged hole in the heavy fabric. Behind the drapes, Fitz found the bullet hole in the wall, recently plastered over and not yet painted to match. He took several photos of the area. "Why would there be a shot fired over here? Was she standing over here first then moved and was shot again?"

Charlie stood there with her hands on her hips, her head swiveling back and forth, taking in the odd scene and trying to make sense of it. "Maybe she fought back," she said, the words so soft she had to repeat them for Fitz to hear her.

There was a question on his lips that he didn't know if he could actually ask. One. Two. Three seconds passed. Finally, he uttered, "What if she was the aggressor?"

Before Charlie could respond, an alarm began to wail.

Fitz knew it was time to run.

CHAPTER 24

They lunged for the door to the Rose Garden. Charlie reached the handle first. Locked. She jerked it to the other side and pulled it toward her. Locked. Charlie whipped around looking for another escape as the voice outside grew louder.

Fitz had anticipated being caught but not in the Oval Office.

Together, they scanned around the room, going for the second door that would lead them further into the president's chamber. The same one Marcus Kane and Henry Coldwell left through that fateful night.

A radio crackled in the hallway – much closer than it should have been. "All units, motion sensors triggered in west wing corridor," a voice barked. "Possible security breach."

Fitz hissed as the loud footsteps approached the main door to the Oval. Charlie grabbed his arm, dragging him through the door to the president's private bathroom. They squeezed inside just as voices reached the main door. Through the crack, Fitz watched flashlight beams sweep the room.

"Check behind the desk," a voice ordered.

Fitz's heart hammered in his chest, the beat relentless and deafening in his ears. He dared not breathe too deeply, afraid the air would give him away. His mind was a whirlwind of thoughts, but there was only one thing he could focus on. Moving. And moving quietly. He glanced up. In their planning, they had talked about the ventilation system. It was quickly cast aside. Fitz knew he was far too big and heavy to be crawling through. Not only might he not fit, the racket it would make would give them away. No, they'd have to snake through the White House back to the kitchen.

Charlie was beside him, her presence a comforting shadow in the dark, but he could feel her tension, too. Her breathing was shallow, controlled – just like his own. He glanced at her quickly. Her eyes flickered back to him, the smallest nod. She was as ready.

He waited until the Secret Service cleared the room, their flashlights no longer glowing through the bathroom door. He stepped cautiously out, his feet taking tentative steps, one after another. Charlie was right behind him.

They slipped down the corridor, hugging the edges of the walls.

Fitz froze, his senses tingling. There was a sound – a low murmur from somewhere ahead. The unmistakable shuffle of boots on marble. Secret Service agents were nearby. His stomach twisted in knots. He held up a hand, signaling Charlie to stop. She did, her eyes narrowing as she leaned against the wall, listening. They waited in the dark, breathing shallowly, hearts racing in tandem.

The footsteps grew louder, closer. Fitz's pulse thudded in his throat. They were in the hall to their right so they went left, moving from room to room sure that the next one he entered would be their last.

Fitz could hear the agents muffled voices just a few yards away. They were scanning the area, calling out to each other in the dark. As they drifted away again, they were on the move. The most dangerous part was still to come. They reached the next intersection, and Fitz held up his hand again, signaling for them to stop. His breath was steady, but his heart was racing faster than ever.

Fitz's chest tightened with every step, the weight pressing down on him. Sweat beaded on his forehead, slipping down into his eyes, but he didn't dare wipe it away.

His fingers brushed against the cold surface of the wall beside him. He saw the door off in the distance. If they could cross the wide expanse there was a metal door. Fitz knew it was a service entrance that would lead to the kitchen. Not the way they had come in but an exit all the same.

Fitz leaned forward looking for any signs of the Secret Service. He held his hand up, counted down from three with his fingers and they bolted toward the door. Fitz ripped it open, nearly tugging it from its hinges. Just a few more steps to freedom.

Once in the narrow passage, he exhaled slowly, as he started to regain a sense of himself. His feet carried him quickly down the hall to the next door. But as he reached for the handle and turned it, he found it locked. Fitz cursed under his breath. As he turned to Charlie to ask what they should do, someone softly called his name.

"Reggie?" he whispered back, barely daring to hope.

"Yeah," came the muffled response as the service door opened, his voice a whisper of relief. "Hurry. Get in here."

Fitz didn't need another word. He moved into the main part of the kitchen with Charlie close behind. The cool air hitting them like a shock to their overheated systems.

"Get to the back door," Reggie instructed, his face taut with worry.

Charlie nodded, her eyes scanning the kitchen for signs of trouble. Fitz could hear the distant clatter of agents, but at least for now, they were safe.

With one last glance over their shoulders, Fitz and Charlie bolted for the door, their steps light but purposeful. The back exit creaked open, and the night air hit them like a gust of freedom.

They didn't hesitate. They didn't look back.

They moved quickly, their breath ragged as they darted through the shadows of the White House lawn, every step louder in their ears than the last. The faint echo of approaching footsteps made them press on, adrenaline thrumming through their veins. Every nerve was alive with the threat of being caught, but they had to keep moving.

Fitz's SUV was parked a few hundred yards away. It felt like an eternity before they reached it, but when they did, Fitz was already yanking open the door, urging Charlie inside without a word. She slid in next to him, slamming the door shut with a soft thud.

No time to rest. Not yet.

Fitz keyed the ignition, the engine purring to life. The headlights flickered on, and for a split second, it felt like the whole world was watching. He shifted the SUV into gear, but just as they started to roll forward, the guard station came into view.

Ethan stood near the gate.

Fitz's heart stopped for a moment.

Charlie's fingers tightened around the seatbelt; her eyes fixed on the agent. She held her breath. The guard station was only a few yards away now. They couldn't stop.

Fitz eased toward the guardhouse, his expression calm but his pulse racing. Would Ethan shoot? Stop them? Turn them over? Ethan was looking right at them, but his hand unmistakenly was near the button to open the gate.

For a second, the world seemed to freeze. Ethan's hand dropped. He pressed the button, the gate sliding open with a soft hum.

Fitz nodded briefly as they passed, no words exchanged. Ethan gave a tight, almost imperceptible nod back.

They were off the grounds.

The White House shrank in his rearview mirror as they drove into the night, leaving behind more questions than answers.

Only once they put a considerable distance between themselves and the White House did Charlie finally speak. "We have proof now that it happened in the Oval. Tangible proof beyond any word of witness. We still don't know who pulled the trigger."

Fitz's hands tightened on the steering wheel. There were so many thoughts rushing through his mind that he couldn't focus on anything long enough to answer her. He expected the Secret Service or the FBI to start a high-speed chase after them at any moment. Surely they were seen by someone. The agent said he'd seen shadows and the other teased him about ghosts. Driving off the lot and down the road toward the guard gate, wouldn't there have been surveillance of them? He desperately wanted to reach out to Reggie to see if the man was okay. He assumed he'd be thoroughly questioned.

"Do you think they are going to flip on us?" Fitz finally asked, his voice not sounding like his own.

"No," Charlie assured him. "If they were going to then Reggie would have stopped us and Ethan wouldn't have opened that gate. They aren't doing this to help us, Fitz. They are doing it because they have loyalty to the United States."

Fitz knew that his features were pained and his hands were gripped too tight around the steering wheel. They were starting to throb. Charlie reached her hand over and tugged at his fingers, prying them loose from the wheel. "We did what we had to do, Fitz," she said her tone gentle.

Fitz knew that but he also couldn't shake the severity of what they had done. He hadn't allowed himself to be too bogged down by it before they left. Otherwise, he would have canceled.

Charlie was talking to him softly, but he couldn't process what she was saying. He also didn't know where he was driving. He was going down roads in D.C., stopping at lights and continuing, waiting for someone to pull him over.

"Pull over, Fitz."

"What?" he asked, coming slowly out of the haze. He glanced over at her. "I can't pull over."

"Pull over," she commanded. "I'll drive. You can't drive like this. We have been going in circles since we left the White House. If anything is going to draw attention to us, it's this."

Fitz pulled the SUV over to the curb and eased off the gas, applying the brake as he put the car in park. "I feel like I'm looking at the world through plexiglass. I'm not even sure what's wrong with me."

"Shock," Charlie said, getting out of the passenger side. He didn't seem to have the energy to fight her on it either. The adrenaline that had been coursing through his body earlier was gone, wiping him out completely.

Charlie ran around and pulled open his door. "Get out."

She took full control and Fitz allowed himself to be led.

Once he was settled in the passenger seat and Charlie was back on the road, Fitz rubbed the sides of his head and chuckled lightly. "Why are you so calm under pressure? First, you rescued Burrows and now me. This doesn't bode well for men in the last few days."

Charlie shifted her eyes to the right and returned his laugh. "I don't panic. The CIA trained that out of me. Burrows needs therapy. He's seen far too much in his time and he needs a break. We used to talk about that all the time. Did you know he used to work on terrorism cases? He was involved in the investigations during the Kenya bombing, the first World Trade Center bombing. He's seen a lot. Part of the reason he's back here in D.C. is because he threatened to quit if they didn't take him off terrorism cases."

Fitz had no idea about the man's background. He had never asked. "Is that how the two of you met?"

Charlie nodded. "At a black site in Poland. I was there interrogating a few suspects after 9/11 and Burrows showed up with the FBI." She turned her head briefly to look at him. "Before you ask, no, I wasn't involved in any of the CIA's enhanced interrogation. I adamantly refused. I never believed that torturing someone would bring about credible intel."

"I didn't think you could refuse to do something in the CIA." If Fitz were being honest, even though he was in law enforcement, he didn't know much about the CIA other than what he read in fiction or saw on the news.

"You can and should refuse any order that isn't legal. I didn't think what we were doing was legal and as you saw with the Congressional hearings after, there is still debate about it. I refused and I threatened to quit." Charlie shrugged it off. "I can be a loud ball-busting obnoxious woman when I need to be. I'm not always so cute and dainty as I am with you."

Fitz snorted. He'd never known a day where Charlie was cute or dainty. "I've been to several horrific crime scenes. I've been on raids. I'm as cool under pressure as anyone. I don't understand what just happened to me."

"Shock, Fitz," Charlie said as she changed lanes, speeding up now on the Beltway. "Not only based on us sneaking into the Oval but of what we found. It was a poor repair job at that. They aren't even trying to hide it. Then again, why would they need to when they can normally control who has access to that space."

"I keep replaying the scene of how it could have gone down and none of it's adding up."

Charlie got off at the right exit and pulled to a stop at the first light. "Let's not worry about figuring everything out tonight. I'm going to call Burrows to ask him to meet. We need some legal guidance on the evidence collection. Our photos are okay but we need an FBI team in there getting actual evidence."

"He's not going to be able to do anything," Fitz said. He agreed with Charlie though, someone actually in government who could do something about it was going to have to get involved. There was only so much they'd be able to do. "What do you want to do next?"

"Let's interview Ian Drake tomorrow. He was in the room when it happened. There was a gunfight. I know we suggested it was Monroe. It could have been any of them and she got caught in the crossfire."

"True," Fitz said, realizing they had made a big leap without the evidence. "I need to call Sebastian to ask if President Monroe had a gun. I think if anyone knew she was armed it would have been him." He noticed the look on her face and changed the subject, "Have you been sleeping well since this started?"

"No," Charlie said. "But I don't sleep well as it is. Never have." She pulled his SUV into the driveway. "I'll pick you up in the morning. I need to take your SUV back to my place."

Fitz was so tired he didn't care if she stole it. He grabbed at the door handle, tugged his house key from his pocket, and said goodnight. When he got to the door, he realized she hadn't backed down the driveway yet. She was staring out the driver's side window. He'd only seen that look a few times and he knew what it meant.

Charlie was ditching him for the night but she was far from done working.

He stood in the doorway and called Sebastian, watching her until she finally left.

CHAPTER 25

Fitz slept like the dead. When he woke the next morning at a little after six, it took him more than a few minutes to adjust his eyes and even remember where he was sleeping. He barely recalled opening the door the night before, finding Amy in the kitchen having a snack, and making his way to his bed. He forewent his nightly shower and threw himself on top of the covers still in his clothes. At some point during the night, he must have gotten warm because he woke in only his black boxer briefs, one arm slung above his head, and the other tossed across the empty side of the bed.

It was only once he pushed himself to a sitting position that he remembered Charlie had taken his SUV last night. Fitz stretched his legs, deciding no matter how he felt a run would do him good.

Fitz stretched lightly in the driveway then started with a light jog down his driveway onto the road. His sneakers slapped against the pavement, rhythmic and steady, as he ran through the crisp morning air. His breath came in controlled bursts, filling his lungs with the cold bite of the morning air, his legs driving him forward like a well-oiled machine. Fitz had always liked the solitude of the early morning run – no crowds, no distractions. Just him and his thoughts.

The city was still waking up. The sky was painted in hues of lavender and pale blue, and the first light of dawn clung to the edges of the houses, casting long shadows across the roads. His mind was clear, focused on nothing more than the steady pace of his feet, the rhythmic beat of his heart.

When he passed an intersection near a row of neat townhouses about two miles from home, something shifted. A low hum. The vibration of a vehicle's engine. Fitz's instincts kicked in, his gaze darting to the side. A dark, nondescript truck was coasting down the street, the driver's side window slowly lowering. He didn't break stride as his body tensed, muscles coiling.

He glanced over and met the gaze of the man in the driver's seat.

Fitz's pulse quickened. His mind snapped back to the conversation he'd had with the Secret Service agent in Rock Creek Park. Wyatt Standfield had told him about the bullets left in the desk. He had insinuated that someone in the Secret Service had known more about the attempted assassination of Monroe than they let on. The man had proven to be right so far.

The truck pulled up beside him, but Fitz didn't slow down.

Standfield's voice sliced sharply through the air. "Fitz," he said with an undeniable urgency. "Get in."

Fitz hesitated, glancing over his shoulder at the empty street. He half expected to see a row of police cars showing up to detain him for what he and Charlie had done at the White House. He couldn't outrun them and even if he did, where would he go? Fitz glanced back. Even with the man's face shadowed, Fitz could make out the hard lines of his jaw, the way his eyes expressed the same urgency as his tone.

With a glance toward the street, Fitz made the decision. He swerved around and jogged to the passenger side of the truck, pulling the door open with a quick yank. The smell of leather and cold air hit him. Standfield's eyes were locked on him, his face grim but composed. Fitz didn't speak as he slammed the door shut, the truck's engine humming as they moved off.

The streets blurred as his neighborhood gave way to the cityscape.

They were heading toward D.C. Standfield didn't say anything at first, his gaze fixed on the road ahead, fingers tight on the wheel.

Fitz's mind raced. Was he being detained? Did Wyatt know what they did? The memory of their last conversation played in his head. Fitz broke the tension. If he was being detained, he still had rights. "What is it you want? You came to me like this before and asked me to investigate. I've been doing that. You were right. The shooting isn't what it seemed. It didn't happen the way it's playing out in the news. What do you want now?"

"You and Charlie," Wyatt finally said, breaking the silence. "You think the Secret Service doesn't know what you did?" His voice was low, but the weight of it pressed into the truck's cabin like a physical force. "Sneaking into the White House. You're lucky they didn't find you last night. You're lucky I'm the one here talking to you right now."

Fitz's eyes flicked to him, but he didn't respond. He wasn't going to admit it. He didn't know if the whole truck was bugged. Was Standfield trying to force a confession?

Fitz did what his training told him – he remained silent.

The truck made a sharp turn onto a quieter road, the streets emptier now, the buildings giving way to the shadow of trees. "I'm giving you a warning," Standfield continued, his eyes never leaving the road. "The whole agency's compromised, Fitz. I don't know who you trust, but you can't trust anyone inside. They all have their secrets. All of them. Do you understand me?"

Fitz's stomach tightened, the words sinking in. "You're not here to detain me? Take me in?" He still refused to say the words aloud of what they did.

Standfield finally looked over at Fitz. "I'm not here to detain you. I'm here to offer you a warning – they know what you did. They know what you saw inside the Oval Office."

"Who else knows?" Fitz asked, his voice steady, betraying the rapid beat of his heart. He didn't want to hear the answer, but it was out there now. He needed to know.

Standfield's fingers tightened on the wheel. "The Secret Service staff in the White House last night. They saw you driving away. Got your tag number and ran the plate. Everyone knows who you are, Fitz. What they didn't know was why you were in the White House until they saw the pillow moved in the Oval Office. They knew then why you were there."

Fitz's first thought wasn't for himself but for Reggie and Ethan. "Did anyone get in trouble?"

Thankfully, Standfield shook his head. "Ethan was questioned about letting you in. He lied and said that you said you had a late meeting with the Secret Service. Everyone knows you, Fitz. They know the work you do. Most would have believed you and let you in." He turned to look at Fitz. "I'm not even going to ask how you got in."

Fitz shrugged. He wasn't going to explain himself. "What's the Secret Service plan?"

"They have no plan," Wyatt said, slowing down for a light. Morning traffic was getting heavy, cars pulled on the passenger side and the intersection had rows of cars waiting for the light to change. When the light was green, Standfield waited for the light and crossed left and then another left, heading back toward the main street. At the light he turned left again, heading them back in the direction they came.

Fitz finally relaxed back into the seat. "What do you mean they don't have a plan?"

"I mean exactly what I said. The Secret Service doesn't have a plan. What are they going to do, tell someone that you broke into the Oval? When they ask what you were doing, they won't have an answer. They'd have to admit that the president was shot there."

"The Secret Service could lie," Fitz said, knowing they probably lied all the time. They were pulling off one of the greatest conspiracies known to history as they spoke.

Standfield brushed off the suggestion. "Your reputation is too stellar. If you're there, it's for a purpose. You're investigating something and that indicates something is amiss. The Secret Service won't admit you got one over them. I'm here to tell you to watch your back."

"You could have told me that on the street." Fitz wasn't buying that was the only reason he was there. "What else is it? What do you know? You were right about the bullets. Tell me about Graham Westbrook. I'm sure it was him who put them in his desk. I know he was there for the shooting, and he didn't go to the hospital. I'm fairly certain he was the one sent to Zachary Steele. I'm just missing two pieces of key information – who shot President Monroe and why? Did she try to defend herself, maybe? There was a gunfight in the Oval. Who else was armed?"

Standfield cocked an eyebrow. "You think President Monroe was innocent in all of this?"

"She's the one who was shot. What am I supposed to think?"

Standfield shook his head, tsking. "You're missing the bigger picture."

Fitz punched his fist into the palm of his hand. "If you know something, stop toying with me. I'm starting to think this is a game for you."

"Not a game," Wyatt said evenly. "You might want to consider President Monroe wasn't shot first. She *fired* first."

Fitz's breath caught. His chest tightened, disbelief making his vision swim for a moment. "Monroe fired first. She was the one with the gun?" he asked, barely able to push the words past the lump in his throat. "How do you know that? Why would she have fired first and at whom?"

Standfield's eyes flicked to him, just for a split second, before he nodded once, sharply. "Someone in that room – someone high up – made a move. The shooting wasn't the end. It was just the beginning. You're going to want to remember that."

Fitz's mind was reeling, trying to make sense of what Standfield said. "You're telling me Monroe shot first?" Fitz's voice was barely above a whisper, as though speaking too loudly might shatter the fragile understanding they'd reached.

"That's right," Standfield said, his voice cold as the air outside. "Everything you think you know. It's wrong. The agency's got blood on its hands. The orders came from higher."

Fitz felt the weight of Standfield's words like a blow to his gut. "I'm tired of your cryptic messages. Either you know something to help us or you don't. What do you know about Graham Westbrook?"

The truck slowed, turning onto a quieter street. Standfield stopped the truck. The silence between them was thick and charged. "He has a connection to one of the men in that room and that man is connected to something bigger."

Fitz cursed softly, tired of the game playing. He opened the door, but before he stepped out, he turned back. "Why are you telling me this?"

Standfield didn't respond directly. "You'll figure it out, Fitz. The nation is counting on you."

With that, Fitz slammed the door in the man's face. Standfield put the truck into drive and sped off, leaving Fitz standing there, the cold wind biting at his face.

He returned to his house to find Charlie sitting at the dining room table chatting with Amy like they were old pals. Fitz walked to the edge of the room, wiping sweat from his brow. He ran hard on the way back trying to process the conversation he had with Standfield.

He cleared his throat, getting their attention.

"I went for a run," he said, holding his arms out to his sides. Fitz locked his gaze on Charlie. "We need to talk."

Amy smiled over at him, reaching for her coffee cup. "I think that's my cue to leave. Charlie, it was nice meeting you." As she passed by Fitz, she patted his gut. "You've got a good partner over there. You better treat her right."

"She'll kill me in my sleep if I don't." Fitz laughed, looking down at her.

"I'll kill him just as easily when he's standing upright," Charlie joked back.

Fitz swallowed hard. That was a true statement if he ever heard one. After last night, he realized he was no match to her mentally or maybe even physically if they got right down to it. He was substantially bigger, but he was sure she had a few tricks up her sleeve to take down a mountain of a man like him.

When Amy left and Fitz heard her hit the top of the stairs, which creaked lightly under anyone's weight, he moved into the kitchen. "I had a visitor on my run. Standfield."

Charlie crinkled up her nose. "The agent who stalked you in Rock Creek Park?" When Fitz confirmed, she asked, "What did he want?"

Fitz wasn't even sure what the man's real intention had been. "They know we were the ones in the White House last night. Neither Ethan nor Reggie is in trouble. I don't think they even know our connection to Reggie. Standfield didn't say anything about him. They cleared Ethan because he told them that we said we had a meeting with the Secret Service. Given my reputation, it was a believable lie."

Charlie's face paled. "Are we being arrested?"

"No," he said with a shake of his head. "Not yet anyway. He said the Secret Service is embarrassed we got one over on them. To discuss what we did, they'd have to come up with a reason for it. It sounded to me like they are desperately trying to keep from the FBI that the shooting occurred in the Oval Office. Of course, on the flip side, they probably assume that to discuss what we found we'd be implicating ourselves breaking into the White House."

"That is true. Where does that leave us?"

"Stalemate for now." Fitz grabbed a glass from the cabinet and put it in the ice dispenser on the fridge. He filled his glass and then filled it with water. He leaned back on the counter, taking a long sip, finally feeling like his mouth wasn't stuffed with cotton. When he was done, he looked back at Charlie. "We don't take our foot off the gas. We have them running scared. We have to interview Ian Drake next. Then we tackle Graham Westbrook."

CHAPTER 26

The decision to interview Ian Drake had been an easy one. Finding him was another matter. It took half the morning, a visit to Ian's residence and the condo in downtown D.C. of his longtime girlfriend to finally get his sister's address.

Fitz pushed the doorbell with a sharp press, his thumb lingering for a moment. The house in front of them was modest, tucked away on a quiet street in Maryland. It had the kind of suburban charm that felt out of place next to the monumental tension of Washington, D.C., only twenty minutes away. The weathered brick exterior was softened by creeping ivy.

Charlie stepped up beside Fitz, her eyes narrowing as she looked toward the street, as though expecting someone to be watching them. "I can see why he chose here to hide out."

"You don't get to be a Secret Service agent by being easy to track." Fitz adjusted the collar of his jacket, suddenly more aware of the cold Maryland air. "I want to know why he's feeling the need to hide out. We know why Sebastian took off. Ian was put on leave too. He felt a need to run."

The door opened, revealing a tall woman in her late thirties, her expression hard to read. She had the same steely blue eyes that Amy had described for Ian Drake, the same square jaw, and dark brown hair pulled back into a ponytail. From the records Charlie had found, they knew her name was Callie.

As Fitz introduced himself, Callie stepped back to close the door. Fitz cautioned her against it. "Ian ran for a reason. If he has information to share about the attempted assassination, he's better off sharing it. Keeping their secrets only keeps him a target."

Callie paused. "How can you help him? What protection could you offer him if he speaks to you?" It was a valid question and the answer was none.

Fitz was honest about that. "There's nothing that I can do personally to protect Ian. It's all up to him. Others are willing to speak. The sooner we get the whole picture of what happened, the faster we can solve this and turn it over to people who can protect him."

Callie hesitated for only a moment before she stepped aside, opening the door wider. "Ian is not doing well. I haven't seen him like this in…well, never."

The inside of the house was cozy – dark wooden floors, muted colors, and shelves cluttered with books and family photos. A fireplace in the corner crackled faintly, but there was no warmth in the air.

Fitz exchanged a quick glance with Charlie before following Callie down the narrow hall, their footsteps muffled by the thick rugs. They stopped outside a door at the end of the hallway, where Callie knocked lightly.

"Ian? We've got company," she called out softly.

There was a long pause before the door creaked open. Ian Drake stood in the frame, a shadow of the man who had once been the sharp-eyed Secret Service agent. His face was pale, and his eyes, bloodshot and dark-rimmed, gave nothing away. He was dressed in sweatpants and a loose shirt, clearly not prepared for visitors.

His expression was unreadable, and the moment he saw Fitz and Charlie, he stiffened. His jaw clenched.

"Do you know who I am?" Fitz asked, not surprised that he might.

Ian offered a curt nod. "I had heard you were looking into…" He couldn't quite get out the words. He left the end of the sentence hanging. "I've been put on leave and so was Sebastian. No one knows where he is. Some say he left the area altogether and won't ever return."

Neither Fitz nor Charlie gave anything away that they knew where Sebastian was and had spoken to him. It wasn't their place to disclose that. "Is there a good place to talk?"

"You can have the living room," Callie called from down the hall before disappearing farther into the house.

"Give me a minute," Ian said, before stepping back into the room and closing the door.

Fitz resisted the urge to stand there and wait for him. He didn't know if the agent was going to try to escape. Charlie tugged on Fitz's arm and jerked her head toward the living room. "He's not going anywhere," she assured him.

They went to the living room. The blinds had only been open slits allowing a shadow of light to pass through. Fitz sat down on a recliner while Charlie took the couch, its back cushions hinting at the years of wear. They were misshapen and bowed forward as Charlie leaned back.

"I had a couch like this once. It annoyed me to no end," she said, pushing it back.

"Callie feels the same," Ian said, suddenly appearing on the threshold of the living room. He had changed clothing into a nicer shirt and a pair of jeans. He had thick wool socks on his feet but hadn't bothered with shoes. "She threatened to toss it to the curb yesterday."

His voice was flat, drained of emotion, but his eyes flickered to Charlie's face for a moment before he looked away. "What do you want to know?"

Charlie leaned forward to look at him directly. "We want to know what you saw. What you know."

Ian leaned against the wall, arms crossed. "The president – she – " He stopped himself, swallowing hard. "I was there. I don't know who did it."

"You were there?" Charlie's voice was filled with calculation.

Ian nodded, his eyes darting toward the window as if he expected someone to be watching. "I was the first one in the room *after* the shooting. Graham Westbrook was in the room when it happened. There was a meeting of some sort. I know that much. Around two in the morning, President Monroe came down to the Oval Office with her husband. They were with Graham. All three of them looked tense. There had been some exchange up in the living quarters. I don't know what it was about. They told me Representative Adrian Mercer, Speaker of the House Victor Graves, Vice President Henry Coldwell and FBI Director Marcus Kane would be meeting with them in the Oval. I was to stand guard at the door."

Both of them.

Fitz wasn't sure he had heard correctly. "You were told that Coldwell and Kane would be at the meeting? Did you see them there?"

"Yeah, they came through President Monroe's private secretary's office. I had to let them in." Ian pinched the bridge of his nose. "They were very clear it was not an official meeting. Kane patted my arm on the way in and told me I was doing a good job. Reminded me that no one needed to know about the meeting."

"The FBI director suggested to you that you were to lie about the meeting?" Charlie asked, her voice filled with confusion.

"Not lie exactly. Just not say anything about it."

"Had all of those people met before like this?"

"Not around me or Sebastian. I can't say for sure if they met when we weren't on shift. I never heard about them meeting *off the record*." Ian took a breath, blowing out threw his nose. "That was the weird part.

President Monroe was known to work through the night sometimes. She had incredible stamina and work ethic. The meetings would always follow standard protocol as if the meetings were midday. This time…" He trailed off, shaking his head. "You have to understand. The Secret Service remains invisible to these people and that's how we like to stay. We blend into the background. We see and hear but are otherwise invisible to them. We are no more than a plant in the room or a chair. During this meeting, they went out of their way to acknowledge me and tell me that this was a meeting I shouldn't mention to anyone. That had never happened before with anyone."

Fitz asked, "Were you outside the room the whole time?"

"Yes. I was standing guard at the door while Graham Westbrook was inside. I'm a more senior part of the team, but I didn't fight him on being in the room. I got the vibe they wanted him there and not me. I didn't consider it a big deal at the start of the meeting."

"That changed?" Charlie asked.

"The meeting went on for a while." Ian hesitated, looking between them. Both remained quiet so he'd go on. "That's when I heard the first shot and immediately drew my weapon. The shot came from inside the Oval and I tried to get inside. The door was locked. I slammed my shoulder into it several times. I'm sure you can imagine those doors aren't meant to be breached like that. I was getting nowhere. I was standing out there banging on it and banging, shouting for access. Begging them to let me in. No one came."

Charlie held up her index finger. "You heard one shot? Just one?"

"Initially, then I heard a few more in rapid succession. I was banging on that door to be let in. I was about to give up and try another access point when I was finally let in by Graham."

"What did you see?"

"At first, I didn't see President Monroe at all. All of them had these horrified looks on their faces like they couldn't believe what happened.

They were huddled around each other. I had my gun drawn and was shouting at them to tell me what happened. I was ready to shoot. To act as my training tells me, only the scene wasn't clear to me. I didn't see anyone with a gun. They were yelling at me that they didn't know who had shot her. Someone suggested it was an accident that Monroe had a gun."

"Accident?" Charlie asked, his tone telling them it had been no accident at all.

Ian held his hand up to stop her. "I knew there wasn't an accident. The shots I heard were in rapid succession. Intentional. I asked who was shot and that's when I saw her, lying on the floor. I tried to rush to her, but Richard Avery stopped me. He said she was already dead. I tried to push past. Speaker Graves stood in my way along with Richard Avery."

"Where was Richard Avery's Secret Service detail?" Charlie asked.

"It was just Graham and I for the night," he said. "The rest of the agents were around the White House doing security checks."

Fitz knew Ian could have shoved past both the men. "Did you see anyone with a gun?"

"Not at first. When Graves and Avery blocked my path, I turned to Graham to ask what was going on. That's when I noticed he didn't have his gun in his hand. It was on his hip. He also wasn't chasing down the threat. He was calm, too calm. He told me he didn't know who shot President Monroe. He assured me he didn't."

"He just came out with it."

"Yeah," Ian responded to Fitz. "It looked bad for him. I'm sure he knew exactly what I was thinking. But before anything else could happen, Marcus Kane grabbed Vice President Henry Coldwell and pulled him across the room to the other door. The one that goes out through the president's private area."

"Did he say anything?" Fitz asked, interrupting.

"Just that they had to get out of there and that no one could know they were there. Marcus Kane repeated that a few more times. He said that the vice president could not be present at the assassination of the president. Then they were gone. As they were leaving, Sebastian rushed into the room."

Fitz wanted to back up to something Ian said. "Marcus Kane said Coldwell couldn't be there when Monroe was assassinated? Is that what you heard him say? Those words exactly?"

"Yeah. That's why I thought President Monroe was dead."

"How did Marcus Kane seem to you? Was he shaken up?"

"I've only seen the man a handful of times. Kane acted fast as I would expect an FBI director to do. What surprised me was that he was pulling Coldwell out of the room. He had to know there would be an investigation. He should have stayed. He needed to be accountable. He would have seen who shot the president."

Charlie asked, "Are you sure he saw who shot the president?"

Ian's eyes grew wide in curiosity. "I don't know how he couldn't have. He was in the room when it happened. They were all acting like no one knew who shot her."

Fitz was trying hard to make sense of the situation. How could the FBI director witness someone shoot the president and do nothing but flee then act as if he had no idea what had happened? It was diabolical. "What happened after Sebastian came into the room?"

Ian gestured with his hand as he spoke. "Sebastian shoved past all of us and went directly to her. He scooped her up and disappeared in the same direction that Kane and Coldwell went. He was running. I didn't understand at first because everyone said she was dead. I assumed quickly enough that she maybe wasn't. I followed because I knew he'd need help. We got out to one of the black Secret Service SUVs and went directly to the emergency room." Ian pursed his lips together. "I know Sebastian believes I had something to do with this.

I swear to you I didn't. I might not have done everything I should have, but I am not and was not involved in this plot to assassinate the president. I had nothing to do with it."

Fitz knew that was going to be for the courts to decide. "Tell me about the cover-up because I know you lied to the FBI."

Ian's head hung low. "I did lie. I did what I was told to do. David Sparks, my supervisor that night. He called me back from the hospital and everything was quickly put in motion. They kept Sebastian out of it for obvious reasons, only sharing with him specifically what he was to tell the FBI and he didn't even get that right. They want to silence him and they are going to want to silence me for talking to you."

Fitz flicked his eyes up at the man. "This isn't the time for fear. You had one job – to protect the president – you couldn't do it that night but you can do it now."

Ian took a deep breath and then told Fitz and Charlie a wild tale that they'd never believe if they weren't hearing it from someone directly involved.

CHAPTER 27

"You think they were all in on it?" Burrows sat at the kitchen table in the safe house staring across the table at Fitz and Charlie. After meeting with Ian, they decided they needed to speak with Burrows immediately. There was no way they could sit on the information he shared. They debated calling Senator Ford first but decided talking it out with Burrows would be a better first step.

They had started with everything Ian had shared about being outside the Oval and only being allowed in after Monroe was found in a heap on the floor. Charlie added, "They told him she was dead. He didn't go and check on her. I honestly think he was too stunned to do much. He went in ready to protect the president and got there after everything was over."

"Did he seem shaken up?" Burrows asked. "Did you believe him?"

Charlie turned to Fitz. They had discussed it on the drive back. Ian had seemed credible to both of them. He had also seemed fearful of his own government and what they might do to him for sharing the truth. Fitz took the question. "We believe him. He was credible."

Burrows wasn't so sure. "In his statement, Ian didn't put himself in the Oval. We don't know if that's true or not. Even Sebastian questioned him at the hospital. Isn't that what the nurse said happened? Sebastian asked Ian if he was involved in the shooting. Ian was in the room when Sebastian broke in. How do we know Ian isn't covering for himself?"

Charlie had one specific answer for that. "Because he implicated himself in the cover-up."

Burrows sighed. "I checked with the guy I know who was in the situation room that night. It's soundproofed, so he didn't hear the shots. That said, he heard from a few others who heard shots that the Secret Service said there was an accident with an agent who was put on leave. That's the story inside the White House. We are going to need solid evidence to push this theory with any credibility."

They still hadn't told him about their late-night trip to the Oval. They were saving it.

In a rush of breath, Charlie admitted, "We have the proof. We went into the White House last night and saw the Oval Office." She waited to see if his expression changed and when it didn't, she went on. "We found bullet holes in the wall and in the couch. The rug has also been replaced hastily. The damage remains in that room. It's clear there was a shooting there."

Burrows leaned forward on the table. "I'm not even going to ask how you got in. Where's the evidence?"

Charlie handed him her phone and directed him to scroll through the recent photos. "That carpet was replaced. As you can see, it doesn't even match. It was done so quickly they did a horrible job of it. Of course, they never expected anyone from the outside to see it. There was only a throw pillow covering the hole in the couch. It was a bullet hole. I'd stake my life on that. There was another one through the drapes that lodged into the wall. That was poorly plastered and painted."

Burrows scrolled through one photo after another. His eyes getting bigger and his breath caught in his throat. "This is evidence consistent with what Ian described."

Charlie had been careful when she shared the earlier details with him. "As you can see, there is a bullet hole in the couch and one across the room lodged in the wall behind the drapes. You know what that means then, don't you?"

"There were two shooters," Burrows said quickly almost to himself.

That's what Fitz and Charlie took from the scene as well. Charlie explained, "We believe they were probably on the couches having a meeting. Then at some point, they got up and things got heated. She took a shot at whoever was standing in that direction and they or someone else fired back."

"How do we know it was Monroe who did any of the shooting?"

Fitz cleared his throat. "Monroe was armed because Sebastian Cole didn't trust those around her. He said so himself. He also admitted to me that he gave her a gun and even took her shooting."

"He took the President of the United States to a gun range?"

"No," Charlie explained, "before she was president. Sebastian has been on her detail for a long time. He was concerned Monroe couldn't trust some of the people around her. He believes this threat goes back some time. He even suggested in the call with Fitz he believes they used her to gain the presidency and tried to kill her to install their own people."

"That would be Coldwell." Burrows stared down at the photo while Fitz provided him with more of Sebastian's theories.

Fitz had learned almost as much on the call as they had in person. "Sebastian believes the party allowed Abigail Monroe to be nominated because Henry Coldwell was unelectable on his own. He doesn't have the charisma and his politics are more extreme than Monroe's. She was the more palatable choice. She beat him in the primary by a large margin. However, her husband and a few in her party convinced her that she should choose Coldwell as a running mate because it brought their party together. Sebastian was completely against it. He saw the writing on the wall early on. They convinced her that if she didn't choose Coldwell, she wouldn't win the election. The ticket polled well and she went for it. Monroe hasn't been open to Coldwell's policy suggestions since taking office. She relegated him to the back of the stage, which happens to almost every vice president. He didn't want to take a backseat to her."

Burrows was slowly absorbing the information as Fitz spoke. "Monroe was a puppet essentially. A way to get them into power because she had the will of the people. Either she was going to play by their rules once elected or they were going to get her out of the way. Is that what you're suggesting?"

"Essentially," Charlie said. "Early on, I thought it might have a financial motive. This makes more sense. Coldwell was completely unelectable on his own. He has extreme policies that aren't popular with the electorate and he has about as much charm as a dishrag."

Burrows chuckled. "That's one way to put it. Do you think he shot her?"

"I don't think he has the balls," Fitz said and he didn't. "We need Graham Westbrook to talk. He was the only one in there when the whole thing went down. He knows the truth."

"How do we know it's not him?"

"We don't," Fitz admitted.

Burrows finished looking at the photos and handed the phone back to Charlie. "Tell me about the cover-up. How did they pull that off?"

Fitz gestured for Charlie to explain.

"Ian doesn't know how the cover-up plot got started or who initiated it. He was at the hospital with Sebastian. All he knows is he got a call about forty minutes after being there asking if the president was alive. He confirmed she was in surgery, and he didn't know anything more."

"Who called him?"

"David Sparks, the supervisor on duty. He was the one directing the cover-up. He also wasn't supposed to be there that night. The regular supervisor was on vacation."

Burrows agreed with that. "I know Samuel Ashford, the Secret Service director. He's not someone who's going to do something like that. I assume the cover-up doesn't reach that level."

"I don't think it made it out of the White House," Fitz explained. "David Sparks was running the show and he got everyone in line. The director had no reason to question what was happening at the White House if the shooting took place at the Lincoln Memorial."

"You're going to need irrefutable proof. Ashford is a fierce defender of the Secret Service." Burrows shifted in his seat. "Tell me how this went. Ian got a call…then?"

Charlie continued. "Sparks made the case that the truth would cause a constitutional crisis never seen before in our country and that the Secret Service had a duty to protect democracy. Ian said Sparks pitched it as this real patriotic sort of thing. Ian wasn't buying it but what choice did he have? If the shooting was going to destroy the fabric of the country, Ian felt like he had little choice but to follow orders. He asked if the director was aware and was told no and that he wasn't to say anything. The order came down from high enough though that Ian knew to follow the lead. Sparks put Ian and Sebastian on leave immediately. He told him that Graham would be on leave too. They were to tell the FBI that they were out for a typical morning run when President Monroe asked to stop briefly at the Lincoln Memorial. There she was shot by Zachary Steele, who had been on the FBI and Secret Service radar for a while given the threats he was posting online. Graham Westbrook shot him dead right there and Ian and Sebastian rushed her to the hospital, leaving Westbrook to handle the scene at the Lincoln Memorial. There was just one big issue with the plan."

"The evidence," Burrows said his tone incredulous.

"We all know evidence can be faked." Fitz leveled him a look. "The thing they couldn't get past was *the timing*. There is no way the president was going to be out jogging at three in the morning. And even if she was, it would have been so far from her normal schedule that Steele wouldn't have known she'd be there at that time. It would hint that he had some insider information, which was the last thing the Secret Service was going to suggest. They had to move the shooting back two hours to make the plan make sense. To do that, they had to convince the hospital staff to lie for the good of national security. You start throwing that term around at civilians and they are going to comply. At least that's what they assumed."

"The nurse?" Burrows asked.

Fitz could feel the corners of his mouth upturning in a smile. "Amy isn't someone who'd comply, even if her job was on the line."

"You like her," Charlie teased.

"Respect her," Fitz countered, not admitting that he had dropped the ball on that relationship. "It was a messy plan and not one they are pulling off well. Anything this big in government is sure to have leakers. They have already gone after Sebastian. Ian has been towing the company line fearful for his life."

"The FBI is rushing the investigation," Burrows reminded them. "While they aren't completely buying the story, I can tell you the agents involved have no idea that something like this occurred. I don't think they'd believe me if I took this evidence to them and suggested Marcus Kane was in the room when this happened. It certainly makes sense why he's rushing the investigation."

Charlie added, "There are others at the Secret Service who aren't buying the story either. It's going to be hard to contain for long. They know Fitz and I were in the White House."

Burrows paled. "What are they going to do?"

"Nothing," Fitz said with a shake of his head. "To admit we were there is to admit we had a reason to be there. I'm sure someone might come after us for the evidence. I think they are more afraid of what we know and probably afraid of angering us."

"Do you think they will come after you?"

Neither Fitz nor Charlie were sure. Fitz was betting on them being too afraid to rock the boat. "If either of us turn up dead there are going to be questions when the evidence is released. They have to know that we are going to keep any evidence we have secure and in multiple locations. I'm betting on them knowing my history to keep us safe."

"They went after Sebastian Cole," Burrows reminded them.

They knew that. "They might send someone after us for the evidence. I don't think they are going to try to kill us."

"You might be right," Burrows agreed finally. He sat back and stared past them. "There's just one big issue in this whole thing. What are they going to do when President Monroe wakes up?"

It was Charlie who spoke first. "They are betting on the chance that she won't."

No matter what had happened one thing remained certain – President Monroe was still in danger.

CHAPTER 28

Fitz cut the engine at the end of the dirt driveway. They had planned for a night meeting with Graham Westbrook. They had no idea if he would talk, but they had to try. Charlie said she had ways of making him talk. Fitz wasn't so sure that was a good idea.

They were in enough trouble with the Secret Service.

Fitz knew based on their trip to the White House, they could be prosecuted and the Warren Circle would hang them out to dry. It was their mission to find answers, but not at the expense of their freedom. He had cautioned Charlie to take it easy.

The address they found for him was an old Victorian deep into Virginia. It sat on an isolated piece of land far from the main street. The lack of streetlights and proper lighting on the property didn't give them much of an advantage to do reconnaissance before entering the property.

Charlie was using night-vision. "It's just an old Victorian, Fitz. A beat-up Ford is in the driveway. A crumbling barn to the right of the house. I don't think anything is in there. It looks like a good strong wind will knock it over."

The property had been listed as Graham's parents' address. An obituary from two years ago indicated that both parents were deceased, the father's heart attack following the mother's breast cancer by two months. There were no children listed other than Graham.

The home was in disrepair probably from years of neglect. Fitz left his SUV at the end of the drive as they got out to walk. The skeletal branches of dying oaks clawed at the sky, casting jagged shadows across the field. A single dim light flickered from an upstairs window, the only sign of life in an otherwise abandoned fortress.

Charlie pulled her coat tighter against the cold, the late-night air thick with the damp, cloying scent of rotting leaves. They moved quickly, sticking to the shadows as they approached the house. Gravel crunched beneath Fitz's boots, but otherwise, the night swallowed their presence.

Charlie pressed herself against the peeling wooden siding beneath a cracked window. Inside, she could make out the faint outline of Graham sitting on a couch watching television. He seemed relaxed and too at ease for a man who had witnessed the shooting of a president and had participated in the cover-up.

"You go first and I'll cover your back," she whispered as they made their way from the side to the front porch.

Fitz knew as soon as he put a booted foot to the uneven porch steps it would creak under his weight. Instead of breaching the house, Fitz called out the man's name instead. He acted on instinct, already going against the plan he and Charlie had made.

"Graham Westbrook!" Fitz shouted once and then again.

A few seconds later, the front porch light turned on, illuminating Fitz and Charlie. The front door of the home eased open, and all six-foot-four wide-as-a-linebacker Graham Westbrook filled the doorway. He had his gun by his side as he peered out at them.

"Sneaking up on a man's home is a good way to get yourself shot. What do you want?"

Fitz took a tentative step toward the porch and Graham responded by raising his gun. Fitz put his hands up. "We just want to talk. That's all. Do you know who we are?"

"Yeah, the two idiots who broke into the White House. What are you doing here?"

Fitz was sure Graham knew exactly why they were there. "We want to talk about what happened. We know the shooting happened in the Oval Office."

Graham dared to laugh. "There's no proof of that. I already gave my statement to the FBI. Get off my property." He started to close the door.

"We know you were in the room when the shooting happened and we also know who else was there. You did a terrible job fixing that carpet and the bullet holes were obvious," Charlie said, her tone tight but unafraid. "You can either talk to us now or we can go to the director of the Secret Service. We have more than enough evidence."

Graham stopped closing the door, sighing loudly. "Whatever you think you know, you don't. You'd be wise to keep your mouths shut if you know what's good for you."

"See now that doesn't make any sense," Charlie said with a laugh. She was calm and cool under the pressure while Fitz willed his heart to stop racing. "If we don't know anything, what do we need to keep our mouths shut about?" She took a step up onto the porch then another.

"I'd stop right there," Graham said.

"Or what? You're not going to shoot me. If I had to guess you have very specific orders not to talk to us but also not to mess with us." Charlie turned back to Fitz jerking her head for him to follow. She refocused on Graham. "Do you know where I used to work?"

"Am I supposed to care?" he asked in a tone too nonchalant for the situation.

Before Graham had a chance to react, Charlie snapped the gun loose from his hand and twisted his other arm back around him, dropping him to his knees. Fitz stopped dead as he watched her limber as a lion attacking its prey. This is exactly what Fitz had told her not to do. Given it was clear that Graham wasn't going to sit and have a nice chat with them, he didn't seem to mind it now they were in the situation.

Fitz leaned against a beam on the porch and watched Charlie do what she did best – take a large man down to the ground and have him at her mercy in seconds flat. Fitz couldn't even see what exactly she had done, but the big man was pleading for her to let go, not able to get out of the twisted hold she had him in.

Charlie leaned down close to his ear. "I worked for the CIA. I've taken down men bigger than you in less time. Slit their throat and watched them bleed out. Now I've had enough of you and this whole fake narrative about the shooting. I'm here to get answers and you're going to give them to me. Do you understand?"

"I'm not," he started to say as she twisted his arm tighter causing him to wince and lean forward, putting his other hand on the porch to stabilize himself. He cursed, his breath hot with whiskey. "You have no idea what you're stepping into."

Charlie pressed her knee into his back, forcing him to keep still. "Then educate us." Graham gritted his teeth, muscles flexing beneath her grip, but he wasn't getting free. Charlie tightened her hold. "Talk, Westbrook. We know about the meeting. We know about Coldwell, Kane, Mercer, and Graves."

Graham went still. The porch light cast deep shadows across his face, accentuating the lines on his face. "It's not what you think. It was just a meeting."

With her other hand, Charlie dug her fingers into his shoulder. "Try again."

Graham exhaled through his nose, then, in a voice that barely reached above a whisper, he said, "She fired first."

A slow, creeping dread settled over Fitz. Confirmation by someone in the room.

Charlie seemed unfazed by it. "Why did she fire first?"

"President Monroe," Graham rasped, not answering the question. He simply repeated what he had already said.

"That isn't what I asked. I asked *why* did she fire and *at whom* did she fire?"

"Let me up," Graham winced, trying and failing to wriggle free. "I promise I'll tell you if you just let me up."

Charlie released her grip on his shoulder and relaxed her hand on his arm, letting it come back to a more natural position. "If you try anything, I'll bring you down again. This time I won't be as nice. Do you understand me?"

Fitz tried to contain his smile. Charlie's whole face lit up when she was in her element. Her eyes shined and she had a confidence – swagger almost – like she was doing exactly what she was born to do. It was hard not to respect it…and, if he was going to be honest, not be attracted to it just a little. He quickly pushed those thoughts aside and focused on Graham.

"Charlie, let him up. He isn't going to do anything." Fitz raised the hem of his shirt to reveal the gun on his hip. "Charlie is armed too. We were crazy enough to break into the White House, so you can assume we are crazy enough to shoot you if that's what the situation requires. I think the rest of the men in that room would be happy to let you take the fall."

Graham flicked his eyes up to Fitz. "You don't know what they are capable of."

"I've got an idea." Fitz pushed himself off the porch post as Charlie released Graham. He slowly rose to his feet, rubbing his injured arm.

"You're fine," Charlie barked at him. "I used pressure points. There's no bone or muscle damage."

Graham glanced over at her. "You were really CIA?"

"I have the scars to prove it." Charlie looked at the front door of the home. "Do you want to go inside to talk or stay out here?"

"Inside. I need more to drink." Graham turned to walk in the home with Charlie right at his heels. She wasn't going to give him an inch to grab a weapon or call someone. He looked down at her. "You don't have to stand so close."

"Yes, I do."

Graham knew better than to pick up his gun from the porch where Charlie had tossed it like a toy from his hands. Fitz grabbed it and carried it inside, leaving it on a wooden table near the door. He was sure Graham had other weapons in the home, but there was no way Charlie was going to give him even an inch to grab for one.

After they were settled in the living room, Graham stared at the pair of them. "I didn't shoot the president," he said his tone as thick as his body. He relaxed back into a worn recliner that seemed to cocoon the man. Fitz was sure it was probably his favorite chair, something modeled from the man's body. "I won't deny that I was in the room when it happened."

"You can't deny that you were in the room," Fitz said with an incredulous laugh. "We have several witness statements from people who put you there. I also know that you picked up bullets from the crime scene and put them in your desk."

Graham looked away, guilt on his face. "I did but I was directed to."

"Who directed you?"

"David Sparks. By the time Dave got to the room, everyone else was gone. I was just standing in the middle of the Oval Office, trying to process what had just happened. Sebastian and Ian were long gone with the president. They took her to the hospital in his SUV. I honestly thought she was dead. I don't know how she survived being shot like that. There was a lot of blood." He closed his eyes and breathed through his nose. "More blood than…"

"Than you thought there'd be," Charlie said, finishing his thought. He nodded in response. "Was that the first time you ever saw someone shot up close?"

Graham dropped his head in a nod. "No one was supposed to have been shot that night."

Fitz had so many questions he didn't know where to start. He figured at the beginning. "What was the reason for the meeting?"

"Adrian Mercer and Speaker Graves wanted to speak to President Monroe about a company called Percepta Tech. Have you heard of it?"

Fitz hadn't. He turned to Charlie and she was shaking her head no.

"It's new burgeoning AI technology used for law enforcement and intelligence."

"That sounds dangerous," Charlie said, the words slipping from her mouth echoing what Fitz was thinking. "I know AI is up and coming and moving at a speed we are never going to slow down. I can't imagine turning over any legal work to artificial intelligence. It sounds like a horror movie waiting to happen."

Graham didn't disagree with her. "The company has benefits but a lot of potential to go wrong. It's why President Monroe wasn't going to roll it out. She wasn't going to give the company government investments to help develop it further at least on the government's dime. My understanding from conversations that I've overheard is that Mercer and Graves were heavily invested in this company and they wanted it implemented. They both endorsed Coldwell for president because he was the one who promised he'd get the company the investments it needed. Coldwell was ready to go. He said he'd start at smaller local police departments then possibly the FBI, CIA, NSA – all those three letter agencies."

Fitz said, "That's a hefty promise and not something I recall ever being mentioned on the campaign trail."

Graham laughed. "You think the American public is going to toss away their civil liberties like that? No one dared mention anything about a government partnership with this tech. They'd be insane to do so. It looked like all hope was lost when Monroe was nominated. There was no way she was going down the path of this technology. I wouldn't say she's anti-AI, but she's much more measured in her response to it. I think we have to be. Some camps say China isn't going to be measured and we need to compete. There are no brakes on this. We need brakes. Kind of like unleashing social media then realizing all that can go wrong with it."

Fitz wanted to ask more about the company and technology, but he felt himself starting to fall down a rabbit hole. He needed them back on track. "That's what the meeting was about?"

"Percepta Tech. All those men were there to pressure her to ensure the company had the funding it needed. They weren't going to take no for an answer. They thought they could strong-arm President Monroe. Even Richard Avery had promised them that he'd get his wife in line."

"His wife in line," Charlie said her tone sharp and biting. "His wife is the most powerful woman in the world."

"Yeah," Graham agreed, "and she wasn't budging. No amount of arguing or strong-arming was going to work. She was as stubborn as I'd ever heard her."

Fitz leaned forward, already knowing the answer. "What happened when she told them no?"

"All hell broke loose."

CHAPTER 29

Charlie was on her feet, not able to sit still. "Tell me specifically what happened. Also, why were you in the room and not Ian?" She asked a few more questions in rapid succession, overwhelming him. He asked her to slow down. "Start with why you were in the room and not Ian."

"I have a prior relationship with Speaker Graves. He's comfortable with me and he assumed that he'd be able to speak to President Monroe in a way that Ian or Sebastian wouldn't allow."

"What does that mean?" Fitz pressed him. "What is the prior relationship?"

Graham's jaw hitched to the side and he mumbled something Fitz couldn't hear. When Fitz asked him again, the agent admitted, "I'm Graves's nephew by marriage. My aunt and he are divorced though. I guess he thought he could trust me."

"Does the Secret Service know about this connection?"

"I assume so. It shouldn't make a difference. I'm still there to do a job."

Charlie stopped pacing. "You allowed someone to shoot the president right in front of you and they are still living."

Graham took a breath.

Fitz wanted to tell her to pull back. They had Graham talking and that's what they needed. Reading his body language and his tone, he was ready to shut down. "How did you feel about President Monroe?"

Graham took his focus from Charlie back to Fitz. "I didn't dislike her. I had a job to do and it's not my business to get into her politics. I didn't agree with a lot of what she was doing. You have to understand I had no idea that she was going to be shot. I also had no idea that she was going to pull a gun that night. I didn't even know she had a gun. I still don't even know where she got the gun and neither does her husband. It was a shock to all of us."

"Where was the gun that night?" Charlie asked, calming down and sitting down next to Fitz.

"She had it in a holster on her side. It was under her shirt. She pulled a gun on Coldwell in the middle of a heated debate when he wouldn't back down."

"Wait a minute," Fitz said. "She was aiming at Henry Coldwell?"

Graham nodded. "That's the direction she was shooting. He was the only one standing there."

Charlie wasn't buying it. "Why would Monroe pull a gun on her vice president? Explain that to me because that doesn't even make any logical sense."

As Graham hesitated to respond, Fitz filled in the silence. "She must have felt threatened somehow." Charlie asked him the same question a few different ways. Graham wasn't budging. "I don't have another answer other than that."

Fitz changed it up. "Why was Marcus Kane present at that meeting?"

That he would answer. "The FBI director was there because President Monroe asked him to be there. He is opposed to AI technology and doesn't want to see it used for law enforcement. He said there are too many risks and flaws in the system. It was Avery, Mercer, and Graves who were pushing for it. Vice President Coldwell certainly wanted the technology. He had invested in the company and stands to gain a good deal of money if it takes off. His policies are much more on the side of a police state."

Fitz blanched at that term. "That's pretty extreme. There's a difference between having more efficient and stringent policing and having a *police state*."

"Coldwell's views on policing in America are pretty extreme. If it were up to him we'd expand for-profit prisons, provide harsher penalties on all crimes, and take away all education or anything in prison systems that prepare people for the outside. He wants people to suffer."

Fitz shook his head. "That doesn't do anyone any good."

Graham shrugged it off. "Those are his views and he was pushing hard for it. I've had a front seat to several arguments between President Monroe and Vice President Coldwell. Marcus Kane was there to be on her side, not that anyone was going to listen to him. When Coldwell is president, Kane is going to be the first on the chopping block."

"*If* Coldwell is president," Charlie corrected him.

Graham gestured in concession.

Charlie started in on him again. "You still haven't told me why Monroe pulled a gun."

Graham shifted his eyes away from them. "I guess she felt threatened."

"*You guess* or she was threatened?" Charlie got up from the couch, crossed the room, and leaned over Graham in the chair. Fitz held his breath waiting for her to strike, but the blows she could have inflicted never came. She lowered her voice, got right in his face, and said, "I'm not going to ask this question again. We have enough information to make sure you spend the rest of your life in prison and don't think we won't do that. This is your time to save yourself. If you didn't pull the trigger and you were taken off guard by what happened, then you shouldn't take the fall for what someone else did."

Graham leaned back, putting space between them. He had a look of defiance on his face. "No matter how this goes down, I'm not going to prison."

"The only way to keep yourself out of prison is to tell us what happened."

Graham nervously licked his lips. "Henry Coldwell suggested that if Monroe didn't go along with their plan they'd make sure she was removed from office. She told them there was no reason to remove her from office, that she hadn't done anything wrong, and that they'd never get the votes. Coldwell knew that. The reality is that Monroe is liked by both sides of the aisle. She might have run under one party, but she's a policy wonk. She's a centrist who was willing to listen to people on both sides of the aisle. She was willing to gather perspectives and research from all sides before making an informed decision. Some people accused her of being wishy-washy and not taking strong positions. That wasn't true. I might not have liked everything she was doing, but she was one of the smartest people I ever met."

"She is the smartest," Charlie reminded him again. "You keep speaking about her as if she is dead. She is still alive and I suggest you remember that."

"Sorry. I honestly thought she had died that night and I can't get past how she is still alive. It's incomprehensible to me." Graham stared past them. "Anyway…Monroe was right. There was no way Coldwell or anyone else was going to get her impeached. Monroe knew it and so did every man in that room. That's when Coldwell suggested there were other ways to remove her from office. He said that and let it hang in the air. We all knew what he was talking about. Marcus Kane tried to intervene. He said we needed to take a break and let tensions cool. He offered to go to the president's private fridge and get everyone something to drink. He wanted to slow things down.

He knew they were getting off the rails. So he left the room, going into Monroe's private kitchen off the side of the Oval Office. That's when Coldwell told her that no matter what Marcus Kane said she was going to be removed from office one way or another. That's when President Monroe pulled a gun on him and ordered him out of the Oval Office. She told him she was taking his threats to Congress."

Fitz was sitting on the edge of his seat then. "What did he say?"

"Nothing. He got up from the couch and moved toward the desk. I don't know what he was going to do. I thought maybe call for Marcus Kane as the door wasn't far from there. He was the only other person in the room other than me who was armed. At least that's what I initially thought. No one said a word, not even her husband. I think they were all stunned. The whole room got eerily quiet. I tried to get her to give me the gun and she wouldn't even look at me. I had no training for that. I couldn't shoot the president. Everyone else got up to go stand with Coldwell. They were trying to protect him. Tell her to calm down. I didn't move because I was right next to her trying to figure out how to get the gun out of her hand before she fired."

Fitz was trying to imagine the scene. He needed clarification. "Are you saying that President Monroe was standing near the United States seal on the floor while Coldwell moved closer to her desk? Then the others gathered around him to protect him?"

Graham confirmed. "They were telling her to put the gun down, saying they could work it out. That Coldwell got overheated and he wasn't serious about the threat. He's a blowhard. We all know that, but he's a wimp. He wasn't going to do anything."

"What about the others? What were they saying?" Charlie asked.

"Richard Avery was telling her she couldn't shoot someone. To be honest with you, he seemed surprised she had a gun too. I don't think anyone knew what to do. I certainly didn't know what to do. If I lunged at her the gun could have gone off. Then someone called for

Marcus Kane and she fired. She fired wide, hitting the drapes and wall behind them. That's when everyone kind of scattered out of the way. More shots were fired and she was down."

Fitz knew what Graham said made sense given where the bullet went into the wall. If the men were near the desk and she shot wide that's exactly where the bullet would have lodged. "What do you mean they scattered?"

"They all moved out of her line of sight. Then one of them fired back at her three shots – pop, pop, pop. It happened before I could even react. I assume someone had a gun out. My attention had been on President Monroe, so I didn't see him pull out a gun. One of the shots grazed by my leg. That's the one that lodged in the couch." He patted the side of his thigh on the right side. "I have a nasty graze where the bullet whizzed by me. I guess that knocked me back and before I could react President Monroe had been shot twice. As she went down, she fell forward near the seal."

"I thought the Coldwell was standing on the side of the desk?" Charlie asked to clarify.

"No, I'd say more in front of it. President Monroe shot wide to that side and that's how the bullet ended up behind the desk to the right. Coldwell and the rest were standing more in front of the desk."

That made more sense to Fitz.

"Who shot her?" Charlie asked, her voice hitched and dry.

Graham shook his head. "I don't know because it would be a guess. I won't guess because that's just wrong. You can beat me, torture me. Do whatever you have to do. I'm not disclosing what I suspect."

Fitz saw the look on Charlie's face and told her to stand down. She didn't appreciate being told what to do, but she remained steady. Fitz turned back to Graham. "Where was Marcus Kane when all of this happened?"

"By the time the president was shot and on the floor, he was in the doorway of that separate area of the Oval Office. I assume he heard the first shot. There's no way he didn't but I know he didn't make it out in enough time to stop anything. It all happened so fast. President Monroe shot then someone immediately shot her almost as if they were ready and waiting. Kane rushed to her, but before he could fully check on her, Coldwell called him. Ian was already banging on the door to be let in."

"What did you do?"

"I rushed to President Monroe, but I swear to you I didn't feel a pulse. I thought she was gone. As I said there was so much blood. As I was bent over her trying to find a pulse, they ordered me to go let Ian in. I tried to tell them I didn't know if she was still alive. I went to let Ian in. Kane pulled Coldwell out of there. He told him that no one else could see that he'd been there during the shooting. Then the next thing I knew Sebastian came rushing in and scooped her up. He and Ian ran out of there through the same door Kane and Coldwell left through."

"You were left with clean-up," Charlie said. It wasn't a question. "Who told you what to do?"

"Mercer called Sparks. I honestly don't know how he wasn't down there already. Mercer told Sparks to wipe the security footage. When he asked what he was supposed to tell people, they told him just to say that there was a glitch. Then they got ready to leave. Before they were gone, Graves pulled me aside and asked me if I was sure the president was really dead. I told him I hadn't felt a pulse. We left that room believing President Monroe was dead."

"If you thought President Monroe was dead, shouldn't the vice president have stuck around since he was next in line and we need a continuity of government?" Charlie asked, her eyes shifting to look at Fitz. He got the sense she didn't believe all of his recounting. Fitz wasn't sure how much he believed either.

Graham didn't have an answer for that. "Kane wanted Coldwell out of that room."

Fitz zeroed in on him. "You're sure that it wasn't Kane who shot her?"

"I don't believe so," Graham said, even though there was a tinge of uncertainty in his voice. "He wasn't even in the Oval when it started."

"You took the bullets from the wall and the couch and put them in your desk?"

Graham nodded. "Sparks told me to. I didn't know what to do with them. I put them in my desk and eventually threw them in a dumpster."

"Why?" Fitz asked, not understanding destroying evidence like that.

Graham didn't have an answer. "I was following orders."

"What about Zachary Steele?" Charlie asked.

Graham clamped his mouth shut. "I'm not talking about that." He looked at his watch. "I've said all I'm going to say. You need to leave." He stood and Fitz waited for Charlie to move on him again but she didn't. She might have felt like Fitz – this was all they were going to get from Graham and they weren't even sure what was true.

CHAPTER 30

The rain remained steady after leaving Graham's house. On the drive back to D.C., a rhythmic tap beat against the windows, as if the sky was trying to wash away the mood that had settled over them.

Fitz didn't want to drop Charlie off and go home. His mind was still trying to work over what Graham had told them. The flickering neon lights of a diner up ahead beckoned him.

"Hungry?" he asked barely above a whisper.

Charlie murmured a noncommittal sure.

He pulled into the gravel parking lot and cut the engine. They filed out slowly as if neither of them had moved in a long time. The rain pelted them as they made their way to the front door.

Inside, the low hum of the neon lights flickered faintly, casting a glow over the retro booths and the cracked linoleum floor. The smell of grease and frying bacon hung in the air, mixing with the dampness of the rain outside. The diner was old, the kind that had seen decades of secrets and broken dreams slide across its counter. The walls were cluttered with old photographs and half-faded posters. It was a place where things slowed down, crawled to a stop.

Once seated in a booth away from the few other patrons – a guy hunched over a cup of coffee at the counter, a younger couple snuggled on the same side of the booth in the back – Fitz leaned back in the vinyl booth, eyes heavy, his dark, unshaven face reflecting the fatigue of a long day.

Before they could even look at their menus, the server dropped two coffees for them without being asked. She must have read the looks on their faces, seen people just like them a million times in her life. Using the diner as some kind of refuge. A break in life.

They ordered quickly, neither one needing to look at the menu. Every diner across America seemed to have the same fare and that's what they both needed – comfort food.

Charlie sat across from him, eyes narrowed, but her gaze wasn't focused on him. She stared at her cup of coffee, steam rising lazily from it. "That interview was helpful but raised a lot more questions. I'm not even sure how much of what he told us was the truth. Maybe I shouldn't have gone so hard on him when we got there."

"You didn't have a choice. If you hadn't, he wouldn't have said anything." Graham Westbrook's face was still fresh in his mind, his answers dancing around the truth like a well-rehearsed performance. The way he'd deflected their questions, how his words didn't match his body language, how he'd shifted his eyes when they asked him who pulled the trigger. That split second of hesitation.

They retreated into themselves until the clink of silverware against plates broke through the silence, the sound almost jarring. The waitress, with her apron stained from countless greasy dinners, slid a plate in front of Charlie. A sloppy stack of pancakes, drenched in syrup, with a pat of butter melting on top. Fitz had ordered the same, though his stomach churned at the sight. The last thing he felt like doing was eating, but the ritual of comfort food was too ingrained. Right now, the routine was all they had to hold on to.

Charlie didn't touch her pancakes right away, her fingers tapping the edge of the plate absentmindedly. "I can't believe he wouldn't tell us who shot the president. We were right there on the edge of finding out what happened and he snatched it away."

Fitz knew what she was feeling. "He has more to lose than Sebastian and Ian. He was there, a witness to it. He took evidence from the scene. He's implicated in that and probably a lot more. Did you see the way he stopped the moment we brought up Zachary Steele? I think we can safely assume he was a part of that. Might have even pulled the trigger himself."

Charlie shrugged, her tired eyes finally lifting to meet his. "I think he's the one who shot Steele. But without proof, we're just spinning our wheels. We need something solid, Fitz. Anything." She let out a long sigh, one that carried the weight of a thousand unspoken thoughts.

For a moment, neither of them spoke. They simply stared at their food, letting the tiredness settle in. The diner's quiet hum, the rain outside, the warm glow of the overhead lights – nothing felt comforting tonight.

They ate methodically, cutting, biting, and chewing. Fitz wasn't even sure he tasted the pancakes as they went down but the food warmed his belly. After several bites, he felt a little of his energy returning. It had just been such a bad situation all around. Every time they turned over one rock, they found several smaller rocks that all needed flipping. Fitz finished off the pancakes before Charlie, who was taking tentative bites as she stared blankly down at the plate.

"We need to snap out of this," Fitz said, more commanding than he meant.

Charlie took one more bite then added her knife and fork to the plate and pushed it aside. She wiped her mouth on her napkin and took one last long sip of coffee. She raised her eyes to Fitz. "You're right. No more pity party. What do we know so far – facts that we can substantiate?"

Fitz ran through the evidence that more than one witness had told them and was backed up by the evidence they saw – the fact that the shooting took place in the Oval, the players in the room, the fact that President Monroe not only had a gun but had shot first, the witnesses had been told to lie both at the White House and at the hospital, and Zachary Steele had been murdered by the Secret Service in the cover-up.

"I don't trust Adrian Mercer," Charlie said after Fitz was through. "I don't even understand why he was there that night."

"Why do you say that?"

"He is a mid-level House of Representative member from Missouri. He doesn't have much of a name for himself, always votes the party line, and hasn't taken a lead in the House."

"He was CIA though? Doesn't that count for something?"

Charlie squinted at him as if she couldn't believe what he was asking. "Everyone else was a senior member of the executive branch. Mercer is nobody. Being a CIA agent isn't the same as being Speaker of the House."

"I'm sure he's been involved in clean-up like that before," Fitz countered. "Maybe they brought him in for his CIA skills."

"It was never Mercer who did the clean-up. We had people for that."

"Maybe he was the shooter. The CIA has overthrown governments before. He might have been the only one to see that up close."

Charlie didn't disagree with that. "Possibly. There had to have been a specific reason."

"Do you believe Graham saying that Coldwell threatened Monroe like that?"

Charlie shrugged. "Whatever the reason, President Monroe had good instincts that they were coming for her. What she didn't have was what a lot of women lack in gun situations – the readiness to shoot someone. That's why a woman having a weapon at home is more likely to have it taken from her and used against her."

"Is that true?" Fitz asked. He had heard safety experts telling women that if they had a firearm in the house they should practice with it. Fitz always assumed that was just so they knew how to use it.

"Both are true – that they are more likely to have their guns used against them and that they aren't prepared to pull the trigger. Thinking about pulling the trigger, shooting at the range, and being faced with an intruder or even worse someone they love trying to hurt them – it's a whole different ballgame to know you're about to end someone's life. I think President Monroe intentionally shot wide to scare them. They were so close in the Oval. I don't think she could have missed. She felt threatened by one of them."

Fitz had been considering that since being inside the Oval Office. Something Graham had said about Kane made him look at the FBI director differently. "Do you think Kane was used that night? I don't think he was involved in the shooting or the cover-up. No one puts him in the Oval at the time of the shooting. Everyone puts him in the room off the Oval. He does serve a purpose though."

"They wanted to implicate him so he'd be sworn to secrecy," Charlie said, capturing exactly what Fitz had been thinking. "It's diabolical. Bring the man who'd be in charge of the investigation into the room so he'd implicate himself in the shooting. Of course, he'd help derail the investigation. He's not going to admit to being there. He's certainly not going to help topple the government in that way."

Fitz wasn't sure how the men knew Kane wouldn't have stopped the shooting or even if he could have stopped them. They knew him better than Fitz did though and what he had learned about the man, hadn't impressed him. "I don't think Kane knew there'd be a shooting, but he's responsible for participating in the aftermath."

"I don't think he knew or participated in the shooting either," Charlie echoed. "If this is all about the AI tech as Graham suggests then I can understand why President Monroe would want him there."

"I don't understand why he left with Coldwell."

Charlie didn't know either. "What do you think about the AI technology as a motive? Would you be against it?"

"I think it's probably broader than the tech. They wanted Coldwell as president. That I can understand. The tech was just the tip of the iceberg." Fitz explained he'd be against AI technology too. It was the kind of thing that could easily be weaponized against citizens. It might prevent some crime but at what cost to civil liberties? He didn't know where Charlie fell on the spectrum. "What about you? What do you know about that kind of technology?"

"Nothing can replace human sources," she said. "I think there's a time and a place for that kind of technology. Look at what drones do for gathering intel. It's safer and gives us more than assets on the ground. We aren't relying on AI to interpret that data alone for us though. I don't want AI to replace human policing. There are a million things that could go wrong with it. There's enough wrong with the criminal justice system and the intelligence field as it is. Technology has a time and place. I've always been someone who expressed optimistic caution."

"I assume Marcus Kane would have thought the same. He certainly wasn't going to be advocating to put the FBI out of work." Fitz tugged his cellphone from his pocket. He thumbed the button for the internet but nothing came up. "We don't have decent cell service here. I was going to pull up the company website."

"We can do that tomorrow. What about Speaker Graves? Do you have a perception of him?"

Fitz put the phone down on the table. "He's not well-liked. He considered a run for president a few years ago. Before you started working with me, his team asked me to pull opposition research on him to see how he'd fare in the public. There was a lot the man wanted to keep hidden – financial debt, shady business dealings, a sexual harassment allegation from years back when he was just coming up in local politics. He had a DUI too and suspected drug use."

Charlie grimaced. "How'd he get as far as he has?" It was a rhetorical question. She knew, probably better than anyone, the kinds of secrets those in politics had. "It was good he didn't bother running. Is that when he backed Henry Coldwell?"

Fitz nodded. "They had been in the House together for several years. Coldwell was more palatable as far as his background. As Graham said, he was never going to be nominated. He wouldn't fare well in a general election. I'm frankly surprised he didn't cost Monroe the presidency. If you remember everyone in the media was going hard at her for choosing him as a running mate. There was nothing in his background like Graves though."

"You think either of them could have shot Monroe?"

Fitz didn't know. "Right now, any one of them including Graham is a suspect."

Charlie sat back and appraised him. "You think he could have shot her?"

As far as Fitz was concerned, they all had some guilt. He just didn't know who among them was the one who pulled the trigger. "The Secret Service is compromised, the FBI is compromised, and the executive branch of the government is compromised. They are all guilty in some way, if only for the fact they participated in the cover-up."

"What about Richard Avery?"

Fitz sat back in the booth. "You know, of everyone present, he is the one I suspect the most. He had the most motive of all of them. His wife was cheating on him. If he had money tied up in this technology and she wasn't willing to implement it, who knows how much he would have lost? He had the most to gain by her death."

"Outside of Vice President Henry Coldwell."

"Yeah, outside of him." Fitz took a deep breath. The cover-up was predicated on one thing – protecting national security. Fitz knew they were both thinking about it. He had no idea what would happen in the United States if the second and third in command were accused of shooting the president. Nothing like that had happened in the history of the United States.

As if reading his mind, Charlie said, "Democracy is far more fragile than people think. That said, I have to believe that the majority wouldn't stand for the attempted assassination of the president in the Oval by anyone, let alone people in their party. Monroe was also popular across the aisle. The lie about national security was just a lie to protect the guilty party."

The server approached the table with a check in one hand while asking if they wanted anything else. They declined and Fitz pulled cash from his wallet and handed it over. Charlie offered but he declined. "It's on the office." Once the server was gone, he asked, "What's the plan now?"

Charlie didn't hesitate. "In the morning we go to Last Covenant and ask about Zachary Steele. I want to know how he got caught up in this plot. We might not be able to solve President Monroe's attempted assassination but we might be able to solve who murdered him."

"That might lead us to whoever is responsible," Fitz said, hoping something was clearer by morning light.

CHAPTER 31

Fitz gripped the steering wheel with white knuckles, the veins in his hands bulging, his mind a hurricane of thoughts. Charlie sat silently beside him, eyes scanning the narrow, winding roads of Virginia. The early morning sun cast long shadows over the fields and trees.

"We're close," Fitz finally said, his voice low and steady. "At least, I think we are."

They hadn't spoken much since they met earlier that morning at the office. They just wanted to get this trip to Last Covenant out of the way. The cult members thought their leader – Paul Berardo – was like a second coming of Jesus. All of his followers believed him to be some kind of prophet. Every three-letter agency in Washington had been watching Last Covenant. Most were too afraid to take action. Afraid it would turn out like Waco. Fitz understood that. Waco had been one mistake after another and an embarrassment for the DEA and the FBI. No one wanted a repeat.

Most thought Last Covenant was a front for white supremacist militia. Fitz figured that was at least partially true. They had weapons – all legal as far as anyone could tell. They were known for a white supremacist podcast. The cult had gone mainstream and high-tech with their message to reach a broader audience. Fitz was warned not to visit and certainly not to visit alone. He didn't think they had much choice. If anything, Fitz was hoping Paul might welcome them, given they were there to exonerate one of their own. That was the hope anyway.

Fitz had been driving down the two-lane rural road for the past half-hour. He had followed the directions meticulously but was starting to feel like maybe he had missed a turn. He'd keep going for another five miles then turn back.

As the third mile passed, the compound emerged like a wound in the landscape. The property was like a forgotten relic. The overgrown fields stretched for miles, choked by a sea of tangled grass that had long since swallowed any trace of cultivation. The air was thick with the stench of damp earth and rotting wood. The road leading up to the compound was cracked and uneven, the asphalt broken into jagged slabs. Dust swirled in the wind, the only movement in an otherwise dead landscape.

The property line was marked by a rusting, dilapidated chain-link fence, its wire taut in some places, sagging in others, and peppered with holes. The gate, twisted and bent out of shape, hung crookedly from a single post.

"Welcome to Last Covenant," Fitz muttered, half to himself, half to Charlie. "You ready for this?"

She didn't answer, but her jaw tightened, her eyes narrowing as she studied the building.

Fitz pulled his SUV to a stop in front of the gate in the sagging chain-link fence. It looked like the wind had knocked it forward. Fitz assumed the next strong storm might take it down completely. Four no-trespassing signs told them to stay out – two tacked to nearby trees and two on either side of the gate. The message was clear but not enough to make them stop.

Fitz got out of the SUV and dragged the gate open, the spikes of the metal leaving tracks in the dirt. From the gate, there wasn't a clear view of the rest of the compound. One of Fitz's law enforcement friends said they had to go around the bend in the road before the rest of the property would come into view. Fitz wondered if anyone would stop them or worse shoot at them before they could make it that far.

He got back into the SUV and inched it forward, tapping the gas lightly.

"Give it some gas," Charlie said, still looking out the front window. "If they are going to shoot at us, they are going to shoot no matter how fast or slow we are going. We might as well move quickly."

Fitz did as he was told, side-eyeing her. Just as he'd been told, as soon as he rounded the bend, the rest of the property stood there like some beacon to the past. The farmhouse was more ominous than Fitz had envisioned. Its once-white paint was now a ghostly shade of gray. Its wooden frame sagged under the weight of years of neglect. The roof, bowed and uneven, looked as though it might cave in on itself at any moment.

To the left of the farmhouse was a massive barn. The main doors hung askew, one partially open. The roof had partially collapsed on one side, creating a jagged skylight that allowed rain and wildlife to enter freely. Remnants of farm equipment rusted in the tall grass around its perimeter, their original purposes now impossible to determine.

The church stood apart – a simple wooden building that seemed to have been transplanted from a century ago. Its white steeple, surprisingly intact, rose above the property. The windows were tall and narrow and a set of wooden steps led to double doors, their original varnish now black with age and weather.

Despite the property's apparent abandonment, there was an unsettling sense of occupation – small signs that suggested life continued here – a pile of freshly cut wood next to the barn, a thin trail of smoke rising from the chimney, the faint sound of voices carried on the wind.

Fitz would have called out and announced them but there was no one around. He came to a stop next to two sedans, one looking newer than the other. An old beat-up pick-up was parked on the other side of the farmhouse. The space offered no clear driveway. Fitz pulled into the well-worn tracks and cut the engine. Charlie reached for the door, but Fitz's hand stopped her. "Wait."

He opened the glove compartment, pulling out another gun. "Take an extra."

Charlie pulled up the hem of her shirt, flashing one gun then did the same with her pant leg. "You know I always carry two."

Fitz put the gun back in the glove box. He had two guns on him as well. He should have known she always carried back up. He had told Amy where they were going and instructed her that if he didn't check in by eleven that morning, she was to call Agent Burrows and alert the FBI. Fitz simply didn't know what their visit would trigger. They had to be prepared for anything.

"We'll play this by ear," Fitz instructed her. While her CIA training might have worked on Graham, they were outnumbered here at Last Covenant. It might look like there was no one around, but Fitz knew their numbers were well above one hundred. Not all of them lived on the compound but there'd be enough to take them out.

Charlie asked, "You think they'll even talk to us?"

Fitz nodded grimly. "If we go in as friends, someone who can tell them they know Zachary Steele is innocent and wrongly murdered by the government, we can probably bridge the gap and get them to talk."

The farmhouse loomed ahead of them, dark windows like watchful eyes. Fitz and Charlie stepped out of the car, their boots crunching on the gravel as they walked toward the front door.

The air was thick with unease. Fitz could feel it in the pit of his stomach – the same feeling he got when he knew they were being watched.

Charlie knocked on the door. The sound was louder than it should have been, echoing across the empty fields. The door creaked open a moment later, revealing a man who appeared to be in his forties, his face gaunt, his eyes too tired to be entirely alert. His brown tee-shirt had a rip along the shoulder and his jeans appeared as if they'd seen better days.

"You shouldn't be here." His voice was low and rough, as though he hadn't used it much lately. "Didn't you see the no trespassing signs?"

"We saw them," Fitz said. "We are here to speak to Paul Berardo."

The man's eyes flickered briefly, hesitation crossing his features. "I don't know if that's such a good idea. Are you cops or something?"

Fitz shook his head. "We are not cops. We think the FBI got it wrong about Zachary Steele and we want to set the record straight. We need Paul's help to do that."

The man eyed him cautiously. Fitz pulled out his wallet to show him identification. The man glanced down at it. "If you're not a cop, what are you?"

"Opposition researchers. We dig up dirt on politicians and business leaders." Fitz hoped describing what he did that way might lend him some good grace. He gestured toward Charlie and introduced her. "Honestly, we are off the record investigating the shooting of President Monroe and we don't believe Zachary Steele is guilty. If anything, we think the shooting was done by someone in the government and Steele was used as a cover-up. We think he was murdered."

"I think you should leave," the man said, his hand inching toward the door.

But Fitz was already moving. He stepped forward, keeping his tone even but firm. "We're not going anywhere until we get some answers. Who's in charge here?"

The man's expression shifted again, this time to one of reluctant resignation. "You should've stayed away."

He stepped aside, opening the door wide enough for them to pass. Fitz exchanged a quick look with Charlie, who nodded imperceptibly. They entered the house.

The interior was dim, lit by flickering candles that seemed to cast strange shadows on the walls. The smell of incense was overwhelming, the kind that made you feel lightheaded. Figures moved in the corners of the room, faces obscured by darkness.

At the far end of the room stood a man with a swath of dark messy hair. Tall and imposing, his features sharp and his gaze cold. He wore a loose-fitting white shirt, almost tunic-like. His hands folded in front of him as he observed Fitz and Charlie with an unreadable expression.

"Why are you poking around in things that don't concern you?" he asked, his voice low and controlled. The man had the look of someone who had dealt with threats before and knew how to play the game. His gaze lingered on Charlie, but he didn't make any obvious move toward aggression.

Fitz sized him up. This man was the leader of Last Covenant, and Fitz had no illusions about what he was capable of. "We're just looking for answers. About Steele. We know his connection here. We thought you could help prove he's innocent."

Paul's lips twitched, but he didn't respond immediately. Instead, he waved toward the shadows, where another man stepped forward. A younger figure, his eyes darting nervously. He looked down at the young man. "Do you think Zachary was innocent?"

"No," the young man said with a shake of his head. "He thought he could make decisions on his own. He was planning things that you didn't allow. He was going outside of your teachings."

The leader of Last Covenant shifted, his gaze flicking to Fitz. "You see, Zachary might not have pulled the trigger that morning, but he was planning in the shadows. His actions disgraced my congregation. He wasn't following orders. That is why he didn't make a good soldier. You know that he was kicked out of the Army for disobeying. I thought I might be able to turn him around. He aligned with us in some ways. But he didn't trust enough. He wasn't faithful enough."

"Was he here much?" Charlie asked and Paul didn't even look in her direction. She narrowed her eyes at him. "Did you hear my question?"

With his gaze firmly remaining on Fitz, Paul said, "You're not much of a man if you let a woman talk like that. You are to be in command at all times. She is to be silent."

Fitz reached for Charlie's arm, knowing any talk like that and she'd have him down to the floor in seconds flat and then they'd be battling with who knew how many men. He ignored what Paul said, "Did you want President Monroe dead?"

"A woman has no right to lead this country. That is not what God made her for. Have you not read your bible?"

"Which one?" Fitz asked off-handedly as the cult leader's right eye twitched in response. Fitz knew this wasn't the path to go down. "Look, you can believe whatever you want to believe. I'm not here to question your faith or to challenge it. If you don't want Charlie to ask you questions, then we won't push that. You're not going to question my manhood or the way I do business though. And you sure aren't going to disparage her. I'm going to ask one more time, do you know anything about what happened to Zachary Steele? If we can clear him of any wrongdoing, then you are clearing Last Covenant. I know that you have the feds breathing down your back. If they think you were involved in an assassination attempt, it's going to be Waco all over again."

Paul swallowed hard. No one wanted another Waco and he knew all too well what the government could do. "When Zachary first got out of the Army, he came here. As I said, he wasn't good at following the rules. While I didn't kick him out, I told him he had to live somewhere else. He was riling up the others too much. When that woman was elected, Steele was bent on taking revenge. He wanted her dead as much as we all did. We just had different methods to go about it."

"I'd be careful admitting that," Fitz cautioned him.

Paul didn't seem dissuaded. "We didn't do anything. I cautioned Zachary not to do anything either. He was posting online and in forums about his displeasure. He was being vocal about something I told him not to be vocal about. The Lord would have told me when it was time to strike and I hadn't been given the orders yet. I told Zachary to stand down. His activities brought them."

"Brought who?" Fitz asked, not sure he understood.

"The other people who wanted her dead."

Fitz stepped back uncertain. "Who was that?"

"The government men. They came here to the edge of the compound to speak to Zachary about three months ago. At first, I thought they were here to arrest him for what he was posting. I was wrong. When Zachary came to me, he told me they wanted to work with him to remove the president. It was clear they had a mission for him." Paul's dark eyes zeroed in on Fitz. "He thought it was some kind of sign that he was doing good. We both know they were lying. They were going to use him. I tried to tell him that. I tried to tell him it wasn't time. That this wasn't the work of God but of Satan. He didn't listen to me."

Charlie remained still at Fitz's side, their arms touching as they stood motionless. She had the good sense not to say a word. It was Fitz who was having trouble finding his voice. "Do you know their names?"

"Sparks was the only name he gave Zachary. There was another man in the SUV. He didn't come out and he didn't speak." For the first time, Paul took a step towards Fitz, who remained firmly planted. "The other man who didn't reveal himself…Zachary was sure it was her husband." Paul held his arms open wide. "Maybe this is the one time I was wrong – maybe it was sanctioned by God. The husband's place is at the head of the family and she usurped his power. He was righting the wrong."

Fitz reached his hand down and gripped Charlie by the arm, both to steady himself and to ensure she didn't propel herself forward like he was sure she wanted to do. Fitz asked a few more questions that didn't yield any more. When he was done, he said through gritted teeth, "Thank you for the information. It was helpful."

Paul wasn't done with him though. "You seem like a good man. You should come back and join us sometime. I could teach you a thing or two."

Fitz stared at the cult leader, hoping to never lay eyes on him again. Their retreat out of the compound was faster than their arrival.

CHAPTER 32

"You should have let me hit him," Charlie said to Fitz as they made their way back to the interstate. "Have you ever seen anyone so smug and self-righteous? I'm not allowed to even speak to him?" She cursed a streak of things she had wanted to say to Paul but had held herself back from saying.

His eyes remained on the road. "If you had hit him, we'd be dead right now," he reminded her again when her rant finished. Fitz firmly believed that had Charlie done anything to step out of line in Paul's estimation they'd be dead. While Fitz couldn't see the other men on the compound, he had acutely felt their presence. If Paul had told them to harm Fitz and Charlie, that's what they would have done, no questions asked. The irony was that it was Zachary's stubborn will to kill the president, going against Paul's orders, that had been the key to his demise.

"Do you believe him?" Charlie asked when they were on the interstate heading towards Zachary's apartment.

Fitz didn't have any reason to believe the man. Yet, he did. "If he's not telling the truth, then he has inside government information. He'd have no way of knowing Sparks was the one who was the supervisor that night. If you remember, he wasn't scheduled to work but was the one there. Ethan, who was at the gate, told us that at the start. His regular supervisor wasn't there that night and had been replaced by David Sparks for no apparent reason. We also haven't heard of anyone else connected to the case with the name Sparks. Plus, he said Zachary recognized Richard Avery."

Charlie blew out a frustrated breath. "I knew I didn't trust Avery. But to hire someone to kill his wife."

"We don't know that's exactly what he did," Fitz said cautioning her. "We don't know that they paid him. We don't know the extent of the conversation at all. While I believe what Paul said about them meeting, and I think we can assume it was about the assassination, we don't know what went down." Fitz felt like he was waffling in his mind about the extent of the plan between the three of them. It was clear from what Paul said that Zachary on his own wanted to kill President Monroe. The Secret Service and the FBI were known to monitor online activity for such things. If they were coming to formally question Zachary about that or arrest him for making a threat, they wouldn't have sent Sparks and they certainly wouldn't have sent her husband.

"You're talking yourself in and out of it, aren't you?" Charlie said with a knowing glance. "I get it, Fitz. It's a hard pill to swallow."

Fitz gestured toward his cellphone. "Call Sebastian Cole while I'm driving and ask."

Charlie reached for his phone in the center console and scrolled until she found the number, the Bluetooth picked up the ringing then Sebastian's tentative hello. "It's Charlie and Fitz here," she said. "Can you tell us about the relationship between David Sparks and Richard Avery?"

"Relationship?" Sebastian asked, confusion evident.

Fitz chimed in. "We don't know much of anything about David Sparks. He's a major player in this situation. He was on duty as a supervisor that night when he shouldn't have been. He was directly involved in the cover-up."

"He was?" Sebastian asked. This time he didn't sound confused or even surprised. "I knew this had to go higher up in the agency. Higher than my team. Sparks was on Richard's detail on the campaign trail before he was promoted. A lot of other good agents were passed over for that promotion. Sparks has been with the agency for ten years, but he's not the best we have."

Charlie leaned forward toward the phone. "Has he ever done anything of concern?"

"No, not directly. He let Richard get away with a lot during the campaign. They became quite close. Not that I can say much given my own relationship."

That told Fitz that the two men had a rapport. It was more than the husband of the president and a random Secret Service supervisor. Sparks knew Richard in the way few would. "Would it surprise you to know that we think Sparks might have been involved in the planning?"

"Nothing would surprise me anymore. What did you find out?"

Charlie relayed the meeting they had with Paul at Last Covenant. "He explained to us that Zachary was motivated to see President Monroe removed from office. He didn't think a woman should have the position. He was posting online a lot. We assumed the Secret Service kept watch for those kinds of threats."

Sebastian confirmed they did.

Charlie continued. "We believe they used those online threats to find someone to kill her or to use as a patsy. We don't know exactly what the three of them planned. We know Sparks and Avery met with Zachary out at Last Covenant three months before the shooting. There was significant advanced planning."

Sebastian cursed with the full force of anger. "That was shortly after the election. She wasn't even sworn in by that point. Are you telling me they were planning to kill her almost as soon as she was elected?"

Fitz had been so focused on the fact that Paul had provided them with names that he hadn't stopped to consider the timing. "I guess you're right. It would have been late November." The implication of that meant only one thing – they had used getting President Monroe elected to install Vice President Henry Coldwell as the actual president. They weren't even going to give her time to get started. Most of her cabinet had barely gone through Congressional hearings.

Charlie's face registered the same disgust that Fitz felt. "We still don't know who the shooter is. Graham told us that the motive might have been software company Percepta Tech. Have you heard of that?"

"Yeah," Sebastian said, his tone sharp. "It was an ongoing debate inside her team while Abigail was running for president. It's one of the main reasons some in the party didn't want them to pick Coldwell as her running mate. Not only had he invested in the tech and for-profit prisons, but he wanted to run things like a police state. He thought there should be harsher punishments for everything. Coldwell thought the more people he could incarcerate, the better society would be."

"The United States already has the highest incarceration rates in the world. We make up twenty-five percent of the world's prison population but only five percent of the world's population," Charlie responded, pulling facts that even Fitz hadn't known. When he questioned the accuracy, she quoted the study where the data came from. "I keep up on these things."

Sebastian cleared his throat reminding them he was there. "There was no way Abigail was going to let AI software dominate our criminal justice system. She was adamantly against it and looking for allies to back her up. It's one of the reasons it didn't come up on the campaign trail. There is almost no one in the criminal justice system in favor of it. Not only would it eliminate jobs but there are so many things that could go wrong with it. It was a non-starter except for a small select few."

"Then why choose Coldwell as a running mate?" Fitz asked.

"Pressure from those in her circle. Her husband more than anyone. He convinced her that she needed him to win the votes of those remaining who weren't convinced a woman could be president. I knew it was going to lead to trouble. I begged her to pick someone... anyone else. In the end, Abigail listened to Richard."

"What about Marcus Kane? Was he for or against the tech?"

"He was against it," Sebastian said with some hesitation in his voice. "He's close to Speaker Graves and they have had some long conversations about the tech. Kane was against it, but I think he could have been convinced to try it."

Fitz only had one last question for him. "If someone told me that Kane was at the meeting because Abigail asked him to be there to help support her position against this technology, do you think that's accurate?"

"Is that who I saw leaving that night?"

Fitz realized then he hadn't updated Sebastian about that. "You saw both Coldwell and Kane fleeing."

Sebastian sighed. He didn't comment further. He answered Fitz's original question. "I know Kane was supportive of Abigail. At first, he was adamantly against the tech. His stance softened over time. I assumed Graves convinced him. He might have bought some stock in the company too. I can't say for sure. All I know is if Percepta Tech was implemented, it stood to make a small group of people a lot of money. It would radically change how we do criminal justice in this country – and not in a good way."

They ended the call and Fitz still wasn't sure which way he was falling on Kane. His guilt or innocence still hung in the balance. He'd need to learn more about the tech and explore its founders. If he was going to bring this to Senator Ford, he'd need to connect the dots.

Fitz headed toward Congress Heights in the southeast quadrant of

Washington D.C. It was an area of high poverty and high crime. When Fitz's GPS announced their arrival, he pulled his SUV to the curb in front of the address.

The street where Zachary had lived was a mix of nice residential homes on one end but a ruin of neglect at the other. The southeast quadrant of D.C. had its share of forgotten corners, and this one was no exception. Rowhouses, once dignified, now sagged under the weight of peeling paint, boarded-up windows, and rusted railings. Streetlights flickered weakly, casting more shadow than light, while the stench of trash filled the air. A distant siren howled, a reminder that crime was never far.

Fitz stood at the base of the rowhouse, shoulders hunched inside his dark jacket, scanning the cracked pavement and broken porch steps leading to the front door. The third floor was their target. The FBI had already searched the apartment. Fitz wasn't sure what they were going to find. Burrows said that Zachary's family wasn't expected to be in D.C. for another week. This would be their only chance to search it.

They climbed the porch and Charlie tried the door first and found it locked. She crouched beside the door, pulling a slim black case from her jacket. Her fingers moved swiftly, extracting a tension wrench and a hook pick, the metal glinting under the streetlamp. Fitz watched her work, keeping an eye on the street. No movement. No curious neighbors peeking from dark windows.

The lock gave a soft click.

"One down." She eased the door open, and they stepped into the entryway. The place smelled like mildew and old cigarettes. The air was thick, damp with neglect. Paint curled from the walls in strips, and the floorboards creaked under their weight. The narrow staircase loomed ahead, climbing into darkness.

Fitz went first as the steps groaned under his weight, the banister wobbling with each touch. The second floor was silent, dark doorways leading into what might have been other apartments. They continued up to the third floor unnoticed.

Charlie picked the lock on the apartment door with the same ease as the first, but this time, she was slower, more careful. The latch clicked. Fitz pushed the door open and they stepped inside. The air was stale, like no one had been inside for days.

As Fitz and Charlie made their way through the small flat the destruction was clear. Furniture overturned. Drawers yanked out and dumped, papers strewn across the floor. The couch cushions had been slashed open, their stuffing spilling like entrails. The TV was gone – ripped from the wall, only the bracket left behind. The kitchen cabinets were empty, doors hanging off hinges. Broken dishes littered the counter.

Fitz stepped over a pile of books, scanning the mess. "They tore the place apart."

Charlie knelt by a pile of clothes and rifled through them. "I wonder if they were trying to find something specific or if they were just grasping at anything."

Fitz scanned around the room. He had an instinct about what he was seeing. "This is more than what the FBI did. This was intentional and they were looking for something specific."

"Do you think Zachary kept evidence of his meeting with David Sparks and Richard Avery?"

"If he was smart, he would have." Fitz thought back to what Paul had told the young man – they were using him. Fitz wondered if the message got through and Zachary started keeping evidence.

Fitz moved toward the bedroom. The bed frame was intact, but the mattress had been gutted, its foam innards shredded. The closet doors hung open, wire hangers swinging lazily. He checked behind them, then ran his fingers along the walls, knocking, listening for anything hollow.

Charlie checked the nightstand, pulling out the drawers and rifling through what was left inside. Nothing other than a few paperback spy novels and crumpled receipts. "They would've taken anything obvious," she muttered, rising to her feet.

Fitz's gaze landed on the bed again. Something about it nagged at him. The frame was metal, cheap, and unremarkable. The worn wooden floorboards underneath. He recalled a case early in his career where a drug dealer had kept meticulous notes in a notebook stashed in the floorboard under his bed. It had been the man's downfall. The notes inside had taken down an entire drug syndicate.

Fitz crouched, running his hand along the wood he could access. "Charlie."

She was at his side in an instant. Together, they moved the metal frame to the other side of the room. Fitz went back to the area where the bed had been, the coloring of the floorboards slightly brighter in color from less wear but more heavily dust-ridden. He walked along the planks in a grid-like pattern until he felt the familiar give of a board.

Fitz bent down, pulling out a small pocketknife. He pried up the loose board. Beneath it, tucked in the shallow cavity, was a small leatherbound book. Fitz picked it up, the worn cover rough beneath his fingers.

"A journal," Charlie said, leaning over him.

"Something like that." Fitz flipped it open. The handwriting was sharp, hurried. He scanned the first few pages, his pulse quickening. Steele's words were erratic, frenzied – anger bleeding through ink. He went to stand holding the book. When he tipped it forward, photos skipped out from later pages.

Charlie worked to scoop them up as Fitz remained focused on the words. He exhaled sharply when he saw the names. Sparks. Avery.

Westbrook. They were just last names but all too familiar to Fitz. He flipped further. Meetings dates and times. Assassination plans.

Fitz's stomach turned. It was one thing to have heard from witnesses about the assassination attempt and the president's husband's involvement, it was quite another to see it in black and white.

Charlie righted herself with the photos and as she started to go through them, a soft curse escaped her lips.

A noise outside made them both freeze.

Fitz snapped the journal shut. "We need to go." He slid the book into his jacket. They moved quickly, careful not to disturb the chaos around them, and slipped out the door. The hallway was empty.

They descended the stairs, each step measured. At the bottom, Fitz checked the street – still empty. They slipped out into the night, disappearing before anyone knew they'd been there.

CHAPTER 33

Fitz guarded Zachary Steele's diary like his life depended on it. He had taken it home with him and with Amy's help they took photos of each page and used his home copier to make another set of pages. No less than two copies of the original was going to satisfy him.

Fitz hadn't had time to go through the entire journal to comb through the wealth of information. He knew from skimming it that the information inside spelled out a broad conspiracy to assassinate the President of the United States.

After he was done, he bagged the journal and the photos in a large freezer-sized Ziploc with the notes of a seasoned homicide detective scrawled on the outside. He had collected what would be the most defining evidence in the case thus far. He noted where it was found, when, and the contents. He would have to admit to breaking into Steele's apartment, but it would be well worth any punishment that might be levied. He had already told Charlie that he alone would take the blame for it and she could continue to run his business. She had protested when he told her that. Fitz didn't care. He felt responsible for getting Charlie involved in the Warren Circle and wasn't going to let her take the fall for any of it.

When they had talked after finding the journal and the photos the night before, there was one thing on Fitz's mind – Paul's words had gotten through to Zachary. As much as the young disgruntled former soldier wanted to kill the president himself, he might never have taken such a bold step on his own. He had written as much in the notes in the journal. Zachary had struggled with coming up with a feasible plan. There didn't seem to be any inroad into actually getting President Monroe in a compromised position to pull the trigger. He couldn't access her schedule, didn't know how to get close enough to her with the Secret Service ever present, and didn't know if it was worth sacrificing his own life in the process. Zachary had felt conflicted about the whole thing, so conflicted that he, alone, had never put a real plan into place.

That is until he was groomed for the job by three men, two of whom were in the Secret Service. It was really the only way it could have gone down. Zachary wrote how they found him based on things he had written online. He was worried at first that they were coming to arrest him for the threats he made. That first meeting at Last Covenant had almost been the last. He wrote that he wasn't sure he could trust the Secret Service. That he assumed at the first meeting they were trying to set him up, get him to participate so he alone would take the fall. It wasn't until he was handed a stack of cash, ten thousand dollars – a down payment – that he believed they wanted Monroe dead as much as he did.

Even if he had wanted to resist, they had made it impossible. There were notes about their persistence in showing up at Last Covenant to speak to him. They never called and they never put anything in writing – they were too smart for that. They told Steele that they would only text him from an unknown number in coded messages and leave him instructions at drop zones. Right away, Paul had told Steele that he didn't trust the men. There were parts of the journal dedicated to how conflicted Steele was between trusting the three men or trusting Paul, who had been his spiritual leader and friend. In the end, the money and the drive to complete the mission had won out. Once Paul asked him to leave Last Covenant, Steele found the apartment in Washington D.C.

There hadn't been time for Fitz to read the rest of the journal last night. There'd be more time for a closer inspection today. The photos were clear evidence – better evidence than Fitz thought they'd have.

What the trio hadn't counted on was how much Paul distrusted the government and how far he was willing to go to protect not only Steele but himself. Paul had taken the photos from what appeared to be the curve in the road that looked out to the front of Last Covenant property. Just outside the chain-link fence at the side of the road, there was a photo of Steele standing at the back of the black SUV meeting with David Sparks. The photos spanned several occasions. Each photo had been printed out and time and date stamped. Fitz would have thought the photos might have stopped once Steele was no longer at Last Covenant, but he said in his journal that Paul had sent someone to take photos for each meeting. After the initial meeting where Avery was present, the president's husband wasn't seen again. All of the interactions with Steele after that point were only with Graham Westbrook or David Sparks.

Fitz was eager today to start going through the journal more thoroughly. Skimming the information didn't do it justice. Once Fitz finished photocopying the pages of the journal one more time, he called from his office. "Charlie, what time are we meeting with Burrows?"

"Thirty minutes," she shouted back as her voice got closer to his office. Charlie appeared in the doorway. "I told him what we found and he's bringing the lead agent for the investigation with him. I stressed the importance of not telling Marcus Kane about this."

Fitz looked over his shoulder at her. "The agent is aware of the situation?"

She shrugged. "I don't know exactly what Burrows told her. I just know that he said she'd be at the apartment so we could all discuss it privately."

"A woman? Agent Isabelle Conklin? Is that her name?" he asked, his voice hinting at a skepticism he didn't mean.

"Yeah, you know we are allowed to work now." She gestured around. "I do more than get your coffee, sir." Her tone dripped with sarcasm.

Fitz rolled his eyes. "There is always a man from the team giving the press briefings. I assumed he was in charge."

"Try not to say anything dumb at the meeting," Charlie cautioned him.

Before Fitz could respond, his cellphone rang. He left the copies and reached for it, looking at the screen. He grimaced. "Kane," he told Charlie as he engaged the call. "Hello."

The man didn't waste any time with pleasantries. "Fitz, I expected an update. What have you been doing?"

"It's a complicated case," he said, a little too casually. "I spoke to Senator Ford the other day. I wasn't aware I had to update you." Fitz had no intention of telling the FBI director what they knew or what they had uncovered about him.

"Ford didn't tell me. You can tell me now."

Fitz chose his words carefully. "We know the shooting didn't take place at the Lincoln Memorial. The evidence doesn't match. It's a little hard to pinpoint where it happened when no one is willing to speak to us. I'm surprised your agents haven't discovered more. The morning news said their case is stalling."

Kane didn't directly respond to what Fitz said. "If you don't believe it happened in front of the Lincoln Memorial but you can't tell me where, how can I take that seriously?"

Fitz tsked. "I don't know what to tell you. We are doing the best we can. You know I've been out of the homicide investigation game for a long time. Maybe my skills are rusty."

Charlie smirked at him and sat down to listen.

Kane grumbled something Fitz didn't understand. Fitz asked him to repeat it. "I said, I don't believe that for a second. I think you found information that you're not sharing. I'm the FBI director, I demand to know what you know."

"Demand, huh?" Fitz said with a laugh. "Last time I checked, I don't report to you. When I find something, I'll let Senator Ford know. Don't call me again." Then he hung up the phone and dropped it back to his desk. He looked down at Charlie. "I'm starting to hate that guy."

"You think he's going to call..." Charlie no sooner got the words out of her mouth when Fitz's phone rang again. He didn't answer it but let it ring twice then sent it to voicemail so Kane would know Fitz intentionally chose not to answer.

"Brutal," she said with a laugh.

"He'll learn or they can kick us out of the Warren Circle, which is starting to feel more and more like a partnership between us than a group effort."

Charlie shrugged as if she didn't mind. "Might be a test for us."

He was starting to regret ever saying yes.

That feeling stayed with him as he put the copies of the journal in Charlie's safe and another set in the hidden safe in his office. The same feeling of regret knotted in his gut on the ride over to the safe house and right up until he entered the apartment and came face to face with the agent standing next to Burrows.

Fitz swallowed hard when he saw her, trying not to stare. To say the woman was beautiful would be an understatement. She had a heart-shaped face, dark inviting eyes, and chestnut hair she wore back in a neat ponytail. She had the body of a woman who lifted weights and could chase a suspect down without any problems but probably never said no to pasta. Fitz wondered if at one point in her life she'd been a little heavier. Her curves certainly hinted at that.

"This is Agent Isabelle Conklin," Burrows said, turning to the woman. "She has been heading up the investigation into the assassination attempt on President Monroe. She has not been happy with the findings or how the investigation has been rushed by our superiors. As I said on the phone to Charlie, she's more than happy to hear any evidence we have to present."

Fitz extended his hand and tried not to trip over his tongue. "Nice to meet you," he said, surprising himself that he could get words out like a normal person. He held onto her hand a little too long and she turned her red lips up in a bemused smile. "Sorry," he said, finally letting go.

Charlie extended her hand as well, side-eyeing Fitz as they sat at the small dining table.

"Nice to meet both of you. You can call me Isabelle. Burrows said you were friends of his and had some information about President Monroe." Her tone was professional but inviting. Fitz could tell that Burrows had only told her enough to get her to the table.

Fitz turned to Charlie but she conceded the floor to him.

He wasn't sure where exactly to start. He began with Burrows coming to ask for help and finished with finding the journal in Steele's apartment. The only things Fitz left out were his connection to the Warren Circle and the fact that Marcus Kane was in the Oval Office.

The presence of Marcus Kane he was saving for later.

Fitz shifted in the chair, locking his gaze on Isabelle. "I've had to do a few things in the case that violated the law to get the evidence I needed," Fitz said firmly, giving Charlie no chance to jump in. "I knew the FBI had already searched the place and I heard that Steele's family wouldn't be here for another few days. There was a window and I took it. If you need to arrest me for that, I'm prepared."

Isabelle's features had remained neutral while Fitz explained every witness they had spoken to and the evidence they had gathered. Now, she offered him a bemused look. "I don't condone you breaking into the apartment. That said, I don't see any reason for an arrest. What do you mean you got access to the Oval Office?"

"We broke in there too," Charlie said without any trace of being sorry for that act. "Burrows wasn't aware that's what we were going to do. He's blameless in that. As Fitz said, if we need to be held accountable, then so be it. We have evidence to show you once Fitz is done."

Again, Isabelle didn't show any signs that she was going to arrest them. She seemed more curious than anything. "How did you get in?"

Fitz folded his hands on the table, considering how to explain without getting Reggie or Ethan in trouble. He found some middle ground. "We had a ruse for the Secret Service at the gate and it worked. If it makes you feel better, we've been informed that the Secret Service knows what we did and isn't pressing charges against us because then they'd have to admit *why* we went into the Oval Office. As you can imagine, that's the last thing they want to do."

Isabelle remained steady, giving nothing away.

Fitz gestured toward Charlie's bag. She handed it to him and he pulled out two evidence bags. He put the first one on the table. "This is Steele's journal with all the information from his meetings with Graham, Sparks, and one meeting with Richard Avery. Everything is dated with where they met, the time and date, and the context of the meeting. He even quoted people directly. There are photos to back up these meetings. I didn't read through the entire thing. There hasn't been time for that. As I said, I just found this last night."

Isabelle took the evidence bag. "You found this in Steele's apartment *after* my team searched it?"

"Last night, and your team wasn't the only ones who searched it. I assume the men who set up Steele might have not trusted him. They trashed the place." Fitz explained how he had come to think about the floorboard. "It was an easy miss. I also spoke with Paul who had told us that he cautioned Steele and told him to keep evidence."

"He wouldn't speak to us," Isabelle admitted. "I went out there personally with another agent. He sent men to stop us before we even made it up the driveway."

"Did you speak to him at all?" Fitz asked.

Isabelle shook her head. "He refused to speak to a woman. Do you think he was involved at all?"

"No." Fitz pointed to the evidence bag. "We wouldn't have that right now if Paul had been involved. He's smart but doesn't trust anyone. In this case, I don't trust anyone either. If that journal goes missing, we have several copies."

"Missing?" Isabelle said with confusion in her voice. "If you've worked with the FBI before you know we don't have evidence go missing."

"Well, there's still one thing I haven't shared." Fitz steadied himself. "Marcus Kane was in the Oval Office the night the president was shot."

CHAPTER 34

For as calm and steady as Isabelle had been throughout, the façade broke at the news that her boss, the FBI director, was in the White House at the time.

"How is that possible? I don't understand. He's never said anything to me about it." She sat back processing what Fitz said while they all waited for her to connect the dots. She got there faster than Fitz would have assumed. "He's pushing for us to close the case. To say it happened at the Lincoln Memorial, despite all the conflicting evidence. Steele is dead. Justice is served. Case closed, according to him."

"The case is far from closed," Charlie said, finally lending her voice. "What about the other man who showed up at the hospital to finish the job? Have you been able to figure out who he is?"

Isabelle remained tightlipped. It was clear she was there to get information, not share it.

It was Burrows who came to their defense. "There's a reason I came to Fitz and Charlie when you told me the case was stalling." He raised an eyebrow in a question to Charlie. The two seemed to be able to communicate without words as Fitz watched her nod. Burrows turned his attention back to Isabelle. "As you know, Fitz was a homicide detective for D.C. Metro. Charlie was a CIA operative in the field. I'd trust the two of them with my life."

Isabelle looked each one of them in the eyes as if she were weighing her decision, searching their faces for some kind of confirmation. Finally, she broke. "No. We don't have prints on file. He refuses to speak. I don't think he's uttered a word to anyone. He doesn't have an attorney either. The court assigned him one, but he's refused to speak to him too. We've kept him at the FBI headquarters in the cells we have, mostly for his safety. I wasn't putting him in general population."

Fitz hadn't realized the FBI building had cells.

"Can I try to question him?" Charlie asked. "I've been an interrogator for a long time. I know how to work within the confines of U.S. law when it comes to interrogation. I was never a proponent of the enhanced interrogation the CIA employed after 9/11. Just give me a few minutes with him, recorded, all above board. If I can't get him to talk, I'll give up."

"He has an attorney," Isabelle reminded her.

Fitz asked. "How'd he evoke his right to counsel if he hasn't spoken?"

"He slid us a handwritten note that told us he wasn't going to speak and to get him an attorney."

Fitz found that odd. "*Can* he speak?"

"We brought in a doctor and there's nothing medically wrong. He smirked when we asked him if there was something medically preventing him from speaking. We believe there is nothing wrong, he's just choosing to remain silent, which is his right. Normally, there'd be identification or something on him or his prints would tell us who he is. Nothing."

"You didn't see him speak to anyone on camera at the hospital?" Charlie asked.

"No, he walked into the hospital dressed as a repairman with a tool kit and badge. He walked through the hospital unnoticed. He looked the part and no one questioned him. He showed up at shift change and the Secret Service agent on watch initially let him pass down into the unit. He must have sensed something was off because he rushed down the hall moments later and stopped him before he even made it to the agent standing outside President Monroe's room. When they went to question him, he refused to speak. He retreated down the hall and then tried again. It was a crazy situation."

"Copycat?" Charlie asked.

"We just don't know. It's also why we were hoping to speak to Paul Berardo at Last Covenant. I was hoping he might be able to ID the other man for us. We were working on the assumption that he was connected to Steele. So far, no confirmation. Then again, we don't have a name."

The last thing Fitz wanted to do was go back to Last Covenant. Paul had been willing to speak to him. "Do you have a photo? Maybe I can ask Paul."

"You think he'd speak to you again?" There was doubt in Isabelle's voice.

"I think he'll speak to me. I don't want to go back out there. The whole place is creepy. Paul wants justice for Steele. He's anti-government. He said the time wasn't right to take out the president. Paul wasn't upset that President Monroe was shot. He wouldn't even speak to or acknowledge Charlie. He's a raging misogynist, but he firmly believes it wasn't time. He also didn't like that any part of the government was involved. He knew from that first meeting they were using Steele."

Isabelle glanced down at the evidence bag, fingering the journal. "Do you think they used Steele as just a patsy and the shooting was always going to take place in the White House, or did they really have a plan for Steele to shoot her?"

Fitz had read enough of the journal that he felt like he could answer that. "Steele believed that they were planning a real assassination. I have to assume that when President Monroe pulled her gun and shot wide, someone in that room reacted and shot her in self-defense or retaliation."

Isabelle stiffened. "Why would Monroe have a gun on her?"

Charlie leaned forward toward the table. "Sebastian Cole was her head of Secret Service. He's ultimately the one who saved her life. If he had chosen not to come back to the White House that night, Monroe would be dead. He's the one who got her out of there. He's also the one who was concerned that something was amiss. Cole told us he couldn't put his finger on what. He had previously given her the gun for when he wasn't around."

"He wouldn't speak to us either," Isabelle lamented. "He didn't technically lie in his statement to us. He just didn't answer our questions. I knew that he knew more than he was saying."

Fitz felt a pull to tell Isabelle the full truth about Cole and his relationship with the president. He had promised the man that unless it was critical to the case, Fitz wouldn't disclose it.

"Let's get back to that night," Isabelle said. "You said you found evidence inside the Oval. Do you have that?"

Fitz grabbed the other evidence bag from Charlie. "We found evidence and the statement of all three Secret Service agents who were there that night. We also have a statement from one of the Secret Service agents who was manning the gate and corroborated what the other three said. In addition, there is the nurse at the hospital who told me a different story than what she was instructed to put in her statement."

Isabelle took in the information. "You believe it was David Sparks who concocted the whole story and instructed the hospital administration to lie to the FBI for national security purposes? Have you spoken to him?"

"We haven't tried. We were working to get evidence before going to any of the major players." Fitz held the evidence bag to show her. "This is the evidence we captured inside the Oval Office. As you'll see in the photos, the room was hastily cleaned up. Not well. The carpet that was replaced looks noticeably different and the gunshot holes in the wall and couch are still apparent. The couch doesn't look like they even tried to repair it. The hole in the wall is covered by the drapes."

Isabelle sucked in a breath making her chest rise as she studied the photos through the bag. She looked at them without taking them out and then set them aside. "This is compelling evidence. Help me to understand what happened at the White House that night."

Fitz knew the information might be hard to stomach, especially because it was still somewhat vague. "As we said, we don't know who ultimately pulled the trigger. Graham Westbrook told us part of the story but not the rest. He also didn't implicate himself, although after reading Steele's journal, he was intimately involved in the planning. He was also the only Secret Service agent in the room. Further, as mentioned, he's the nephew of Speaker Graves. While I believe he was telling us the truth at times, I can't say that his full statement to us was accurate."

"What do you know that you can confirm?" Isabelle sat back and gestured for him to continue.

Fitz named each of the men who was in the room when the shooting occurred. He could see that she was still having trouble believing her boss was there. "Both Ian and Graham said that Kane was in the room. Cole said that when he entered, it was either Kane or Coldwell, who was fleeing out the other door with someone. He wasn't able to see who it was or that it was two men."

Isabelle stopped him. "Everything at the White House is recorded. I can just pull the video feed."

Fitz shook his head. "Ian said David Sparks shut off the video feed before the group arrived. They didn't follow any protocol that night. There is no official record of the meeting."

"Why? If the shooting was spur of the moment, why not follow protocol?"

That was a good question. One for which Fitz didn't have the answer. "I believe given the topic of conversation, no one wanted it on the record." Fitz had also held back the motive for now. He didn't want Isabelle or Burrows to go off on a tangent without hearing the bulk of the evidence. When Isabelle asked him for the reasoning, he asked if she could wait. It was clear to Fitz she wasn't the kind of woman who liked to be told how to direct the interview.

"Please, just hear the rest of the evidence first."

Isabelle dismissively waved at him to continue.

"We don't believe Kane was the one who shot Monroe. Graham said Kane was trying to slow things down when the conversation got heated. He suggested they should take a break. He left the Oval Office to the side room where there is a bathroom and a small kitchen stocked with drinks and snacks. He was out of the room when President Monroe fired the shot wide and when she was shot, according to Graham. We were told she was shooting at the vice president but that's not confirmed. We also don't know who shot her. There are just a few unknowns left. But Kane was there."

Isabelle didn't show her hand. "I'll take that under advisement."

"What does that mean?" Charlie asked.

"It means I need more proof before I accuse the FBI director of being involved in the plot to kill the president."

Fitz couldn't fault her for that. He would be the same way. "Percepta Tech," he said finally, throwing out the motive. He watched how both Burrows and Isabelle reacted. It was clear by the wide-eyed serious expressions on their faces they knew exactly what the company did.

It was Isabelle who spoke first. "What does Percepta Tech have to do with anything?"

"That's why they were meeting that night," Fitz informed them. "According to Graham, there had been many conversations about this technology. Many meetings like the one that night. Monroe was adamantly opposed to it. The others not only wanted it implemented, but it had been the reason for the push for Coldwell to be vice president. This plot to get rid of Monroe was started as soon as she was elected. She was the one who could get elected where Coldwell couldn't. They want this implemented. We've heard conflicting reports about whether Kane is for or against it."

"Against," Isabelle said, turning to look at Burrows. "Do you know anything different?"

Burrows shook his head. "We've had briefings with senior leadership at the FBI. Other intelligence agencies joined us. No one thinks this technology is a good idea. We know AI is coming and we're going to have to continue to address it. There are too many things that could go wrong with it. Kane has always been against it. I've never heard him take a favorable position about it."

"That's the reason Kane was there that night." Fitz had wanted Isabelle warmed to the idea of Kane being there before he had delivered the final nail in the man's coffin. He could see the expression on her face that she was coming around to the veracity of it.

Isabelle said, "If Kane was there, then he's protecting whoever shot the president."

"Not necessarily," Charlie cautioned her. "Graham put Kane out of the room when it happened. I don't see any reason for him to lie about that. He could have just as easily put Coldwell in the other room during the shooting. It didn't strike me that Graham would have any reason to protect the FBI director. I don't believe that's who they are trying to protect with this whole thing."

"Then who?"

"That's the question that remains," Charlie said with a sigh.

The four of them sat still now that they were all up to speed. The tension hung heavily over them.

It was Fitz who finally broke. "What's your plan for the investigation?"

Isabelle put her hand on the evidence bag with the journal. "Review this thoroughly before I take any action." She raised an eyebrow. "If you're asking me if I plan to tell the rest of my team or run to Marcus Kane about what you've brought me… No. There's been something off about this investigation from the start. I want to find the truth and that's exactly what I'm going to do."

Fitz did not doubt that. "We plan to keep digging until we know who pulled the trigger."

Isabelle cracked a smile. "I'd have expected nothing less. Burrows can let me know if you need to pass on any more evidence." She got up to leave thanking them again for sharing it with her. She turned back for a brief moment. "Charlie, meet me tomorrow and I'll let you interview the second suspect. Fitz, if you want to see Paul again, I'll text you the photo." She gave Charlie the address to meet her in the morning and got Fitz's number before she left.

As the door to the apartment clicked shut, Fitz turned to Burrows. "For the first time, I think we might actually be getting somewhere."

CHAPTER 35

By the time Fitz made it to the office the next morning he had received a text from Isabelle with the photo of the man who had tried to kill the president at the hospital. Fitz sat back in his desk chair, staring down at the photo of the man with cropped dark hair, even darker eyes, and olive skin complexion. He stared straight ahead at the camera, not smiling or smirking. His features were relaxed and completely neutral. If someone asked Fitz to guess what the man had been thinking, he wouldn't have a clue.

Fitz forwarded the photo to his email and then downloaded it onto his laptop. He ran a few scans on the internet searching the image and came up blank. He knew the FBI had taken the photo, so this particular photo wouldn't be online. He was curious to see what other photos of similar-looking men the internet might find.

He scanned through the images, growing increasingly frustrated that there wasn't a match. Not that he thought it would be this easy. Fitz was sure the FBI had done the same thing. He sat back and considered his options. Ditch was the only name that came to mind.

Fitz reached for his phone and punched in a familiar number. Ditch – born as Kevin Detrich – had been the world's best hacker. He was wanted by governments around the globe. A special unit in the FBI had snatched him up and put him to work for the United States. Fitz had the good fortune of meeting Ditch sometime back right after he started working for the FBI. He was running a side hustle helping businesses and the like, against the government's wishes. Fitz assumed they knew they had to keep the temperamental man happy to keep him employed. Ditch could easily change sides and source himself out to other governments less friendly with the United States.

The phone rang five times before a groggy-sounding Ditch mumbled a hello.

"Time to get up, buddy. It's nearly nine."

"Late night with some hot girls and some coke. My head is pounding."

"I didn't think you did drugs. You told me it messes with your skills." Fitz had never known the man to do drugs. He had to keep his skills sharp at all times.

The sound of rustling covers and the mummer of a woman's sleepy voice echoed through the phone. Another woman's voice followed and Fitz rolled his eyes. "Call me back when you've gotten yourself together. I need help with something."

"I'm here," Ditch said, more awake now. "It wasn't me doing the coke. It was the lovely ladies I brought home with me. I'm in D.C. You at your office?"

"Yeah. I don't need you to come here unless you want to. I just need you to use your facial recognition for someone in FBI custody who won't talk. The man hasn't said a word since they got him into custody."

"Well, that's the way to do it." Ditch yawned loudly. "His prints didn't come back? No identification on him? Where was he found?"

Fitz explained that the man had been caught in the hospital trying to finish the job on President Monroe. "The FBI is stumped. Charlie is with the agent in charge right now. She's going to interview him."

"Waterboard him, you mean."

As soon as Charlie had confided in Ditch that she had been CIA it was the first thing he had asked her. Then had had the audacity not to believe her answer. It had been a big argument between the two of them in the office one late Friday night. The argument ended when Charlie threatened to waterboard Ditch in the kitchen sink.

"I thought you learned your lesson the first time. Charlie isn't someone you should antagonize."

Ditch let out a breathy sigh. "You know the fact that you have a spook working for you is the number one reason I was hesitant to do any work with you."

"Wasn't it the CIA who got you out of the hands of the Russians?"

"Yeah. I'm not sure who's worse though. The CIA had me in their grips for four months trying to get information out of me before my current boss released me from their clutches." Ditch yelled something to one of the women then got back to Fitz. "Listen, send me the photo and I'll search right away. I can do that from here."

Fitz attached the photo in an email and waited on the phone until Ditch confirmed receipt. "Call me when you know something. I'm supposed to drive to Last Covenant today and check with Paul Berardo and that's the last thing I want to do. If you can get me some information, I might be able to avoid the trip."

"Isn't that the cult guy?"

"You've heard of him?" Fitz didn't hide the surprise in his voice.

"Yeah, he's an equal opportunity hater. I see his people in some of the chat rooms in places where most wouldn't go or they'd never sleep at night. My boss has me watching for any real threats."

"Do you think he's a threat?"

"Not to you and me," Ditch said with another yawn. "If you're not a straight white guy, then he's definitely a threat. You're not bringing Charlie out there with you, are you?"

Fitz recalled the disdainful way that Paul had looked at her, the way he wouldn't speak to her, and having to hold Charlie back. She had said later that she could have ripped him limb from limb and Fitz knew she was telling the truth. "It didn't go well last time. I'll be going alone this time."

"If you brought her out there and she made him angry, she's now going to be on his watch list."

"What's that?"

"He's got an enemies list. They have gone after people before, Fitz. A few of their members have been arrested for various reasons – assaults at protests and such. These aren't good people. They aren't religious people either. Paul uses religion as a shield to spread his message. It's why the feds are hesitant to break them up. You know, Waco. Just remember certain factions of the government like having groups like that out there doing the dirty work."

Fitz nodded even though Ditch couldn't see him. "Do you think Charlie is in any kind of danger?"

Ditch laughed. "Charlie is the danger. I'm sure she will be able to handle herself. Just know she's on the list and tell her to take some extra safety measures. I'm sure we don't need to tell her that though."

"It almost sounds like you're softening on her."

"She's hot. Just don't tell her I said that." Ditch mumbled something else and Fitz had him repeat it. "Are you two…you know…."

"Don't ask me stupid questions."

"Well, that's *not* a no."

"Just search the photo and get back to me." Fitz hung up before Ditch could say anything else inappropriate. He tossed his cellphone back on his desk and stretched his arms overhead. He knew he was stalling on going to Last Covenant. Not only did Fitz not want to see Paul again, but he also didn't want to make the drive.

Fitz got up and went directly to his safe behind a wall photo of the Oregon coast. He pulled the photo back, punched in his six-digit security code, and pulled the safe door open. Fitz pulled out the stack of journal pages and carried them downstairs to the big table. He poured himself another cup of coffee and got down to work. While he waited for Ditch, he could finally go all the way through the journal. There might be nuggets of information he missed.

Fitz skimmed the beginning pages of information he had previously read. Then he moved on to later pages where the writing got more pointed and darker. Steele was preparing for murder and Fitz could see it in his writing. He was being buoyed by David Sparks and Graham Westbrook. Every time Steele expressed a doubt about being able to shoot Monroe, they were on his heels reminding him he was a Patriot and doing it for the good of his country. That Steele would be a hero and save the country.

Steele expressed frustration that the agents wouldn't let him meet with Richard Avery again and wondered why Monroe's husband wanted her dead. The agents refused to give him any clear motive as to why they wanted to kill the president. When pressed, Sparks would tell him that it was above their pay grade and it was something that needed to be done for national security. It was the same refrain that had been used during the cover-up after the shooting.

Fitz knew many things had been done under the guise of national security that had, in his opinion, been wrong – clear violations of people's civil liberties. It was a good threat though for people who didn't know better.

Fitz continued to read until he reached the end of the journal. There had been a plan in place. On March 1, during President Monroe's morning run, Graham Westbrook was going to divert the run because of a called-in threat. They'd get her to the Lincoln Memorial to keep her from the open air but in a position where Steele could take a shot.

Graham assured Steele that in the aftermath of the shooting he and the other agents would let him get away. By then, there'd be enough money in the man's bank account and a new passport waiting at his apartment for him to flee the country.

Fitz knew that was an outright lie. They were never going to let Steele live. Ian and Sebastian were not in on the plot – there was no evidence of that. No one was going to let Steele get out of there alive. Fitz's gut churned at how easily Steele had been duped. There was nothing in his writing that indicated he didn't believe them.

Fitz kept reading until he reached the name of another contact who was supposed to be in touch with Steele. Gray Wolf. It was a code name. Steele didn't know the man's real name even though he asked countless times.

He was supposed to meet with Gray Wolf shortly before the scheduled assassination. Gray Wolf would be there as backup in case Steele lost his nerve. He'd be waiting in the shadows to make sure the shooting was carried off without a hitch.

The code name was only used five times in the writing then never mentioned again.

Fitz wondered if that was the man sitting in the FBI cell. He jotted down the name on a notepad and kept reading. The last entry was dated the morning of the shooting. Not so much in the morning but in the middle of the night. Steele noted the time – 3:22 a.m. Graham Westbrook texted him and told him that it was go time. Steele had to be at the Lincoln Memorial within the hour, ready to go. It wasn't what they had planned. Everything was moving fast and sooner than the date that had been chosen. Westbrook said it was time, so it was time. Steele wrote that he was nervous but ready to get this over with and onto his new life. That was the very last entry.

Fitz closed the journal and sat back. He felt a pang of empathy for Steele that he didn't like. Fitz told himself that he shouldn't be feeling sad for a young man who was willing to kill the President of the United States. Yet, he saw in the writing that it had only been an idea for Steele that was cultivated by powerful men. Young, disenfranchised men had been used by more powerful men for centuries to do their dirty work. It was the way governments were toppled, wars carried out, and the downfall of just about every civilization that had collapsed. Exploiting young, male anger was an effective way to carry out a mission.

Fitz pushed the feeling aside as his phone chimed. He picked it up and read the message with a pang of disappointment. Ditch didn't come back with anything from the photo. The facial recognition didn't pick up anything.

Fitz texted back the name Gray Wolf and asked Ditch to pull what he could find. He sent another text to Charlie with the same code name.

Immediately, she responded. "Where did you get that name?"

Fitz could feel the pointed way she asked the question. "It's in Steele's journal towards the end. Gray Wolf would be there as a backup. Does the code name mean anything to you?" He sent the text then waited five minutes…ten…twenty.

Her text finally came with an urgency Fitz hadn't been expecting.

Get to the safe house now.

CHAPTER 36

Fitz rushed to the FBI apartment. He didn't know what he was going to find once he arrived or why she so desperately wanted him there. On the way over he had ignored two calls – one from Senator Ford and another from Marcus Kane. It seemed the FBI director was not going to give up trying to get information from him.

Arriving at the apartment, Fitz climbed the stairs to the third floor, knocked once, and Charlie pulled the door open. Her face was flushed and her nostrils flared.

"What took you so long?" she barked as he entered.

"What is going on?" he asked, looking past Charlie at Isabelle sitting at the table. Burrows wasn't there as Fitz had expected. "Where's Burrows?"

"No, no, Fitz." Charlie shook her head. "We can't read him in on this. He shouldn't know."

"Shouldn't know what?" Fitz had never seen Charlie like this. Wild-eyed, flushed, and nearly panting. "I don't understand what's happening. Did you figure out who the guy is?" He wondered now if she hadn't been responding to his text, but instead, to the interview she was supposed to be conducting.

"He refuses to speak. I tried everything I know to do outside of hurting him." Charlie looked back at Isabelle sitting at the table. "As much as I would have liked to apply that kind of pressure, it's a no-go for the FBI, particularly on United States soil."

"It's okay," Isabelle said to Charlie. "I didn't think you'd get anything. I wasn't expecting you to. I sent in the FBI's best interrogators and the man still refuses to talk." Where Charlie seemed amped up, Isabelle was as calm as she had been the last time Fitz saw her.

He made his way over to the table, pulled out a chair, and sat across from her. Charlie remained in the center of the room. He looked over at her. "You're starting to worry me. I've never seen you like this. You can't be this worked up because the guy wouldn't talk."

"I wasn't until you sent that text," she admitted, finally coming over to the table. "Do you have any idea who Gray Wolf is?"

"No. That's why I asked you."

Charlie raked her hands through her hair, tucking strands behind her ears. "Gray Wolf is a ghost in the spy world. People were already telling me about him around the time I started working for the CIA. He was an assassin from Eastern Europe. A murder for hire kind of guy. Not your average domestic killer, Fitz. He's high-level and takes out the most powerful. Do you remember when the Russian diplomat was killed in London back in 2014?"

"I remember some of it." Fitz strained his memory for the details. He hadn't paid much attention to it at the time. He didn't much care that a Russian diplomat had been shot. "What about it?"

"Gray Wolf," Charlie said. "The investigation turned up nothing. No one saw anything or knew anything and even those who were suspected of knowing weren't talking. Inside the CIA, MI-5, and MI-6, we had heard rumblings that it had been the Gray Wolf who was hired by the Russian government to take out one of their own."

"Does Gray Wolf work for the Russians?"

"No," Charlie said emphatically. "He doesn't work directly for anyone. He doesn't answer to anyone. There's only been one name connected to him and that's Luka Petrović, who was a Serbian national. There was speculation for a long time that he might be Gray Wolf but that was never confirmed. Luka disappeared and no one has heard from him since. I can't tell you the operation where we discovered the name, so you're just going to have to trust me."

"I trust you," Fitz said, trying to piece this together.

"Tell me exactly what you saw in the journal." Charlie remained standing, hovering.

"You're going to have to sit down so we can talk. You're making me uncomfortable. You're like a lion tracking its prey and I'm not prey." Fitz pulled the chair out for her and waited until she sat.

"Now, that's better. Steele mentioned he was going to be aided by Gray Wolf during the assassination. He never said he met the man. Didn't know his name and knew nothing about him. Graham Westbrook told him that if something went wrong and he wasn't able to pull the trigger or that he missed, there'd be backup. I don't know if it was another lie told to Steele. He thought he was going to get away with it. Just show up at the Lincoln Memorial and shoot the president, only to flee back to his apartment where there'd be another stack of cash and a new passport waiting for him."

Isabelle stopped him. "I have one of my agents going through the journal today. I haven't received an update yet. You're saying the journal specifically states that Graham Westbrook had a specific plan to shoot President Monroe. Was there a date mentioned?"

"March 1. Clearly, it happened sooner. The last entry is from the wee morning hours when Westbrook called him and told him to get to the Lincoln Memorial, that it was go time. Steele was a bit thrown off guard by the immediacy but expressed relief that it would be all over." He glanced over at Charlie who hadn't said anything then back to Isabelle. "Has the FBI heard of Gray Wolf?"

"No," she said with a shake of her head. "I searched after Charlie told me the name and we have nothing like that in our database."

"The FBI wouldn't know," Charlie reiterated. "This was CIA. We've been trying to track him for decades. He doesn't leave evidence behind. No one has ever caught him on video and there has never been a credible witness."

Fitz asked, "Should I assume then that the man sitting in custody isn't Gray Wolf?"

Charlie couldn't say for sure. "He won't speak. He's as much of a ghost to us as Gray Wolf. That said, the Gray Wolf that the CIA was tracking would never walk into a hospital like that to finish the job. He was easily caught. I assume he's some kind of copycat and probably not connected at all. It was announced on the news what hospital President Monroe was in and it was easy enough once in the hospital to figure out she was in the ICU. I'd stake my career that the man sitting in that cell isn't Gray Wolf."

"Okay," Fitz said slowly, trying to figure out why Charlie got all worked up. "Isn't it possible then that this might not be the Gray Wolf the CIA was chasing? Couldn't someone else have used the code name Gray Wolf?"

"No," Charlie said adamantly. "This is him."

Isabelle raised an eyebrow as she locked her gaze on Fitz. It was clear to him that she had tried to talk some rational sense into Charlie and she was getting more and more dug in. "We don't know anything. It could be him or as Fitz suggested it could just be a name Steele wrote down."

Fitz needed to correct that. "It wasn't something Steele came up with. He used specific names in the rest of the journal. He didn't put anything in code. He got the name Gray Wolf because it was given to him by Graham Westbrook."

Isabelle conceded the point. "Why have a second shooter? Why choose the Lincoln Memorial?"

Fitz had been considering those details. "The Lincoln Memorial was along her running route. If the Secret Service wanted her to stop and get off the road, there's enough cover up on the memorial that they could have gotten her out of sight. Back her into a corner of the space behind the statue of Lincoln. It also gives them a line of sight down. I think it served a purpose in being believable that Sebastian and Ian wouldn't have questioned it."

"You believe that Sebastian and Ian are innocent of all of this?"

"Yes, I do," Fitz said. "I wasn't sure about Ian at first. He was believable in his statement to us. More than Westbrook. He was, by Westbrook's account, not in the room when the shooting happened. He's not mentioned at all and neither is Sebastian in the journal. Ian also left with Sebastian to help get President Monroe to the hospital. He might not have made the best decisions once he got into that room and he participated in the cover-up as was directed by David Sparks. But, no, I don't think Ian had any idea what was going to happen that night."

"Why the second shooter?"

Even though it was Fitz she asked, Charlie answered. "Steele was the decoy made to believe he was going to be the shooter. They needed a dead man to limit the investigation. Steele had the right connections to Last Covenant and had already threatened the president online. He made the perfect patsy, which makes me believe that someone in the administration reached out to the real Gray Wolf. He was able to carry off the assassination."

"Wait. Wait." Isabelle got her bearings. "Maybe that was the intent. The shooting happened inside the White House. Are you suggesting that this assassin was inside the White House and we aren't looking at one of the men who we know were in the Oval Office as the killer?"

Fitz wasn't sure what Charlie was saying either. He reminded her, "We know the shooting took place inside the Oval Office. How could

Gray Wolf get access? I thought you said no one has ever seen him."

"Mercer," she said in a rush of breath. "He was CIA. He knows what I know about Gray Wolf. Maybe he knows more. There's just one problem. No one has ever seen Gray Wolf and lived to tell the tale. He's as good at clean-up as he is at assassination."

"Is he a murder-for-hire?" Isabelle asked. "Could someone have contracted with him to take out President Monroe?"

"That's exactly what he is. I can guarantee though, whoever set it up, if they saw that man's face and could identify him, he's dead now. He'll go after every single one of them that were in that room that night."

Fitz felt the urgency now. "We need to warn them."

"Wait!" Isabelle raised her voice to stop the frantic energy building in the room. "You're all over the map. First, you think one of the men shot her. Richard Avery was involved in the plot to kill Monroe using Zachary Steele. It was supposed to happen at the Lincoln Memorial but it happened in the Oval Office. I can't keep up. You're chasing each piece of evidence like it's the linchpin." No sooner had the words left her mouth than her phone chimed. She tugged it out of her coat pocket and lowered her head to read it. Her eyes widened.

"What's wrong?" Fitz asked, seeing the distress blanket her face.

Slowly, she raised her eyes from the phone and looked right at Charlie. "He's dead. Someone got to him in his cell. I need to get back to the FBI building immediately."

"It's Gray Wolf. He's cleaning up." Charlie was off her chair to the door faster than Isabelle could tell her to hold back.

"We're going with you," Fitz announced as he pushed himself up from the chair and followed them both.

Isabelle didn't put up a fight.

Without another word, they all filed out of the safe house, the weight of the situation settling in Fitz's bones. Charlie might very well be right about the whole thing. They piled into Isabelle's SUV and she pulled out, weaving in and out of heavy D.C. traffic like a pro.

Before Fitz realized it, the FBI building loomed ahead, the concrete monstrosity that dominated the city skyline. She pulled her SUV to the front of the building, jumping the curb slightly as she put it in park, and cut the engine. "Stay with me."

The building felt like a fortress. Fitz had never liked the Brutalist style of the building with its concrete design and deep bronze-glass recessed windows. The inside of the building felt even more suffocating. Isabelle moved them quickly past the front security and made a beeline to the bank of elevators.

She hit the down button without explaining. They got in and she waited for the doors to close before swiping her badge against the keypad. She hit a combination of numbers and the elevator started its descent.

As they stepped off into the corridors of the FBI's holding block, the air felt thick with tension. The block was a maze of reinforced steel doors and tight hallways, designed to keep those on the inside contained. Isabelle's boots echoed sharply on the concrete floor as they made their way toward the isolated cell where the prisoner had been held.

When they reached the small viewing room, the scene was already set in a cold, clinical light. A few agents milled about, talking in hushed tones. No one was looking at her. No one was looking at anything, really. The walls seemed to close in, and the air was so still.

An agent with features drawn tightly gestured toward the body. "Headshot. Clean, point-blank. An alarm went off in another area of the building. We were focused over there. After we found the body, we noticed that the video had been cut. No one even saw the killer come in or out. It was like a ghost killed him."

Isabelle didn't speak. Her eyes were locked on the cell door, and the dark figure inside.

Inside the cell, the body lay sprawled across the floor. Fitz's stomach twisted, but he couldn't look away. The blood had already started to congeal, dark and sticky, staining the floor. As Fitz scanned down the body he stopped at the chest.

"Is that something pinned to his chest?" Fitz asked, not sure he was seeing it correctly. It looked like a small card-size envelope.

"It's addressed to someone named Charlie," the agent said, looking at Isabelle for an explanation. "We didn't open the envelope. We figured you'd want to do that."

Isabelle nodded, snapping on the gloves he handed her. She moved through the other agents to the body, bending over and tugging the envelope free from the dead man. She turned back to Fitz and Charlie as she tugged the card free from the body. The outside was a river scene painted in hues of blue and green. She flipped it open and read the card.

I should have killed you when I had the chance.

Gray Wolf

The words landed like a punch. Charlie stepped back into Fitz. His large body braced hers.

"It *was* him," was all Isabelle said.

Fitz could hear her breath catch in her throat. "We need to finish this before he finishes us. We have to warn the others."

CHAPTER 37

As Fitz raced to Graham Westbrook's house, he reflected on how calmly Isabelle portrayed herself in front of them and her team. The only sign that she had been shaken had been the slight catch in her voice. As soon as Fitz said they had to warn the others, she launched into action, splitting up her team to go to each person who'd been there that night. Protecting their lives from Gray Wolf outweighed them overplaying their hand in the investigation.

Fitz reasoned if they showed the slightest fear about Gray Wolf then that alone would be a confession – both in knowing the name and understanding why he'd now be a threat to them.

Charlie was headed to David Sparks while Fitz would meet with Graham. He was hoping to both warn the man and get some information out of him at the same time. Isabelle had warned him that anything Graham said could be used in court. It was a warning not to screw up a case that hadn't even entered the legal system yet.

Fitz hit the gas harder, flying at least twenty over the speed limit. He had tried to call Graham twice but it went straight to voicemail. He had called Ethan after that to see if Graham was at the White House that day. Ethan explained that Graham was still on paid suspension after the shooting.

The only other place Fitz knew was the house in Virginia.

Fitz got off the exit and flew down one narrow rural road after another until he turned into the familiar dirt drive. A cloud of dust billowed around his tires as he aimed toward the house. He pulled up next to Graham's truck, jumped out, and raced toward the front door.

Fitz's boots hit the cracked front steps of the old Victorian, the sound echoing. The first time he'd been here he tried to be quiet, hoping not to engage in a confrontation with Graham. This time he wanted to make noise. The old screen door was firmly shut but the wooden door behind it had been left slightly ajar.

Fitz called out for Graham, his voice the only sound. "Graham! It's Fitz."

He pulled the screen door toward him, the rusted hinges groaning in protest. He pushed the wooden door, old paint flaking off against his palm. He called the man's name again and was met with nothing but silence. Not a creak or a shuffle of movement – only the heavy weight of inevitability hanging in the air.

Fitz's hand instinctively went to the gun at his side, but he didn't draw it. Not yet.

Fitz stepped farther into the house. The air was thick with the scent of decay. He moved through the dimly lit hallway, his boots barely making a sound as they padded over the dust-covered floors. The house felt colder now, empty in a way that made Fitz's skin crawl.

Fitz took a deep breath and entered the living room. It wasn't hard to spot the body.

Graham's enormous lifeless form lay sprawled in his chair. His legs kicked out in front and his arms splayed wide. A bullet wound burned in the man's forehead; his brains shot across the wall behind him. Fitz's throat tightened as he reached for his gun. Yet, instinct told him he was alone in the house.

Gray Wolf was long gone.

Fitz clenched his jaw and fought the rising wave of frustration that threatened to engulf him. He needed answers. Fast.

The room was cluttered with papers, old books, and unopened mail. He moved swiftly, searching for anything that could lead him to the next piece of the puzzle. Something to indicate who Gray Wolf was and how the rest connected to the conspiracy – if they did at all.

Did Gray Wolf really pull the trigger that night?

Fitz needed something – anything.

As he rifled through a drawer in a nearby side table, Fitz's gaze landed on a sight that made his heart pound in his chest. Graham's cellphone. He snatched it up without hesitation, his fingers brushing over the screen.

The phone was locked, but that wouldn't be a problem. Fitz's mind worked quickly, running through the possibilities. It was about the last thing he wanted to do but he didn't have the luxury of time. He pressed the phone to Graham's cold, lifeless thumb, and after a moment of processing, the screen flickered to life.

Fitz stood right next to the man's lifeless body as he scrolled through the messages, his eyes scanning the lines of text with practiced speed.

At first, it was nothing noteworthy – just the usual text chains, work appointments, the mundane conversations of a life lived. Then, in the content of a message, a name Fitz recognized jumped out at him: Gray Wolf.

The text was simple and direct. A payment had been made, but the job hadn't been completed. Gray Wolf would not receive the rest of the payment promised. Graham dared to argue with a well-trained assassin. The Secret Service agent had been in over his head and drowning fast. Gray Wolf threatened him enough that Graham finally relented saying that the man would be paid.

That was the final text between the two. The number was one out of D.C. A number Fitz was sure was no longer operational.

Fitz quickly scrolled back through the other messages, and then he found it. A chain of texts between Graham and Adrian Mercer dated months back. The messages were short, coded, and unsettlingly calm, considering the gravity of their content.

Adrian Mercer: "I left you how to contact Gray Wolf. Do not mention my name."

A week later a reply.

Graham: "It's done. Gray Wolf is in place."

Adrian Mercer: "What's the next steps?"

The next few messages were brief, but they spoke volumes. There were no names mentioned, but Fitz knew enough to understand what this meant. Mercer had been involved – complicit in the plot to take down President Monroe. He already knew Richard Avery was involved too. The others – Marcus Kane, Speaker Graves, and Vice President Coldwell were not mentioned.

Fitz's fingers hovered over the screen. He searched through more of the texts and one months back, dated right after the election, made his blood run cold.

Graham: "Are you sure about this?"

Richard Avery: "One way or the other it's already in motion. We have to take control, or we lose everything."

Fitz shoved the phone into his pocket, his mind racing with more questions than answers. He needed to get out of there and warn the others.

Fitz turned to leave the living room but a distant sound stopped him cold.

A footstep. Then another.

His heart was pounding as he reached for his gun and aimed it at the doorway.

Fitz's mind raced with how to get out of the room. There were two closed windows and one hallway exit where the footsteps originated. His mind raced through the possibilities. Would Gray Wolf come back? Fitz didn't think so. Why would he when the job was done?

The stiffness of Graham's body told Fitz it had been a few hours since the assassin had been there.

The footsteps echoed again. "Graham?" a man's voice, low and controlled, called out. "Graham, you in here?"

A silhouette stepped into the dim light of the hallway in front of the living room. Adrian Mercer, dressed in an expensive suit that looked too perfect for this decaying house. He turned and stared at Fitz with his gun raised. The recognition flashed across Mercer's face like a flicker of lightning. He didn't even flinch as he surveyed the room with sharp, calculating eyes.

It was the first time the two had come face to face.

"Connor Fitzgerald," Mercer said. The Congressman knew his name. "I didn't expect to find you here." The congressman's lips curled into a tight smile, his eyes narrowing.

Fitz didn't move. His eyes locked onto Mercer with a mix of anger and disgust. He didn't have time for games. "Graham's dead," Fitz said, with no trace of emotion. "The more important question is why you're here."

Mercer's expression barely shifted, his eyes betraying no emotion, but Fitz could see the slight tension in his posture, the faintest tightening of his jaw. "I was here..." his voice trailed off as he stepped into the room without hesitation. "Graham and I had some things to discuss."

"A representative and a Secret Service agent. What could the two of you possibly discuss? Wouldn't any requests you have go through official channels?" Fitz didn't lower his gun. Mercer might not have pulled the trigger but he was still involved in the attempted assassination of a president. He was a man with a lot to lose. He had also been a CIA agent.

Mercer seemed stumped for a response. The smooth calculating demeanor was quickly crumbling. "We...I..." He stared at Fitz. "Why did you kill Graham? I'm going to call the police."

"Please do. While you're at it, call the FBI. I can give you Agent Isabelle Conklin's number or maybe Agent Josh Burrows." A flicker of recognition lit Mercer's face.

"Why would we need to call either of them?"

Fitz stood to his full height and let the gun fall to his side. "You don't even seem surprised that Graham is dead. Why is that?"

Mercer released a breath. "He wasn't a good man, Fitz. Involved in a lot of shady underhanded things. You know Congress is even questioning what he might know about the shooting. He was there with President Monroe when she got shot. Some are starting to question Graham's relationship with the shooter Zachary Steele. There's talk, Fitz."

Fitz wanted to laugh at the absurdity of this man trying to convince him. He had no idea what Fitz knew. "Let me see if I understand this. You think Graham might have been involved in an assassination attempt and yet you came here alone to what? Question him? I'd think if you are making an accusation like that, you would have brought backup or questioned him formally. His house, early in the evening, alone. No, that doesn't make any sense."

"I don't know what to say, Fitz. Duty got the better of me." Mercer went to put his hands in his pockets and Fitz pointed the gun at him again. Mercer extracted his hands and held them up. "I'm not armed. I wanted to know from Graham what happened that morning at the Lincoln Memorial."

Fitz took a step forward, lowering the gun. He let out a chuckle filled with sarcasm and anger. "Don't you mean what happened in the middle of the night in the Oval Office?"

Mercer's smile faltered, and for just a moment, Fitz saw the slightest crack in his carefully constructed façade. It was gone in an instant, replaced by the same cold, calculating gaze that Fitz had come to recognize in men like Mercer.

"I don't know what you think you know, but you're wrong. You'd better think about what you're suggesting. I know that you like your little business. It's brought you a lot of power and money and I'd hate to see it fail. Things have a way of failing in D.C. People who don't play ball have a way of being run out of town. It's not my rules, Fitz. It's how the game's always been played."

"Mercer, men like you have tried to buy, bribe, and threaten me before. They found out quickly that it only enrages me. You and I are out here alone. I've got a gun. I already found one body. What's to say I didn't find two." Fitz had no intention of hurting the man. He just needed Mercer to know he could.

"Are you threatening me?"

"Nope," Fitz said with a shake of his head. "Let's stop playing games. I know exactly why you're here. You were behind the whole thing – the assassination attempt. Graham, Avery, Sparks, and you. You used Zachary Steele. You probably used Graham too. Now you're out here trying to cover your tracks and make sure the truth stays buried forever."

Mercer didn't even try to deny it. "The world is changing, Fitz. People like you who get in the way don't last long. We needed to save this country and Abigail Monroe wasn't going to get the job done."

"You got her elected then eliminated her. Was that the plan all along? Just use her too?"

"We tried to get her to play ball, Fitz. We really tried. She was a headstrong woman. She wasn't going to give in to what we wanted. She had time to save herself."

"Last time I checked, she's still alive. Who was the killer?"

"Zachary Steele. He's a troubled guy, Fitz."

Fitz shook his head.

"Give it up, Fitz. You're on a crusade for nothing. Monroe will never serve as president."

Fitz's stomach twisted, the truth of Mercer's words sinking in. He wasn't wrong. Monroe's recovery would probably take what would have been her entire first term. "Did Henry Coldwell know about the plan? He was there that night. So was Marcus Kane and Speaker Graves. Were you all in on it?" Mercer's smug grin didn't falter. "You are going down; you might as well take the others with you."

Mercer shook his head. "They are innocent. President Coldwell will take his rightful place and do what needs to be done. Now, I'm going to leave and you're going to forget we ever had this conversation."

"You're not going anywhere. I'm taking you into the FBI," Fitz said, his voice hardening. "I'm not going to let you or Avery get away with this."

Mercer's smile returned, but it didn't reach his eyes. "You think you have the upper hand? You're alone, Fitz. You're not going to be able to prove any of this."

As Mercer turned to leave, Fitz asked, "Aren't you wondering who killed Graham?"

That stopped him. He turned around. "I honestly thought it was you."

"No," Fitz said his tone icy cold. "Gray Wolf is going to kill anyone who knows the truth. You should have thought better than to hire an international assassin. You were CIA. You know the man always cleans up his mess. You're in over your head just like Graham."

Mercer's eyes flashed, the smile disappearing completely. "There's nothing that ties me to this, Fitz. You're the one who is in over his head."

Fitz laughed at the man's bravado. He slipped Graham's phone from his pocket. "It seems Graham wasn't so careful. The texts are right here on his phone. It implicates you. If I saw this, then you can bet Gray Wolf did too." He watched the blood drain from Mercer's face.

"The FBI already knows you're involved. The only way you live now is to let me take you in."

Mercer turned to leave again but only made it a few steps.

"Take another step and I will shoot. I'll leave you alive so Gray Wolf can finish you off."

Mercer didn't move to fight Fitz or argue further. All the fight in him was gone.

CHAPTER 38

Even though Mercer didn't fight being led out of the house, once they were outside, Fitz slipped zip ties from a bag he kept in the back of the SUV and fastened them around Mercer's wrists. He did it in front of the man's body rather than behind, leaving him more dignity and comfort than he deserved. Even after patting him down to ensure he didn't have a weapon, Fitz didn't trust Mercer at all. He had put him in the front seat of the SUV and then walked back into the house.

He stood in Graham's living room and called Isabelle, updating her. She listened to him and barely commented then instructed him to bring the phone with him. When Fitz asked about the others, she said she'd update him once they were all back at the FBI building. She left no room for argument.

It left Fitz with one more task before leaving the house. He went back to Graham's body and pressed the dead man's finger to the screen. He unlocked it once more and Fitz was able to navigate to the settings and remove the security entirely. There's no point getting the phone back to D.C. to not be able to open it again.

Fitz took one last look at Graham, thinking what a waste the man's life had been to go down this path. He could have been a rising star in the Secret Service. He had chosen the wrong side of history and gone down a terrible path. If he would be remembered at all, it would be in infamy.

Fitz left the house without looking back again.

Once back at FBI headquarters and Mercer was sitting in one of the interrogation rooms, Fitz stared at him through the window. "He admitted everything to me," he said, turning over his shoulder to look at Isabelle. Her head was buried in the phone going through the text messages. He left the window and walked over to the table, putting his palms flat on it and leaning over. He didn't want to interrupt her but he had been the first one back and he wanted an update on Charlie, who wasn't answering her phone.

Fitz cleared his throat. "Have you heard from Charlie?"

Isabelle held her finger up to stop him. She finished reading and raised her eyes to him. "This is good information, Fitz. I appreciate your help on this."

"No," Fitz said with a shake of his head, suppressing a frustrated smile. "Tell me about the others. You've kept me waiting long enough."

Isabelle leaned back and crossed her legs. "You don't like being told what to do, do you?"

"Whatever you are thinking about me right now, you have it wrong. I worked with Burrows just fine. I don't have an issue with the FBI. I want to know about Charlie. You wouldn't even be close to the truth about this investigation if it wasn't for us."

"Fair enough," Isabelle conceded. He slid into the chair. "David Sparks is dead. Charlie found him shortly after you found Graham Westbrook. She also found evidence about the dead man in the cell."

Fitz's eyes got round and big. "You know the identity of the second shooter?"

"Terry Sparks, David's cousin. He's some lowlife who didn't have a job and was living on David's couch. He'd been with David when they were planning this whole thing. When Gray Wolf didn't finish the job and no one could get hold of him, David sent Terry to finish her off and to scare Sebastian Cole. He's the one who shot out his windows. She found text messages between them."

"He wasn't a good assassin. He didn't even get through Secret Service."

"They were desperate," Isabelle said. "If Monroe wakes up, she's going to talk. Sparks had told Terry if he got caught to say nothing to anyone. Sparks knew Terry wasn't in the system anywhere and figured they'd sort it out later. I assume Sparks was going to let Terry take the fall once everything was said and done. Then we put his photo on the news looking for anyone who could identify him and that set off a chain reaction."

Fitz didn't understand something. "Why did Gray Wolf kill him? They wouldn't have had any contact."

Isabelle shook her head. "I asked Charlie that. She seems to know him a little better than she let on. She said that since the FBI didn't know the man's identity, Gray Wolf didn't want anyone thinking he'd gotten sloppy and got himself caught. He also might have wondered what David Sparks had told him."

"Why show himself at all? Gray Wolf couldn't have known that Zachary Steele wrote about him in the journal or that Graham Westbrook sent texts about him."

She gestured to him and smiled. "We think alike. I asked the same thing. Charlie said that she would expect Gray Wolf to put tracking on the phone of the person who hired him so he could monitor what they said. He has strict rules and if they aren't abided by, he doesn't complete the assignment. Charlie believes everything that possibly could go wrong with this hit went wrong."

"There's still so much I don't understand," Fitz admitted. "Do you have Richard Avery in custody?"

Isabelle pointed toward the door. "He's the third cell down on the left. He already asked for an attorney. I'm not able to question him. I need to interview Mercer. Do you think he'll talk?"

Fitz wasn't sure. "What about the rest of them?" What Fitz wasn't saying was *what about Marcus Kane?* But he didn't want to pressure her.

"There's only five implicated right now. David Sparks and Graham Westbrook are dead. Cousin Terry is dead. That leaves us Mercer and Avery. We have no information that points the finger at Speaker Graves, Acting President Coldwell, or FBI Director Kane. They were in the room and hadn't disclosed what happened that night. They are withholding information from the FBI. There are criminal charges we could levy, but it isn't going to get us anywhere. They will lawyer up and we'll make a politically charged situation even worse."

"The three of them will walk? Coldwell will become president?"

"He's already acting. But yes, Monroe's cabinet under the 25th amendment will remove her from office and Coldwell will be the next President of the United States. There's nothing to stop that now outside of some evidence that he was involved." Isabelle held her arms open wide. "I don't have an ounce of evidence that suggests they were involved. They didn't report, but I don't have any evidence to suggest they were involved in the plot or cover-up."

Fitz couldn't say one way or the other. He didn't like how it went down. They were still culpable and he didn't like just letting them walk. "Can I get a crack at speaking to Avery?" When Isabelle didn't respond, he explained, "I'm not law enforcement. I'm not even acting as an arm of the FBI. I was working on this investigation as a private citizen. I have no ability to arrest."

A smirk formed on her face. "You brought Mercer in wearing zip ties."

"For my protection. He was CIA," Fitz said not containing his smile. "Let me go talk to Avery and if he doesn't say anything, he doesn't say anything. No harm, no foul. If he admits to something, I assume this whole area down here is wired for sound."

"Video too," Isabelle added. She shifted her eyes up to one of the cameras. "No, Fitz, you can't interview Richard Avery. His attorney will be here soon, probably within the next thirty minutes. You can stay here though while I interview Mercer." She locked her gaze on him and Fitz got the message loud and clear. She couldn't give him permission.

Isabelle rose from the table. "Will you still be here when I finish?"

Fitz nodded. "Not going anywhere."

"Good," she said as she left the room, leaving the door slightly open for him.

He waited until she was in the interrogation room, sitting down at the table with Mercer. Fitz slipped out the door and headed straight for the cell holding Avery. He found the man sitting with his head tipped back against the wall with his hands folded in his lap.

"That bench can't be comfortable. Certainly not what you're used to at the White House," Fitz said as he walked up to the bars and leaned against them.

Avery opened his eyes and looked over. "Who are you? I asked for my lawyer."

Fitz held his hands up. "I'm not with the FBI. I'm not here in any official capacity. Just thought we might have a little chat."

Avery folded his arms across his chest. "I told that other FBI agent that I don't have anything to say. I should be at the hospital with my wife."

"I heard they aren't letting you see her." That was something Mercer had told him on the drive back from Virginia. The Secret Service had kept Monroe's husband away from her even in the hospital. She had other family there with her but not Avery.

"It's a Secret Service decision. How'd you hear about it? It wasn't on the news." Avery turned his body to face him more, even though he left his arms folded. "Who are you?"

"Connor Fitzgerald. I run an opposition research firm. Although lately, I've been doing a bit more than that."

"You look familiar."

Fitz shrugged. He wasn't going to admit he'd been a homicide detective. He wanted Avery comfortable and underestimating him. "I get that a lot. I've been around D.C. for a long time. Why is the Secret Service keeping you and President Monroe apart? That doesn't seem normal."

"I don't know," he responded dismissively. "Why does the Secret Service do anything? I didn't know how much control over my own life I'd be giving up once she became president."

"That's a hard role for a man to take. I'm sure you had to give up a lot for your wife."

"I did and no one ever thanks me for my sacrifice."

"Well," Fitz said with a smile. "I'm thanking you. I understand how hard that must have been."

Avery looked at him square in the face now. "What do you want?"

"I guess you could say I heard a few things about you and I'm having trouble believing it."

That sparked his interest, stroked his ego. Someone was talking about him instead of his wife.

Fitz let him relish the feeling for only a moment. "I heard you might be mixed up in the assassination attempt. I guess the FBI heard those rumors too."

A line between the man's eyes folded in. "Do you have any idea who is saying that?"

"I do," Fitz said with a little enthusiasm. "Adrian Mercer." He watched as Avery went from mildly interested to concerned, even though he tried to hide the shift in his features. "Can you believe that? We know Mercer is directly involved with David Sparks and Graham

Westbrook in planning the assassination attempt. We also know who they used. There are a few things we still don't know though."

"How do you know all of them are involved? That's a wild accusation."

Fitz smiled broadly. "It's not an accusation. I'm the one who figured it out."

"Figured what out?" Avery was trying to sound casual about it. The more he did, the more his voice had a squeak of fear he couldn't seem to shake.

"Oh, I probably should have told you. My partner Charlie and I were the ones who figured out the shooting took place in the Oval Office." He gestured for Avery to come over to the bars. When the man got up and took a few tentative steps, Fitz showed him photos on his phone. "The Secret Service was too sloppy in cleaning up. Not only that but Graham Westbrook didn't delete the texts between him and Mercer. We know about Gray Wolf."

At the mention of the assassin's name, Avery shivered. He peered down at the photos, blinking rapidly at the evidence. "I don't know anything about this. I'm not sure what you want me to say."

"Truth might help you."

Avery retreated from the bars and went back to sit on the bench. He stared at Fitz but didn't utter a word. Fitz continued "No problem then. I thought you might want to set the record straight. I just brought Adrian Mercer in and he's in there right now telling Agent Conklin how you set up this whole thing. That you're the one who wanted Abigail dead so you could continue with your affairs."

"You think I wanted my wife dead because of an affair?" he scoffed. "She's been sleeping with her primary Secret Service protection for years. Our marriage was open."

"I see. Maybe that wasn't your motive then." Fitz grew quiet on purpose, waiting to see if he'd fill in the blanks. When he didn't, Fitz added, "I guess it was because of Percepta Tech."

When Avery didn't respond, he asked, "Do you know that Graham Westbrook and David Sparks are dead?"

Avery glanced down at the floor shaking his head.

"Gray Wolf took them out. That means FBI agents are tearing through their homes right now looking for evidence. Let's hope Sparks was a lot more discreet than Westbrook. I'm the one who found his body and the treasure trove of evidence against you all is unmatched. It was enough that I think Westbrook might have been gearing up to blackmail all of you."

"It doesn't matter what Graham Westbrook or Mercer says, I didn't have anything to do with this. I wouldn't kill my wife."

"Would you kill your president?"

Avery's eyes darkened. He opened his mouth to speak but didn't utter a word.

"What about what Zachary Steele said?"

At that his head snapped up. "He's dead."

"Yeah, he is. A sacrificial lamb to your devious plan." Fitz leaned against the bars. "There's just one thing you didn't consider. That vile preacher out there, Paul Berardo, didn't trust any of you. In fact, he snapped a photo of you in the SUV on that first trip. That was dangerous of you. I know you didn't get out of the SUV. I don't even know why you'd risk being seen. Paul doesn't trust the government and he told Steele to stay away from all of you. Steele wasn't going to do that. Paul told him to keep a record of everything."

"You're lying," Avery said with the fear rising in his voice.

"Not lying. I guess sometimes dead men do talk. The FBI has all of Steele's information – the journal and the photos. If Mercer points the finger at you and the other two are dead, who do you think is going to take the fall for this – a well-known member of Congress or the president's jealous husband?"

Fitz left him and walked away. He made it halfway down the hallway when Avery called him back.

"I want to make a deal!" he shouted to Fitz. "I'll make a deal."

Fitz smiled to himself. He took his time walking back to the cell. "I can't promise you anything. As I said, I'm not FBI. You can tell me one thing right now, were Graves, Coldwell, and Kane involved in the plot?"

"No," Avery said shaking his head furiously. "They didn't know. Coldwell can still be president. He must be. Otherwise…" he trailed off.

"Otherwise, this would have been for nothing."

Avery's gaze met Fitz's. "They really weren't involved. It wasn't supposed to happen like it did."

"Who pulled the trigger?"

"I assume the man they call Gray Wolf, but I never saw him in the Oval that night. I really don't know. I didn't see anyone shoot her. It was all so confusing."

Fitz wasn't paying attention to him. His phone buzzed in his pocket. He reached for it and read the text from Sebastian Cole: *"Abigail is conscious and wants to see you."*

Fitz didn't know how Sebastian knew President Monroe was awake and it didn't matter. All that mattered to Fitz was that the president would live.

"Did you hear me?" Avery shouted at him as Fitz was already making his way down the hall to leave the FBI building.

Fitz only stopped once. He sent off a quick text to Agent Conklin that Avery was primed and ready to talk. As much as Fitz would have liked to get more, when the president summons you – you go.

CHAPTER 39

Fitz felt the weight of the silence pressing in as he walked through the hospital's sterile, fluorescent-lit hallways. Each step echoed in the otherwise hushed corridor, the sound of his shoes on the polished tile floor amplifying the nerves tightening his chest. His eyes flicked from one end of the hallway to the other.

He had never been in this part of the hospital before. This section was sealed off from the rest, a hidden area beyond a labyrinth of hallways. The hospital guards, the tightly controlled security checkpoints, the tightlipped staff all added to the sense of unease swirling around him.

Fitz adjusted the collar of his jacket, trying to steady his thoughts. He reached the first checkpoint, where a pair of Secret Service agents stood guard. The one on the left, a woman with a sharp gaze, flicked her eyes over his identification before gesturing for him to stand still. Her partner, a tall man with a stone expression, patted him down with meticulous precision. The process was invasive, but necessary. Fitz kept his expression neutral, his heart racing beneath the surface. They took his sidearm, after he informed them that it was there. They would hold it there until he returned.

Fitz didn't argue. There was no way the Secret Service was letting him into the hospital room with a gun. If he'd had time, he would have left it back at the office.

When they were satisfied, the woman stepped back. "You're cleared," she said, not looking at him as she motioned for him to move on. "Your partner is already in there."

Charlie. That was the first time Fitz had considered her. He hadn't bothered to text her, figuring she was busy with other things. Sebastian had obviously contacted her too.

Fitz stepped past the checkpoint, navigating a series of long, narrow hallways that smelled faintly of antiseptic. The white walls were interrupted by the occasional framed photo of medical staff, their smiles frozen in time.

At the end of the hall, a door loomed, the type of door that seemed designed to keep people out – a solid wall of steel. As he approached, the door swung open with a soft hiss, revealing a small nurses' station with a woman who glanced up at him and pointed directly across the short hall to a room with a large front window where the staff could look in on President Monroe without having to go into the room.

Fitz stood in the doorway for a few seconds, steadying his nerves. Charlie flanked one side of her bed while Sebastian stood on the other.

President Monroe lay on the bed, her dark eyes locked on him the moment he entered. Her hair was slightly disheveled, a stark contrast to the crispness of the sheets that enveloped her. Despite the pallor of her skin, there was an undeniable strength in the way she looked at him, an intensity that made his nerves flare.

He swallowed hard as he stepped into the room. "Madame President," he said, introducing himself.

A faint smile creased her face. "I know who you are. I asked for you."

"Of course," he said as he approached. He glanced over at Charlie who looked like she'd been through a battle. Her face was pale, her hair a halo of waves around her face, and her eyes for a rare time showed a hint of concern. He wished he could pull her out of the room and have a conversation with her before speaking to President Monroe.

"Fitz," President Monroe said, her voice quiet, but there was no mistaking the authority in it. "Sebastian told me that you and Charlie have been investigating who shot me. He said it's quite a mess, the investigation, but that you have been working to uncover the truth."

Fitz moved to stand right next to her bed so she wouldn't need to strain her voice. She had a mess of tubes and monitors attached to her. Her body was propped up by pillows on all sides. Sebastian stepped back to allow him the space.

"We have," he said and explained about the official FBI investigation and then added what they found. "We know the shooting happened in the Oval Office and we think we know who shot you. There are still some questions about who was involved."

"The man behind the drapes," Monroe said, looking up at him.

Fitz wasn't sure he had heard her correctly. "What do you mean?"

She swallowed and licked her dry lips. Sebastian held a cup of water for her as she sipped. "We were arguing about technology when I got up. I couldn't sit there and listen to them blather on anymore. It was the middle of the night and they were all trying to strong arm me into implementing it. It's too dangerous and too unknown. Of course, when I got up, they all got up too and started moving around the room. Marcus Kane, the FBI director, was there because he was against the technology as well. Marcus noticed how stressed I was and said he'd go get me something to drink. He headed out of the Oval to my private kitchen. When I turned to ask him a question, that's when I saw the man. His black shoes are what I saw first, at the bottom of the drapes. I'm sure he meant to be fully covered but they were there."

"Were you aiming at him or just trying to scare him?" Fitz remembered the shot had been wide of the drapes.

Monroe explained, "You have to understand the rest of them were all together talking. I had to aim around them at the man behind the drapes. Coldwell was in my way. I was trying not to shoot him, but he didn't move fast enough. No one moved fast enough. They were all clumped together when I fired." Monroe closed her eyes. "It was mayhem."

Fitz saw the pain in her eyes and hated that she was having to relive it. "What happened after you fired?"

"They all scattered, completely unsure who I had been firing at. They were shouting at me as the man behind the drapes stepped out and fired three times then retreated back into position behind the drapes. My world was upside down. As I fell to the floor, I could hear them arguing about who had shot me. They were blaming each other. I tried to speak, tried to tell them about the man. No one could hear me. I don't think I was actually speaking. I lost consciousness soon after. The last thing I heard was Marcus shouting about what had happened. He said he was in the bathroom and couldn't get out of there fast enough. He was demanding to know who shot me. He was screaming about a gun but no one admitted to having one. That's all I remember. I don't have any recollection of getting out of the Oval Office or the hospital or anything."

"I've filled in the rest," Sebastian said, his voice strained. "I can only assume one of them took her gun because it wasn't near her body when I arrived."

Fitz assumed that it had been Graham Westbrook. He had also dug the bullets out of the wall and the couch.

Charlie stepped forward. "Who called for the meeting that night?"

Monroe turned her head to look at her. "Richard. He had gone to lunch earlier that day with Coldwell and Graves. He said they wanted to talk off the record and I should hear them out before making my final decision. He offered the meeting without checking with me.

That's when I called Marcus and told him he had to be there too. I don't know who called Adrian Mercer, but he was there too. I assume Richard."

"Were meetings like that common?"

"Yes, at night. But never off the record," Monroe said. "I didn't like unofficial meetings. I wanted things on the record. There had been so much fighting about this technology from Percepta Tech. It was a real mess."

Charlie explained, "They were pushing you so hard because they were invested financially in the company. It sounds like Coldwell had ideological reasons too."

"Of course," she said as she closed her eyes. "That's how it always is. Money wins out. Not that night though. I wasn't giving in." Monroe rested for a moment while they watched her in silence. Fitz knew talking to them was probably expending a lot of energy she didn't have. When she opened her eyes again, she asked, "Who was the man who shot me?"

"Gray Wolf," Charlie said and explained about the elusive assassin. "You can request CIA information. There's files upon files about the man. I'm frankly surprised he took a job on United States soil. We have been chasing him for decades. Did you see his face?"

Monroe gestured toward her face. "He was covered head to toe in black. I saw his eyes – piercing blue. A color I don't think I'll ever forget. I don't remember anything else about him. He had black gloves too. The gun was black. It was a blur of movement. Then I was down."

"It's probably good you didn't see his face," Charlie said. "He's been cleaning up."

"You think she's still in danger?" Sebastian asked.

Charlie didn't even need time to consider. "I think you have to assume so."

"My recovery is going to take a long time. The doctors said it's going to be a while before I'm even up and around walking normally. I'm going to give the presidency to Coldwell."

Fitz winced, knowing how difficult a decision that was for her. "Are you sure?"

"I don't have a choice. I have to accept where things currently stand. It's the only way." There was a catch in her voice when she spoke. "Tell me who else was involved. An assassin didn't just walk off the street into the Oval Office. Someone hired him and someone let him in."

"Graham Westbrook and David Sparks with the Secret Service let him in. They must have given him access before the meeting started and got him out of there when it ended."

"They will be prosecuted then," she said confidently.

Charlie told her that wasn't going to happen. "They are dead. Gray Wolf doesn't leave anyone alive who has seen his face. He must have known they could identify him somehow. There were others involved too." Monroe looked at her expectantly. "Adrian Mercer as well."

Before Fitz lost his nerve. "Your husband, too."

It didn't seem to surprise Monroe. "I assume he had a lot of money tied up in Percepta Tech and he knew I wasn't going to agree to it. If they didn't get a government contract their company would be worthless. Our marriage hadn't been good for a long time. He never wanted me to run for the presidency. Did he admit to what he did?"

Fitz explained that he was sitting in a jail cell. "I just came from there. I think that he'll provide the FBI with a statement about what he's done. He insists the others – Graves, Coldwell, and Kane aren't involved."

"Kane was there for me. He didn't even want to come to the meeting. I had to beg him."

"The others?" Charlie asked.

Monroe gestured dismissively. "While I disagreed with Coldwell on many things, he was someone I trusted." Monroe closed her eyes and soon she was softly snoring.

Sebastian ushered them into the hallway. When they were out of earshot of Monroe, he looked at Charlie. "When she's well enough to be moved, should I take her away from D.C.?"

"Will she be willing to go?"

Sebastian looked through the window at her sleeping. "She's willing to go. We've already talked about it. I want her out of D.C. and protected by me. I don't trust anyone else."

"You shouldn't trust anyone else," Charlie said, agreeing with him. "When you can, go and don't look back."

Sebastian promised them both that he'd keep Monroe safe. "We aren't going to alert the news that she's awake. We aren't going to tell them anything. We will give it a few days then discreetly contact Coldwell to permanently transfer the power to him. I want to be out of D.C. at another hospital with her before we disclose that she's awake. There are already plans being put in place."

Fitz couldn't blame him for the lengths he was willing to go. He extended his hand and they shook. "It was David Sparks's cousin, Terry, who shot at you that night. He's dead. You never saw Gray Wolf, so you should be in the clear."

Sebastian thanked him and extended his hand to Charlie. "I can't thank you enough."

"Consider us even," Fitz said. "Without your information, we'd still be spinning our wheels. Tell her we wish her well."

Charlie and Fitz walked back down the hall together, collected their guns from the Secret Service, and made their way out of the hospital.

"I'm the one who found David Sparks. Gray Wolf didn't torture him. Just shot him in the head," Charlie said once they were outside in the parking lot. "I warned Ian too. He's left the city for someplace safe. He didn't see anything though, so I don't think he is in danger."

Fitz wasn't concerned about any of that. He reached his hand out and gripped her shoulder, pulling her in for a hug. Charlie wasn't usually affectionate, but she allowed herself to be surrounded by the embrace. "Are you doing okay?"

"Not really," she said as she stepped back from him. "I got close to catching Gray Wolf once and he nearly killed me. That's what he was referring to in the card he left on Terry's body. He ambushed me in Kenya. I barely made it out alive."

"Will he come for you again?"

"I don't know. I thought I had put all of that behind me. As I said, I'm surprised he came to the United States at all."

The silence hung heavily over them. They were both tired and the case had sapped whatever energy either of them had left. Fitz's phone buzzed against his hip and he groaned as he looked at the screen. "Senator Ford wants to see us." He raised his head to Charlie. "You go home and I'll handle this."

"Are you sure?"

"I'm positive. Marcus Kane will be there too and you're not up for the confrontation we need to have."

There was no argument from Charlie. He watched as she turned and walked the short distance to her car. Fitz stood there as she drove away and he gathered what little strength he had before heading to the meeting location.

CHAPTER 40

In the basement of Ford's Theater, Fitz found Senator Ford and Marcus Kane deep in conversation at one of the small round tables. The anger at seeing Kane rose in Fitz's chest. While he believed Kane hadn't been involved in the plot, he also hadn't been forthcoming with information with Fitz or with the agents in his ranks.

"You wanted to see me," Fitz said, not able to hide the edge of anger in his tone. He locked eyes with Kane and didn't look away. "I'm sure you called for this meeting once I refused your demand for an update."

"I called for the meeting, Fitz," Ford said, gesturing to the chair next to him. "Please sit and speak with us. We do need an update. As you know, there are broader issues at play."

Fitz didn't take his eyes off Kane as he walked over to the table, pulled out the chair, and sat.

"We aren't enemies, Fitz," Kane said, his tone gentle. "I know that you think—"

"You don't know what I think," Fitz spat, cutting him off. "What I *know* is that you were in the Oval Office when the shooting took place and you lied to my face. Sent Charlie and me on a wild goose chase, just like your own agents. All along you knew the truth. You were going to let your agents sell the public a false narrative of what happened. You were going to let that be the official record. You stymied the FBI investigation at every turn. How can I trust you? How can anyone trust you? How can the Warren Circle trust you?"

Kane didn't back down. "I did what I thought was best. I didn't know who pulled the trigger. None of us did. I searched each of them for a gun. The only one who had one in that room as far as I can tell was Graham Westbrook and he had his holstered. He took Monroe's gun too. I didn't even know she was armed. I got Coldwell out of there to safety as fast as I could."

"Where were his Secret Service agents that night?"

"Outside the Oval Office. They were as confused as anyone by what had happened. I called them as soon as Coldwell was safely in my SUV. They came running after that." Kane turned to Senator Ford then back to Fitz. "I told Ford everything earlier today. If I felt like anything would have been helped by me disclosing I was there, I would have. I don't know who shot President Monroe. I assumed by telling you all of this it would have cast suspicion on the wrong person and we desperately needed a smooth transition of power."

"What if Vice President Coldwell had been in on the plot?"

"He wasn't," Kane said, forcefully. "I've known him my entire career here and he'd never do something like that. I was sure he wasn't involved. I had no idea whether he was going to be shot next. I got him out of there quickly before a second tragedy happened."

Fitz still didn't understand the man's reasoning. It was clear that he wasn't going to admit to anything else no matter how much Fitz pushed him. "Agent Conklin has it under control now. All I had to do was point her in the right direction."

"I know. She interrogated me today. She might resign over my actions. I've begged her not to. The FBI would suffer a great loss without her." Kane sat back in the chair. "Like you, she said she isn't sure she can trust me. I understand it. I didn't want my presence there to cause a distraction."

"You didn't want suspicion to fall on you," Fitz said, seeing that he was right about that as Kane glanced away from him.

"That too," he admitted, surprising both Fitz and Ford. "I didn't even want to be at that meeting. Then the shooting happened while I was in the bathroom. Can you imagine, the FBI director was there but was indisposed and had no idea what happened? I was trying to keep my name out of the whole thing. I also wanted a smooth power transition."

"Did you think I'd ever find out the truth?"

"Honestly? No."

"Well, thanks for that vote of confidence."

"I didn't think the team assigned at the FBI would get to the truth either. It's nothing personal, Fitz."

"Okay," Ford said as a way to break the tension. "Now that's out of the way, can you tell us what you know?"

Fitz assumed the information would come out sooner rather than later. He leaned on the table and gave them the play-by-play of everything he had uncovered to date, leaving out that he had spoken to President Monroe and that she was conscious. He did add in what she had told him. "One of the people we interviewed believed the shooter was behind the drapes. It makes sense that's where Monroe was aiming. We can only speculate that David Sparks or Graham Westbrook let this person into the Oval Office that night and escorted him out. They are both dead – shot by the same perpetrator. Adrian Mercer and Richard Avery are in custody as we speak. Both admitted to me their roles in the plot. Agent Conklin is in the middle of interrogating them. I'm confident she will get the information she needs."

Senator Ford had sat stone-faced as Fitz laid out the information. "What about Speaker Graves? My understanding is Coldwell is going to ask him to be his VP. We have to know if he was involved."

Fitz wasn't surprised by the news. "We aren't going to know until Conklin is done. Honestly, those are the only two who know the truth. Steele's journal and photos and the information in Westbrook's phone and whatever evidence they find at Sparks's home. Plus, the evidence found in the Oval Office. There's enough there for a strong case with or without their testimony."

"You still didn't tell us the name of the person who pulled the trigger," Ford said, staring across the table at him.

Fitz realized then that he hadn't. "Gray Wolf is the man's code name. That's what the CIA and the international intelligence community call him. Charlie is familiar with him. Mercer would have been familiar with him too. If Steele hadn't written it down, I don't think it would have ever come to light."

Ford turned to Kane. "Is that name familiar to you?"

Kane shook his head. "If he was hiding behind the drapes, it makes sense why I missed him. I was focused on the other men in the room."

"Some of them were involved in the plot. They just didn't pull the trigger," Fitz stated again.

"Where is Charlie?" Ford asked. "I wanted to meet with her too."

"Not tonight. Charlie has had a rough few days and the appearance of Gray Wolf has her rattled like I've never seen her rattled before. I want her to take some time to regroup."

Senator Ford knew better than to ask about Charlie's past connection with the assassin. "Is there anything else we need to know?"

Fitz sat back and raised his hands palms up. "I'm done with this. It's in the hands of the FBI. I don't fully understand the Warren Circle. I didn't get any help with this investigation and now I'm not even sure how much I trust your members."

"I sent you help," Ford said, his eyes narrowing.

Fitz started to say no but then remembered the Secret Service agent. "Wyatt Standfield?"

Ford nodded. "I send help when I can. Each of us has a role to play and we get involved when the time is right. Please trust me that your experience and expertise are of great value to the Warren Circle. The same for Charlie. We want you to continue with us."

Fitz made no promises. He got up to leave. "We're just going to have to see how things play out." Before leaving, Fitz expressed his concern about Percepta Tech. "If Coldwell enacts this, we might all have some issues going forward. It seems like a civil liberties nightmare."

Kane agreed with that. "As you said, we are going to have to see how things progress."

With that, Fitz headed out of Ford's Theater to his SUV. He drove back to his house in silence. As he entered, Fitz called Amy's name a few times but was met with silence. He found the note in her scrawled handwriting on the kitchen island propped up against a tin of cookies she had made for him.

Amy said she was going back home. Now that the threat was over, she wanted her bed. She referenced Agent Conklin giving an update about the case on the news, explaining that the FBI was close to finalizing the investigation and that arrests had been made. Amy thanked him for taking care of her. She told him she'd call him soon.

Fitz wasn't sure if she would. He wasn't even sure how he felt about it. He dragged himself up the stairs to the shower. He flipped on the light, pulled his shirt over his head, shoved his pants down to the floor, and stepped in. He let the hot water do its job.

Later, after he had eaten, he texted Charlie to check on her. She was at home recovering from the events and told him she was taking tomorrow off. He sent the thumbs-up emoji. He tried Agent Burrows but got no reply.

Fitz settled into the couch and caught the news segment that Amy had mentioned. Isabelle had spoken eloquently about the threat against President Monroe and the ongoing investigation including the turn in the case with the factual information about where it had happened. She announced the three deaths and the two suspects in custody. Partisan talking heads were already trashing the investigation and conjuring up conspiracy theories. Fitz assumed that was just going to be part of it. He turned to one of the late-night talk shows and lost himself in another world.

When the doorbell rang a half hour later, it jolted him back to reality. Fitz made his way to the front door and looked out the side window, surprised to see who was standing there. He regretted the ratty old tee-shirt and blue plaid pajama bottoms he had on but there was no time to change.

He ran a hand through his hair as he pulled open the door. "Isabelle," he said her name but nothing else came out.

She held up a six-pack of beer and pizza. She offered a sheepish smile. "Burrows told me where you live. I hope you don't mind. I thought we could talk. I feel like I owe you a lot after today. Richard Avery was begging me for a deal by the time you got done with him."

Fitz stepped back, still struggling to find words. He couldn't believe she was in his house. "Sorry," he said as he closed the door behind her. "I moved in not long ago and haven't decorated."

"I don't mind. Kitchen in the back?" Before he could answer, she kicked off her flats and carried the beer and pizza to the kitchen. She found herself two glasses and plates in the cabinet. Pulled two slices for each of them out of the box and handed the plates to Fitz, who carried them wordlessly over to the table.

She carried over the beer and glasses, setting them down on the table. "You're conspicuously quiet. More so than I would have thought."

"You thought about me?" he finally said and wished he could immediately take it back.

Isabelle laughed as she sat. "I thought about you. I thought there was a connection here. Am I wrong?"

Fitz had never met a woman who spoke so directly to him. "You're not wrong. I just didn't think you liked me much."

"I don't like anyone meddling in my investigations," she said, taking a big bite of pizza. As they ate, she gave him the rundown of the case from Mercer and Avery. Both confessed to their part in the assassination attempt and directing the Secret Service agents who were sympathetic to their plan.

As suspected, Mercer knew of Gray Wolf and used his connections to put out word that he was needed. He hadn't explained to Isabelle how he had tracked down contact information for the international assassin but admitted it had been his idea. After he obtained the information, he passed it on to David Sparks and Graham Westbrook. They had contacted Gray Wolf and came up with the plan including finding a patsy in Zachary Steele. Neither Mercer nor Avery knew who ultimately had shot Steele.

When she was finished, Isabelle said, "Mercer and Avery are going to spare the public a trial. They will plead guilty and the other three are dead. I think that's about as much justice as the public will get. Graves was never implicated and neither were Kane or Coldwell."

"What are you going to tell the public about Gray Wolf? You mentioned the conspiracy on the news without mentioning the assassin. You alluded to Westbrook as the one who pulled the trigger."

"The American public can't handle the truth. We'll lay the blame on Westbrook and the rest of them. It's just what we have to do. The CIA has been notified and they are going to increase their operations against Gray Wolf. I don't think Charlie is going to let it go."

"I don't think so either," Fitz admitted. "What about Coldwell and Graves? They are going to be the president and vice president. How can we be sure about them? Graves is Graham Westbrook's uncle. Can we really believe he wasn't involved?"

"I don't have the evidence," she said evenly.

"We both know that doesn't mean anything." He stared at her across the table and wondered at her ability to be unwavering about this. "We just have to accept it?"

"We just have to accept it. You know better than me, Fitz, all politicians are terrible. Some are just a little less terrible." Isabelle sat back and smiled. "Are we done talking about the case?"

"I think so," Fitz said even though he didn't want to be. He still couldn't believe she was in his house.

Isabelle finished off her beer. "I think Burrows has a crush on Charlie."

"I think Charlie has a crush on Burrows," he countered, realizing then she wasn't there only to discuss the case. "They had a thing a while ago. I don't think either of them want to admit their feelings."

Isabelle took a sip of her beer. When she put it down on the table, she said, "Let's be smarter than them. Are you going to ask me out?"

Fitz let out a nervous laugh. "Dinner tomorrow night at seven. I'll pick you up."

"Make it Friday," she countered. "I'll wear a pretty dress."

Fitz leaned into the table. "I don't much care what you wear. You've already got me hooked."

"Good," she said smiling broadly, her gaze never leaving his face.

Fitz didn't know if it was good or not.

Good for her, but maybe not good for him.

Fitz had fallen for her fast – and that never ended well for him.

About the Author

Stacy M. Jones was born and raised in Troy, New York, and currently lives in Little Rock, Arkansas. She is a full-time writer and holds masters' degrees in journalism and in forensic psychology. She currently has four series available for readers: the completed cozy paranormal Harper & Hattie Magical Mystery Series, the hard-boiled PI Riley Sullivan Mystery Series, the FBI Agent Kate Walsh Thriller Series and the new Connor Fitzgerald Thriller series. To access Stacy's Mystery Readers Club with free novellas, visit StacyMJones.com.

You can connect with me on:

🌐 http://www.stacymjones.com

f https://www.facebook.com/StacyMJonesWriter

🔗 https://www.bookbub.com/profile/stacy-m-jones

🔗 https://www.goodreads.com/StacyMJonesWriter

🔗 https://www.amazon.com/stores/Stacy-M.-Jones/author/B07DHYT9CS

Subscribe to my newsletter:

✉ http://www.stacymjones.com

Also by Stacy M. Jones

Watch for the next Connor Fitzgerald Thriller in Spring 2026

Access the Free Mystery Readers' Club Starter Library
 PI Riley Sullivan Mystery Series novella "The 1922 Club Murder"
 FBI Agent Kate Walsh Thriller Series novella "The Curators"
 Harper & Hattie Mystery Series novella "Harper's Folly"

Sign up for the starter library along with launch-day pricing and special behind-the-scenes access. Hit subscribe at http://www.stacy mjones.com/

Please leave a review for Sparrow Down. Reviews help more readers find my books. Thank you!

Other books by Stacy M. Jones by series and order to date:

FBI Agent Kate Walsh Thriller Series
 The Curators
 The Founders
 Miami Ripper
 Mad Jack
 The Fuse
 Dead Senate
 Close Killer
 Diamond King
 The Magician
 Helix Syndicate

Connor Fitzgerald Thriller Series
Midnight Judge
Sparrow Down

PI Riley Sullivan Mystery Series
The 1922 Club Murder
Deadly Sins
The Bone Harvest
Missing Time Murders
We Last Saw Jane
Boston Underground
The Night Game
Harbor Cove Murders
The Drowned Boys
What He Saw
Fear City
What Stays Buried

Harper & Hattie Magical Mystery Series
Harper's Folly
Saints & Sinners Ball
Secrets to Tell
Rule of Three
The Forever Curse
The Witches Code
The Sinister Sisters
Scandal Knocks Twice
A Treasure Most Deadly

www.ingramcontent.com/pod-product-compliance
Lightning Source LLC
Chambersburg PA
CBHW032336310726
48973CB00007B/1730